We hold these truths
to be self-evident that ...

The Empty House

The house sat empty for so long that no one remembered who last lived in it. The main ridge beam of the roof had cracked, and loose shingles allowed decades of cold Wisconsin rain and snow to permeate its once resplendent interior. The house wasn't fancy. It was a farmhouse. It had been used for generations by those who toiled the land as a place of safety, comfort, and family. Then, as it does with everything, time took its toll, cracking the windows, peeling the paint, and taking its wooden skeleton and inflicting wounds of dry rot so great that the finest architects in Spring Green and contractors from Madison indicated that it simply could not be saved.

How do you say goodbye to a tribute to your own life and that of your family? It could not simply be destroyed. There were countless memories etched deeply into the walls that made the site more of a shrine than a residence.

My name is James Terrill. I am a farmer. I have been a farmer my entire life, as had been my father and his father and his and his, and as I hope and pray my children and children's children and children's children's children will be as well. The land has been our sanctuary and in our care for nearly two hundred years. We borrowed it from God and Mother Nature, and we reap the bounty of its harvest.

The decision was made to say goodbye. My wife, Susan, and I decided that the house needed a farewell party. We gathered our neighbors and relatives to see it one last time before the bulldozer came and leveled the place. Over two hundred people showed up ...

friends and descendants who came simply to pay their respects to an empty house and to the heritage and meaning it provided to us all.

As it had been for the reunion when our little one-room school closed during my early childhood, so it was for the house that had stood so long. It was a grand event with lots of laughter and even a few tears. We served Sprecher Root Beer and Spotted Cow beer. We roasted a pig and served cheese curds and corn on the cob. More than one discussion took place about the Packers and the Wisconsin Badgers and how they would look in the fall. In the end, it was more like a funeral, I guess, than a house party, and yet it went on.

As the event ended, my wife and I took one last look at what had been. It was decided that we would carefully traverse the hallowed grounds of yesterday one last time. We couldn't allow others in, as our liability insurance wouldn't allow it.

We had carefully planned how our memorial was to be removed with the architects, who were so used to creating something that I think it came as a bit of a surprise when I asked them to develop a plan to take something apart. They created an operational protocol that would dismantle the house in sequence, which would not only allow for recycling but also allow for the limestone walls to be put to use elsewhere. The family voted that we should create a stone fence around the family cemetery. What better place than to surround those who had lived within?

The following day, the workers arrived and commenced with the first phase, which consisted simply of removing all the windows and doors from both the first and second floors. Within a few hours, they had been extracted and placed in a dumpster. The window panes shattered like brittle bones of yesterday, but it didn't matter as they were no longer needed for looking out nor peeking in.

On Tuesday, a small crane arrived and began removing the roof. Within a matter of minutes, what had taken months to create was gone, leaving in its place a hollow shell that freed the memories previously encased to ascend to heaven and reunite with those who had made them.

The contractors began the process of removing the interior walls using a bucket to lift the debris. Just as one would clean a deer carcass, the interior walls were stripped away. First the second story and then the first ... walls and floors ... everything that had been planned and constructed, everything that provided warmth and shelter to a family across the generations was coming to an end.

Some folks thought we should sell the wood for picture frames. Others thought a huge bonfire should suffice. Our idea was simply to remove the debris and bury it on our land, much like you would a dear friend who had passed away.

After two days, all that remained were the exterior limestone walls. The house was but a shell of what it had been. I entered the basement one more time, using the storm door on the east end. This door had been used to provide refuge and safety from storms, both natural and social, in the past. As I entered, I looked down upon the packed earth floor, thinking about those who had come before me seeking refuge, seeking respite, seeking the confidence of wellbeing that only comes when one feels secure in mind, body, and spirit.

Standing in the middle of the cellar, I could look up, as if through a huge chimney, and peer deep into the cloudless sky, feeling the warmth of the summer sun as it began its relentless task of drying the cool, damp floor and basement walls that had been encased for what seemed like eternity.

Even the door to the root cellar was gone, and behind it stood the cool darkness where, for so many years, crops had been stored. Jams and jellies, potatoes and pumpkins, fruits and vegetables had all been hidden here until they were retrieved for the dinner table. The old wood shelving had already been removed, and all that remained were the harvested stones worn smooth by a millennium's onslaught of rushing stream water that had been traversed and placed atop each other for safety, security, and substance so many, many years ago.

With the sunlight pouring in, I saw everything from a different perspective than that as a child. Now everything seemed so small. Now it all seemed so passionless. Now it all seemed so distant from my thoughts, my memories, and my emotions. I stood and peered around the cellar for the longest time, recapping all that had transpired. I breathed in the deep aroma of silence and nestled my soul in the fact that this had been the home of my ancestors and it would soon be gone just as they were, so many years ago.

As I was about to turn and leave, an aberration caught my eye. One of the stones seemed askew. Something was out of place in a pattern of symmetry. I walked towards the wall and realized that the mortar around one was not the same as that which encased all others. It was softer and by color looked much younger. Darkness had hidden this aberration from others. The sunlight had opened it to me.

I took the liberty of grasping the stone and realized that it was loose. With a gentle tug, I removed it and was able to peer within. Even in the bright sunlight, it was still very dark, and yet I realized that I had discovered a small alcove surrounded by rocks creating a tiny, functioning grotto—a safe receptacle within which who-knows-what could have been stored. Money, deeds, documents, jewelry? This had been my ancestors' safe ... a place they felt confident would escape discovery ... a place secure from the ravages of storm and fire ... a place where memories could be stored without the threat of annihilation. As the years passed and its existence forgotten, the now-stripped wooden shelves had been placed in front of the spot, and it was simply unnoticed and unseen.

Without a flashlight, I plunged my hand deep within the hole. Expecting not to find a thing, yet hoping there would be something that would link me to my heritage. I felt the smooth, moist ridges of the rock walls and then the rough gravel of what consisted of the waist-high, enclave's floor. The entire vestibule was less than two feet tall but was more than an arm's length deep.

I was about to conclude the grotto was empty when my finger-tips touched an alien surface. My heart jumped. There was something within! I took my arm and extended it as far as I could. I felt a smooth, flat, almost sticky surface. My hand could not traverse its width nor height. My fingers wouldn't allow my mind to comprehend what they were in contact with. I extended my fingers and thumb and found what felt to be a crease. I grasped the upper edge and very slowly began pulling my discovery from its resting place. Inch by inch, I was able to slide the contents until my hand reached the back.

Was it a small box? Slowly I pulled it forward. I was now able to reach the back of the prize with my hand and pulled it from its resting place.

Looking down, I saw what appeared to be a rectangle carefully wrapped in an oil cloth that had then been covered with sealing wax. Whatever it was, it had been intended to withstand the ravages of both time and the elements. I turned the package over and examined it carefully. Whoever had placed it there had done so with purpose.

I carefully slid my bounty beneath my arm and walked out of the basement storm door. Susan and the contactors were waiting in the sunlight, having allowed me to savor my moment alone in such hallowed ground.

"What did you find?" Susan inquired.

"I don't know" was my response as I held it up for her to see.

"Let's take it home and open it up," I offered.

We climbed into the truck and gave the workers the nod. I would never see the house again.

We drove the mile to our house and quickly went to the kitchen table. I found a box cutter in the kitchen drawer and slit the wax seals so that the flaps that had been folded so long ago could stretch and bend, allowing the contents within to be free.

Carefully, I opened the oil cloth and peered at a tin box. Gingerly, I pried open the lid and found a pile of handwritten papers nearly six inches thick and an old Bible. I had no idea what I had uncovered. I had no idea their source. I certainly had no idea their meaning until I began reading and realized what it was. My God!

I sat down at the kitchen table and began to read. There was first a letter and then a biography. The story of our farm and how it began. More importantly, it was the recollection of a time long ago and the honor and dignity that my ancestors possessed. I share this story of my family and our farm from its very beginning. I share the thoughts and deeds, fears and emotions, laughter and tribulation of my ancestors, and do so with great pride and profound joy.

What a treasure for my children and me ... the story of Waldwick ... our home, our life and our destiny ... the very words of my great-great-great-grandfather George Terrill and a letter from my great-great-grandfather. I only hope and pray that those within this story are at peace that I have shared it with you for I feel that to leave it buried for all of time would have certainly not been what it was intended for.

Henry Terrill

My name is Henry Terrill, aged 54. The year is 1874. The date is October 23rd. Ten days ago, I placed my father, George, in the ground next to my mother, Elizabeth, who passed away six years ago. They are buried on a hill not far from where our house has stood since I was a child. It is a peaceful place where my mother and father would sit after evening chores and watch the sun go down. In the summer, there is a gentle breeze that comes up from the valley below, bringing with it the sweetness of the evening dew that has already settled in with the darkness. My father chose this spot as it was his and my mother's favorite.

I was not aware of this book until the death of my mother. It had been wrapped in oil cloth and placed in a tin box and buried beneath the floor of our house, lest there were a fire and everything burned. My father spoke of it only to me and then only with my word that nothing would be opened and nothing read until he had joined his Elizabeth.

While I have memories from my childhood and thoughts still fresh of all that has been, it is this book and the passages I read that have given me a better understanding of who I am and why this land called Waldwick bears forth the fruit of my family's labor. Now it is my turn to look back, rekindling my thoughts and memories and placing them here, beside those of my father to sleep their long sleep until they too are roused by my demise to be shared with those with whom they shall come in contact. Before taking a journey back into my past, I must fill in the spaces between my father's last entry and his departure, as it will end his story the way that it should end.

George Terrill lived to the age of 76 years, and so you know that he was born in 1798. I cannot understand why he didn't continue to write because there was so much more that he could have said. I guess he shared his memories when he did because he had reached an age older than his father's and yet young enough to remember so much. I also think that he had said what he wanted and decided to let me carry on with my stories of what all has happened.

From the time of this writing until one week before he passed, my father worked the farm. He rose in the morning and helped milk the cows. He helped with the planting and harvesting, and in between, he would help mend the fences and fix all of our tools. He was a powerful man, capable of doing the work of those many years younger than him, and he never once complained about the life he had, because the life he had was his dream ... a dream that he carried in his mind and in his heart from those days so long ago in Cornwall.

In the end, my father died more from a broken heart than anything else. After my mother passed away, he no longer had his best friend. I would watch him as he would go to the edge of the meadow and sit on the fallen log next to her grave and talk as if they were still together. But then, perhaps they still were. Only God knows for sure. Near the end, his only dream was to be with his Elizabeth, and finally his dream came true. What follows is his and my mother's love story that I share with you.

Sincerely and with honor,

Henry Terrill

Mother Earth

I, George Tyrrell, have reached that point ... ten times seven ... ten cycles, and my time has come to share. I sit alone. The love of my life has departed. I write from my memories, and so I can only say that what I write is what I feel is true. As time has changed my appearance, so has it changed what I carry within ... my thoughts, my passions, my memories. I have waited until now to share these thoughts, not out of avarice or lack of will, but to give my mind the temper it needs to share my journey with balance, not fraught with glee nor anger but with the experiences that have shaped who I am. In my life, I have learned that the extraordinary belongs to those who make it, and without a dream, there can only be reality.

I have as my only goal to give you meaning, to provide you with those experiences that have made me what I am. I cannot, will not, and do not apologize for what I am ... for I am simply a common man, a man who has been bound to Mother Earth in many ways, who will someday soon return to her and give back my body so that others may follow.

I did not start out to write what I have written, but as my age has crept upon my soul, I began to accept that there comes a point in everyone's life when their head begins the eventual turn and they start looking back on how they got where they are as much as they look forward to where it is they think they're going. It's not a part of youth. Youth is only tomorrow and immortality. It's not a part of being old when the reality of mortality makes one peer back at yesterday, grasping at memories of what was and what could have been. Somewhere in between these two crossing points is the zone called middle age ... when there are still more than enough of both yesterdays and tomorrows to keep both interesting.

I guess we all reach that point ... sentimental about the past, anxious about the future, thriving on today's today. And yet, like those who have passed through these gates before us, our head has started its gradual turn, and we feel an urgency to bank our memories before too many years paint too many coats of experiences over the details that were once so clear, leaving us with only fuzzy generalities of what once was and was perceived to be.

There are many more chapters harvested from things that I was told that I could have shared ... some funny, some sad, some filled with anger and frustration ... all filled with lessons learned and lessons forgotten. I wonder how many people had promised themselves they would record their lives just in case some day, somewhere, someone should care.

For most of us, there are only five generations that we will personally encounter in our lifetimes—the two generations that preceded us, our own generation, and the two that will follow us. Beyond that, in either direction, are generations we will never know. Those before us are nothing more than a name, linked by a set of lines in a genealogical chart for the benefit of family members who are curious enough to want to know. Gone are the actual family members. Gone are the people. Lost forever are the tales of the elements that made up their lives.

When I was young, my great-grandparents were already gone. If they had still been around, I would have been much too young to remember them. Their stories, like so many drawings stored in a bureau drawer, have faded away because each storyteller eventually stops telling their tales. The stories are those of strangers. We don't know their faces, and often times not even their names. They preceded us on earth, and we are bound to them forever. And yet they are lost in so many yesterdays.

Sadly, unless they were someone great or some great scoundrel, all we have is a dotted line to someone who was conceived, nurtured, and probably mourned at their passing. Nothing more, nothing less ... just a name frozen in time and space. How sad that we can't contact these people and share their stories ... what made them happy and what made them sad, what they feared and what they loved. What would they share with us to make our lives better, happier, and more productive?

Three generations after us, we too will be lost. Our names and images will be all that will be preserved of us by unknowing strangers. How sad, and yet how true. As sad and true is the reality that for many of us, we also will not share of all that we explored, discovered, learned, loved, and feared. Instead, all that we are and done will be dispersed like so many leaves in the autumn wind.

In just two generations, today's grandchildren will become grandparents. Today's events will become distant memories. Unless we take the time to record the small bits and pieces of another day, another era, and to appreciate the essence of a time when everything was bigger, slower, and a lot less complicated it too will be lost.

As we march toward the day when a second generation is following us, I wonder how we will be remembered. Will Grandma and Grandpa be seen as being as kind, generous, patient, and loving as our own grandparents were? Will there be a continuing increase in life's pace so that our lives, our problems, and our worries seem quaint by comparison? We can only hope to be remembered as we remember our grandparents ... as common people who were full of love and pride with a dignity that made them strong.

If we are truly lucky, we share our lives with our parents well into our own adulthood. We had firsthand knowledge of their happiness and comforted them in their times of sorrow. We were the recipient of their unrequited love and nurturing. We were allowed to grow and mature. We continued to increase our independence from them, from a point when our actual lives were reliant on their love and care to a point when we were on our own. Their love and compassion for us gave them the ability to look past our shortcomings, consider us special, and willingly accept the fact that there is a natural inability that comes with age to fully adjust to and comprehend all the change that comes with the passage of time.

As the years pass, in many instances, our parents became more and more like our own children ... reliant on us to protect and nurture ... to defend and oversee ... to comprehend the changes in life's rules so that they could, at least marginally, play the game. This is a natural evolution of the family. This is the way generations before and generations after must adapt. One generation alongside the other ... interwoven yet distinct, reliant yet independent, sharing the joy and fabric of this concept called life.

If we are fortunate, we will share the lives of our children well into their adulthood. Hopefully, we too will have firsthand knowledge of their joys and excitements, sustaining our role as protector from the scrapes and bumps, both physically and emotionally, that they will encounter in life. If we have done our job properly, we will have filled our children with the confidence that only comes from feeling loved ... the confidence that they are accepted for what they are and not for what they want to be ... the confidence that they will always be loved, honored, and respected ... the confidence that, as their years pile up like so many waves upon the sand, they too will be allowed the freedom and independence to journey the road that beckons, unbridled by the vestiges of their ancestry, capable of assuming their position center stage, and willing to accept the risks of life along with its rewards. The hope is for them to be confident that, when it's their turn to play the role of parent, they will do so willingly and with grace, sustaining all that is necessary to provide the same environment for their children that they had provided to them. In today's world, this is a difficult challenge. The world isn't as nice as it once was.

When the day comes that we move to the wings and our final curtain is drawn, we must hope that we are remembered for who we were, what we were, and above all else for our living legacy ... our children. Our houses will fall ... our money will be spent ... our possessions disbursed and eventually consumed, but our family and its character can carry on forever. A parent's deepest wish must be that we precede all of our children to the grave and that we truly rest in peace for doing so.

While looking back appears to be a gradual preoccupation, as we grow older, all of us eventually reach a point when our heads are violently jerked backward. The assumption that life goes on forever is coldly shattered, leaving us grasping for the past as if it were the seeds of milkweed abruptly scattered in the wind.

For all of us, there are times, there are people, and there are events we will always cherish. When we wake up one day to the news of the passing of a special person ... a parent, an aunt or uncle, who was the last member of their generation ... and we realize that the bridge to a previous generation is broken, not only is the loss of the person traumatic, but so is the reality that there is no longer a path of communication to the past. We shudder at the realization, and at the lost opportunities. The questions never asked ... the stories never told ... they're gone ... lost to us forever.

As my head has turned, I have taken it upon myself to share our story. I feel that I owe it to my children and their children's children, too, to simply write down who we are and how we got to be that way ... to share with the unknowing the heritage that made us who we are, what we are, and where we are going. While the pages written here are quite long, what you communicate need not be long or profound ... only a brief outline that will keep those who are interested locked into reality, capable of understanding a little more about who they are, why they are, and how it is that they got on the path on which they journey.

I suppose I could take you back before my time and tell you the tales that were passed to me. I could, but I won't. In the end, those tales all center around but one thing ... the earth ... where my father and his before him and his before all carried on their labor, like me. Our family had been simple farmers in Cornwall who had hoped to return to the land until the Enclosure Act of 1801 forced many off their land and into the earth. Don't ask me why I followed those who came before me. I simply did, and this is my story.

Cornwall

Within the bowels of this great earth lie riches waiting to be taken, scooped out in so many buckets to satisfy the cravings of those above. In the cold, dreary climes of the South of Cornwall, Mother Earth spreads her legs, letting mankind slip beneath her skin ... chiseling their way far beneath her belly, extracting, ever so slowly, the soft, pliable riches of tin.

Since the times of the sound of Roman chariots beating their pulse across the limestone surface, men made their daily trek, scraping up this bluish white ore for use throughout the world ... for armor and cans and even tin soldiers, I have heard.

The exercise within God's earth was not for the common man, nor the foolhardy, for the days were long, the risks incredibly steep, and the rewards ... yes, the rewards ... barely enough to keep a man, let alone a family, alive.

As each century turned to another, the task has become that much more difficult, not only within the miles of hot, damp tunnels burrowed deep within Mother Earth, but upon the surface as well. Slithering on your belly into a hole barely larger than your shoulders, illuminated only by the slight flicker of a solitary candle, always invited disaster. For those who entered the mines at thirteen, as an apprentice like me, the celebration of twenty years of darkness was a shallow victory, filled with the memories of those who simply did not make it.

In my time, the miners were, in a sense, their own men, but the game they played saw them as objects rather than men, parts of the mine rather than parts of life. They were more like crude, raw, phenomena rather than human beings, trailing from the bowels below, gray-black, distorted, with one shoulder higher than the other, stooped from another day within hell's fury, slurring their heavy boots and raspy breaths with underground gray faces, whites of eyes rolling, necks cringing from the narrow shafts within which they had stood ... distorted clowns with shoulders out of shape, bodies asunder, souls reeking, rasping, with nothing more than the equivalence of a living death to show for it.

To slither like a snake within the ground. To grovel for a few pence. To slide asunder beneath the roaring sea. This is not what a man was supposed to be. Yet we did and we did and we did, hoping and praying that there would be more. Hoping and praying that the end was near in one way or the other. Hoping and praying that our children and our children's children would escape the hell in which we labored so that they might breathe the air of freedom.

Men. Men. Oxmen! Nothing more than cattle that had been whipped to do their deed. Alas, in some ways patient and good men. In other ways, non-existent beings, bearing the onslaught they should have given their lives to quell. Instead, moving on, moving on, moving on, until all of us had become nothing but mannequins unable to fight the tyranny that was bred to rip out our heart and souls, numbing our minds with our bodies until all that mattered was here and now and never yesterday, nor tomorrow. Yet we were men and we did what was expected.

Dig. Dig. Dig. And then at night feel the warmth of our lover's body next to ours, motivating us, stimulating us, arousing us, to bring forth heirs to take our place when we could no longer carry our load. We, the miners and those who came before us and our wives and their wives, begot children whose destiny was no more than to become a part of the system built with keen skill to ensure just enough food and only enough dreams to create the next set of workers, when our generation finally met its demise.

What terrible, terrible thoughts. Yet so very, very true! We were men who were good and kindly. But we were only half men, only the gray half of a human being. And yet, we were "good" men, spilling with incarnate ugliness, half dead and yet alive. What would become of us all? Perhaps with the passing of the tin, those like us, so foolish to follow in our footsteps, would disappear off the face of the earth or be swallowed up by the swarming sea as it came crashing down, interloping, dominating, cascading ... taking lives, swallowing those within its path but giving that liberty called death ... the peace, the tranquility, and finally that balance to which we all aspire. Still, what can I say for life that goes on? The human existence is, was, and always will be a good deal controlled by the machine of external circumstances ... a monster more powerful than all, taking, taking, taking until all is taken. Times have certainly changed, for nature has run its course, and Mother Earth is now in the power of this machine.

The men before me had appeared out of nowhere, in the thousands, from which only a few hundred would ever be needed, when the tin man called them. Perhaps for those who came before me and my friends, we all were simply weird insects that existed because of the tin. Were we nothing more than creatures in simply another reality? Were we not just one element serving the elements of tin such as the metal workers were nothing more than yet another set of elementals, who took what we had harvested and melded it into what the tin became? We were, we are, and those who followed were/are/will be elemental creatures, weird and distorted, of the mineral world ... deep within the earth's bowels. We belonged to the mine, to the tin, to the clay in which we dug ... nothing more than the fish who belonged to the sea above us and the worms below who squirmed into the bodies and souls of those departed. Thus was and so is the life of a miner, the animal of mineral disintegration, incarnate ugliness, and yet alive. Breathing, sighing, hoping, praying, but above all else, dreaming, dreaming, dreaming that tomorrow will not be as bad as today.

I would have changed everything if I could have. Sadly, I couldn't and realized at an early age that no man could. Brave of heart, strong of mind, weak of spirit, I too went along, silently wishing, quietly hoping, forever praying for a way to leave. Yet, gnawing at my heart, even today, is the festering reality that the physical sense of injustice is a profoundly dangerous feeling that buries itself within one's soul like some sort of cancer, that, once awakened, must have an outlet, or it will eat away the heart, the mind, and even the soul of the one in whom it is aroused. It is called freedom, and that is what I write about. Freedom, echoed from the highest hill. Freedom, whispered in the darkest night. Freedom dreamt about, thought about, fought about until the sweet nectar is on the very tip of one's soul as one sensed that without freedom, there is only oppression.

I was a miner, and what I share is about freedom. Should you follow in my footsteps and that day arrive when you reach such a milestone, the cough within your lungs from the dust and soot you swallowed will also reverberate off your stooped back and rounded shoulders, making you wheeze, as I do, to simply whisper your joy. The profound risk I met was not leveled with profound reward, but equated by the terror of seeing yet another life taken either abruptly or slowly, as Mother Earth takes you back ... ashes to ashes, dust to dust ... leaving nothing but your name to fade like a fallen timber upon the ground.

Blessed are the women brave enough to marry a miner. Many a widow has shared her grief with those around her as the solitary bell at the mouth of the mine rang out to announce the terror below. And yet, for many, at least there was a sense of peace ... their living hell replaced by a placid sense of tranquility that we call death.

For over a thousand years, the boys came, and the men went, in a slow procession, laughing, joking, praying, that their day's entry would result in an evening exit to share a few precious hours upon the surface before they went back down again. For forty generations, it had been the same. For forty generations, Mother Earth allowed my fellows to reap a bounty that kept father and son and grandson continuing on.

It is normal for young men to have unlimited confidence in themselves and their ability, to feel certain that they can get anything they wish out of life and accomplish anything they decide to accomplish, and it's up to them to do what it takes to achieve their goals. Reality is that not all dreams come true, and those of grandeur and dominance are the ones most left behind as each and every dream of one man is countered by that of another and that of the world in which he lives. Realized dreams can come true if a young man functions according to the nature of man, the universe, and his own proper morality as such. This is when small dreams can come true.

While Mother Earth remained calm and filled with equity, taking only those stupid or unlucky enough as her toll, those who remained upon the surface slowly changed the rules, making certain that those who played could never win the game of life.

At first, the Romans used their captured enemies as slaves, working them until they could work no more, feeding them, housing them with just one purpose ... to keep them digging, digging, digging ... to satisfy their hunger ... like a ravenous bear awakened from a deep winter's sleep.

Just as winter turns to spring, conquerors came and conquerors fell, and yet the mines kept going. The Crown Mines of Botallack stood as reminders to all who came of all those who went. Houses sat perched close to the sea, and the mine's diagonal shaft reached down over 240 fathoms below the sea and then almost as far beneath the Atlantic Ocean.

By 1811, the Queensland Mine matched that of Botallack in size, intensity, and misery, reaching 1,700 feet beneath the surface in its primary shaft, then reaching out, like the fingers of an empty glove, for a distance of 5,000 feet beneath the cold Cornwall shore.

As we labored, dripping our salty sweat into the soft, moist ground, the waves of the ocean pounded above us, beating out a never-ending rhapsody to which pick and shovel sustained their cadence, like so many heartbeats within. Each day, I became buried, as if dead. Each night, I was resurrected, gasping for the sweetness of life.

In a time of relative peace, in a land so wrought with war that plowshares were beaten into swords three times within my first twenty years, we were still conquered ... not by soldiers but by the system. In a period of a few brief years, in a time of our great-grandfathers, the bounty had been lean and, in place of a free worker, what had become known as the factory system had been born ... developed at first as a temporary structure. But, after nearly four generations of existence, the system had been finely honed, like the finest of watches, where every piece neatly fit together, and all parts moved in unison, against the call of freedom.

The Company owned the mine. All that was taken belonged to the Company. We knew the system, and yet still we played the game—too dumb, too fearful, too ignorant to move on. Hoping, hoping, hoping that it would be different. Praying, praying, praying that we would be the lucky ones. Knowing, knowing, knowing that all was against us. Aware, aware, aware that what we dug was our own grave into which we would someday fall.

My Family

Our family consisted of my father, James, born in Cornwall, the son of John and daughter of Clara; my mother, whose birth name was Adele Huxstable; and their two sons. I am one of those sons, and my brother, William, who was ten years older than me, was the other. Two children, who had been born between us, both died. We lived in Waldwick, a small spit of land near the sea, between the towns of Botallack, Levant, and Geevor. My parents lived there their whole lives, as had my father's father before him and his and his and his. All of them had farmed or worked the mines all the way back to some point when all the dreams of tomorrow had been was totally washed away, faded like the pile of soft sand upon the shore by the waves of time until nothing, and I mean nothing, was left of what had been.

What a drop this was in our fate! I heard stories that we were descended from lords and ladies and that we had ancestors from France, where we could count dukes and kings amongst our kin. Waleran, Count of Vexin, and Edelgard, daughter of the Count of Flanders, who was a great-granddaughter of Alfred the Great of England, were some of my forebearers. Waleran died in 965. His son, Walter I, who succeeded his father as Count of Vexin, was also in my lineage. Somewhere, these ancestors met with those of Pepin le Gros, Charles Martel, Duke of Brent, and even Charlemagne, also known as the Great Charlemagne, King of Hearts, Savior of the Roman Catholic Church.

It also has been passed onto me that Walter I married Eve and bore a son, Ralf de Tirel who married heiress of Landry, Count of Dreux. The fourth son of Walter I and Eve, Ralf de Tirel had lived in his castle near the village of Tirel on the banks of the Seine, a short distance below Paris. It was from this village that Walter I took his surname of Tirel. Ralf De Tirel married the daughter of the Seigneur of Guernanville where, in time, he became Seigneur of Guernanville, the Chatelain of Pontoise, and Viscount of Amiens.

The second son of Ralf De Tirel and his wife, Faulk De Tirel, became the Seigneur of Guernanville and Dean of Evreux. He then married Crielda, who was the daughter of Richard I, the third Duke of Normandy. The son of Faulk De Tirel, Walter Tyrell, Lord of Poix, Castellan of Pontoise, and Baron of both France and England, accompanied his cousin, Duke William of Normandy, in the expedition which led to the conquest of England and also was present at the Battle of Senlac on Hasting in 1030.

From Charlemagne, we had descended from dukes and duchesses, and yet here we were, like so many generations before us, digging like rats in the ground. How this happened, I cannot say. All I know is that something had gone terribly, terribly, wrong.

We grew up within the shadow of the mine. While it was simply a dark hole in the ground, you never felt free of its presence, you never escaped the threat that it could one day take your life, and you had a constant fear that your destiny was never more than one bad decision away. The mine was where all boys were trained to work, and by the age of thirteen, I already knew the "game," as my father called it.

There were four points to this "game." First was what we were paid for our labor or, as we called it, our "tare." From our tare, we paid for the despicable roof under which we and our families ate, slept, and dreamt, along with the few victuals we could put on the table to feed our lot. Nothing fancy like meat, mind you, but a few eggs, flour, and what vegetables we couldn't grow. Finally, we paid what we could to send our children to school ... a school I might add, owned by the factory ... hoping that at least they could escape our self-inflicted misery, but knowing all too well that someday the boys would end up beside us, while the girls married them to keep the cycle going.

What we were paid was a simple matter. Each month, the estimator would work his way down into the mine and check the progress, measuring each vein of ore to see whether it was thick and full, like some small stream after a spring rain, or whether it had narrowed and become thin and sparse as the hair on an old woman's head.

When the vein was thick and full, the estimator set the tare low. It would be easy pickings, and no one was allowed to earn his keep without paying his due. To do that would be to allow someone to climb above the hole into which he had fallen, and that was simply not the plan.

When the vein was thin and narrow, the estimator would raise the tare. Work was still difficult, but the carrot on the end of the stick would dangle there, begging you to pull the sweat from your brow and dig, dig, dig to keep the mine and your life going.

I remember my childhood in bits and blabs as it blurred before me. And yet, there are points as sharp as that of a needle that stick within my brain. We played sea captain and dreamt of sailing away, fresh air in our lungs. We played soldier and dreamt of marching away in clean, bright uniforms, believing that bullets were only meant for others and none for us. We dreamt of tomorrow but quietly, oh so quietly settled for the confinement of today.

I was two and twenty and had nine years within the shafts. This is when most things seem to have come into focus. It was the year when so much began to happen to change what followed.

The years had made me strong of back, and I only prayed that I could breathe the freshest of air every day, sweet with the nectar of freedom. At eighteen, I had married Sarah Lawrence, a pretty girl of fourteen. We had known each other our entire lives, and it was meant to be. We lived with my parents, sleeping behind an old blanket that served as our privacy ... listening to my father's raspy breathing, measuring each sleeping breath as if it were his last.

Our house was owned by the mine. It was a row house, simply one large room with a fireplace for both heat and cooking. It was but twelve paces wide and nine paces deep. The roof was thatched, and there was one small window made of glass so distorted that the light that shone through meandered upon the floor, drunk with the disdain of neglect, muddied with the tears of those who had lived there, died there, and cried there before us. Within the room sat one table and four chairs. Beside the table sat one bed with a rope that reached from post to post upon which a curtain had been sewn. The privy was out back and was shared with the seven other families who called this ramshackle arcade home. There was always some sort of noise ... people laughing, people crying, people arguing, people fighting, people taking their innermost frustrations and spewing them into the air for everyone to breathe.

Late at night, the sounds would subside. Silence would envelope our existence and smother humanity in solitude. When all was still, I could hear my mother's tears. She knew that my father's time upon this earth would be short, and soon she would join the others ... alone, afraid, angry ... wondering what each day would bring for a woman of forty-three ... young in years but old in body and, more importantly, ancient in spirit.

When the moments were right, Sarah and I would have our time together, quietly enjoying each other. We would whisper our secrets and smother our laughter, knowing that our actions, thoughts, and hopes were bouncing off walls and ears so very near.

In our third year, Sarah became expectant. It was time, and we felt ready. From the first day, all was not right. She was sick and frail, and soon she began to bleed from down under. As Mother would later say, "It was God's way." When Sarah got her strength back, she became expectant once again. For the second time, God chose a different way than we had intended. After nearly five years, we had no children. Perhaps it was a blessing for what was to come. I don't really know, but that's the way it seems to me now.

For all those years, I had watched my father grow old and then the fallow set in. At first, it was a little stoop in his back, and then the cough was more intense. Soon his strength was leaving him, and the foreman was on his back. Either dig harder and deeper or get out of the mine. There were others waiting to take his place ... younger, stronger, more willing. My father endured as long as he could, the cold sweats of night filling the bed with his misery.

My father was a common man, with only simple dreams ... a roof above his head, a meal upon the table, someone to love him, and every now and then a pint and a laugh to make him forget his lot.

Even with such a common thread, he had his wisdom that he would share with me and my brother. "Get away," he would say. "And never tarry another breath for another man beneath the earth. A man is only a total man when it is his land and all the sweat and tears are simply for himself."

I thought my brother was the lucky one. He was never of the mind to work within the mines. Instead he made his way to sea until one day he sailed for America and jumped ship, taking with him only the shirt on his back and a head filled with dreams of all that could possibly be. He settled in Virginia, and those dreams ... many of them ... came true. But I'll speak of that a bit later, you'll see.

I remember that cold sixteenth day of March of my twentieth year as if it were yesterday. A deafening silence arose from beyond the blanket. My father's staccato breath no longer beat out its rhythm. Silence overtook our home. Father had succumbed at age forty-eight. Our moans were such that the neighbors on the other side of the wall came rushing over. They knew that his time had come, and they were there to comfort. Like so many others who lived in the row houses, attached side by side, soul by soul, life and death were an everyday occurrence that you hoped and prayed would stop at someone else's doorstep and not your own.

It was a workday like so many others, and the grief in my mother's eyes fell as tears that burned her cheeks with desolation. My heart pounded with sadness. The stillness of my father's face beckoned me to look deeper at the man who had always been there for me.

Though surrounded by others, I sat somehow feeling all alone, seeking answers to all that was and all that had been. How I wanted to stay with him, to say my goodbye, to tell him how much I loved him, to listen to his whispers one more time. And yet, the mine called, and I knew that it was me who was being beckoned. My sadness turned to anger. My anger turned to fear. Now I would have to carry on. Death did not stop Mother Earth's calling.

As I stopped in the doorway, one last time, I remember looking back over my shoulder trying to memorize the image of all that there was. I slowly, quietly, reluctantly, walked towards the shaft to take me down to my purgatory. I prayed to God to let me escape from the Hell within which I lived. By the time my shift had ended and the sweet nectar of life was upon me again, my father had been buried. Forever, he was in the ground he had learned to hate.

My Friend Henry

Within the bowels of Mother Earth, no man with sense ever walked, worked, or lived alone. To rely on another was not only what all men must do, but it provided that source of consistency that allowed the life to go on above and below, within and beyond, today, tomorrow, and always. As one grew in experience, he also grew in dependence. One man alone could not succeed. You needed a trusted friend, a partner, someone to live with, someone to laugh with, someone who was there for you as you were there for them.

My friend Henry was just such a man. Henry and I had grown up together, played together, dreamed together, and entered the mines together. Henry was the other brother I never had. At first, we worked as apprentices, hauling the ore-filled buckets that the older men had picked, dropping it in the carts to be hauled to the surface. As we grew in stature and experience, our bonds grew with them, and our lives became intertwined as we became partners in work and in life, sharing hopes, dreams, and fears of the today, tomorrow, and always that which seemed to lie ahead.

As partners in life, we shared our manly secrets, telling tales, sharing dreams, talking of the loves that gave our lives meaning. For me, it was my Sarah. For Henry, it was his Elizabeth. We had all known each other our entire lives, first as playmates, then as friends, and finally as lovers of our wives. Because Henry and I were partners in the mine, we came to rely on each other. Because Henry and I were friends up top, our wives' lives also became intertwined.

As I have spoken, crawling on your belly within the ground was never something one did alone. Falling rock, broken timbers, unexpected gasses, and floods meant you had to have someone into whose hands you could put your life. I placed mine in Henry's. He placed his in mine. I had the better of the deal. Henry was larger, stronger, and much more powerful than I. I stood but five feet four inches and was always thin. Henry stood nearly a half foot taller than me, with broad shoulders and a powerful back capable of doing the work of two men. My job was to crawl into the crevices and pluck the ore. Henry's task was to protect and defend me from the risks at hand and then carry our tare to the measuring point to ensure that we got our proper credit. We worked as a team, equal partners, trusting, relying, sharing our bounty and our risks.

Nearly one in five of our fellows would enter the darkness of the mines never to see daylight again. Their living death would prevail, and they would succumb, without ever breathing the sweet nectar of the fresh air again. You never knew when death would call. Henry and I were always careful. Henry and I never tempted fate. Henry and I felt that what befell our fellow workers would certainly never come to pass with us. We were wrong ... tragically wrong.

It was a gray November Tuesday in the same year as my father's death. We had gone, like we had so many times before, deep within the belly of the mine. As I slid into the darkness, my candle caught sight of a vein so rich that my eyes glistened as my heart pumped in excitement. The mine chief had not been where we were. He had not seen the bounty. We could reap the reward and move us one shilling closer to our goal ... freedom. Freedom from the mine! Freedom from the oppression above! Freedom to leave our horrible world! Freedom to move to America and all that we heard it offered!

In our haste, we began to dig in earnest. In our haste, we let all that we were taught go asunder. In our haste, the care and reservation needed for simple preservation was lost. Instead of making certain that our digging was secure, we simply dug with glee, and then our excitement turned to horror. Within a heartbeat, our world crashed down around us.

For an instant, I thought we had dodged death's dagger. For an instant, I sensed that all was well as I looked into Henry's eyes and he into mine. Quietly I coughed the dust from my lungs and tried to speak from within the rubble.

"Henry" I whispered. "Henry, are you there?" There was no reply.

"Henry," I said with greater urgency. "HENRY." My eyes caught his glimpse, but his eyes did not move. The glisten that had been there was gone. He lay still, without expression. My greatest fear had come true. My friend, my partner, the man I loved more than life itself, was gone. As we lay there for what seemed like an eternity, I could only think of all that was. No longer were there dreams. No longer were there plans. No longer was there anything more than the reality of the emotionless silence that had almost become our common grave.

Within the mine, even under the most wretched of conditions, there were measures taken to satisfy the bonds of those within. Even though we worked in pairs, we also worked in teams. When a pair did not report in, did not bring its tare to the collection point, then everyone knew that trouble brewed, and all those within the mine stopped harvesting the ore and started collecting one another.

I lay beneath the rubble trapped by the rocks, trapped by my fears, and trapped by the reality of the silence of death. Soon I heard the sounds of the rocks being moved and the excited voices of my rescuers. As the men dug, their voices became louder. I began to respond to let them know that I was alive. After what seemed like an eternity, my dust-filled lungs captured the first whiff of the dampened air. The men kept up the vigil to release me from my premature grave. I had been saved by the size of the boulder that had taken Henry's life. I was the chosen one, either lucky or doomed to continue on. Hell had been at my doorstep, and I had survived.

Upon the surface, the lonely bell began to toll, telling all within our small world, that death had once again come to its doorstep. Hearts stopped. What little laughter there was in such an ungodly place stopped. Life stopped, as everyone quietly walked to the mouth of the mine hoping and praying that it wasn't their life that was being forever altered.

Sarah and Elizabeth met and looked into each other's eyes, for some reason sensing that it was their lives that were at risk. They grabbed each other's hands and squeezed with all their might hoping to press the bitterness of death out of their souls, like one would squeeze the last drops of juice from an orange.

Finally, the last boulder was levered from my purgatory, and I was freed. I had been pinned between two rocks, and they had saved my life. I had a badly cut leg, but the pain of the injury was numbed by the pain of my loss of my dear friend. Carefully, my mates lifted my body and placed me in a small ore cart. I was offered a sip of water to clear the dust from my mouth and then a cup of alcohol to numb my pain.

I refused to leave alone. I was not going to rise to the surface without my partner. My mates understood. We had grown together, and he died with me at his side. I would rise from what could have been our common grave to make certain that those above understood. For what seemed an eternity, my fellow miners hammered and chiseled, breaking apart the crucible that had squeezed the life from Henry. When at last, they could free my friend, they carefully placed him beside me in the ore cart. I looked into Henry's now lifeless eyes and pulled the lids down, knowing that I would never look into my dear friend's eyes again, never hear his voice, never laugh at his laugh, and never feel the warmth of his friendship for eternity.

As he lay beside me, I could sense his peace. All that had troubled him was gone. All that was left was the reality that stood above waiting to learn our fate. Carefully, I took a cloth and soaked it with water and began wiping the blood and dust from his face and from his hair. As I finished, I did something I had never done before and would never do again. I bent over and kissed his forehead and then began to cry.

The journey back to reality seemed to take forever. As we neared the surface, I caught hold of myself and became composed for what I most dreaded. Word had already reached above of what had happened. No one was certain what the conditions were. Prayers were to be answered. Prayers were to be shattered like a delicate glass upon a stone floor.

As we reached the surface, I caught a glimpse of Elizabeth and Sarah. They could see my and Henry's heads. I could see their collective relief as they thought we were both alive. Then both women caught my eye, and Elizabeth, sweet Elizabeth knew, like an arrow piercing her heart, that something was terribly, terribly wrong. She let out a screech and fainted dead away. Had not Sarah caught her, Elizabeth would have tried to join Henry in eternity.

How sad the abruptness of death. How permanent the thoughts of forever. How tragic when things that should have been said, things that should have been done, things that should have been shared lie, like fallow seeds upon the ground, never reaping their bounty.

The Sea

Henry and I had agreed. If either of us were to die in the mine, the last place we wanted to spend eternity was in the ground. It was agreed that we would be wrapped in sail cloth and buried at sea, where the fresh air would be the last thing that caressed our bodies, before moving on to another world. And so it was, we took what few shillings we could spare and set about to meet his wishes. The dark gray November skies spewed forth the cold winter rain, washing away our salty tears as we silently sat in the small boat until we reached a point from which the current would carry Henry to his final resting place above the tip of the mine that lay below.

Elizabeth sat mute, in total shock, aware and yet denying what was ... that nothing could change her reality. Two days after we had both been buried in the ground, Henry was again buried at sea, this time forever.

Death is a strange bed partner. It takes the routine of life and distorts it, making life seem slower for those affected, and yet reality moves on, marching to the pace of its own drummer. As we took Henry to sea, that reality had already set in at what had been Henry and Elizabeth's home. It was owned by the Company, as they owned our lives. With the knowledge that Elizabeth could not pay her rent for the next month, the time was convenient to expel her from their lodging while we were away. There would be no arguing. There would be no scene. There would only be the stark reality of the mine and the fact that Henry was no longer there to pay his and Elizabeth's way.

Upon our return, we found what had been Henry and Elizabeth's meager belongings stacked outside what had been their home. Their hopes, their dreams, and their memories stood piled, like so many pieces of chopped wood, soaking in the November rain and waiting to be taken away. This was the reality of the mines. This was life in its cruelest form. There was no time for mourning, only time to move on.

Elizabeth stood silent and lost. Her parents were both dead and gone. Her husband was dead and gone as well. She had no means of support and, unbeknownst to anyone but her, she was expecting. The cold rain washed down upon her life, and she looked to Sarah and me for answers.

"Come live with us," I responded, knowing that she would say no.

"I can't," she replied.

"If only until things are straight," Sarah added.

Elizabeth knew she had no choice. Quietly, we gathered her items and walked the few houses to our own. As we opened the door, arms loaded, Mother's eyes caught mine, and she knew. Without a word, she pushed the table out of the way so that we could spread the wet items out to dry.

"Only until I get sorted," Elizabeth added.

Silence filled the room.

"Only until I get sorted."

How strange to live with three women ... mother, wife, and best friend's widow. Daily, I would go to the mine seeking a new partner to share life's realities. Nightly, I would return home burdened by the weight of supporting all with one.

Those first nights with Elizabeth in our quarters were filled with the sobs of reality. Reality is cold and reality is stark and reality is brutal as dreams are smashed upon the floor. Elizabeth kept expecting Henry back, especially at night. I knew. Oh, how I knew that she would keep waking up thinking: Why is he not in bed with me? It was as if her heart would not accept that he was gone even though her brain told her so. Elizabeth shared with Sarah that she just dreamed that he would return, if only for an instant, and lie against her so she could feel him with her. That was all she wanted, to feel him there, his warm body next to hers.

As the reflection grew, so did her depression. Her dread was not the dream or even the consequence, but the nights when she could not sleep. As she lay there, it was awful indeed, when annihilation pressed in from every side. Like a small slip of paper that was being slowly unfolded to press the letters d-e-a-t-h into her heart one letter at a time until the entire consequence began to appear before her. Death is ghastly on those who live to exist alone at night. Aloneness can be so cruel, especially when all else is at peace. It is like being alive yet without life, where the stillness of serenity becomes your enemy, smothering you in silence so that only your thoughts shine forth.

It took time for her heart to mend. Yet, in one corner, I knew she felt that if there was a heaven above, he would be there, and he would lie up against her, soft and warm, again one day, so that she could finally sleep the deep sleep that only comes from happiness.

Sarah and I kept our curtained quarters while Elizabeth took the place of my father, sharing my mother's bed. How strange to think of two widows sleeping together when less than one year prior, they had been sleeping with their men. How strange what people will do when they must and accept it as reality! We adjusted, and life began, once again, to move on. They say that time heals all wounds. Only time could tell how long it would take for the broken hearts gathered under one roof to heal. Only time could tell when even the slightest bit of laughter would return and joy would once again make its way across our doorstep. Only time could tell what changes would take place that would alter all that we were or ever could be. Those changes had already begun, and we just didn't know it.

The Departure

The winter of 1820 was one of the most severe anyone could remember. The cold winds came early, and with them, the rains. When someone already has a broken heart, it isn't long until their body becomes broken as well. The consumption that had squeezed the life from my father had made its way into the lungs of my mother. In her weakened state, the cold, harsh winter began to take its toll. What had been a young woman became stooped and old. What had been a face filled with the shades of life became faded, with all life washed away. Soon the cough that had been the sound of my father became that of my mother. By January 1821, she was frail. By February, she had become so weak she could not leave her bed. In March, we placed her beside my father. Her troubles ended. Her pain gone, she was at peace. Now I lived with two women and soon my best friend's child.

With the reality that Elizabeth was with child, we knew that all my work would never allow all of us to escape to America. We also knew that we could never keep up with the costs of the Company simply to live. My Sarah had been educated, something few girls were in Waldwick. She had learned to read and knew her numbers and was intelligent.

One day, she took it upon herself to walk to the mine office. She had been before, but only to collect my pay. Sarah learned that widow Daniel was moving to America to live with her son in some place called Illinois. Sarah knew that the pay wouldn't be much, but she also knew that we were in dire straits, and even a few shillings each week would help, especially with Elizabeth's baby coming soon.

Old man Fitzgerald had been with the mine since before my time. He was a rough, crude brute. He had a reddish complexion that matched his hair, and he always had a snarl upon his face. The mine had been good to him and his wife. They lived in the big house upon the hill and had all the fineries of life. Fitzgerald's wife was an ugly, old hag. When we were upset or felt that we had been shorted, we'd make fun of her ... crooked nose, crooked teeth, and crooked spine is what Henry would say. But then they deserved each other.

Sarah had shown Fitzgerald that she could do the numbers, and he took it upon himself to make her an apprentice in the payroll office. He made quite certain to all that he was doing this out of sympathy for my father and the fact that we had taken Elizabeth in and all. Everyone knew that Old "Fitzie," as we called him, liked to keep his eye on pretty lasses, and my Sarah was certainly one of those.

At first, Sarah's place was simply to construct the weekly tare sheets. She would add up the totals and make certain that they were correct. Old Fitzie told her that any mistakes would come from her pay. She wasn't paid enough as it was to afford any deductions.

It wasn't long before Old Fitzie realized that Sarah could do much more and had her figuring pay and deductions owed. It always broke her heart when a woman would show up to claim her husband's pay only to find out that the total of the rent and food was greater than what they had earned and they got nothing but the knowledge that they would go further into debt to the system.

Old Fitzie had developed a way of keeping track so that he knew who was near the breaking point ... that point where a man would give up and risk debtor's prison to spending one more day digging in the mine. At that point, Old Fitzie would call in the tare master and fore-man and make certain that the team was given the richer veins so that they could get closer to the top of the hole. How strange that a man so heartless could play God, and yet he did, day after day, week after week, year after year ... making certain that no one could ever escape.

Every now and then, someone would try and sneak off and head for the ships and to America. The problem was that Old Fitzie had an agreement with all the sea captains, and he would give them a bounty simply for turning someone in. When they were caught, they would either be sent to debtor's prison or come back and lose all privileges, working the worst part of an already terrible job.

My Sarah was an honest soul. She wouldn't have cheated anyone. I guess that's why we were so poor. As the months went on, she began to realize that the numbers didn't add up. Not only were there adjustments to the amount paid for the tare, but figures would be short as well, and Old Fitzie would pocket the difference. She would make them correct and then, when it was time for pay, they would be changed again. The poor, stupid bastard who'd given his soul wouldn't receive his fair share and never even know that he'd been robbed. When you had no way with numbers and couldn't read, how could you ever really know?

Sarah knew that she couldn't speak of what she knew. To do so would have been the end of her job and would have put what little we had at risk. She kept it to herself, except when it came to figuring my tare, she always made certain to let Old Fitzie know that she had double-checked the numbers. I guess that was the reward for keeping her mouth shut. We weren't being cheated!

As spring came, it was Elizabeth's time. In early April, her son, Henry, was born ... named for his father, and rightfully so. With Henry, our little house changed again. The sound of a child made Sarah and me want our own all the more, but it was not to be. With the baby, our lives became full of routine. Sarah and I would work, and Elizabeth stayed home and took care of the house and the baby and made certain that all was as good as it could be.

The fact that my pay was all mine and Sarah was working soon helped us get closer to reaching zero than ever before. It was still a hard climb, but we secretly began hiding money for the three of us to leave for America.

The Proposition

For about six months, things went along quite smoothly, and all seemed well. Then one day, Old Fitzie called Sarah in and told her she was dismissed. He said that he thought she was stealing from the company, something there wasn't a shred of truth to. My Sarah was taken aback. She denied any wrongdoing. She begged Old Fitzie to double-check her work. But he would have none of it. Our dreams were put on hold as our funds began to slowly disappear. We were desperate.

I learned that the three of us could book passage from Ireland to America for about half the fare they were charging from Liverpool, England. All we needed, I thought, was some way to get to Ireland. We were still short of funds. We still owed the mine. We were still as far from tomorrow as ever and yet, we could almost sense the sun rise when it had always been so dark before.

I did some figuring and learned that we could skip across the sea by ferry from Wales and then, if need be, walk to the western side of Ireland to Cork and the ships. Old Fitzie had us, and he knew it. I worked as hard as I ever worked in my life. I dug and dug and dug until my body ached, and yet, without Sarah in the office to check the numbers, I had no way of knowing whether we were getting our fair pay.

It wasn't until many years later that I learned that one day when Sarah and Elizabeth were at home, there came a boy to the door. He had a message for Sarah that Old Fitzie wanted to see her. Sarah thought he had need for her in the office, and she went quickly.

Had I known what happened, both Old Fitzie and I probably would have been dead long ago. Sarah kept it to herself and made Elizabeth promise to never tell what happened. Because I was not there, nor had any way to share my words with others, I can only write what I can imagine.

It seems that Old Fitzie had learned that we asked about Ireland and was afraid that others would realize that they could escape that way, too. Old Fitzie was also afraid that Sarah would begin to tell people about his pay scheme and that there would be trouble. It also seems that Old Fitzie knew about how much money it would take for us to escape from his hell, and he was going to make certain that any effort on our part would require more than we would ever expect to pay.

Once again, I must say that what I am about to share comes only from putting the pieces together and seeing if it didn't make a picture as Sarah never spoke a word of this to me or anyone else. Here is what I have put together ...

One day, Sarah made her way up to the mine office, I am certain thinking that she was about to get her job back. Instead, Old Fitzie told Sarah that the bookkeeper had audited her work and found that she had stolen fifteen shillings intended for pay, that she had been stealing from the miners, and that he was intending to let them know that it was her who had caused all the problems.

Sarah was of sharp wit and she had the correct answer. She told Fitzgerald that it wasn't true and that it would be her word against his. She told him that no one, including me, knew of the pay adjustments and that any accusation of wrongdoing would only open up a whole mess where everyone would begin to question each and every pay stub ... where every single week there would be doubt in the miners' minds as to whether they had been cheated. To lose a miner every now and then was one thing. To have all the miners stop working at once would be a totally different matter that would not only threaten the mine, but Fitzgerald and his way of life.

Sarah had outsmarted Old Fitzie, and he knew it. She was much smarter than he thought. He needed some form of leverage to make certain that she never breathed a word of what was going on to anyone while getting rid of her along the way.

Sarah knew, to the shilling, how much it would take for all of us to escape. For Elizabeth, Henry, her, and me to leave Cornwall forever, it would take a pound to reach Ireland and then another nine pounds, sixpence to travel from Ireland to America. Each week, she would count what we had saved and keep track of how much more we needed.

Old Fitzie, I can only imagine, knew that she was aware of the figure and made her a proposition. She could earn enough money for all of us to leave if he could have his way with her just once. The thought was so repulsive to Sarah that I can imagine her disdain, and yet my Sarah, sweet Sarah, also knew that in a matter of a few moments, we could be free. No one would ever need to know. No one but her, God, and Old Fitzie would know that she shared his bed.

I can imagine her catching her breath as her mind raced forward to Ireland and America. I can imagine the look in Old Fitzie's eyes as he watched for her decision, enjoying every second of her degradation. I can imagine his shock when she said "yes," but only if there was a way to ensure that she would get paid. Fitzgerald had taken Sarah to a level she did not know. Fitzgerald had moved her to a point of total submission, where subhuman acts are done, not out of pleasure, but out of desperation.

It was agreed. Sarah would come to the big house to service Fitzgerald while I was in the mine. It was agreed that she would receive ten pounds, enough for passage. It was agreed that our debt with the mine would be wiped away. All this was agreed, first to satisfy the sick needs of one despicable man and second to make certain that Sarah would never speak the truth of all that was going on. She was willing to forget Exodus 20:14. Her belief was that this was our exodus to freedom.

Sarah and Elizabeth had become like sisters, and they could easily read each other's emotions. When Sarah returned home, Elizabeth knew right away that the meeting wasn't about her returning to the office, simply by the look on Sarah's face. Elizabeth later hinted to me about their conversation. Elizabeth later told me that she had sensed what was going on, for she had heard that Old Fitzie had had his ways with many before her, taking their virtue and their dignity. Elizabeth also later told me that Sarah told her she had agreed so that we would all be free ... one small passionless act for a lifetime of dreams. Elizabeth told me that she warned Sarah that others had been given the same offer only to have Fitzgerald not honor the payment, and there they were, without money, dignity, or their own self-worth. More than one had walked off the cliffs and into the sea, with nothing more than the knowledge that they were victims of his treachery.

Elizabeth said that it was at this point that a plan was hatched to make certain that Old Fitzie would not make Sarah his next victim by making Elizabeth her accomplice. These are from Elizabeth's words, and not just mine. Sarah wrote it and put it away in case it ever became known what had happened.

The Act

Sarah and Elizabeth made their way up the hill to Old Fitzie's house. Sarah led, and Elizabeth followed ... close enough to see what was going on, but far enough away so that no one would realize that they were together. Sarah had been told to come in the back door, and she went around to the side of the house. As she entered through the kitchen, she left the door slightly open so that Elizabeth could follow.

Old Fitzie was in the parlor when Sarah walked in. He had a cruel smile on his face as she entered the room. As Old Fitzie started to stand, Sarah crossed the room and sat on the chair facing him, making certain that his attention was on her and also giving her enough time to hatch her plan. As Sarah sat, she slowly rocked forward in her chair, more out of nerves, I guess, than anticipation.

Old Fitzie's eyes watched her and slowly, mentally, undressed her. She was to be his prize. She was to be his reward. She was to be yet another conquest in his life.

Sarah coyly smiled and watched Old Fitzie's lips curl in anticipation. Her smile was not one of joy, but because she had seen Elizabeth quietly slide into the house and up the stairs. Their plan was in place.

Soon, Old Fitzie beckoned with his hand, and Sarah stood. He raised himself from his chair and, using the same hand as a guide beckoned that she follow. Up the stairs, the ponderous beast climbed with Sarah behind. She had learned from the cleaning woman which would be his bedroom and had instructed Elizabeth on where to hide.

As they entered the room, Sarah's senses caught the mustiness of stale air and the darkness of what lie ahead. The soft light of the almost forgotten afternoon shed its bleakness across the bedroom floor. Sarah stood there, motionless, her fear fighting only her repulsion for what lie ahead.

Carefully, Sarah glanced towards the wardrobe door, knowing, hoping, praying that Elizabeth stood behind ... her sentry, her guardian, our only hope for freedom. She felt that all of our dreams and all of our joy would begin once she had endured.

Fitzgerald beckoned her, his massive hand pulling her in as if she were nothing but a kite upon a string. He knew that she had never done anything like this before, and this is what excited him ... to take another man's woman and have her for himself ... taking away yet another dignity. As he stood there, his breaths became filled with anticipation ... short, staccato gasps of what he dreamed lie ahead.

Slowly, Sarah's hands reached her shoulders ... first her left and then her right. Gradually she pulled upon the blouse that had protected her from Fitzgerald's glances. As the sleeves fell, her milk white breasts tumbled from beneath, catching the old man's attention. Her shoulders arched as if in pain ... not from some unknown injury but from the burden she was about to place upon her soul. She knew that these moments would be branded into her memory as if they were seared by a white-hot iron.

Fitzgerald sat upon the edge of the bed, his huge belly plunging down across his thighs. Once again, he gasped in anticipation.

Now Sarah's anxiety began to boil as her nipples turned hard ... not in excitement, but in fear. Could she do this? Could all that was so very, very wrong finally come to an end, simply because she was willing to submit herself to the man she despised more than anyone, anything that she had ever hated before?

Once again, Fitzgerald let out a long, deep sigh.

"More," he whispered. "More."

Sarah's eyes darted to the window, where the last rays of sunlight were settling upon the face of the mine. She knew that I would soon begin my trek back to reality, and the deed would need to be quickly done.

Once again, she glanced at the closet … hoping and praying that Elizabeth was there, wondering if Elizabeth really understood and accepted what she was about to do. Or would Sarah carry this indiscretion alone and forever?

Sarah's eyes caught Fitzgerald's. His impatience was growing as was the craving within his loins. Perhaps, just perhaps, she could satisfy him without having him violating her, and it would be enough.

Again, there was the hand, beckoning her, telling her that there was more to be done.

"Please let him use it upon himself," Sarah prayed, but she knew that was not to be the case … not tonight, not forever.

Fitzgerald's eyes looked upon Sarah's face, and a tepid sneer pierced his lips. "Come on, little lady. You know you want it. Let me see what ya come to show me."

"Not until I see the money."

"What, ya don't trust old Fitzie, after all I've done fer you and yours?"

Slowly Sarah began to back up, never taking her eyes off the old man. "Not until I see ten pounds, do you get to see any more."

Fitzgerald grunted as if he knew that her will was strong. Slowly he pulled himself up from the bed, with the groans of a man nearly twice his age. There he stood, in his long underwear, buttons split by folds of his skin as if desperately holding the man within.

"Here's your money, wench," Fitzgerald said as he tossed a small bag upon the table. "Now come and satisfy me ... if you can."

"Let me count it first," Sarah said, taking the sack within her hands, feeling its dampness from Fitzgerald's sweat.

Quickly she counted the coins.

"Still don't trust me, eh?" Fitzgerald countered.

"Just want to make sure there's no misunderstanding. You'll get what you're paying for, Mr. Fitzgerald. I'll promise you that."

Without trying to have him notice the degree of her intent, Sarah quickly placed the money sack upon the top of the wardrobe.

"Why you puttin' the money up there?" Fitzgerald asked.

"So that it'll be near my clothes when I take them off."

Sarah's answer seemed to satisfy Fitzgerald's concern, and he slowly sat down upon the edge of the bed again.

"Come on, dearie, show me what ya got."

Sarah knew that the time had come. Behind her was her destiny, wrapped up in a sweaty leather sack. In front of her was her misery, waiting to take her dignity and shatter it, like so many pieces of looking glass upon the floor.

Once again, Fitzgerald was breathing deeply. Once again, the huge hand was beckoning her closer.

The light was now nearly gone from the window pane. Perhaps, in darkness, it wouldn't be so painful.

Now Fitzgerald was again rising to his feet. Labored, he slowly made his way to the table where the money had once been. He took the glass chimney of the oil lamp and raised it. With his thumb, he split the head of a match, igniting it in an instant.

"Gotta see me pleasure, you know," he said with a crooked grin of his yellowed teeth.

Sarah's breasts took on the soft, warm glow of the light, and for some reason, she was suddenly at ease with herself. Perhaps it was resignation. Perhaps, indifference! Perhaps nothing more than exhaustion, physically, emotionally, and even spiritually, as the earth sucked all the energy and youth that had been hers and left her drained and virtually lifeless. She knew the time had come and she would have to succumb, but for some unknown reason, she no longer cared. Her eyes closed one last time on innocence and opened to reality.

She took her right hand and slid it behind her. She could feel the oil upon her skin that comes whenever one sweats, and she could only imagine that which was upon Fitzgerald as his mind raced to a point of concupiscence where his ardent desire erased any and all sense of reservation and his primal urges overtook his patience.

Slowly, she reached for the button upon the back of her skirt and unhooked it. As her fingers expanded to their open position, the skirt fell, sliding down her hips, bouncing off her knees, tumbling to her ankles. There she stood, only her undergarments keeping her from total exposure to only the second man in her life.

Without taking her eyes off Fitzgerald, she quietly stepped back, leaving her skirt, like a puddle of humility, upon the floor. Looking still at Fitzgerald, never taking her eyes off his face, she slowly bent forward to pick up her modesty. Her breasts had fallen forward, no longer supported by the bones of her chest, as the twinkling firelight made them glisten.

Fitzgerald was becoming more aroused. His breaths becoming shallower and more pronounced.

"More," he exclaimed between his gasping.

Slowly, Sarah righted herself and stood before him.

"More."

Again, her hands were to her sides, slowly pulling down her last vestige of modesty. As her pants slipped below her rounded hips, they too fell to the floor.

Again, without taking her eyes off Fitzgerald, Sarah slowly bent down and picked them up.

Now, Fitzgerald was breathing deeply, aroused by the woman who stood before him.

Without taking his eyes off her body, he began to unbutton his underwear. With each button, his body jumped from within, exposing his girth and the years of overindulgence. Soon he was at his waist and the bulge within his pants was straining to be released. With that, Fitzgerald's hand stopped, and he caught himself. He knew that this would only happen one time and was determined to make the most of it.

"Let down yer hair," he quietly said.

With that Sarah, took the comb from atop her head and released her tresses, letting them fall upon her shoulders like so many feathers to the ground. Quietly, she shook her head as if in disdain so that her hair fell to each side, caressing her shoulders as it slid to the middle of her back.

Fitzgerald leaned back upon the bed, peering at her. He focused first on her eyes, glistening in the candlelight, then his attention slid to her face that stood emotionless and drawn. Next his eyes slid down to her breasts as they hung, limp and mundane, no longer filled with anger or excitement. Finally Old Fitzie focused on her pubic area, memorizing its dark hair moist from the sweat of her torment. "Don't worry, missy, yer gonna like this and beg for more."

Sarah stood mute watching the old man saunter in his self-proclaimed abilities.

"I'm quite the cocksman ... you'll see."

She wondered how many had come before. Had they too come only to escape ... to free themselves from the tyranny that surrounded them? And what of his wife? Did she know or care ... as long as he left her to her ways?

With that, she took a short step towards the bed. "Come on, old man, let me make you happy." Why she said that, Sarah didn't know ... only that it sounded like something he would expect her to say.

Fitzgerald slowly bent forward taking her by the wrists and pulling her in. His hands were much softer than Sarah expected and soon they were behind her.

Fitzgerald looked up into her face.

"I've wanted you since you were a child, and tonight you are mine ... just like your mother was, once upon a time."

With that, Sarah pulled back in disgust.

"What's the matter, little girl? You don't think you're the very first, do you? There're been many before you ... including your mother."

Now Sarah's head was turned away, and revulsion had returned.

"Ten pounds is a lot of money for a little tart like you. Do you want it or don't you? If not, get your clothes on and get back to that man of yours. But, remember, things can get pretty dangerous down in the mine, you know."

She knew that he had won. She knew that he had taken her and broken her spirit. She knew that the time had come to succumb. Simply get it over with, she thought. Her head turned forward, and she slowly walked towards him. Once again, his hands circled her waist as she stood before him while he sat upon the bed.

Slowly his hands slid down upon her buttocks, pulling her closer. Now she could feel his warm breath upon her abdomen. Now his hands were softly gliding upon each cheek, softly circling, sliding slowly lower to where they met the tops of her thighs. Now this wretched old man was sliding his fingers along this ridge and, for some unknown reason, Sarah was becoming excited.

Quietly, Fitzgerald pulled back and looked up at Sarah's breasts. As he put his hands upon her waist and slightly pushed down, Sarah knew what he wanted and stooped to let him begin to lick each nipple. Soon they were erect, standing out from ambivalence as Fitzgerald sucked, like a newborn babe, making all the sounds of a child nurturing itself upon its mamma.

Sarah's head rolled back, and her eyes fell shut as she began to sense revulsion. As she tilted her head forward, her glance went towards the wardrobe, and she could see that Elizabeth had opened the door a crack ... standing mutely, a witness to her situation. With anguish now filling her body, Sarah tried to pull away, but Fitzgerald's grasp was too strong, and she knew that she was trapped. With that, Sarah closed her eyes in deference, shook her head, and licked the tears that streamed down her face, moistening her lips with her sadness.

"Come on, tart, enjoy this." With that, Fitzgerald tilted his face down and began pressing his lips upon her abdomen while he rocked back and forth, pushing, then pulling her in and out, in and out counter to his motions.

Fitzgerald looked up at her and smiled. "And you thought it was all going to be misery."

She couldn't answer. Her breaths were simply too deep. Old Fitzie's fingers slid between her thighs, and he began rubbing. At first, Sarah was repulsed, but then the erotic motion became narcotizing. Her breaths became even deeper as her head tilted back. She had never felt anything like this in her life. She wanted it to end, but never end. She forgot all about the money and Elizabeth. Now she only wanted one thing ... for Fitzgerald to enter her and take away the incredible longing she felt. She had reached a parallax. She was at a point she had never known ... excitement, yet revulsion. Arousal, yet profound fear. Wanting, yet hating every heartbeat. How could she be so attracted and yet so repulsed at the same precise instant?

Slowly, she pulled away. Her body was quivering in an aroused state of anticipation, and she felt urges unlike anything she ever felt before.

"Now you want it, don't you, missy? Now old Fitzgerald ain't so bad, is he?"

With that, her head turned from side to side, and she ached for him to finish.

With his fingers, he took her hand and pulled it to the button of his underwear where he pressed it upon the lump within. She knew what he wanted and slowly unbuttoned the buttons. As she knelt down to pull them off, her head was near his thighs and she felt his hands upon her head. Slowly he pulled her up until her face was within inches of his erect penis. Even in the shadows, she could still see its bulges of excitement.

"Ya want yer money now, don't ya? Well then get busy, little girl."

He forced her down so that her lips met his arousal. As she surrounded his erect appendage with her lips, she thought, "My God, what am I doing?" This was not a dream. This was a horrible nightmare and she was caught in it.

Sarah began to suck. With that, the old man took Sarah's hair and pulled her off of him. "Don't want to short-change meself if ya know what I mean."

Quietly, Fitzgerald pulled her up beside him and began to fondle her breasts again.

"I think the time has come." With that, Fitzgerald stood and laid Sarah on the bed. As she lay looking at the ceiling, all she could think about was America ... fresh breezes ... children ... laughter. She knew what she was doing was wrong, and yet after ten years, it was the only way to freedom.

Soon she felt his hands upon her ankles and she knew it was time to submit. Slowly she spread her legs and felt the bed bend beneath Fitzgerald's weight. Soon his knees would be at hers, and then he would be upon her ... or so she thought.

As he knelt, looking at her, Fitzgerald's hands slipped again between her thighs and once again, the slow, methodical motion began and she found herself perplexed. She had no idea what was transpiring.

Now her hips began to undulate, and soft moans came from within her lungs. These were the signs Fitzgerald needed, and he quickened the pace. Soon, Sarah's back arched and gave, arched and gave, and her moans grew deeper and more frantic.

The feelings were hers! The unspeakable motion that was not really motion. Whirlpools of pure sensation that swirled deeper and deeper through all of her tissue and consciousness, permeating her entire body until she was enveloped in one perfect, concentric fluid, suspended in a feeling that transcended her existence. She had never felt anything like this before. She hated him, and yet she needed to prove to him that there was no need for force or threat. She had reached that point of complete absolution where the deed no longer mattered. All that mattered was the consequence ... freedom. Freedom from the tyranny! Freedom from the oppression! Freedom from here and now to think and feel about tomorrow! She lay beyond any realm of reservation and was willing, regardless of how, to service his physical and then her own emotional needs and do so with one simple justification ... "as long as we were free."

This was so wrong, and yet to her it was so right. For all her willingness, there was still great fear. This was a monster who had forced himself upon her, and she was afraid that her efforts would not be adequate and she would die a lonely death, encumbered with the memories of pleasure that he had provided ... realizing that it was wrong ... understanding that nothing would ever be the same again ... accepting that this one time had changed all that there was and all there would ever be again.

From within the wardrobe, Elizabeth peered in total disbelief. Never had she seen an event like this, nor even imagined it. Now Sarah's moans were staccato, and her breathing quickened with each undulation as Fitzgerald kept on. Now Sarah was pulling on Fitzgerald's hair and pulling at his skin, scratching him in ecstasy. He, too, was breathing hard. And then, it happened, Sarah's back arched and her body jolted as if hit by lightning. A tremendous rush shook her entire body, and she laid there quivering, emanating flashes of nervous exuberance that she had never experienced before. "Told ya, you'd enjoy it," Fitzgerald barked.

Before she could catch her breath, he was upon her again ... pumping, pumping, pumping, making her move as if she were a rag doll. Rolling his head back in pleasure, eyes closed, devouring every moment, every thrust, every heartbeat that was both hers and his.

In his euphoria, the old man didn't realize that the wardrobe door had opened, and Elizabeth reached up, grabbed the sack, and slipped out the door. Old Fitzie was too busy submitting to the most primal of pleasures to recognize that the insurance policy had been put into effect.

Soon, Fitzgerald was also spent, and he slipped upon her in exhaustion, breathing deeply waiting for his heart to stop pounding in his head.

Sarah gingerly slid him off her and quickly glanced towards the wardrobe door. It was slightly open, and she knew that her plan had worked. Elizabeth and the money were gone, along with her innocence. He was a beast, and yet he had made her feel like she had never felt before. He was a monster, and yet his way with her had filled her body with a rush unlike anything she had ever felt before. This was not what was intended, and yet it had been what it was, and with it, all had changed. How could life ever be what it had been before? Without a word, she arose and slid her fingers through her hair. Quietly she moved to the wash basin upon the table and began to wash herself.

"Told ya. Told ya you'd enjoy it, ya little tart."

With that, Fitzgerald was up and headed toward the wardrobe.

"Ya didn't think I was really gonna pay ya ten pounds fer one fook, now did ya?"

Sarah stood, composing herself, not saying a word as she felt the coolness of the evaporating sweat slowly bring her emotions down.

Fitzgerald reached up to where he knew Sarah had placed the money. "Where's me money, ya little bitch? Gimme my money."

Sarah turned and reached for her clothes.

Fitzgerald stood before her.

"Gimme my money."

"Get outta me way, ya bastard, or I'll run outta here naked and say ya raped me. Wanta explain that to the missus or to all the boys comin' up outta the mine? They'll string ya up and cut that thing of yours right off."

"It'll be my word against yours … ya little whore."

"Not quite, ya see. I was a walken with my friend Elizabeth, and she saw ya pull me inta yer house. If I'm not outta her in the next five minutes, she's ta go to the constable and tell him what happened … that you raped me. Now get out of my way, before I cut it off meself."

With that, Sarah pulled up her underclothes, put on her skirt and top, and walked to the doorway. "Should I go quietly, or do ya want me to tell the misses I'm leavin'?"

Sarah made her way down the stairs, tears streaming from her eyes. She had not been the first and was certain not the last. Her guilt was not the deed, but the pleasure she had experienced. Quietly she walked into the night. The cool air was upon her, and the chill of guilt made her cold. Sarah looked neither left or right but simply walked straight on, avoiding glances, avoiding stares, hoping that no one could possibly understand all that had just happened. As she slowly walked, she sensed someone next to her. It was Elizabeth. Not a word was said, only a slight tug upon the sleeve and the leather bag was transferred. Freedom was now within their grasp. Dreams would replace the nightmare.

What price we pay for freedom, and yet within the conscience of our own mind, we all can justify almost anything.

In the end, when the turmoil had subsided and her emotions clamed, Sarah was simply afraid. Afraid of her today. Afraid of her tomorrow. Afraid that she would never, ever find the peace and tranquility for which we all so yearned.

Recompense

That night, I returned home from the mine. Even after all these years. I remember it as if it were just yesterday. As I entered the cottage, I could tell something was wrong. Sarah's eyes had a blank stare, unlike anything I had seen before. Her face was flush as if bitten by the winter's wind, and her hair, normally so much in place, was askew. I had learned not to ask too much, and so that night I kept my mouth shut. I do not know what would have happened had I learned the truth right then. Would I have taken after Fitzgerald? Would I have taken after Sarah? Time heals all wounds, softens all pain, and makes even a broken heart beat again.

Elizabeth spent the night taking care of Henry, avoiding meeting the eyes of either Sarah or me. How strange it was with three people under one small roof and yet it was as if we were worlds apart. As we pulled the curtains closed and lay down for sleep, Sarah turned away from me, and I could sense that she was crying. I did not know why. Nor in my wildest dreams would I ever had imagined. Slowly, the darkness of night pulled down the lids of my eyes, and I fell asleep, unaware that the person lying next to me would not close her eyes, nor share in any of her solitude, for fear that her living nightmare of that day would play out within her head. Things would never be the same, but that then, is like all of life. One path altered leads us all to a different destiny.

How strange that I can tell so much, and yet, it was as if I was there, but I was not. Sarah had written it all and neatly placed in within the lining of our Bible. As I arose the next day, I remember that I could sense a change. I just couldn't imagine what it was. As always, I headed for the mine. Little did I realize then that for the very last time my body would make that trek. For the very last time, would I breathe that pungent air. For the very last time would I stoop before another man who had but one goal ... to strip my soul and leave me, like the earth before me, empty of all that had any value at all.

Whilst I was there, Sarah and Elizabeth took what few belongings we had and placed them in whatever they thought we could carry. Around noon, Sarah came to the head of the mine and told the foreman that I was needed because there had been some problems at home. Word reached me in about an hour, and I worked my way to the top. How strange to see the bright sunshine. I walked home as quickly as I could, only wondering what the problem was.

As I entered the house, I could see that the women were packed. "Come, we're leaving for America," Sarah commanded. Where we were, what we were, and how we were mattered not, for at that point in time, the profound allegory of existential change lie on the precipitous edge of reaction concluded by emotion more than reason ... by hate more than logic ... fear simply of tomorrow more than of today.

"But."

"No buts. We're packed and leaving now." With that, we walked out of the cottage and headed up the lane. I remember turning back and wondering how far we would get before we were caught. We walked the rest of the day and made our way toward Wales. The journey was rough with a babe and two women and the constant thought that we would be caught and put in debtor's prison. It took three days to make it to Pembroke, Wales, where the ferry left for Rosslare Harbour, Ireland. How strange we must have seemed—one man, two women, one baby, walking, walking, walking towards freedom, constantly peering over our shoulders, expecting to meet our maker. Nary a word was spoken, and I did not ask. I only knew that things were different, and I was glad. It would be years before I learned what really happened that night.

That first step upon the ferry is with me today. I knew not where the pound and sixpence came from and whence I stood upon that boat, and I really did not care. That first sense of freedom! That first glimmer of hope that no one was coming to take us back! The reality that, as that little boat slid quietly from the shore, all that had been would no longer be ... all that was would never be again ... tomorrow had become today, and with it came liberty while the euphoric shudder made any-thing seem right as long as I smelled the sweet, sweet scent of freedom.

I remember little of Ireland except that it was green even in November and full of hills. We walked and walked and walked some more, and with each day the city of Cork got that much closer. The skies were gray, and yet we traveled on. Every now and then, a passing farmer would see the queer sight of a man, two women, and a baby and would stop and give us a ride in the back of his cart, like hogs going to slaughter. We would stop and spend a few shillings on some bread and something to drink. Elizabeth would nurse baby Henry, and we would continue on. At night, we would depart from the road and find a safe haven where I would build a fire and we would share our dreams of America. For six more days, we walked across hill and dale with each minute, each hour, each day, taking our strength but increas-ing our resolve. From Wexford to Waterford to Dungarvon, across the hills we walked until our feet were blistered and our backs hunched, our stomachs growled and our heads swirled in a maelstrom that only comes from exhaustion. It was the hills from Dungarvon to Cork that almost did us in and yet we continued on, existing only on a dream of a better tomorrow.

We would meet strangers, walking mute along the paths of righteousness, who shared our dreams and our peril. Like us, they, too, were walking away. Away from oppression. Away from tyranny. Away from that which had kept them down. Walking toward a dream. Toward a passion. Toward a prayer for nothing more than a new beginning, a new life and, above all else, freedom.

As for the Irish, people are all alike, with very little difference. The Irish were like those of Cornwall. They all wanted to get money out of you. Our journey quickly taught me that, if you were travelers, they wanted even more, like squeezing blood out of a stone. Ireland. They spoke of its beauty, and yet when all you wanted to do was to leave, Ireland seemed so destitute ... like Cornwall, replete with poor mountains and poor landscape that had all been squeezed and squeezed and squeezed again, to simply provide for today and never for tomorrow. Where there were once trees, there was only grass and rocks and more rocks and then even more. In the dead of winter the growling wind cried out in shame, for nowhere was there a place for it to hide, nor to subside in its passionate search for tranquility.

Few other words were spoken, but then few were needed. We were not the first, nor the last to head for America. We were not alone in our journey. Many had come before, and many would follow our path from England and Ireland itself and all of Europe to a land we dreamed would welcome the tired and the poor and those huddled masses who gave up everything but their dreams. We set out so filled with excitement ... so innocent ... so stupid as to think that all would go as planned. Little did we know, little did we sense, little did we see what would lie ahead.

When we arrived at the other edge of what we thought was the world, we were in Cork and headed straight for the docks. It was a dirty seaport full of shenanigans and hooligans where bars and brothels mixed with churches and stores, where few hands were clean of the filth that comes from taking advantage of others.

We had learned correctly what was needed, and Sarah had saved the money. We booked our passage and had but three days wait for our journey to begin. While the weather had been quite good as we walked across the land, the winter storms brought the rain and cold winds that can chill a man to the bone. With nowhere to stay and what few belongings we had strapped to our backs, we sought shelter wherever we could find it. As I said, we were not the first to come and so, there had sprung up an industry of farmers letting barns and then, while you slept, thieves making off with what you had.

We were careful, and even when two slept, the third kept watch. Our last night was filled with anticipation, for the next day, we would be heading for America. As we slightly dozed, Elizabeth and the baby tried to keep warm near the small peat fire that I had built. Perhaps, it was the warmth, perhaps, simply exhaustion, we will never know. All that I remember is that the first rays of the new day awakened us to the reality that all that we had carried was gone. We had but what was on our backs and the Bible that Sarah had used as a pillow beneath her head.

Sarah had hidden what little money we had left upon herself. While we felt that we could make it, little Henry would be the challenge. Thieves have no soul when they take that which belongs to a child. Elizabeth volunteered to stay behind. We would not hear of it. Passage had been paid and the opportunity would not come this way again. She and Henry would be alone on the docks. If she would not go, then we would all return to England and do what we could to survive.

We had but a few hours before the ship departed and so, we took what little money we had to purchase a warm blanket for Henry, along with what little food we could afford.

The Sea

Once again, I can see the image before me, as if it were just yesterday. As we neared the dock, we saw a huge number of people. I thought they were there to simply say goodbye. Instead, they, like us, had paid their fare for the voyage. In a ship where the hold could handle no more than 200, 343 souls were jammed. While our belongings had been stolen by thieves, the thieves who ran this ship had stolen our space and simply took the belongings of those who had come and left them sitting on the docks. You had paid for your passage and not that of your treasures, they said. Our memories or anything that wove a tapestry to our past had to be left behind. For us, they had been taken the night before.

As we boarded the ship, all we had were the clothes on our back, what little food we could carry, and the family Bible that Sarah kept beneath her cloak. As we made our way below, the fear of 11 days in cramped quarters was upon me. I looked upon the crowd and wondered how many would simply perish along the way. I wondered how many would lose loved ones. I wondered how many dreams would come to an end as we huddled and prayed and hoped and dreamed and promised ourselves: Never again! Never again! Never again!

As we slipped from port, the full force of the merciless ocean was upon us. It was late November, and the thrusts of winter tossed the boat like it was simply a toy. The cold damp weather from land was soon replaced by the bitter cold of the sea. I can still remember the sounds as if they were still being played. First it was the sound of the sails snapping in the wind. With each change, there would be a dull crack as if God himself was whipping the souls of those on board. Next would be the creaking of the wood of the boat, a soft, high-pitched moan as if it were crying out to all those it carried to forgive it for what was being done. Finally, I will never, ever forget the sounds of people crying, coughing, breathing ... simply trying to live one more day, one more hour, one more minute of their dreams.

Three hundred forty-three people tried to sleep, tried to eat, tried to survive. With weather so rough, the challenges not thought of became apparent. Relieving oneself could not happen above, and so, the small trap door to the ballast below became our only portal from which we could all go.

Within two days, the stench began to fill the below decks and mix with the smell of 343 bodies ripe from lack of bathing or cleaning one's mouth and that which lay below. What little food was guarded at all times, as it represented the only manner anyone could think of surviving. The results of the cold, damp journey that had taken its toll on the bodies of our fellow passengers began to show. Seasickness and vomiting became common, and its stench quickly blended with all the other unpleasant circumstances that attacked our senses. We were weak. We were dizzy and we were cramped ... too many people ... too little room ... not enough to eat.

I guess when you are in such a situation, you don't realize the gradual changes that are happening around you. The first small itch upon yourself seems like nothing until you begin to see those around you scratching and realize that you are all infested with lice. The pale gray color of those near you seems normal until they no longer move and their fallow eyes lose their gleam. The slight coughs from a few days prior are now a symphony of raspy throats spewing forth in cadence from within. Illness was upon us, and all but the very strongest were at risk.

The first to go was an old woman. She probably should have never boarded, but she did. On the fourth day, her body was taken above and dumped into the sea. Sarah, pulled out our Bible and read the 23rd Psalm. "The Lord is my Shepard, I shall not want. ..." By the tenth day, that Psalm had been read 13 times. As each of us prayed for the lost soul, we thanked God for just a little more room, a little more water, and hopefully a little more quiet.

Elizabeth, Sarah, and I took turns watching little Henry. Elizabeth would nurse and then we would take our time watching him. Because our rations had grown so small, Elizabeth was not eating properly and soon she could not produce the milk that Henry needed. It is so very difficult to listen to a baby cry out in hunger. It is even more difficult to hear the roaring silence when the crying stops because a little one is too weak to cry. Young Henry was the 15th to visit the deck. We wrapped him in the blanket we bought and bound it with a bit of rope the crew had given us and said our prayers. "He maketh me lie down in green pastures. ..."

As we stood there, the three of us, with salty tears being washed away by salty spray, said goodbye to our little Henry and to the father he never knew. Death had come to both of them before their time. Death had visited Elizabeth, and as she looked into our faces, I knew that she wanted to join her Henrys, but God would not allow it. "He leadeth me beside still waters. ..." Without a word, we slipped Henry into the sea, drank in the last bit of fresh air we could, and headed below decks.

In our misery, we had forgotten how vicious people could be. The space that we had protected had been claimed by others. What little food we had saved had been devoured. What dreams we had of America virtually drowned in our own tears. When it is three against the others, you quietly accept that you are beaten and move on, vowing to get even ... some way, somehow, someday.

As the trip continued, people turned to catching the rats aboard the ship and roasting them. It was meat, they said, to give them strength. With each day, I saw the three of us fade a little more. With each day, our strength was less and less and less. With each day, our vivid dreams turned in the faded sky, and we wondered just what it was we were thinking so long ago when we were still in Waldwick.

They say that sleep is the nearest to death that one can get. Each time my eyes closed, I hoped it was the last. Each time my lids slid down upon each other, I prayed that my journey had ended and that I would be the next to find the peace we had dreamed of. Each time, when I would awaken, I would realize that my dreams were just that and that my nightmare was all around me. I hated crawling on my belly within Mother Earth. I came to hate even more the sea and the death it brought, promising myself that I would never, ever sail again.

We were but one day from Baltimore and our reality when I looked at my beloved Sarah and began to realize that her voyage was about to end. Her face was pale and drawn and the cough that had been the end of so many others rang deep within her lungs. As she lay beside me, she looked into my eyes, too weak to speak, and she quietly mouthed "I love you." I gently squeezed her hand and nodded that I loved her, too.

"We're but a day away," I quietly said. "Please wait for me."

Again, she looked into my eyes and softly nodded towards Elizabeth ... without making a sound. I knew what she was saying ... that Elizabeth and I could carry on. Once again, she looked into my eyes, and then her lids closed, and the faint grasp that she had on my hand was gone...as was she. My Sarah had died. We were but one day away, and yet the ravages of the sea had taken her from me. "Yea, though I walk through the valley of the shadow of death, ..."

I remember as if it were a fortnight ago that when I touched her, she lay very, very still, receding into a silent and strange motionless distance, far, farther, farthest than the horizon upon us, and with her travel, my heart began to weep. I could feel her soul ebbing away, leaving me there like a stone upon a shore. She was withdrawing, her spirit was leaving. I knew she was gone, and in real grief, I was tormented by my own double consciousness. Had we stayed in Cornwall, both Sarah and Henry would be alive. It was my dream that killed them both, and I began to weep ... soulful melancholy sobs for which I took no notice to those around me, nor did I care. The storm of regret welled within my heart until my weeping swelled and shook me, and those around me covering me in a tidal wave of despondence. This would be my final memory of Sarah. Quiet, still, alone, cold, gray in thought and mode. How profound that it would be one of sadness, but then, for the living must this always be the case for those who are dead?

All that we do, all that we think, all that we feel, never cease to exist. They can always be found some place in our soul. Yet, some memories remain like mountain peaks jutting above the land, as pinnacles of joy or sorrow or guilt or regret forever marking a point in time that permeates our heart and impregnates all the other memories that are associated with it. Such is sadness, an infectious disease that many cringe and seek to avoid until it is their own that prevails.

I looked at Elizabeth, and she at me, and we knew right then and there what need be done. We simply made it look as if Sarah were asleep. Sarah was not going to be dumped into the sea. She was going to be buried with her dreams ... our dreams ... in America.

Those last hours before landfall seemed to be forever. The seas had calmed, and so many of those that I had learned to hate moved topside for air and to give themselves the first chance to see their tomorrow.

Elizabeth and I stayed with Sarah waiting for that moment when we could, once again, step foot on dry land.

As we sidled up to the pier in Baltimore Harbor, the rush began. Of the 343 who had started the journey, 296 made their way off the ship so that only Elizabeth, Sarah, and I remained. Forty-seven had died along the way, including little Henry and my Sarah. Slowly I took what little strength I had left and lifted Sarah. What had been a strong woman had become nothing more than a wisp that even I could easily carry.

We simply wanted to bury her in America, and so our wish was granted. In an unmarked spot next to so many others, Sarah was anointed ashes-to-ashes, dust-to-dust, the 23rd Psalm read again as it had been written. "Surely goodness and mercy shall follow me all the days of my life; and I shall dwell in the house of the Lord forever."

Elizabeth and I held each other and cried ... sobbing great tears of sorrow ... sobbing great tears of relief. We were in America, and we were free. Our dream had come true, but with it, nightmares so permanent that they would never, ever be forgotten.

I opened the Bible to read from it when I noticed the small slip of paper. It was what Sarah had written about that time with Old Fitzie and what she had done to earn the money that awarded us our freedom. At first, I shook with anger and then with remorse as I realized and recognized that I was the one who had been so selfish. I was the one who had only thought of his own feelings, his own satisfaction, his own needs, and never those of Sarah. How weak I had been. How shallow. How so self-centered. Her sacrifice had been for all of our good, and yet her pleasure was so profound that, from the grave, it burrowed into my mind and tore through my heart and my soul, making me an invalid, unable to comprehend how I could have been so rough, so crude, and so alone in my satisfaction.

She was not a repository of my senses, and yet that is what she made me feel. I had lost her physically that night in Old Fitzie's domain, and for the very first time, I realized how inadequate I had been. I now understood why she had been so different. It wasn't simply the act that she had done, but the fact that the pig had made her feel what I never had, made her sense what I never did, made her be aroused unlike any time when we were ever together. As I stood there, stoic and emotionally isolated, a cold shiver of remorse trembled my shoulders and made me realize what I had been, and I fell on my knees in the soft ground of her grave and prayed that she would forgive me ... for my dreams, for my aspirations and above all else, for my indifference.

Our voyage taught me that hate can be a growing monster like anything else. Hate is the inevitable outcome that results from forcing ideas onto our life ... fomenting one's deepest instincts, darkest intuitions, and primal intents into our beliefs and feelings to such a point that thoughts result in hate instead of love, turmoil instead of peace, and insolence instead of humility. A simple twist, a minor turn, one slight variance, and what should have been good can be bad, what should have been happy can be sad, what should have been attractive turns ugly to the point of revulsion. It is a fine line between love and hate, and I wonder if people hate to love or even love to hate. Such are emotions. Such is life.

Elizabeth pondered my expressions and began to realize that the secret that had been hidden was now shared. She understood my perplexed soul and gave me comfort. From her, the forgiveness I so deeply needed came forth. She was my bedrock. She was my soul. She became the earth beneath my outstretched fingertips who gave me the strength and courage to carry on. I knew that at some time when all was right, we would share what happened that night, but not at this time and certainly not when and how we stood or where we stood ... together.

Beyond the grave stood the office of immigration. We needed to cross over into the world for which we had held out so many hopes. I remember there was a sign on the outside of the building that began, "We hold these truths to be self-evident, that all men are created equal, that they are endowed by their Creator with certain unalienable Rights, that among these are Life, Liberty and the pursuit of Happiness." I learned later that it was from the Declaration of Independence ... that of a people, that of a nation ... that of those who came forth in the search of freedom.

With so many following the dream, there were rules. It had been set that only the living came to America. If you were sick, you were quarantined until you either were better, died, or went back to where you came from. We were given bits of food and water and, three days later, were presented to immigration. Should we affirm or deny freedom? Should we accept or acquiesce the liberty? How can one know when they have never peered through the thickness of constraint to examine the other side?

In 1820, the government began registering everyone by name and where you came from, and we were some of the first. As we stood in line, I looked at Elizabeth, and she at me, and we knew what had to be. Upon reaching that point of registration, I signed George and Elizabeth Tyrrell, husband and wife. Without looking up, the officer took note and recorded George and Elizabeth Terrill. I tried to explain to the officer, but not a word was spoken. In the stroke of a pen, we had become man and wife and our last name was changed forever. *Welcome to America, land of the free.* We stepped across the threshold into our destiny.

The New Land

How incredibly strange to set foot in this new land. All that we had imagined just wasn't there. The streets were not paved with gold. They were of mud that stuck to your boots and made your feet grow cold. The folks who came and went did nothing to help, as we had thought they would. We were strangers to them ... interlopers who came from afar, looking for that proverbial pot of gold, and they wanted no part of us. We were cold and hungry and smelled of death. Those of us who made the trek stood as strangers amongst strangers, wishing, hoping, praying that something could happen that would send us on our way. Amongst those who were, we became those who would be, the chasm of which seemed simply profound ... bubbling to the point of emotional disarray of love and hate, desire and disdain, acceptance and profound rejection, simply for not having and profoundly being a have-not.

If it were for a moment, it would have been one thing. If it were for an instance, it would be another. But we were looked upon and hated simply for being and sadly, so sadly, hate can be a growing thing like anything else. It's the inevitable outcome of forcing ideas onto your life ... of forcing one's deepest instincts, one's darkest intuitions and one's most somber intents into your primal feelings that results in hate instead of love, turmoil instead of peace, and insolence instead of humility.

In our voyage upon the sea we had learned so much about ourselves and about others, to the point that I would have thought a person would have died of shame to endure what we had and still exist the way we were. Instead, the shame died. Shame. What a sad word. What a sad state of existence. I began to realize that shame is nothing more than fear. Deep, organic fear. Physical fear, which crouches in our body and in our roots only to be chased away by the lust for life, tendered by the fuel of dreams about something better than what we trusted and endured.

As we left the immigration office, Elizabeth and I thought that we had reached the bedrock of our nature and were essentially shameless. We were naked to the world in thought, emotion, and purpose. There was nowhere that we could perceive we could ever go that would be any lower. Yet, we felt a triumph, almost a vainglory that comes from feeling that nothing could ever be worse than where we stood that winter's day. Cold, hungry, filthy and with no means, we were at the bottom of the bottom, looked down upon in disdain, avoided at all costs, shunned like lepers upon the stage of life, regardless of our circumstance. Welcome to the land of the free and the home of the brave.

So, that was how it was. That was life on that first day of freedom. That was how it really was. There was nothing left to disguise or be ashamed of and no time for recompense. We vowed that we would dig our fingers in the muck of life and pull out what little we could upon which to build anew with the commitment and perseverance and the vow that we would never ever forget where we had been.

As the joy of the new land grew faint within our hearts, reality set in. Maryland was colder than I had imagined it would be. Folks like us who had been on a ship and those before stood huddled around burning fires, trying to keep warm. Thoughts lingered in each of our heads … food, warmth, freedom. Each day there were less of us from the ship as yet another walked away in search of a better tomorrow.

Elizabeth and I needed money, and we needed a plan, and Virginia seemed a long way away. I had no time to write to my brother, William, before we departed, and there was no way for him to know where we were. The last words that had been written were over a year old when our mother died, and he did not respond. I hoped that he would take us in until we got our feet back on the ground. I prayed that he would welcome us as I would have welcomed him. However, I also understood that we had never been close, never really been brothers ... just two lost souls who happened to have the same parents and lived in the same house, who never shared our dreams.

Elizabeth and I had searched for any form of employment, and none was to be found. When your trades are miner and mother, there's not much for you to do in a city like Baltimore. Slowly our world expanded beyond the docks and the shysters and whores who frequented there. We slept where we could for three nights until I could take it no more.

I remember that it was Saturday, and we had seen many people who looked like they had money entering a long brick building. We felt awkward and yet were enticed by the welcoming respite from the winter's wind. The roof was low, and there were three chimneys eliciting the warmth of the fires that burned within the roiling heaters. Our intrusion, however brief, meant we could enjoy, at least for a few moments, some degree of comfort and relief. As we entered, we saw long rows of benches and behind a space for common folk like us to simply stand. We were outcasts and were looked down upon with great disdain, and yet nary a word was spoken to or against us, nor did any eye meet ours. Within the large room was a small raised platform. At first, we thought it was for play acting, but it was the middle of the day.

Soon they were brought in ... a group of 20 to 30 dark people. Slaves. I had never seen a dark-skinned person before we set foot in Baltimore. They were all chained together in a row ... men, women, even children, some the age of eight or nine. I could only imagine what was in their minds. They had been torn from their families and their ways of life and placed upon a ship.

I could only imagine what their voyage had been like. Ours had been filled with terror, and we had paid our way. They had been thrown into the ship's belly not knowing where they were going, only knowing that is was far, far away from where they had been. I could only imagine the fear that resided within them. Their futures were unknown, and whips and chains had replaced the freedom that they once knew, here in the land of the free.

As we peered across the room, the first of group was unlatched from the others and brought forth. These were the smallest children. They did not know what was happening. They were too scared to do anything. One little boy wet himself, and for that, a man four times his size beat him with a club until he fell upon the ground. No one moved. No one said a word. Not a single soul defended that small boy.

The children were grouped in threes and fours, and the bidding began. Those who rose to make their presence known talked of breeding stock, investments and long-term returns, and it made me sick. These were human beings with souls and the grace of God within their hearts, and yet to those in the fancy dresses and fine cloth breeches, they were but property much like someone buying a calf or even a lamb.

As the bidding ensued, the price was raised at first by dollars and then by cents. Three boys and a girl, linked together in misery, bonded forever for the tidy sum of $40.20. Four lives. Four sets of dreams. Four children sold for ten dollars and five cents each. How sad! My only hope was that they would live in peace and dignity ... that their lives would be spared the brutality that comes from domination and subservience. My God, how inhuman humans could be.

Within minutes, the children were disposed, and the procedure took itself to the adults. First the smallest and the weakest and therefore the cheapest until there were only two left ... this auction's prizes.

How easy it is to forget so much and yet how easy one can remember some things as if they are burned into your heart and soul forever. I will always remember him. He was wrapped in nothing but a cloth that wound between his legs and around his waist on the coldest of days. He was led to the stage, and his arms were shackled such that they were spread apart, like an angel. Next his ankles were positioned the same way so that he could not move ... shackled apart. I remember the look within this man's eyes ... anger, fear, hatred, burning like hot coals, searing into everyone's memory.

I will never forget what happened next. The foreman walked up and untied the man's cloth so that he stood naked before all. Soon, both men and women arose and began "inspecting" this man. At first, it was a casual glance, and then they began prodding ... poking here, grabbing there; inspecting as if he were a horse or just a piece of meat.

One woman in particular remains with me to this day. She looked the man over from top to bottom, pulling his lips apart and checking his teeth. Squeezing each hand and pressing on each muscle and then grabbing him by his privates, squeezing to make certain that they were in place. Without emotion, without any reservation, without any thought, this woman inspected what would soon become someone's "property" to make certain that he was "all" there.

"Good breeding stock," I heard whispered, and at that, I was so repulsed I wanted to set the man free. We had come to America for freedom, and there, before us stood a man, a proud man, who had no freedom. In Cornwall, we at least could make some decisions. In America, land of the free, for some, there were to be none.

The bidding began, and the auctioneer announced that what stood before us had once been the leader of his nation. What stood before us was a former powerful leader of great skill. What stood before us was a man who could be used to enhance one's "property" and increase one's "value." There was no consideration for love or passion, only for an increase in the number of slaves one owned. Freedom was not for all. The bidders sat in all their finery looking so prim and proper ... so superior to what stood before them. The system was already built when we arrived. Supremacy wasn't only used to justify slavery but to keep in line the Southerners who weren't slaveholders as well. A tiny minority of slaveholders controlled everything. The government! The economies! The ways of life as they ruled over the entire population!

I looked in the man's eyes and saw his anger and his pain. I watched as each labored breath was simply his breathing out his independence and his dignity as he knew that he had been beaten. I was aware that he knew that his freedom and his honor and dreams were simply gone, replaced by the shackles of tyranny that come when one man controls the life of another simply because of the color of his skin. Although nothing that has been experienced ever ceases to exist, some are relegated to the unconscious simply because they are irrelevant and unimportant to our lives. However, others burrow into our soul, leaving an indelible mark that transcends who we are and what we truly want to be. So was this man upon the stage. Once you have seen a hidden image, it is easy to see it again. The profound challenge is to darken the sky so that you cannot see it and then bury the thought so that it is once again hidden ... dormant ... and in refuge from our "now" even though it remains there still, and deep, as the dream of regret. So was this man upon the stage.

The man's head tilted back as the bidding continued. I cannot say what his thoughts were, but I can only imagine. I am certain that he was looking to God for salvation. I am certain he was asking God, why was this happening? I am certain that he was praying to God to simply take his life and let it end, but this was simply not to be. So was this man upon the stage.

The bidding stopped at $250 ... a large sum, enough to buy three horses. The man was led away with his new owner and chained to a post, as the man had chained the horses for his wagon. So was this man upon the stage ... burned into my soul ... forever.

Next came a female. Again, proud. Again, filled with fear. Again, desperate to return to what had been her reality. Her arms were shackled and, as she stood there, the process began again. Her clothes were removed, and inspection began. This time it was not for her ability to work hard, but her capability to breed. As those who inspected moved close, tears welled in her eyes and slowly trickled down her face. A hook was used to pull her legs apart, and every single inch of her was inspected.

I watched as her eyes darted around the huge hall as she sought the man who had been before her. Could it have been her husband? Could her dreams of sustaining some sense of consistency be before her? Could it be that she was simply looking for a sympathetic eye? I do not know.

I looked at her face, full of scorn and full of sadness, and knew that she realized her life as she had known it was over. Her eyes grew wide so that I could see the whites all around their middle. She let out a scream that only resulted in the hook being used to beat her across the buttocks. How sad, how incredibly sad. What more can I say? Even after all of these years, it was burned into my heart and into my soul for me to carry forever.

The bidding began and soon stopped at $180. A human life for one hundred eighty dollars! The process was the same, the bidding stopped, and she was unchained from the posts and pulled away. As her head turned back, she caught the man's eyes, and in one fleeting moment, their lives, their dreams, their hopes for their future evaporated forever. As she walked, her legs buckled, the man leading her grabbed her by the hair and pulled her up, and they stumbled out the door.

What we saw that day was nothing to what we heard. The whip represented the everyday violence of life, and few slaves went through their lives without experiencing this form of punishment at one time or another. The pervasiveness of rape and violence was part of the nature of the system itself and was also used to discipline the workers. Humans were dehumanized. They became chattel ... nothing more than a piece of property to be bought, sold, used, and abused.

I could watch no more. The freedom that was ours was not to be theirs. The dreams that were now Elizabeth's and mine would never come true for them. All that was supposed to be would never be, all in the name of commerce. I remember looking at Elizabeth, and she understood. We would never, ever, own slaves. How could one come to America in the name of freedom only to take it away from another?

As we walked out into the cold, reality hit us as if it were the winter wind. We needed to travel to Virginia, and we needed to do so soon. As the participants of the auction began to appear, I took it upon myself to quietly ask if we could trade our services for transportation, should anyone be traveling to Virginia. Some ignored us. Others said no, they weren't traveling that way. Others said they had no room. Finally, I came upon a couple who had made the journey and did not acquire any slaves. They said they were headed for Virginia and we could have a ride if we were willing to help drive the team and prepare the meals. We agreed and set about getting prepared for the journey.

As we traveled, we learned that these folks—the Wilsons, I think their name was—had come from England as children with their parents and had settled outside Richmond, Virginia. They grew cotton and tobacco and owned several slaves. While they did not think it was the right thing to do, they also rationalized that they needed them to work the farm as they could not do the labor themselves. They seemed like good God-fearing people, and they were proud of the fact that they treated their slaves well, keeping families together and giving them all the necessities.

To pass the time, we spoke of Waldwick and of our dreams. We shared our hopes and aspirations, and they smiled at our youthful determination. When they spoke of the slaves, they called them the coloreds. What a strange name I thought. Coloreds. Weren't we all colored in the eyes of God?

Amity

After one and one-half days, we came to a point outside Richmond. We departed and thanked the Wilsons for their assistance. We took what little money that remained and purchased some bread and hot broth. We still needed to travel to my brother's home in Amity, but we were in Virginia.

When one lives so far away, we all think in generalities. Ireland seemed distant, and yet we had traveled there. America seemed distant, and yet we had traveled there. Virginia seemed distant, and yet we had traveled there as well. Amity could not be that far away. Little did we know that Amity was a greater distance from Richmond than Baltimore. Little did Elizabeth and I know that the walk would not be across flat land but hills and valleys. Little did we know that the area between Richmond and Amity would be filled with people who did not welcome strangers. Had we known, we probably would never had ventured, and yet we began. For five days, we walked in the cold of December asking directions, foraging for food, doing nothing more than trying, trying, trying to make that very last part of our journey happen as quickly as possible and with as few of threats as we could endure.

When both of us had just about given up, we came to a small road with a sign that said, "Amity Four Miles." We were just four miles from where we had set out to end. Just four miles from family and warmth. Just four miles from safety and security. Those were the four longest miles of the entire journey, and yet on December 17, 1821, we arrived at the home of William Tyrell, my brother. We must have been a strange sight ... two haggard, skinny waifs, clothes dirty, unkempt, wreaking of the stench of six weeks in the same attire.

As the door opened, my brother stood before me, his mouth agape. He had no idea that we were coming. I shall always remember the look upon his face ... one of disbelief, then one of joy and finally, one of concern.

"How ... ?" was all that he could murmur before I opened my mouth.

"We left Cornwall six weeks ago. We paid our dues and saved our fare and Sarah, Elizabeth, little Henry, and I came for America."

"But ..."

"Sarah and little Henry are in God's hands. Elizabeth and I have journeyed on."

"Where?"

"We need a place to stay until we can get our strength, and I will look for work."

"But ..." was all he could get out when behind him approached a woman ... tall, erect, strong, with deep red hair.

"William, who are these people?" she asked.

"My ... my brother," he replied.

"Why have they come here?" she asked.

"They had nowhere else to go," he responded.

Elizabeth and I sensed immediately that all of our hopes of shelter and acceptance were not to be.

"All we ask, is for some warmth, a chance to bathe, a change of clothes, and we'll be on our way," Elizabeth added.

"No, no, heavens no," my brother responded. "It's just that we're ... we've ... we are just so surprised. Please come in."

With that, he stood beside the door, and we walked in. The house was large by Cornwall standards, with several rooms. The floors were made of wood instead of dirt. The fireplace was large and contained no rod for cooking. Its warmth was such that I will always remember its welcome as it took the cold from my body and filled my spirits with hope for a better tomorrow. On the walls were paintings and tapestries, and I could see the woman's touch.

"Please, please, sit down," William said.

With that, we moved a little closer in. However, I could tell by the woman's look that she didn't want us to sit.

"Perhaps, we should stand," I offered.

"Nonsense," William quickly replied.

"I don't think we should be sitting when we're as dirty as we are."

"I think a hot bath for each of you would be best," William agreed.

Turning to his wife, he said, "Can you ask Clara to prepare two baths in the smokehouse?"

Without a word, the stern woman turned and exited through the door.

"She doesn't take to surprises much," William said. "She's a good woman and means well. We have worked very hard to make a life for ourselves, and she just doesn't realize what you have been through to get here."

"You'll need new clothes," he added. "Let me see what we have."

With that, we were alone and looked at each other in disbelief. We stood in my brother's house and did not even know his wife's name. We stood, afraid to sit, dressed in rags, covered in filth, and coated with lice. We had come thousands of miles, had lost two of our loved ones, risked everything we had, and now stood with nothing … no money, no clothes, no food, no lodging, and above all else, no more dreams. Reality had shaken its ugly fist and thrown our souls against the wall, like some unwanted rag doll tossed out of tantrum by a small child.

My brother returned with clothing for both of us, trousers and a shirt for me and one of his wife's plain dresses for Elizabeth. Just then, his wife returned, and you could tell by her silent stare that she did not appreciate William giving her dresses away.

"The baths will be ready forthwith," his wife announced. "You need to go out to the smokehouse." She said, pointing to a small stone building with smoke coming from the chimney.

Elizabeth and I backed out of the house and made our way to the small building. The room was warm from the fire, and the walls held carcasses that had been smoked and stored for the winter. The rich aroma of hickory filled our nostrils and scented our bodies as if we, too, were nothing more than sides ready to be cured and hung for later consumption.

Inside stood a large, dark woman with sweat beading on her brow. She handed us each some long grass whips and a bar of lye soap and closed the door behind us. I noticed her hands, broad and strong and yet gentle. The light on the table gave off its reflection, and we saw two large wooden tubs, both filled with steaming water.

As we stood there, I realized that I had never seen my "wife" without her clothes, nor she without mine. As the shadows played upon our bodies, we attempted to not look at each other as the clothes we had been wearing dropped to the floor. Slowly, we stepped towards the large vats and slid in. The hot water at first repulsed me as its shock attacked my senses. After but a minute, my body met the challenge and the warmth began its magic.

Quietly, we took our bars of soap and began to wash ourselves with the lather quickly making a foam upon the water. I had forgotten how good a warm bath could feel. Slowly I washed every part of my body that I could reach and slid beneath the surface. As my head arose so that I could catch my breath, I looked at Elizabeth and saw that she was watching me. For the first time ever, our eyes locked on each other in a way unlike any other. We both smiled, and we knew that our union was meant to be.

Soon the air of the room took its toll, and we both dipped below the water's surface. As we sat there letting the trials of our journey wash themselves away, the door opened, and the large woman returned. With her, she brought two more kettles of hot water that would re-excite our now-cooling pleasure. As the hot water mixed with that in which we were sitting, I felt a cold liquid upon my head. It smelled of some form of alcohol as this dark stranger began to work it into my scalp.

"You gots lice," she said. "This will kill them all."

With that, she worked the tonic into my scalp and turned to Elizabeth and repeated the process.

"Doan you wash it out now, hear. Gots to sit till I say so."

There we both sat, like two drowned rats … hair sticking up … stinking of the worst concoction I'd ever smelled. It seemed like an eternity before the woman returned.

"Wrap these around you and comes outside," she said, setting two large blankets beside us and walking out. Carefully we both arose. In the darkness of the smokehouse, we both glanced at what had only been imagined, we both saw what we had only thought of seeing. We both memorized each other's body so that the tomorrows of tomorrow would begin again.

At first, I was concerned that the cold would make us ill, but this woman had spoken with such authority that I did not dare protest. With that, we both obliged and, letting the cold ground attack our feet, walked outside … making us tingly all over.

The woman took us to a spot where we could kneel and lean for-ward. Here, she poured more warm water over our heads, washing away the concoction from our hair.

"Dis 'ill wash 'em all away. I hates dem lice."

In an instant, the warm water washed away all the smell and was replaced by the sweet smell of clean hair.

"Come back in 'fore you catch a death."

Again, we obliged and walked back into the smokehouse. While we had been outside, two young boys had entered the small building and were quickly dipping the dirty water out of the tubs with pans, throwing it out a now-open window.

"You stay here and keeps warm. We bringing fresh water so you can rinse off."

As we stood in the corner watching the boys, two men carried in buckets of steaming water and began filling the tubs again. It wasn't long before both tubs were full, and the party left us to the silence of the room.

Without concern, the blankets were dropped, and we stood before each other exposed in both flesh and soul. I remember looking in Elizabeth's eyes and pulling her close to me. It felt so good to feel her body next to mine. It was if we had washed away all the pain, all the suffering, and all the disappointment we had faced. As we stood there, dripping wet, wrapped in each other, our lips met for the very first time and there was peace.

We both climbed back into our warm tubs and sat soaking. Her hand slid across and grasped mine. We sat, hand-in-hand, letting the warm water rinse away our misery. As the water cooled, we looked at each other, and when the time came, stood and pressed our bodies against each other letting the warm moist air dry us off.

As we began getting dressed, the feeling was as relaxed as if we had just been together physically. We knew that the time would come when that, too, would happen. For now, it was simply returning to reality as we walked hand-in-hand towards William's house.

As we approached, the door opened, and it was as if there was someone different behind the door. William smiled and welcomed us back in. His wife came out of the kitchen, and the look that had been was replaced.

"This is my wife, Priscilla," William said. "I am sorry if we were so surprised when you first arrived. We didn't know you were coming."

"Sarah sent a letter," Elizabeth said. "Mailed it about two months ago."

"Don't mean much, those letters," Priscilla replied. "They can take some months to get here."

The moments elapsed, and we began to feel a little more welcome. News was shared of home and all that had happened. How our father had died and our mother and what had happened to all of our friends and of William's farm and the 47 acres he planted. We both spoke of how often our father would say that a man was only a man when he owned his own land. We talked of the mine and how it took away a man's soul, leaving him hollow and desperate, weak and old before his time. William shook his head and lifted his eyes and noted how glad he was that he had never set one foot in what he called "the grave" where every man went to die.

The hours passed, and soon darkness was upon us. It was quite strange to sit and feel the hunger within your belly and not have a single morsel offered.

At once, Priscilla yawned and looked at William as if to ask, "When are these people leaving?"

"So, what are your plans?" William asked.

"We would like to find some land and begin farming, like you have done," I replied.

"Well, if you go much further west, you will be in Kentucky, and it will be easy to get land, but more difficult to farm," William said.

"So what are your plans right now?" Priscilla asked.

"Well, if you wouldn't mind, perhaps we could sleep in the barn tonight and then head out tomorrow," I answered.

Elizabeth looked at me with eyes of disdain. She knew we were too weak and too poor to travel, and we needed to ask William if we could stay awhile.

"The barn will be fine for tonight," Priscilla answered, looking at the two of us. "I'll have one of the boys spread some straw for you to sleep on."

As she rose, William stood as well.

"They don't need to sleep in the barn. They can use the other room upstairs, Priscilla. This is my family."

I could sense the problem and offered again to sleep in the barn.

"I'll not hear of it. If my own brother can't spend one night in my house, then I am not his brother."

In just a few words, William let me know that our visit wasn't expected and any extended stay would not be welcomed. Times change, people change. We all must move on.

"So be it," Priscilla said. "I'll set out some quilts. We arise early to milk the cows. Breakfast is served when we call."

With that, we all retired. The steep stairways led up to a large room cold with the December night. As I lit the oil lamp, I could see my breath. Quickly, Elizabeth and I took off the clothes we had just put on and slid beneath the warm down comforter. There we lay, naked, in each other's arms, too tired for romance, simply at peace with each other and the world.

The night slipped quickly by, and we were awakened by the sharp scream of Priscilla's voice.

"Come quickly. There's been an accident. Come quickly."

I jumped out of bed, slipped into my new trousers and buttoned my shirt on my way down the stairs. The front door was open, as was the door to the barn. I ran across the clearing and found William lying on his side, in obvious pain. His right arm and leg were broken.

I learned later that William had gone up in the loft to get hay to feed the cows. As he picked up some hay to drop down to the floor, he accidentally kicked over the lantern and lunged for it so that it would not fall, break and start the barn on fire. In so doing, he had fallen from the loft, breaking his arm and leg.

When you grow up in a mine, you are around accidents all the time. Through watching and doing, you quickly learn what needs to be done. I had set many a man's broken bones. My brother was to be yet another.

I asked Priscilla if they had any whiskey and she looked at me stunned.

"Of course not," she replied. "We're not that kind of people."

"Then get me a piece of leather to put in your husband's mouth."

She ran and brought a piece of belting leather that I put between William's teeth.

"Bite down hard," I commanded.

As William bit down, I took his broken arm bones and pulled them far enough apart so that the pieces could be put back together. I could see the pain in his eyes, yet knew he could tolerate it. When the bones were in place, I took a board and placed it on his arm and wrapped some cloth around the splint to hold the bones in place.

Next it was his leg. He had been lucky in that the bones were broken but still nearly in place. I needed help, and so Elizabeth grabbed William under the arms, and we both pulled until the leg was also back where the bones should be. Again, I took a board and wrapped cloth so that the bones were secure.

"Go get your helpers," I told Priscilla. "We need to carry him into the house."

Priscilla was gone before the last word had come from my mouth. Soon she returned with the two men who brought the hot water the day before. We took a longer board and laid it on the ground and carefully slid William on it. Next the two men, Elizabeth, and I carried William into the house and put him in his bed.

"Now what are we going to do?" Priscilla asked. "What about milking and planting this spring?"

"If you want, we will stay and help until he can work again," Elizabeth said.

"We can't pay you," Priscilla replied.

"Did we ask for anything more than a roof over our head and perhaps some food?" I answered.

"You can't stay in the house. You will have to live in one of the quarters," she replied.

"Fair enough." I knew that William would be unable to work for several months, and it would give me a chance to learn about farming.

That morning, I began the life of a farmer, something I have done almost every day since. It was a difficult way to begin, but it was a beginning.

Elizabeth and I moved into one of the slave quarters. It was small and warm, and we made it our home. The slaves at first did not take a liking to us being there, white folks and all, but as time went on, they seemed not to mind so much as I treated them not as slaves but as individuals ... people who could teach me farming ... people who I learned to respect for their kindness, generosity, and humility.

Within days, the routine was set. We would arise, and Elizabeth and I would milk all eight cows. Then we would tend to the animals, cleaning the stalls and feeding them. As spring began to arrive, we looked at the fields and planned the crops. Each day, Priscilla would make breakfast for us and had it delivered to our quarters. Each night, we would go to the big house as we called it and eat dinner with her and William, who would spend time teaching me about the farm and the crops and the animals. As night drew near, Elizabeth and I would go back to our small house and lay awake holding each other, sharing each other, comforting each other, dreaming of our tomorrow.

After several weeks, William was able to leave the house for short periods of time. The slaves would load him in the back of the wagon, and he would come to the fields and watch me work the plow, teaching me tricks that would save time and my muscles. Soon the crops were in, and most of the spring work was done. As had always been the custom in these parts, there was to be a party when all the neighbors would get together to celebrate the spring planting.

I remember Priscilla and William getting dressed in their finest. I remember Elizabeth and I riding in the back of the wagon with the slaves, dressed in our work clothes. I remember the looks we got from both the white and colored folks when we got to the church and I helped Clara down from the wagon. It was a look of disdain that I would never forget.

As we got down and went to meet the others, we were the outsiders. No one knew who we were because William never introduced us. Rumors spread that we were sharecroppers. Others called us white slaves. Still others simply walked away. When you work hard and honest, you should get some respect, no matter who you are. When someone called my Elizabeth a name I shall not write in this good book, I took it upon myself to make absolutely certain that this man understood that I resented his comment. I was William's brother and had helped him by doing all the work while he was injured.

This "gentleman," as I shall call him, didn't accept that we were brothers because we never did look that much alike. William was tall, and I was short; he had black curly hair, and mine was straight and brown. With that, I had had enough. "Come here," I said and took him to William. "Tell him I'm your brother."

"Yes, he is," William responded.

The gentleman was still not convinced.

"Look at my hands, and look at his. Look at our fingers," I said. "See the shape of the fingernail. It looks like a perfect fan. All the men of our family have the same hands. Big or small, the hands are always the same. The fingers are always the same. Look at anyone else, and you will see that only William and my hands are the same."

The gentleman looked, and a wry smile came across his face. "You are his brother. But you must be a fool to allow him to make you out as someone so below him."

"My brother was injured while we were at his home. Our father and mother would never have forgiven me, if we had not stayed to help until he was well enough to work again. If not for family, what do we have? If not for family, how can we define who we are?" I asked.

The night drew to an end, but we realized that we truly were being used by my brother and his wife. We had become nothing more than free slaves. We knew that our time to leave would come soon. The next day, I went to William and told him that we were planning on leaving so that we could earn money to buy a farm. Instead, William offered to pay me five dollars per month and also reward me with one-third of whatever money we earned when we sold the extra crops at the end of the year. We shook hands on it, and the agreement was made.

As spring turned to summer and William's strength returned, the load of work began to go down and our time spent together with it. It was then that Elizabeth announced that she was expecting our first child. We made plans. If a boy, he would be named Henry; if a girl,

Sarah, of course. The baby would come in the spring. We would stay and help with the harvest and then move on.

Some nights after dinner, Elizabeth and I would sit on our little porch and listen to the crickets and count our blessings. Other nights, we would walk down to the meadow and count the stars and think of both Henrys and Sarah looking down at us from heaven. Still other nights, we would stop by the slaves' quarters and just sit a spell, chatting with those folks. Such kind, peaceful, generous souls wanting nothing more than to know that their lives together were secure. There were ten of them—two adult men, three adult women, and five children ranging from two to about fourteen, I would guess.

In many ways, William was good to the slaves compared to others. Sunday was a day of rest for everyone, and in the summer, every Sunday night meant a picnic where everyone would sit out, drink fresh squeezed lemonade, and eat fried chicken that would melt in your mouth. Music would be played, and a fire built, and we would all join in singing some church songs that Priscilla had taught, along with the Negro gospels that the slaves sang almost every day to everyone.

Each night, Elizabeth and I would retire and hold each other and thank God for all that we had. One hot August night as she slept in my arms, I decided to arise and get some fresh air. Without wanting to awaken her, I slid out, without the lantern, and sat upon the porch. The moon was full, and you could see as if it were a cloudy day. As I sat there, I saw the front door of the big house open and a dark figure walk down the steps. I could tell by the limp that it was William.

At first, I thought he was going to the outhouse, but he kept walking straight towards the slaves' quarters. I kept in the shadow so that he could not see me. Quietly, he lifted the latch of the small house and within a few moments he reappeared with Anna, the twelve-year-old slave girl, dressed in her nightgown. William had his hand on the back of Anna's neck and was marching her toward the barn. As he opened the door, he looked around to see if anyone had seen him. Shivers of fear went through my body as I began to realize what was about to happen. Did I interrupt? Did I keep to myself? We had too much to risk with Elizabeth expecting to cause any sort of trouble. To this day, I regret that I did nothing.

In a few moments, I heard some soft crying and knew my fears were coming true. A few moments later, the barn door opened and Anna ran back to the slaves' quarters while William walked back to the big house and quietly went back to bed.

The next morning, I saw Anna and I could tell by the sadness in her eyes that all was not right. Her childhood was gone. Reality had set in. Her innocence wiped away with just one indiscretion. I was full of anger. I was full of hate. I had come to loathe my own brother and his wife. Everything that he and I had escaped was being played out in his life. The oppression, the fear, the hate was all there, and all in the name of commerce. I wanted to confront William but elected not to. The time was not right, and there was too much at stake. Instead I waited, and as we worked together, I would talk about our parents and freedom and all that we had dreamed about when we were so very, very young. William was older and I thought wiser than me, and some of what he said I normally thought made truth. And because he was older, he always talked down to me as if I were still a child.

William spoke. "Well, if you want the truth from me, my brother, it's this. The world goes on, and with it our society and culture. The earth stands and will go on standing. The world is more or less a fixed thing, and externally we have to adapt ourselves to it and not try to change it to meet our whims and fancies.

"Socially, and in my private opinion, we must please ourselves even when it means acting upon some sort of stage. Emotions change. You may like one person this year and another next. But the earth still stands. Stick by the social order as far as the order sticks by you. Then please yourself. But always remember you'll get very little out of making a break with society. You can make a break if you wish, but the risks are great, and the rewards can be much smaller than your dreams."

As the conversation moved on, I began to talk about the slaves and what kind of people they were. William told me that he didn't think they were "people" like white folks and that he needed them to provide for him and Priscilla. He told me that they were better off with him than on other farms where they were often whipped and kept in chains. He told me that he thought they were better off in America than in Africa. In the end, he had justified everything in a way that let him sleep at night.

I wanted him to know that I suspected what he had done with Anna, but knew I had better not confront him directly. One Sunday in late August, when we were having our dinner, young Daniel, the smallest of the slaves left his momma and came toward me. I picked him up and set him on my lap and began playing with him, trying to make him laugh. As we were playing, I spread his hand in the palm of mine and happened to glance at his fingers. His hands were shaped just like mine. His hands were just like William's. His hands were Tyrell hands. He was William's son. My own brother had his own son, who was a slave.

As the night grew on, I called Joshua towards me. He was age five. Again, I looked at his hands. Again, I found hands like mine. Again, I saw that my own brother had fathered another child and put him into slavery.

I thought back on our conversation about slaves being nothing more than property. I looked at my brother and then at Daniel's hands and William knew I understood what he had done. I looked at Anna and wondered if he had impregnated her as well, so that he could get more "property." I wondered what had happened. I wondered how my own brother could do this and think nothing of it. Perhaps the Sunday dinners were his way of making some amends. I wondered if Priscilla knew. Perhaps that was why she was always so cold towards everyone.

My conversations with William became distant. He had taught me many things about farming and about life. Through his actions, he also taught me that I wanted nothing at all to do with slavery and that Elizabeth and I would travel north to make sure that we did not need to be reminded of the injustice we saw before us.

By mid-October, all the crops had been harvested and stored, and William and I went to town to sell the excess. As I said earlier, it had been our understanding that I would be paid one-third of whatever money was earned from what was sold for all my efforts. As we sold the crops, I counted the money ... $240 ...and I knew that I should receive over $80 for my year's work.

As we loaded the wagon with winter supplies and began the journey back, I turned to William and asked for my pay. He looked at me and said that after he took out for food and using the house there was nothing left for me to have. Now I am an honest man. I live by my word and expect others to do the same. I have always been this way and will always be.

While William was larger than me, he wasn't nearly as strong, and when I grabbed the reins and pulled the wagon to a stop, he knew that there was to be a big problem.

"That was not our agreement," I said in total anger.

"What agreement? You show up at my house, eat my food and live in one of my quarters. What do you expect?" he replied.

"I expect to be paid, as promised," I responded.

"As promised? By who?"

"By you."

"Don't remember ever saying that. I gave you the five dollars every month. That is enough."

"You bastard," I replied.

"Bastard? Me? I'm not having a child with a dead man's wife. You're the bastard, as will that child of yours when it comes."

"Me a bastard? You son of a bitch. Who was it that fathered Joshua? Who was it that fathered Daniel? Who was it that took poor little Anna into the barn and raped her? It was you. I've seen the boy's hands, and they're like yours and mine. I saw you walk across the yard in the middle of the night and pull Anna from her bed and take her into the barn."

"Big John didn't father a single child. He was someone I should have sold a long time ago. He hasn't provided any return on my investment. I should have sold him a long time ago. Instead, out of MY generosity, I have kept him here with his wife and let him live as if there were a family," William roared.

"These people are not cattle. These are human beings," I countered.

"They're just slaves," he responded.

"Just slaves? Those boys are your own sons. You have placed your own sons in slavery."

"And Anna?" I added. "You are having sex with your own daughter?"

"She's not my daughter, nor is she Clara's, I traded two fine horses for her."

"Horses?" I responded. "Horses. You traded two horses for a human life? Why?"

William and I were both getting angry, and our voices rose as our breaths became short. I could see the anger and the frustration boiling within him, and he could see the same in me.

"I needed to expand my breeding stock, and we all know that bad things happen when you propagate within the same bloodlines. With Anna, look at those features. Look at those lines. Look at her beauty and she's only twelve. Her children will be worth a fortune."

"Bloodlines? Propagate? Breeding stock?" I was incredulous. These were people, and he spoke of them like farm animals, nothing more than chattel ... inventory that could be bought, sold, bartered, or used with recompense and done so without remorse.

"And what did father do to us?" he replied. "Didn't he put us in slavery? Didn't he take you down into those God-forsaken mines? What's the difference?"

"The difference is that we got out of there. We had a way to make our lives better. Your own sons cannot escape, even from you. They will be slaves until they die."

"But you don't understand. We need the slaves to work the farm," William replied.

"I understand. I understand that you have put money and material possessions above everything else. When you fell and broke your leg, we stayed and helped. Even when that wife of yours continued to insult us, treat us as if we were nothing more than sharecroppers, we continued on. When we went to meet your neighbors, we were made to feel as if we were nothing."

"Well, you are, God damn it," he screamed. "You show up at our house stinking and covered with lice. You had nothing but yourselves, and we take you in, feed you, clothe you, pay you, and this is the thanks we get. You are not my brother. My brother died in Cornwall. May he rest in peace."

"Give me the money you owe me, and we will be gone before the sun rises. Cheat me, and I promise you, I will go to Priscilla and bring the boys and show her where you have been spending your nights."

"The boys are her idea," he cried. "She said we needed more workers and we couldn't afford them. Women slaves with children don't run away, and if they're boys, they can bring top dollar when they are older."

"You bastard. You would sell your own sons?"

"They're not my sons. They're slaves. Damn it. They're slaves."

"So there is to be no money?" I asked.

"Let's not start again. No money!" he replied.

It is always difficult when your anger reaches the point of violence and yet you can't do anything about it. It is always difficult when you know that you have lost. There's a sick feeling in your stomach, and you want to cry. William picked up the reins and slowly marched the wagon back to the farm. Not another word was spoken. Not that night. Never again, for a long, long, time.

When we arrived, I went to Elizabeth and told her what had happened. She cried, but knew we had to move on. We packed what little we had and prepared to leave. Before leaving that little house one last time, I took one of William's coats and ripped the collar. William would know what this meant ... I was dead and out of his life, and he of mine. For many years I never spoke of him nor recognized his name and it was then that Elizabeth and I truly, emotionally, and permanently, in not only the law of the land, but the law of God, became Terrills and not Tyrills. We were to have no association with him in any way ... or so I vowed.

Elizabeth and I went down to the slave's quarters and met with all of them. We told them that what happened and that we were leaving. Clara began to cry. "Youz good people. We gonna miss you, Miss Elizabeth, Mr. George. Youz good people."

Big John asked us where we were going, and we said to the North where there would be no slavery. He asked how we were going to get there, and I said we would walk. He said "no" that there was an old wagon out in the field that would not be missed until spring. With Elizabeth being with child, it would be better. He told me to put one dollar on the table and take one of the work horses and to write out a receipt for the horse. The horse was only worth about five dollars, and William and Priscilla would keep the money and not cause a problem. He would make certain of that.

As I took the money from my pocket. Clara looked at Big John and said, "John, you know we got no needs, you give them what we'z got."

John knew what Clara meant and went to the back wall of their little cabin. Lifting a small board, he took out a small leather bag and carefully opened it. Within were two five-dollar gold pieces.

"We'z been savin' them for something special. You folks is that somethin' special," Big John noted.

I leaned back. This was their entire savings. Every single dime that they had ever acquired in their lives, and they were willing to give it to Elizabeth and me.

"I can't take your money," I stated.

"You takes it. You needs it more than we'z do. Go on now, takes it," Clara insisted.

"I won't take it, but I will borrow it. I give you my word. I will return, and when I do, you will be repaid."

With that, the money that had been theirs became ours. With that, we knew it was time to go.

We went and got old Ed, a dapple gray that had seen his better days. As we hooked him up to the wagon, Big John told me to follow him. He had something else for us. We took the wagon and Old Ed and went over the hill and into the forest. Soon, we came to a hill, and Big John told me to come with him. Slowly we walked down the hill until we came to what looked like a shallow cave with brush piled in front of it. Quickly, Big John pulled the brush away, and to my surprise, he showed me two muskets wrapped in oil cloth, a barrel of powder, flints, two hunting knives, and even some blankets.

"We'z been keeping these in case the day come dat we'z could head north," Big John said. "You and Miss Elizabeth, you been good to us. We want you to take all this, we will save again for da nex' time."

Big John had been hiding everything they needed to get out of Virginia and away from my brother. He and his family were willing to give up their dreams for us. Big John was a gentle man who had a kind heart and a kindred soul. He wanted nothing more than to live in peace, and the hope of freedom would be dashed upon the rocks of reality each time he heard another story, another event, another circumstance of someone who tried to get away.

We sat on a rock, and he shared with me the life of a slave and all that transpired. He explained what happened to those who tried to run away and got caught. He spoke of what they did to runaway slaves who were captured and tortured, and my mouth dropped open.

Little had I heard of the wheel torture, and when Big John was done, I hoped and prayed I would never see it take place. The word was spread throughout the South that, periodically, examples had to be made of those who tried to get away. Whippings. Lashes. Castration. Hanging. Those were the easy ways. When it looked like there could possibly be an insurrection, an example had to be made, and the runaway slave would be tethered to a large wheel with their hands and feet spread wide with their ankles and wrists strapped to it. As the wheel slowly turned, slave masters and even forced slaves would take turns using a steel sledgehammer, pounding on the runaway's body.

At first, it would be the forearms and lower legs that would be shattered. As the wheel turned and the weight shifted, the change in weight would put different pressure on the broken bones as the captured slave cried out in pain. Next the upper arms and legs would be shattered and the wheel could continue to slowly turn. Again, the pain would be excruciating. Next it would be the shoulders and the hips. By now, there would be no support, and I can only imagine the pain. Finally, the hammer would be used to break all the ribs as the captured slave was positioned upside down. If they collapsed and became inattentive, water would be thrown in their face until they were awakened.

They were to endure the pain. It mattered not if it was a man or a woman. All the slaves and especially the children would be paraded to see the naked, broken slave as he or she gasped their last breaths and begged for mercy ... not to live, but simply to die. The process could take up to three days, and all would be forced to watch. The pain, the terror, the sight of destruction would be burned into the memories of all those who were captives so that they understood the consequences of insurrection. While hope is the greatest of all motivators, fear comes in a close second ... and fear is what kept slaves as slaves.

I shook my head in disbelief as our conversation resumed.

"Probably not have made it anyway," he said.

"But, Big John," I protested.

"Nonsense, you takes it. We will save again."

With that, we loaded all the munitions in the wagon and headed back to the farm. Clara placed an old horse hide cover in the wagon that we have to this day. Then she and the men slid three sides of pork, a barrel of flour, four loaves of bread, and a round of cheese in with us.

"Just a few lashes is all we get," she said.

We looked at the slaves one last time and did something they had never had done before. I shook the men's hands and kissed and hugged Clara. Elizabeth kissed them all. These were good people.

"Thank you. We will never forget you. You tell William that when you came to awaken us, we were gone. Tell him that we stole the food and give him the money for the horse."

Kentucky

With that we set out west, toward Kentucky. We knew that we would have a few hours' lead and that William would never come after us. As for the slaves, we hoped that William would trust them and that they would be treated fairly … anyway as fairly as someone can be who has no rights, lives with the fear of being sold and understands that life for them does not contain words like freedom, liberty or justice … words written in the Declaration of Independence for all.

At first, Old Ed walked quite quickly, and I felt comfortable with our head start. After a while, the old horse slowed his pace, like he thought he was still plowing, but it was better than walking ourselves. Soon the fear of being chased by William left us, just as those fears of Old Fitzie chasing us had left us long ago. We were on our way to Kentucky and away from my brother and his wife.

While the fall days provided warmth, the nights were cool, and it meant finding someplace sheltered where we could sleep. After three days' travel, we were in the middle of Kentucky. While Virginia had been rolling hills, Kentucky meant more mountains, and it became more difficult to travel. We ate as little food as we could and tried to conserve our energy and that of Old Ed's as much as we could.

When the cold rains hit on our fourth day, we found a small cave and settled in, building a fire for warmth and placing as much brush as possible over the opening to keep it as warm as possible. We had hoped to continue on, but the road had turned to mud, and Old

Ed just couldn't keep pulling the wagon.

To save what food we had, I began hunting. At first, I tried shooting, but found that my skills just were not there. Instead, I turned to trapping and caught rabbits, squirrels, and other small animals that gave us meat. In addition, we harvested nuts and the fall berries. There was a small stream nearby, and so we had food and water.

While we had planned to move on, November turned bitter, and we decided to keep our cave for the winter, stacking wood and brush for the fire and making the entry as tight as possible to keep out the winter wind.

When we had everything just about set, we had our one and only visitor. I guess, as we had been with William, our visitor was quite a surprise. It seems that we had decided to spend the winter in a bear's den. I really can't tell you who was more surprised, the bear or us, when he decided to knock down the brush and found us living in his house. I just know that he was not happy and decided to make us leave.

I had never seen a bear before and an angry one at that. He stood nearly ten feet tall on his back legs, all growling and ready to attack. His coat was white, his eyes were red and his nose pink. When you have never seen a bear, you had no idea that this one was not like other black bears. Well, I can tell you, I still thank Big John for the gun. I had one shot before he would have gotten to us.

As he stood there, I raised my weapon and fired just as he was about to lunge. Even with a shot to the chest, he came forward. I could see by the look in his red eyes that it would have been him or me. Old Ed was skittish and tried to move further back into the cave. I screamed to Elizabeth to move further back.

Once again, he rose on his hind legs, and then his will was gone. He stood for an instant, and then a puzzled look came across his eyes. All of his anger, all of his passion, all of his energy flowed forth, and he fell before me, gasping for one last breath. As I looked down at him, our eyes met ... I the victor, and he the vanquished. Then it was over. His breathing stopped, and he lay there in total silence characterized by the stillness that only comes from the finality of death.

Now I'm not one for killing, but when it's you or him, I think it was all right. I took that big old bear and butchered him and skinned him and thank God to this day that he was sent to give us the food and warmth that we would need to survive the winter.

It took Elizabeth, Old Ed, and me a great while to recover. My hands shook, and I could feel my heart pounding within my chest. I had never killed anything, and it upset me unlike anything that I had ever done before. It took me almost a day to put the brush back in front of the cave, and this time, I tied some really big branches together and made a door so that the only way a bear could get in would be if he knew how to open it.

Old Ed seemed like he understood what we were doing with the bear and all, and yet I still wonder what he thought. When the nights were warm enough, we let him sleep outside. When the cold of December and January came, he moved in with us. We tried to keep track of the days when we thought it was Christmas time, we talked about Christ Jesus in the manger and how he lived and died for us.

I would forage for food for Old Ed and give him some of the nuts. He seemed to like those most of all, and we learned that if we dried his manure, it would burn to help keep us warm. In the end, it was Elizabeth, Old Ed and I in the winter of 1822 living like I had vowed never to live again, within the ground.

As early spring came, Elizabeth's belly had grown large, and I knew it was time to move on. We loaded our belongings, including the bear skin, in the wagon and said goodbye to the cave in which we had lived. Old Ed seemed as anxious as we were to move on. As we headed west across Kentucky we looked for land that we could farm. It appeared that many others had the same ideas, as all the flat land and valleys had farms already in them.

Soon we were in a place called Indiana where we met some folks who had traveled from New York. They spoke of the land west of Indiana before some big river that I learned later was the Mississippi. They said that the Indians were peaceful and that commerce had already begun. I asked if the land was rich and flat for farming, and they said it was. Based on the words of two strangers whom we spoke with for only a few moments, our lives changed, and with it, our destiny.

We headed for the village of Chicago. It was a ramshackle place built next to a swamp. The people were rough and tumble with a lot of taverns and just about as many fights. Old Ed was getting tired of pulling the wagon, and Elizabeth was about to have our child. We took a little bit of the money we still had left and got Old Ed some oats and Elizabeth a warm bed at a boarding house. The people who owned it were real nice and kindly, and the lady helped with the birth. Two days later, our first son was born. Henry James Terrell, he was. It was March 4, 1823.

Galena

As I was now a father, it was my need to find gainful employment. I only knew two things, mining and farming, and you couldn't do either in Chicago. When it came to farming, you had to own a farm, and I didn't think we could buy much with the $13.12 we had in our pocket, and so I asked about mining and learned that near the Mississippi River there was a town where lead mining was going full steam. The town was called Galena, and they had discovered lead on the Fever River. Most of all, I learned that if you worked hard, you could quickly get your stake.

When young Henry was just nine days old, we set out for Galena ... Elizabeth to raise our son and me to do what I had vowed I would never do again. Much to my surprise, when I got to Galena, I learned that the mining they had talked about in Chicago wasn't like Cornwall at all. Instead of crawling into the ground on your belly, you just dug into the hills, and you could find lead near the surface. By working hard and working alone, you could make a good wage without the system that we had before.

Galena was a lot like Chicago when it came to the people. There were roughshod drinkers and fighters who clashed with whores and gamblers, which scared both Elizabeth and me. The town itself was built near the Mississippi River. The big boats would put in and load the crops and lead and take them down river, depositing in return the riffraff that comes with any place where you can get away easy.

While Chicago was flat, Galena was built into the hills, a lot like Cornwall. We found a small room and paid our rent and found a stable for Old Ed, and our routine began. Each day, I would set out early and find a spot along a creek, which some folks called the Bean River and others the Fever. Here the spring waters would expose the silver gray metal, and you could actually see the veins of ore in the ground. I would dig a shovelful of dirt and ore and take my buckets and wash the ore and place it in the wagon. I would do this sunrise to sunset six days each week. Sunday was my day of rest when I would spend time with Elizabeth and Henry. On a good day, I could earn as much as a dollar. On a bad day, I would sometimes earn next to nothing.

Old Ed seemed to enjoy himself, as each day meant new grass and not much work. His only job was, at the end of the day, pulling the loaded wagon back to Galena. Some days, it was hard, and others it was easy because it was just me, wondering, wondering, wondering where this all would end. As we slowly made our way, I would look for the lead plant because it was supposed to indicate the presence of minerals. Sometimes the plants grew in straight rows, sometimes curved, sometimes in patches. Even with my untrained eye, I could find them even when they were short and close to the ground. In the late spring and early summer, when their bluish-purple flowers were in bloom, they even looked pretty. As summer came, the plants would sometimes be four feet tall. After a few trips, I could spot them as they stood out among the hillside grasses. Because the Indians had mined the land for the French and other settlers were trying their luck, finding the lead plant with even a slight indentation of the land got my heart afluttering. Unfortunately, most of the time, it meant nothing, and Old Ed and I would keep on our way.

Because the pickings were so easy, there were a lot of miners to compete against. As the summer moved on, we found ourselves moving further and further north, away from town. We were just dumb miners. We didn't know anything about land and boundaries and treaties and such. All we knew is that we needed to keep moving north to dig more lead. The Fever River, which had been wide, kept getting smaller and smaller and smaller until it was just a small step across. Because you needed water to rinse the ore, many of the miners gave up and didn't continue north. We all kept to ourselves and didn't tell anyone that, just a few miles upstream, the banks were high and the ore deep and there were only a few of us working the area.

After a few months, the journey from Galena got to be too much to do every day, and so I would start out on Monday and stay until the wagon was full. If it took one day, that was fine. If it took longer, I began sleeping under the wagon with my rifle by my side.

I mined the lead all summer and fall and when I could in the winter. The weather here was much colder than anywhere I had ever been before, and so there were many a day when I would simply stay in Galena with Elizabeth and Henry.

Word of the lead spread like wildfire, and those hungry enough for good fortune set out for Galena to strike their riches. Throughout the spring of 1827, the pioneers came on foot, horseback, wagon, or river craft. Narrow Indian paths became dusty roads as even more miners came. The Mississippi boats that moved upstream with miners and supplies returned loaded with lead and stories of incredible wealth. Miners, merchants, rivermen, gamblers, trappers, and Indians came to Galena, jostling through muddy streets, crowding saloons and stores, and sleeping anywhere they could—in houses, tents, or wagons, or even under the open sky. At night, campfires glowed all along the Fever River flats, and the saloons stayed open twenty-four hours a day. Each day, Galena would change its personality as one group of miners left to seek their fortune and another group arrived to take their place.

By that spring, we had saved nearly $300. I wanted to mine one more year and then purchase our land and begin farming. As spring came, I set out further up river than ever before and found a different stream that they called the Pecatonica. As I came to where two branches met, I had to make a decision, and it was one of the best decisions of my life. The lead was easy pickings, and I had left the others so far behind that it was to a point where I was the only person on the river. Mind you, I didn't know anything about treaties and the like. All I was interested in was taking lead out of the ground and earning enough money to support my family.

As I worked my way further away from Galena and the other miners, the land seemed better for farming. I began to notice how the hills were flatter, the soil deeper, and the rocks fewer, and I felt that I had found a place where we could settle. One day as I was working a small vein, I looked up and saw Indians watching me. I had heard about them and wondered what they wanted. As I turned towards them, they looked the other way and rode off. When my wagon was filled, Old Ed and I headed back towards Galena. As we neared town, I saw the constable riding towards me. I didn't think I had done anything wrong and so thought nothing of it. I was wrong.

As he approached, the constable asked me where I had been, and I told him upriver. When he asked how far, I told him I didn't know, as I really didn't. It was then that he told me that I had crossed the border from Illinois into Sauk territory and was causing a ruckus with the Indians and needed to be careful.

I told him that all I was doing was getting lead. He told me that the Sauk thought it was Indian lead and that unless I was invited by them, I had no right going into the territory again. I asked how I got permission and he said I couldn't. So, I said, "In other words, I can't go upriver anymore?" "'Bout right," he replied.

I promised to stop going that far upriver and kept my word for two months until I found out that nigh on twenty miners had been working where I had been before without a problem. At that point, I decided to go back.

One trip, I took Elizabeth and Henry with me. As we came around a bend, we saw a valley with the river running through it. We both knew we were home. We learned that five families had preceded us, and four had dug out small caves across the valley from the river and were living in them until they could get their houses built. The other family, the Hoods if I remember correctly, built a shelter of poles and bark.

Little Henry was now nearly seven years old. Elizabeth was expecting again. I guess one of those cold nights was just one too many. I needed to mine more lead, but didn't want to be away from her much longer. We decided that we would move to the new diggings as soon as I could build a house. In a single year, the population of the Fever River mining camps grew four-fold. Sadly, our baby died at birth. Something was wrong, and God took her from us. We both cried, looked at each other, and then cried some more. There is nothing more defeating than the loss of a child.

Red Bird

There are many lessons that we can learn from the mistakes of others. A long time ago, I realized that, except for what I see with my own eyes and hear with my own ears, nothing is what we think it to be. Stories are told, and our world is enhanced or taken down, spun or even pulled out of context to the point that it can even be made more extreme than it really is simply because the thoughts, ideas, and actions have come from someone, somewhere else. I feel that this can lead to a great deal of risk when you react only to what you read or hear. When you are mining alone or live on a farm, you spend most of your time isolated, and when you do go into town, most of the stories you hear are gossip. You always try to sort things out—good and bad—so that you have some idea of what really happened. One thing was true. There were many lead miners moving into southwest Wisconsin, and this, along with some untrue stories about the Indians and an event sixty miles from where we were mining, led to one of the saddest moments in our friendship with them.

As the mining camp grew, the number of Indians we saw became less. They came by periodically, but their numbers were fewer as were their smiles. The Winnebago nation spread across the land where the Fox and Wisconsin Rivers flowed into the Mississippi on both sides ... from Missouri and Iowa on the west side to Illinois and Wisconsin on the east. The Winnebago lived in small villages along the rivers and relied on farming, hunting, and trapping as a way of life. The leader of one Winnebago village north of Prairie Du Chien and along the Mississippi River was a man named Red Bird.

Red Bird was no ordinary man. People said that he was about six feet tall and straight but without restraint. A newspaper story I once read said that "his proportions were those of the most exact symmetry, and this embraced the entire man from his head to his feet." It noted that "his face appeared to be a compound of grace and dignity, of firmness and decision, all tempered with mildness and mercy. When he was ready for battle, Redbird's face was painted ... one side red; the other, green and white. He wore a collar of blue and white wampum, interspersed with claws of a panther and a Yankton dress made of beautiful elk skin that was almost pure white. Across the chest diagonally was his war pipe that was at least three feet long, ornamented with dyed horsehair, feathers, and bills of birds." Red Bird had learned that it was best to live in peace and was always welcome in Prairie du Chien, where he often ate and drank with the settlers in their homes.

It seems that during the maple sugar season of 1826, a family in Iowa had been murdered by a couple of Winnebagos for stealing their maple sap. The Winnebago offenders were found and brought to Fort Crawford in Prairie Du Chien. While the Winnebago prisoners were there, a flood on the Mississippi left Fort Crawford temporarily underwater, and the army moved the two prisoners to Fort Snelling in what became Minnesota.

In the spring of 1827, an Indian from the Sioux Nation came into Red Bird's village and reported that the soldiers at Fort Snelling had killed the Winnebago prisoners and chopped them into little pieces. Red Bird had no reason to doubt this brave, believing his story. It cost him his freedom and his life.

After hearing the tale, Red Bird and his village wanted justice and demanded that the ancient Winnebago law be upheld, which meant killing two-for-one of their own killed. What made this difficult was that Red Bird had many settler friends and didn't want to hurt them. However, pressure within his village was strong, and he finally, reluctantly, agreed to lead his little war party into Prairie du Chien. He and a small band went to the village and returned saying they couldn't find anyone to kill. Story was that his young warriors mocked Red Bird as being too old, too weak, and too much of a friend of the white man.

On the morning of June 28, 1827, Red Bird and three companions set out to fulfill the tribal command. After stopping for a while at Prairie du Chien, the four men went on to the farm home of Mr. Registre Gagnier. The family invited the Indians to eat and, I heard tell, was preparing food for them, when the braves opened fire. The story was that Gagnier and his hired man, Solomon Lipcap, were killed immediately, and Gagnier's infant daughter was scalped and flung to the floor. Gagnier's wife managed to escape with her son to Prairie du Chien, where she spread the alarm. This was not the end of it, but I'll let another tell the story of the Winnebago War.

Mr. John Reynolds, the governor of Illinois, wrote of the event, and I share his thoughts that another event "of such brutality that it is painful to record." It seems that shortly thereafter two keel boats moved up the Mississippi, carrying supplies to the garrison at Fort Snelling. Red Bird's clan appeared around a river bend north of Prairie du Chien, and the two crews put in to shore. There, according to Reynolds, the "boatmen made the Indians drunk and no doubt were drunk themselves when they captured six or seven squaws who were forced on the boats for 'corrupt and brutal purposes.' Not satisfied with this outrage on female virtue, the boatmen took the squaws with them to Fort Snelling. When the remaining Indians became sober, they realized the injury done to them."

Two days later, the boatmen believed they could simply drop the squaws off and be on their way. As they reached the mouth of the Bad Axe River and were about thirty feet from shore, reports were that the sailors heard blood-chilling yells and war hoops and then experienced a round of bullets. A voice asked if the crew was English, and when they said yes, the voice then invited them ashore to which, it was told, the crew answered back insultingly. Thus commenced a second round of fire from the shore, and one of the sailors was killed.

There was a gun battle that was supposed to have lasted nearly all day. Of thirty-seven Indians from the village, seven died and fourteen were wounded. I don't know who counted them or what was true, but the rumor was that the Winnebagos put 693 bullet holes in and through that boat and then fired on a second boat later that night. The keelboats got away, and when they reached Prairie du Chien, reported what happened. The settlers, including those who considered Red Bird their friend, were terrified and left their homes, crowding into Fort Crawford for protection. Now I am of man of religion and of peace. However, if someone took my Elizabeth under such circumstances, I too would have responded the way Red Bird and his village did.

Sadly, the attacks of those two days turned one incident into what was called the Winnebago War. Because of one lie told by one Sioux and the actions of some drunken sailors, everyone overreacted. The soldiers responded, and the commander of Fort Crawford captured the elderly Winnebago chief named Old Dekauray, who was a frail old man trying to live in peace in a world that was rapidly changing. The commander demanded that if Red Bird were not turned over, the chief would die instead. The old man didn't like confinement and promised that he would return each night if they let him out during the day. The commander let him out, and true to Dekauray's word, the old man returned at dusk.

With so much ruckus, soldiers and the volunteer militia moved north from St. Louis, and more soldiers and even more militia came down the Fox River from Green Bay to an area called Portage. I was told that there was a meeting between the Winnebago elders and the soldiers and that the Winnebagos were warned that the existence of their entire nation depended on the surrender of Red Bird and the killers of the one sailor and two settlers.

Red Bird was said to be near Portage, and the militia wanted revenge for all three deaths. I think the Winnebago realized that this was the end of life as they knew it. Their land was gone. Their livelihood was gone. Their dignity was gone. All that was left was their existence, and to some of them, that wasn't worth the price they had to pay.

On September 2, 1827, a single Indian arrived at the soldier's camp carrying a white flag. He promised that before the sun went down the next day, Red Bird would surrender. Red Bird kept his word. As Red Bird stood on the opposite shore of the Fox River, the soldiers heard him singing which was said to be his death song.

Red Bird reported that he had accompanied two of the three other braves, but indicated the other had escaped. He asked for kind treatment with no irons for the prisoners and food and tobacco for his starving people. Red Bird stood up when the white men finished talking and faced a Major Whistler and said, "I am ready. I do not wish to be put in irons. Let me be free. I have given my life away. It is gone." People say that he stooped down and took up some dust between his thumb and finger and blew it away. "I would not take my life back. It is gone."

Red Bird was supposed to have written: "I do not know that I have done wrong. I come now to sacrifice myself to the white man because it is my duty to save my people from the scourge of war. If I have done wrong, I will pay for either with horses or my life. I do not understand the white man's law, which has one set of words for the white man and another for the red. The white men promised the lead mines would be ours, but they did nothing to the men who took our possession away from the lands. If an Indian took possession of something belonging to the white man, the soldiers would come quickly enough. We have been patient. We have seen all this. We have seen our ancient burial grounds plowed over. We have seen our braves shot down like dogs for harvesting corn. ... We have seen the white men steal our lands, our quarries, our waterways by lying to us, cheating us, and making us drunk enough to put marks on papers without knowing what we were doing. When first the Long Knives came, the prophets told us they would never be honest with us. We did not believe them. We do now. When word came that our brother was slain, I went forth and took meat. I did not know the report was false, so I did no wrong. I fulfilled the law of the Winnebago. I am not ashamed ... I come because the white men are too strong, and I do not wish my people to suffer. Now I am ready, take me."

Red Bird and his Winnebago companions expected that they would be executed. Instead, they were jailed at Fort Crawford. I heard that imprisonment to Red Bird was worse than death, and the Winnebago concluded their captors were too cowardly to inflict capital punishment. With his surrender, tensions eased somewhat, but there were always rumors that the Winnebago intended to launch more attacks on farms like ours. Many in the U.S. government felt that if Red Bird were tried and put to death, war would break out.

Red Bird died in prison the next year, and the two other braves, who were convicted of murder, were released by President John Quincy Adams himself so that they could go back to their families. It was hoped that this would end the trouble between the Winnebago and the settlers.

Based on the actions of Red Bird and five men, the entire Winnebago nation was forced to agree in 1828 to relocate across the Mississippi River. As a consequence, both the Sauk and Fox nations were also to be removed from Wisconsin as well and forced to settle on the west side of the Mississippi River. With it, we became part of the Wisconsin territory in the minds of everyone. With the territory came even more soldiers and even more people, and the peaceful co-existence that we had enjoyed with the great leader, Black Hawk, and his people were forever changed. Because of a few crazy acts on both sides, many people in Washington, D.C., began to think that we all could not live peaceably together and that all the Indians should be moved west of what was now "our" land. The men who had marched to war returned as victors without firing a shot. They laid down their guns and went back to their diggings on Indian land.

Few of the newcomers planned to stay. Even after the Winnebago War, this was still Indian land, and the Indians were still restless. Most miners came for lead and the profits of the lead industry. They planned to get rich quick, strip the region of its wealth, and do so for as long as the Indians remained quiet. But any hint of trouble, and the miners would be gone, making life unstable for many who wanted to stay. Towns appeared wherever strikes were made and disappeared whenever the veins ran out. Miners went from one digging to another while entire families lived for years in tents, wagons or dugouts, caves, and even sod huts, waiting for that lucky strike that would quickly bring them wealth that they would probably just squander.

Periodically, an Indian family would come by looking for food or a way to earn some money. Their sadness and frustration could be seen in their eyes. While we thought that things with the Winnebago and Sauk were finished, they were not. The settlers didn't respect the Indians and treated them as fools. They got them drunk and made a mockery of their beliefs and their way of life. These kind, brave, peace-loving people were turned into buffoons through whiskey and mistreatment. They were hungry and defeated and disrespected in many ways. Their dignity was lost. Their lives shattered. Their families destroyed. Black Hawk must have seethed at the indignities. To his death, I am totally certain he felt that his people had been cheated and mistreated by the white man who hid behind the Treaty of 1804 that he argued was not only illegitimate when it was signed, but not in force because the government had only paid the $2,500 for everything. So little for so much. Life, liberty, and the pursuit of happiness regardless of whose life, liberty, or happiness stood in its way.

While we had been quietly digging for a long time and had success, 1828 saw a new miner named Nat Morris come up from Galena. Either he was really smart or just plain lucky. None of us ever found out which one. Nat found a rich vein of lead that ran through a steep ridge just above the river that the rest of us had missed. The vein was positioned so that it stood at a point in the river, and he called his claim Mineral Point. This deep, plentiful vein made Nat Morris rich and gave our town its name ... Mineral Point. And so it began.

Even mining amongst roughshod men needs a set of rules. Because lead had been mined in Missouri for many years, rules of Missouri Lead made the most sense because they helped protect everyone against lead thieves and land speculators. The rules were quite simple ... a prospector could work only one claim at a time. Each claim was limited to 200 square yards. A miner could not cultivate the soil, cut the stands of timber, or settle on the land. Each prospector had to take all the ore that he raised to a licensed smelter who would deduct 10 percent of the total yield as rent due the government. If the miner gave false testimony, stole ore, set fire to the prairie or woods, cut forbidden timber, sold his lead to an unlicensed smelter, or did no work on his claim for eight straight days during the mining season, or in any way violated the rights of other miners, he would lose his permit and forfeit his holding. Each prospector was required to settle disputes about discoveries and claims directly with other miners and the smelters. When agreements could not be made, the government agent would step in, and his word was final. These were the rules in the new Mineral Point, and we all pretty much lived by them.

The men who built log houses across from the diggings all planned on being miners forever and never farmers. As folks came, stories would be told about how it was when we first arrived. Now miners like to tell stories and tall tales. Some of them were about the weather and about the vermin, but one held true. In the beginning, we all lived in hollowed-out holes in the sides of hills just like badgers ... tough, mean, and protective of what was ours.

The Land I Love

Because I had been north so many times before, I had scoured the area for land and found some fertile grassy plains about three miles southeast of the Mineral Point. The land was hilly but well drained, and a small spring-fed creek meandered, making sure that there would be drinking water all the time. On one end of the horizon, there was a deep forest that would provide the lumber we needed to build a house and barn someday. This is what I had dreamed about and fallen in love with. This was my unbridled passion. It was a romantic, fantastic love affair ... not with another woman, but with a time and place where my dreams could come true. I had fallen in love with the land as it reached out to meet a smear of sky in the distance. This was something that those in Cornwall had never seen, even when they glanced out upon the sea and looked at the tiny boats disappearing along its edge.

How can I speak of the land I love except to begin at what I believe is the beginning? I am not a man of science nor do I have much education, but I do know the land and believe I know how it came to be. In a time before time, my land was untouched by the great glacier that made its way across what has become Wisconsin. While much of what became Wisconsin had its start beneath the wrath of that mighty sheet of ice, our land and that of my neighbors remained a lone island in what must have been the sea of ice. The never-ending wind, frost, and rain carved the land into deep valleys and steep slopes, eroding the less resistant rock, even exposing the lead that had been deposited so long ago.

I remember that first time I stood upon the hill and breathed in the succulent spring air filled with the scent of tranquility. I looked north, and dark knots of oaks and clumps of bluestem grass and wildflowers pierced my heart with beauty and aroused my imagination of all that could be. I stuck my shovel beneath the earth's crust and felt the depth of its richness. The gnarly rocks that had punctuated our homeland were simply not there, and the soft sweet breezes of summer washed away the brittle cold from whence we had come. This was a land ... an amalgam of fire and ice, of earth and water where Mother Nature had splendidly opened her womb and poured forth her bounty. Behind me played a symphony not made of musical instruments but instruments of God. The sound of the whippoorwill calling to its mate. The chirp of the redwing blackbird upon the branches. The hoot of the great owl, calling out its lonesome song. These are the sounds of nature that called to me, enrapturing my mind, my body, and my heart, making me aware that we are never, ever alone ... that God is always with us.

One day when Henry and Elizabeth had made the trip from Galena, I took them to see the land for the first time. Elizabeth stood speechless, in awe at that point where the quietude of our singularity called and enveloped her in tranquility. She was home, and she knew it. She had awakened from her dream to realize that it was reality. Like me, Elizabeth fell in love, and the transcending rush of unification wound itself around her heart until she felt that this majestic experience could only have but one single name ... home.

The land had a wide valley ringed by sharp bluffs. There was also a high, open prairie where we could grow our crops. We walked the land for the first time as a family and saw willow, elm, basswood, and poplar trees in the valley while the bluffs above maintained a sentinel, worn by water and wind into a variety of shapes. As we looked towards the horizon, we saw the fields covered with many species of tall grass. When the wind blew, the grass looked like waves across the sea, and yet the cold gray of the sea that we saw in Cornwall was alive in Wisconsin with splendid colors of the prairie wildflowers, where plants such as the dark purple Masonic weed and the gold sunflowers and soft reds of Kansas gayfeather stimulated our eyes, arousing our imaginations. As we looked deeper into the sea, we saw low-growing violets, the delicate Pasque flower, the snowdrop, and many varieties of aster. Elizabeth was in heaven, her mind racing wildly about all the beauty that she could bring home. Over-shadowing all of the grass with its great height was the compass plant, whose leaves point north and south and serve to guide those who come across the treeless prairies. God had given us directions, and we were home.

The clear stream started below our land and crept from beneath the limestone rocks, and yet the bounty of the earth was so great that by the time it reached beyond our hills, it was full of brook trout, pike, bass, and another fish I did not know the name of. Between the grass and the prairie were hills covered with white oak, black walnut, basswood, along with apple and hickory trees that shadowed fields where gooseberry, black currant, and raspberry thickets grew. I could imagine the spring resounding with the drumming of ruffled grouse and deer, and knew that we would never go without food as the land would provide.

Having immediately fallen in love with the beauty all around her, Elizabeth said we needed to purchase the land. I agreed, but didn't know who we would pay for it. Was it owned by the Indians or the government? If it was owned by the Indians, which nation did the land belong to, and who did we purchase the land from?

I was told by the government about the agreement with the Indians, called the Treaty of St. Louis, which was signed in 1804 and included a payment of $2,500 for a swath of land stretching from northeast Missouri through almost all of Illinois north of the Illinois River as well as a large section of southern Wisconsin. I also knew that miners were forbidden to farm the land, but a lot of us felt we could build a house and have a small garden if we chose. But the question arose ... what does "small" mean and to whom?

While many white men considered all Indians to be the same, I learned that there were differences between the Fox, Sauk, and Winnebago nations based on not only their language but their beliefs, just like there were differences between the French and the English or between different religions. The term "Winnebago" was a name given to the people by the neighboring Algonquian-speaking nations, such as the Fox, Sauk, and Ojibwa. I also learned that the 1804 treaty was deeply resented by the Sauk, especially their Chief Black Hawk, who felt that the two elders of his nation who were present at the signing were not authorized to sign treaties.

I guess I should have known there would be issues. Change always creates those situations where some will win and others will always lose. Little did anyone realize what the consequences would be. In 1828, America elected a president by the name of Andrew Jackson: a man nicknamed "Indian killer" and "Sharp Knife" who built his reputation on killing Indians. In 1830, a year after he became president, Jackson signed a law that he had proposed—The Indian Removal Act—which legalized killing any and all Indians, even women and children, which he encouraged.

It wasn't long until I realized that Black Hawk understood that times were changing and that his role as head of the Sauk was to ensure safety and security for his people against the settlers. I learned that, after attempting to resolve the issue with the Winnebago, Black Hawk went to Missouri to settle the matter. While there, he explained his feelings in an article in a newspaper. It wasn't until 1832 that I read what was written, but feel I need to share it with you so that you understand what transpired between our family and this great leader. Here is what Black Hawk wrote ...

"On our arrival at St. Louis we met our American father and explained to him our business, urging the release of our friend from his prison. The American chief told us he wanted land. We agreed to give him some of the land on the west side of the Mississippi, likewise more on the Illinois side opposite Jeffreon. When the business was all arranged we expected to have our friend released to come home with us. About the time we were ready to start, our brother was let out of the prison. He started and ran a short distance when he was SHOT DEAD.

"This was all myself and the nation knew of the treaty of 1804. It has since been explained to me. I found by that treaty, that all of the country east of the Mississippi, and south of Jeffreon was ceded to the United States. I will leave it to the people of the United States to say whether our nation was properly represented in this treaty? Or whether we received a fair compensation for the extent of country ceded by these four individuals?"

When there are no rules, you do what you think is best. We were in love, and we decided to settle on the land and call our home "Waldwick" after where we had come from; after where we had dreamed so much about; after all those who had come before us and never had the chance to live what we were about to live. Our camp had officially become Mineral Point, and in 1828, Mr. R.C. Hoard and John Long built the first smelter there so that raw ore wouldn't need to be carried all the way to Galena.

About the same time, William Roberts and his family arrived to mine. Now Brother Roberts was a very religious man who thought it was his calling to bring the faith of God to all of us. He was like a stern uncle, and we all called him Uncle Billy. I don't know if he liked the name, but he sure liked preaching. Uncle Billy didn't have any formal education, and so what he preached and the songs he sang were quite limited. He didn't know the words to too many songs, but he always did sing "Jerusalem, My Happy Home," which all of us miners would stop and listen to when he sang. It was so popular that many of us began calling the natural springs that fed the panning creek and the valley "Jerusalem." That summer, the first store was opened by Erastus Wright, and so supplies didn't require the long trip to Dodge's Grove when they were needed. With the Wisconsin winters being as harsh as they are, many miners would head south in the fall, while the rest of us would hunker down for the cold spell.

With so many miners coming, the Mineral Point Hotel opened in March 1829 just a short time before the miners and prospectors began to arrive for another season of digging. I remember that year as a long line of men and wagons from the South crowded the roads in even greater number than before. Those of us who stayed the winter had names for them all ... "Suckers" from Illinois, "Corn-Crackers" from Kentucky, "Hoosiers" from Indiana, "Buckeyes" from Ohio, and "Pukes" from Missouri. Wagon camps were set up, and shelters built, and the diggings reopened. Newcomers, with no common sense, dug everywhere for lead. Everyone was out to strike it rich, and when they failed to make a strike, they simply moved on without filling up their shafts. Soon the prairie grass grew over the scarred ground, hiding the dangerous holes, and night travel became so hazardous that many men simply stopped in their tracks when darkness fell, refusing to stir until dawn. In some areas, it was so bad that travelers preferred using oxen to horses. If an ox fell into a mineral hole and broke its neck, its carcass could be used for beef. With a dead horse, nothing could be done.

1829 was quite the year. On July 4, we all got together to celebrate our independence with 110 couples dancing until the musicians fell asleep over their fiddles. That year, Mineral Point had its first wedding when Miss Lovey Roberts married Mr. Joshua Brown. It too was a grand time with much joy and laughter. Also, the Mineral Point public school opened with eight students who were taught by a Mrs. Harker, if I remember right. In November, Mrs. Hood gave birth to a boy named John who was the first child born in Mineral Point.

Also in 1829, our county was formed and named after the Ioway Indians. First off, we run all the Indians out and then we name our county after them. Now, I guess Ioway didn't sound right, and so it was named Iowa County. Mineral Point became the county seat covering all the lead-mining lands within the borders of the Michigan territory. With over 4,000 people, Mineral Point had more residents than the towns of Milwaukee and Chicago combined, and I hoped we had fewer problems. Drunks and whores littered the streets, and anyone with two nickels could open a saloon or a whorehouse and make themselves comfortable. The miners came and the miners went, and with them came a flush of money as those who thought they would strike it rich would only make small deposits towards the wealth of others before departing for another dream, another adventure, another disappointment.

Mining was so good and so productive that additional smelters opened in Mineral Point to purify the lead. The problem was getting the lead to market, which meant all the way to New England. The river at Galena was the nearest port of commerce. Up to forty tons of smelted ore were loaded on carts pulled by slow-moving teams of from four to twelve oxen, driven by teamsters using twenty-seven-foot-long whips that coerced the beasts to pull ... pull ... pull as they dragged the lead over the forty-mile road, if you wanted to call it that. Now the term "road" was loosely used. In truth, the road to Galena was a hard road to travel as it was cut up by the ore wagons and in many spots rendered almost impassable. Because Galena was where one could catch a boat to anywhere, three or four coaches with six-horse teams carried passengers and mail over the roadway each day as well with returning teams carrying provisions to the camps and towns along the way. Every few miles, there were inns, taverns, and rest stops "where refreshments were served to man and beasts," and where teamsters or stages might stop when night overtook them.

We would experience the hustle and bustle of Mineral Point when we visited, but would tire of it quickly and meander back towards Waldwick where life on what we hoped would be our farm wasn't always work. Elizabeth and the children and I enjoyed our time in each other's company. Instead of the daily ritual with men whom you depended on for your life and your livelihood, most of the time you are alone. To this day, farming has always reminded me of how the solitude within one's fields allows you to concentrate and yet isolates you from both good and bad. As time progressed, there would be days and even weeks when I didn't see another soul and would yearn for their company. Yet, I have always loved the peace and tranquility of being alone where the only sound in the summertime is that of the breeze through the tall grasses. Elizabeth and I would take the boys and walk the land enjoying the flowers, the view, and the warm summer breeze. At night, the sound of crickets kept pace with the warm earth, reminding us that we were all just visitors. While we all hoped the good times would go on forever, they didn't. A depression hit the country hard, and the bottom fell out of the price of lead. 1830 was not going to be a good year. None of us realized just how bad it was going to be.

Black Hawk

I need to back up a bit to make some sense. You see, I began mining from sunrise until early afternoon. Then I would hitch up Old Ed and head out to the site we had chosen for our cabin. I would try and cut one tree per week and drag it up to where the cabin was going to be built. To make Old Ed and my journeys worthwhile, each day I would load some of the smooth river rocks I had mined into my wagon and take them out for the fireplace. Then before dark, I would head back to the Mineral Point and sleep in the lean-to that I had built.

Our first cabin was designed as simply one large room. I made it so that we could add walls inside as the children got bigger. The fireplace was for heat and cooking. There was to be an outhouse and eventually a barn. That first winter, Old Ed would sleep inside with us. After two months, I had most of the walls up and needed help with the roof. I brought Henry and Elizabeth with me from Galena, and we had the help of other families in putting the roof on. The floor was dirt, but I promised Elizabeth that someday it would be made out of wood. She said she really didn't care as long as the house was filled with love and happiness.

By fall, we were ready to move into the cabin. We took time to gather acorns and hickory nuts. We cut the tall grass for Old Ed and went hunting for deer, quail, squirrels, rabbits, and ducks. My aim got better, and we had more food for winter. On October 11, 1829 our second son was born ... Thomas Michael Terrill, first born at Waldwick.

In the spring of 1831 I continued to mine, but with lead prices so low, I spent less and less time doing so as I needed to break ground and plant crops. I knew I was breaking the law, but, like everything else, people's minds were on much larger things than one farmer digging up some ground ... especially when we were told we could have gardens. While Old Ed had served us well, we bought another work horse, Jackie, and built a stable for the two of them. I think Old Ed resented Jackie at first, as he was so used to getting all the attention, but after a few weeks, I could see that Old Ed and Jackie had become good friends. There's something about being around your own kind that can soften even the hardest of souls. Elizabeth would take the two of them out and stake them in a field, and they would eat to their hearts' content. When it was time to come home, she would simply pull up the stake, and they would head for home.

All seemed peaceful and natural until one day I looked out the window and saw ten Indian braves on horseback heading towards the house. We had seen them off in the distance, but never up close. They seemed to tolerate us but never wanted to come that near. As they approached, I remember Elizabeth asking if I needed the gun. I thought, "Ten braves and me?" I didn't think my chances were too good, especially when my aim wasn't there. As they approached the house, I stepped onto the porch and raised my hands so that they could see that I was not armed. I told Elizabeth to keep the boys inside, and so I shut the door.

As the Indians stopped, I motioned for them to get down from their horses and offered them water from the cistern. They ignored me. I didn't think I could speak to them, so I guess I must have looked pretty stupid standing there making all kinds of gestures with my hands. It must have been so bad that one of them started laughing, and soon all of them were sort of amused. Finally the leader spoke.

"Where is your squaw?" he asked.

"In the house with the children," I replied.

"Is she afraid?"

"No," I answered.

"Then have her come outside."

I turned and opened the door and told Elizabeth to come out with the children. Gingerly, she appeared in the doorway holding the baby and Henry's hand.

"Why have you built your house on our land?"

"Because we did not know this was your land. I am willing to purchase it from you if you like. I am sorry, but we thought we were still in Illinois," I lied.

"You know better than that. You have been coming here for three summers."

"I am sorry. You are right. We are just simple people and wanted to farm this land."

"What are you willing to pay for the land?" the leader asked.

"Do you want money?"

"What good is that?" he replied. "We have all that we need given to us by our great father. We had food and water and safe places to raise our children until the white man came. We have weapons and all that we ever wanted until you and your people came and brought with you guns and whiskey and sickness and took our land, which has been ours since before the sun. We have tried to be honorable people and live with your kind. We have taken our nation and attempted to create a settlement with your government, but no matter what we do, no matter what we give, it never seems to be enough. We are of the Sauk nation, not the Winnebago or the Fox. We have our land and our rules and our way of life, and yet all white men do not see us as the Sauk and the Winnebago and the Fox but as simply red men you lump together like clay that you then try to mold to the white man's ways."

I could tell he was irritated and frustrated and more importantly angry—not only at me but at what we were doing to his land and to his people—and yet I knew that for me to simply give up and leave would only mean that in a few weeks or months some other settler would arrive and take my place. The door was open, and sadly, with the open door, what had been all theirs was no more.

"Perhaps we could trade you for the land," I offered.

"What have you got that we could use?" he asked.

He looked around and got down from his horse. He was much taller than I had expected, and his hair stood on end and was tied with a single white feather in back. Even though he was much older than me, his arms were powerful, and he walked with the gait of authority. He was the leader, and he knew it. He walked past me and into the cabin. He looked at the pots and pans and roughly made furniture that I had built and shook his head.

"There is nothing here that we need. I think you should leave my land now and forever."

My heart sunk, and I knew he could see my disappointment.

"This land has been ours for all time, and you people think that you can come and simply take it."

Elizabeth spoke for the first time. "That isn't true. We just didn't know who to ask about the land or who to pay. We are honest people, and we will do what you ask. If you insist that we leave, we will pack our belongings and leave. If you want money, we will pay you what we have and pay you more when we get it. If it's belongings you want, we will give you anything that is a fair trade."

I could tell that the leader was impressed that she had spoken.

"She speaks well. You should let her talk more often," he said with a wry smile.

As he turned, he froze when he saw the white bear skin in the corner.

"What is this?" he asked. For the first time, there was fear in his voice.

"We lived in a cave a few years back in Kentucky, and after we were settled, this bear came back, because it was his den." I replied.

"Something like today?"

"Something like today," I agreed

"Will you shoot me, like you did the bear?"

"Only if you decide that you want to sleep in my bed," I answered.

This brought a nervous chuckle from the leader. "You have done much and have done it alone. I have much land and feel that you will not bother my people. I will let you live on this land, but in return I will need three things from you."

"What?" I asked.

"First, I want you to give me this bear skin and his claws."

I handed it to him with no hesitation. I sensed that the land would soon be ours and there was no need for trepidation.

"Next, I want you to teach my people how you make the bullets for our guns. The lead we make is not pure, and the bullets do not shoot straight."

"Done," I said.

"Finally, I want you to give me your word that you will tell your people that we are people of peace only wanting to live our lives so that our children can live theirs."

I looked him in the eye and said "done" one last time and stuck out my hand to shake on it. Instead, he turned and walked out the door with the white bear skin over his shoulder. All of the others looked at him with envy. He had something they had rarely, if ever, seen before. Was this a sign? Was there a spirit that came from within the soul of the great, white bear that would give this man power and respect and authority?

As they mounted their horses, I looked up at him and said, "You are a great leader. What is your name?"

"Black Hawk," he replied as he turned and rode away.

"Black Hawk?" I whispered. "Black Hawk."

With that, the farm was ours in regards to the Sauk. Black Hawk and his people lived up to their side of the agreement, and we to ours. His men came back, and I showed them how to clear the lead of its impurities and then how to melt it and form it into balls for the guns they had acquired. Whenever anyone spoke of Black Hawk, I replied that he was a man of honor and dignity as he had lived up to his word.

For the most part, in the beginning, we all got along. I'm certain that the Indians did not appreciate our coming on their soil and never leaving, and yet I think they also realized that with each passing day, there were more of us than the day before. Along with Mineral Point, there were towns called Platteville, Shullsburg, Belmont, and New Diggings that sprang up around mines.

For some of the miners, the word "peace" had a much different meaning ... piece," since all they cared about was grabbing as much as they could take. Some were a rough and tumble bunch who drank a lot, swore a lot, gambled a lot, and whored a lot. They weren't good people, and when they got a few drinks in them, they would brag about how much they hated the Indians and what they wanted to do to them and their squaws. As more and more miners arrived, it became a real mess, and the confrontations with the Indians became more and more and more. Anger was everywhere in a land so peaceful that only God could have made it.

We kept to ourselves and enjoyed our solitude. When it was really hot and we were feeling in the mood, we would go down to the stream to cool off. The fall meant crisp air and blue, blue sky ... so blue that it made you wish it went on forever. Winter always meant white silence, as the snow muffled the sounds of life and nothing stirred as we kept waiting, waiting, waiting for the first drop of warmth that meant yet another sun would rise and warm our hearts as it bared the earth and made her ready for her rebirth. Spring was met with the sounds of birds telling us that life was about to burst forth once again, and with it the joy that came with long summer nights filled with a symphony of sounds whispering in our ears, telling us to live life and enjoy.

One of my favorite memories was a time when the boys were still quite small and were napping. I don't remember the year, and so forgive me, but I wanted to share with you the event. It was one of those hot, humid, late summer afternoons when, no matter where you were, you could not get comfortable. It was miserable and simply too hot to work. As I looked out the cabin door toward the horizon to the west, I saw the storm clouds rising. Not a bad one, mind you, but rain was on its way, and I knew it would quickly burrow its energy within our souls.

Soon the rain began pouring down. As Elizabeth and I peered out through the doorway at what had become a torrent, she acquired a girlish grin upon her face. She glanced back at the sleeping boys and began swiftly pulling off her clothes until she stood naked in front of me. Then, and without warning, she ran out, with a crazy little laugh, holding up her head to the heavy rain, spreading her arms and twirling in the onslaught. At first, it seemed strange that my Elizabeth would be so free, and then I realized that the womanish bonds that had restrained her were broken and she was nothing more than a little girl wrapped up in the moment as her body became caked in the finest of Wisconsin mud, begotten from the finest place on earth ... Waldwick and the Terrill farm.

As the warm rain poured down, her head became enveloped in her crimson hair as her body glistened with glee. It was a strange sight to see, and a smile creased my lips. Freedom! Total, unequivocal freedom! I leaned back and watched her merriment. At that point, Elizabeth became Lizzie, my love ... a name I saved for only those moments when we were alone but together.

Lizzie, her hair all wet and sticking to her head, turned her exuberant face and saw me. Her blue eyes pierced my heart with excitement as she turned and began running out of the clearing and down the path, the wet wisps of tall grass whipping her loins. What a perfectly wonderful sight to see the majesty and grace of the woman you love embodying the purest of purity with a sense of innocence that formed a rainbow of joy around her body.

Hastily, I removed my clothes and joined her in the cascading onslaught. Awash in laughter, bathed in freedom, unrequited by the social bonds that held us so tightly, we were but children playing. The path had become a waterway, and as I caught her, we both slipped and fell in the mud, laughing at our plight. As I went to stand, she reached down and took a handful of mud and slathered it upon my ass. She wanted to play. With that, I responded with mud of my own and proceeded to cover her as well. Soon, we were both covered from head to foot, highlighted by trickled streaks as the rain worked hard to wash it all away. For moments, we looked at each other, laughed at each other, and loved each other with as much intensity as that summer's rain. Nine months later, our first daughter was born. I wanted to call her June, but her name was Sarah as we had always promised.

We were all glad to see 1830 and 1831 go and reveled in singing Auld Lang Syne ...

Should auld acquaintance be forgot
And never brought to mind
Should auld acquaintance be forgot
And days of auld lang syne
For auld lang syne, my dear
For auld lang syne
We'll take a cup o' kindness yet
For auld lang syne
And surely you will buy your cup
And surely I'll buy mine
And we'll take a cup o' kindness yet
For auld lang syne
We two have run around the slopes
And picked the daisies fine
We've wandered many a weary foot
Since auld lang syne
For auld lang syne, my dear
For auld lang syne
We'll take a cup o' kindness yet
For auld lang syne
We two have paddled in the stream
From morning sun till dine
But the sea between us broad have roared
From auld lang syne
For auld lang syne, my dear
For auld lang syne,
We'll take a cup o' kindness yet
For auld lang syne
We'll take a cup o' kindness yet
For auld lang syne

The winter of 1831-32 was especially hard on all of us, but particularly the Indians. January and February 1832 turned out to be bitterly cold months with a deep snow cover that existed over much of the North Country to the point that, at the end of February, I heard even the Great Lakes were almost completely covered with ice, which set the stage for still another month of severe winter weather. When things did begin to warm up in late April, there was nothing but mud, and planting crops simply could not be done. If that wasn't bad enough, the summer was too hot and too dry, and nothing grew.

By spring, many miners were in such bad straits that some had no food. While the government had lowered the tax on the mined lead from 10 percent to 6 percent in 1830, it was still difficult to make ends meet. Now not having a drink or two was one thing, but not having food on the table was another, especially when the land stood fallow. That spring, the superintendent of the Dodge County Mining District let it be known that because of the hard times, he would no longer enforce the laws forbidding land cultivation. This was all I needed, and within one week, I went from being a full-time miner and part-time farmer to a full-time farmer and part-time miner. Our prayers had been answered, and when the price of lead increased, those of us still remaining began to see light at the top of the mine.

The Black Hawk War

As I wrote earlier, the Terrill family got along well with the Sauk nation and with Black Hawk himself. He was their leader and had become our distant friend. We respected each other because we both kept our words. I kept to my land that I had purchased from him and helped him better understand what little I knew about farming, and he taught me about leading people.

The Sauk built their villages in an area called Saukenuk, where there was plenty of water, good land for growing everything from corn to pumpkins, and many animals for food and clothing. I learned that the entire Sauk nation had come from the northern part of New York, where they were pushed out by other Indian nations and settled in Wisconsin and made decent lives for themselves.

As more and more people came across the border, Black Hawk found himself with a real problem. This time, instead of Indians, it was people like me. While there had been a treaty that said we had to stay in Illinois, we broke it. I guess we all thought that a few people in a land so rich wouldn't make that much difference. The problem was that there were thousands of people who had the same idea ... a little bit of someone else's land wouldn't matter much.

Even though the Sauk had been forced to move to Iowa, Black Hawk and his people were starving and, like any proud leader, Black Hawk was angered by the loss of his birthplace. In 1830 and 1831, he came across the Mississippi to Illinois several times in search of food. In June 1831, the government forced Black Hawk to sign a treaty stating that he and his people would never return to their homeland on the east side of the Mississippi River without government permission. In return, he and Keokuk, the other Sauk elder, were promised enough corn and food to feed their people throughout the winter. We had taken their land, and now we were taking his pride. No man should suffer like that, and it is understandable why he was angry.

The government never provided the promised food, and so with little food and tribal members starving, Black Hawk elected to return to his homeland. In April 1832, encouraged by promises of alliance with other Indian nations and Britain, Black Hawk moved what was called his "British Band" of more than 1,200 people, composed of a few hundred warriors and old men, women, and children of the Sauk, Fox, and Kickapoo nations, back east across the Mississippi River. He initially came simply in search of the food that was promised to where his former cornfields were to harvest what crops had grown. Who would have thought that something as basic as wanting to feed your family could lead to war, if you want to call it that?

I heard that the settlers who had moved into Saukenuk got real nervous. They had fenced in what had been the Sauk fields, and their animals had trampled the vegetables that Black Hawk's people came for. The Indian leaders heard about the ruckus and went to the settlers carrying a white flag, meaning they meant no harm, simply to tell them that they had only come back to harvest food for their families. The settlers didn't seem to care about the Indians or the white flag or the fact that Black Hawk's people only wanted to eat. Instead, their excuse was that they didn't speak the Sauk language, and they killed two Indians, white flag and all. Black Hawk was enraged and began killing white settlers. Now this wasn't right, but what happened next cannot be explained or justified.

The Sauk nation's "incursion" into land that was once theirs, simply to find food, was considered an invasion by the United States government, and volunteers were sent to fight Black Hawk and his people. Now, I'm not here to say that all that Black Hawk did was right, as there were issues on his side as well, but what we did to those poor people can never be excused.

In May, the volunteer militia was supported by regular U.S. Army troops, who combined to drive Black Hawk and what was left of his followers to a point of exhaustion and starvation. With his supplies running low, Black Hawk sent out a truce party bearing another white flag of surrender. The volunteers saw the three representatives and rushed out and killed one while capturing the other two. The "soldiers" then pursued five warriors who had followed the truce party, killing two of them, and "attacked" Black Hawk's encampment, saying they didn't speak the language. Needless to say, Black Hawk was enraged that the dignity of surrender could be sullied and that integrity did not exist. Black Hawk took his men to battle and dispersed the militia, many of whom simply went back to their homes without ever firing a shot.

Black Hawk made plans for war because he didn't believe the volunteers were warriors. He used small groups of warriors to randomly attack while the women and children remained safe in the marshes of Koshkonong. No one knew where the next attack would be, and fear was rampant throughout all of Wisconsin, including Waldwick and Mineral Point. The armed forces attempted to stop Black Hawk, and for four months, the "war" went on as the Sauk nation eluded capture by leading the forces around southern Wisconsin. The toll on Black Hawk and his people, who had no food or water, was tremendous.

In late July, what was left of the Sauk nation was traveling through the four lakes area called "Tychobera." They were traveling between two of the lakes with the soldiers in pursuit. We learned, with our heads shaking in disgust, that, as the malnourished and exhausted stragglers fell behind, they were simply shot by militia throughout the day. One by one, these starving people were destroyed as if it were a sport ... a game ... a competition to see who could kill the most. It wasn't difficult to track Black Hawk's nation, as flocks of buzzards and carrion crows swooped above the bodies as they fell in exhaustion or, if lucky, in death.

As darkness was setting in, what was left of the Sauk nation reached the Wisconsin River at a point called Wisconsin Heights with troops and militia in pursuit. Black Hawk had a choice: continue to watch his people die one by one as they fell behind or try to get back to safety in Iowa. It is my understanding that Black Hawk knew that the existence of his entire nation was at stake. He took fifty warriors and moved about two miles from the river, leaving the balance to help the old people, women, and children cross the river. Another seventy warriors volunteered to fight to save their families and their ways of life.

Black Hawk and his half-starved warriors repeatedly attempted to surrender, only to be met with volley after volley of weaponry. When they reached the Wisconsin River, they defended the pass against nearly thousand soldiers and militia, while the remainder stayed with the women and children and could be seen crossing the Wisconsin River. Shots were fired, and the battle commenced until all family members were safely across the river, at which time Black Hawk and his men retreated and made their way across the river themselves.

They continued northwest above Prairie Du Chien to the Bad Axe River, where some families fashioned rafts and floated downriver toward the Mississippi, as they believed their only hope to save themselves was to get back to Iowa. Few escaped. They either drowned of found themselves facing soldiers who stood on the steamer "Warrior" and simply killed the women, children, and braves as they floated by. The soldiers didn't seem to care that these people begged for mercy and again waved white flags, desperately trying to surrender. The soldiers simply shot them. One story told was of a little Indian boy, starving, his arm half-blown away, begging for a piece of bread. Instead he was shot with those of his nation. As they fell into the river, their bodies floated away, and the river, as Captain John Throckmorton so vividly boasted, "blushed to a scarlet red" with Indian blood, washing away their hopes, their dreams, their love for life, and the land that had once been theirs.

Those who hid in the reeds along the shore were hunted down and bayoneted to death. About seventy who escaped across the Mississippi River were hunted like animals by bands of Sioux at the direction of General Atkinson. Of the 1,200 followers of Black Hawk who came "home," less than 150 lived to tell of the horrors they experienced.

Black Hawk surrendered to an Indian agent named Joseph Street at Fort Crawford in Prairie du Chien. He was a tired, broken man, no longer able to fight for his freedom, no longer willing to fight for his people who were, for the most part, decimated by disease, hunger, and the never-ending tide of settlers. They took Black Hawk east and made him a spectacle. He learned the power and might of the government and realized that his way of life was forever gone. Gone was the peace. Gone was the tranquility. Gone was the harmony with God and nature, replaced by the ever-growing insidious presence of a mankind hell-bent on controlling everything and making it work for them.

They took Black Hawk to New York City and let him see all of the people. It convinced him that his fight was futile. His people were dead, and each day there were more white men than the day before. They say he died of a broken heart somewhere out in Iowa—Iowa, land that was supposed to be the Sauk's forever. I wanted to go to his funeral and pay my respects, but I was told there wasn't one. Then I heard some grave robbers dug up his body and paraded it around for more people to see. Black Hawk went from being a great leader to a great sadness all because of someone else's dreams. While lead was the main reason people came to southern Wisconsin, all the news about the Black Hawk War that filled the newspapers out east with stories of the lush land played a big part in shaping our destiny as it portrayed Wisconsin as some sort of cornucopia of wealth and prosperity where even more settlers wanted to live.

There are many things that I am proud of in my life, but what I am about to tell you is not one of them. The Indians were good, honest, caring people. They had dignity and grace and understood what the word humanity was all about. When they went to war, they went as warriors to fight warriors and left the women and children alone. Only once in my adult life, did I ever get into a fight, and it was over the Black Hawk War. We had gone into town, and I went for a pint when one of the fellows at the bar began talking about how these poor starving people had been killed. He was laughing as he went into all the details about how they died.

I took it for as long as I could and then, when I couldn't take it anymore, went to where he was standing and asked him if he had ever met any member of the Sauk nation. He said "no," but that all Indians were alike and the only good one was a dead one.

I told him of my many encounters with the Sauk and what I thought of them. I told him that when old women and children raise a white flag in mercy, even the worst soldier doesn't shoot them down and watch their bodies float down the river awash in their own blood. I told him of how noble Black Hawk had been and how I had come to respect him as a man of honor who kept his word.

I don't know if it was the smirk on the man's face or the fact that he spit on my shoes that took me over the edge, but for the one and only time in my entire life, I pummeled the man. I beat on him until I was afraid that I had killed him.

It took four men to get me off of him. Four men!

They saw a side of me that even I didn't know existed. There was anger unlike any I had ever felt before. There was disgrace unlike any I had ever known before. There was sadness that had only previously touched my life when my friend Henry, Sarah, our baby girl, and little Henry had died. There was a need inside of me to get rid of the poison and the guilt that I felt, as I felt that it was because of people like me that these people had all died. With the passing of Black Hawk, we all knew things would change, but I guess none of us really understood how much different they would be.

The Deer Hunters

My boys grew quickly, and soon it was time to teach them about farming and gathering food, how to plow, when to gather and, just as importantly, how to hunt. The fields and forests kept us satisfied with wild game so that we could keep our farm animals to help provide money for other things.

After recovering from the depression, the little town of Mineral Point once again began to quickly grow as word spread of the rich lead deposits. When possible, we would go into town and meet with others. There was always someone new whom we had never seen before ... good, bad, old, young ... people simply trying to move ahead in life. With so many folks moving in, we knew that our solitude would soon be challenged.

When Henry was fourteen and Thomas was eight, it was decided that I should teach them how to shoot and to hunt. We would set up targets, and I taught them about the gun's sights and the wind and how to gauge your target. As the boys grew, they became the marksmen, and I remained the novice, as they could hit a moving target from fifty paces.

As for hunting, I first taught them how to track as Black Hawk's men had taught me. Next, I taught them safety so that they would not end up accidentally shooting each other or me for that matter. We learned to work as a team, each of us understanding where the other was to make certain that we weren't in the line of the other's shot.

The fall the boys were fifteen and nine, we went hunting deer. We had seen them in the fields and knew that they would be in our second wooded ravine. Quietly, we worked our way down towards the small stream that had cut its way through the valley. Henry was to my left and Thomas to my right so that we made a triangle-shaped party.

As I neared the valley, I heard a rustle and thought it to be a deer. I peered into the woods and caught sight of two miners, one holding a young Indian girl who was crying. I knew what they had planned. I knew what the outcome was to be. I also knew that we had to stop it. This girl was maybe fifteen, and they had torn her clothes away. She stood trembling in fear and embarrassment.

I looked to my left and caught Henry's eye. I motioned to him to circle to the left about thirty paces. Next, I let out a soft whistle that I had learned so that Thomas would hear me. I motioned so that he also saw what was happening. I motioned to him to go to the right thirty paces so that we had the miners in our crossfire. Then, I began slowly walking towards the miners. My gun in front of me, cocked and ready, I remember taking a deep breath and moving further until I caught their eye.

"What do you think you're doing?" I asked.

"What is it to you?" the one replied.

"You're on my land," I answered.

"Won't be long, and we'll be gone," the same one replied.

"Leave the girl and go now," I said.

"No," the other replied. "Not until I'm done with her."

"What you're doing is wrong."

"Just a goddamn Indian."

"What you're doing is wrong, and you are to stop right now."

With that, the first miner picked up his gun.

"You think you can use that?" he asked, pointing at my gun.

"It's not just me," I replied.

"That so?"

"Yes. Now put down your gun and let the girl go."

With that, I remember the miner releasing the girl and moving towards his gun.

"As I said, I'm not alone."

I remember his grin as he thought I was pretending. As he reached for his rifle, Henry let go with a shot that splintered his gun's butt, kicking the gun about ten feet from where it had been.

"As I said, I am not alone."

Now the other began to circle. I guess young Thomas thought he was a threat, so he let go with a shot that hit the miner in the leg right above the knee, knocking him to the ground. The first miner went for his pistol, and I took a shot, hitting him in the shoulder, ripping his shirt as the blood splattered out the back.

The young girl stood frozen in fear. She had two men shot lying near her, and she stood naked. Quickly the three of us moved in just as the one who had been shot in the leg pulled his knife. With that, Henry took aim and hit the man in the temple. I remember watching the interloper's eyes roll back and then come forward. First there was disbelief and then a total loss of any emotion as his head jerked back and he saw part of his skull lying on the rocks beside him.

With all of the noise from the gunshots, we had not noticed that the Indians had also come. At first, they assumed that we had been the cause of the problem and appeared ready to attack. We raised our arms and dropped our weapons so that they could see that we were not a threat to them. With that, the young Indian girl quickly put on her clothes and crumbled to the ground crying. We could see that the Indians were angry ... at us, at all white men ... at everyone who had promised peace and brought lies, disease, and corruption.

One Indian came forth and bent down next to the girl. She looked up and I think began to explain what had happened. The Indian looked at me, then at Thomas and Henry, and finally at first the dead and then the living miner. Quickly he stood and went to the miner who was still alive. Without hesitation, he took out his knife and slit the miner's throat. I remember hearing the gurgling sound as the miner gasped for air before falling into a puddle of his own blood. While the miner was still alive, the brave pulled the miner's head back and scalped him, pulling the hair and flesh from his head before pushing his now expressionless face into the dirt upon which he knelt.

My boys stood watching, their mouths open. They had never seen a man die before, and to watch them go the way they did had left them without words. I was concerned for Henry, as he had killed a man. I was concerned for Thomas because he was so young. I was also concerned for the young Indian girl, as she had been taken to the edge and threatened to the point that she would never forget what had happened.

It seemed like forever, then without word, the Indians melted back into the forest. Our hunting for the day was done. We were all trembling as we looked each other in the eye and started walking home. Nary a word was said that entire afternoon. The bodies were left for the wolves or whomever it was that would stoop so low as to eat vermin. We walked back to the cabin, and I quietly told Elizabeth what had happened. She pulled her skirt to cover her face and grabbed each boy and held them tight. It was only later that she said how sorry she was for the little girl. But, like all parents, she wanted to calm her own children first.

Discussions were had as to whether to go to Mineral Point and inform the constable. I said I would do it the next day and take him where the miners' bodies were. Soon it was time for bed, and I remember looking at my boys and realizing that in just a few moments their childhood had disappeared like the morning dew and they were now little men. As Elizabeth and I lay in bed, holding each other, I cried for the first time since Sarah had died. I cried for the dead miners. I cried for my boys, and I cried most of all for the little girl, knowing that she would not sleep without nightmares for many nights, if not forever.

When morning came, I sensed something different, but didn't know what. It wasn't until I opened the door of the cabin that I saw what had changed. There, hanging from the front support post, was a cleaned deer. The Indians had come and presented it as their way of saying thank you for what we had done.

The Farm

While there have been several events that have made up my life, in between there have been long periods when things just went on. Days began, and days ended, with nothing different or special in between. But then again, that's how life is supposed to be. Starting anything is always difficult. Starting a farm on land that had never seen a plow before was even more difficult. What can I say?

You rose with the sun and worked until you couldn't see anymore. Your body ached until you didn't think you could go on, but you did, for it is your dream and not someone else's. It is your land and not someone else's. It is your life to live as you see fit and not controlled by someone else. While there is no such thing as true freedom, for that would mean absolutely no responsibility, working our farm was as free as we could possibly get.

As the seasons moved, so did the work, with spring and fall filled with the burdens of planting and harvesting, and summer and winter filled with preparing for the other two. Each of us had our chores, whether it be breaking the land and planting the seeds or gathering eggs and making dinner. In the end, we were a team ... a family ... a well-organized group whose only goal was to live life to the fullest the way we wanted it to be.

There are many things I love about my farm. The most important is the peace and quiet it has given me. To sit on a warm spring day and hear nothing but the soft breeze whispering in the tall grass is as beautiful as any hymn ever sung in church. To stand at the end of a fall day and watch the sun go down as it takes the red and golden leaves and makes them glisten for one more instant is as beautiful as any picture ever painted. To walk within the ears of corn and feel them brush against your arms is as soft as the down on a goose, for you know that it is your corn and that you were the one who planted it, nurtured it, and helped to make it grow. This had been our dream way back when, and this had become our reality.

I will not tell you that farming is an easy life. It is filled with danger and struggles, and the risks you take day after day, week after week, month after month, year after year, have made many a man look elsewhere. And yet, for us it was what we had always wanted. When you are a farmer, you have but one goal: to grow as much as you can with some of it to eat and some of it to sell. You quickly learn that every person and every animal must play a role in allowing you to reach that goal. You can't be sentimental, and yet all of those beings who help reach that goal must be rewarded. Whether person or animal, they must be asked not to do more than they can, yet do their fair share and in the end reap the bounty.

Life on the farm is all about routines. You set your schedule based on the part of the year and the time of the day. Our goal was to help our little farm grow, making certain that with each new row tilled and each new calf born our ability to support ourselves would become greater and our lives more secure. Farming can also get pretty lonely. It's not like mining where you depend on someone else all the time. In farming, you're depending on the members of your family, and that's about it. Farmers do stick together. We help each other build barns and houses, asking nothing in return but the same favor when it is truly needed.

Farming is also like gambling. It all runs in streaks. Sometimes everything goes your way … just the right crops planted at just the right time that get just the right amount of sun and rain to make them grow. Other times, things don't go so well. It's too hot or too cold or too dry, or there are bugs all over everything. Then you hope and pray that God is looking down on you and you can make it until the next year. When you have two or three of these bad years in a row, that's when you wonder if it will ever be good again. Then, you'll have a good year, and it makes you forget about all your problems. If you want to see a farmer smile, watch his face when there is a gentle rain on a dry July day. He knows that God is taking care of him.

There are always too many tasks to be done on the farm. In the summer, haying was one of the big tasks. Henry had the job of driving the horse that pulled the hayfork into the barn. The horse was named "Mable," and she had great big hooves. Henry would lead her through the basement of the barn, and her big feet were always trying to dig into the cobblestones. Henry was always afraid that she would step on his feet. I used to laugh so hard at this great big boy and how afraid of that horse he was. Yet, he respected her, and I think she respected him as he never laid a hand on her in anger or frustration.

Haying is really important, as it was the food for the cows during the winter. Too little, and the cows could either starve or we would have to pay for food—and this meant losing precious money. We had dozens of acres in hay, and harvesting it three times a year would last for many weeks. The children were off school to help, and I'm certain that it seemed to them that most of their summer vacation meant doing more chores around the farm. While Henry was leading Mable, I would be in the barn mowing the hay, making certain that the stacks were even. Of all the chores on the farm, this was next to my least favorite after having to put one of my cows down. Mowing is hard and hot work, and I would come out of the barn soaked with sweat and simply exhausted.

The other big task was threshing time when oats and barley are harvested. All the farmers would come and help, and then we would help others with their harvests. This is what farming is really all about. The shocks of grain had to be brought in from the field and fed into a threshing machine that separated the straw from the oats. The oats had to be hauled to the granary, and the straw stack built. The children were always cautioned not to slide or climb on the straw stack, but I know they did and always smiled when I told them not to. They worked too hard not to have some fun.

All of the men who helped during threshing, usually around fourteen or fifteen, had to be fed lunch and supper. The men were hungry, so Elizabeth had to cook a big roast, boil potatoes, and make pies. Fortunately, some of the neighbor wives came to the farm to help with the meals, and Elizabeth would do in kind for them. Unless we had butchered, the meat had to be purchased the day before in Mineral Point. All our milk, butter, and fresh meat were kept in the root cellar on a swinging board, and that meant many trips had to be made to the cellar every day.

Besides the animals, we had to save food for ourselves for the winter. Elizabeth always had a large garden with all the vegetables and a large strawberry patch. She would take the children to where she knew blackberries or black-raspberries or raspberries grew, and they would come home with buckets to can. During the fall, Lizzie and the children would go "nutting." Hazelnuts grew in the back forty, and there were hickory nuts and black walnuts as well. Elizabeth also canned beef using a large kettle of boiling water. The beef was packed in quart jars and then boiled. It made its own gravy. I never told Elizabeth that I didn't care too much for the canned beef, but it was better than only eating vegetables.

We saved cabbage and carrots from the garden along with asparagus, cucumbers, rutabagas, tomatoes, and potatoes by putting them in the root cellar as well. Whenever we butchered or shot a deer, we made our own sausage. To help preserve the meat, it was frozen and placed in bags during the winter. We had little variety in meat during the winter as it was too difficult to go into Mineral Point every day, and so we ate sausage and cured ham and bacon as we built a smokehouse, just like my brother's, to bathe in and to cure our meat.

Like the farm animals, we all had accidents and sick spells. If one of the children said, "I feel chilly; I think I am getting a cold," Elizabeth would say, "I will fix you some hot toddy," which she made with brandy, hot water, and sugar mixed together. It was a warming drink, and if they went to bed, it helped. If you had a chest cold and cough, Lizzie would soak a flannel cloth in goose grease, mixed with a little turpentine. This flannel cloth would then be pinned to your night clothing. It was a greasy, smelly mess, but it worked. Also the children were given Dr. Drake's Croup Medicine, which was green and thick and horrible and even made me gag.

Being around the cows, pigs, and horses meant that we were all exposed to their vermin, including worms. Here, the children were given a vermicide (we call it vermiafuge) for worms even if the children had no signs of worms. A precautionary method, I guess. Elizabeth would take sulfur and honey and mix them together. What a concoction! The children loudly protested, but to no avail. Lizzie said this evil concoction was supposed to clear their blood. I don't think it did a thing except clear their lungs from the noises they made.

When the Sauk nation came from New York, they brought along apples. As they ate them and threw away the cores, apple trees sprung up. We took the small seedlings and planted our own orchard. In the autumn, our family would pick the apples and grind some and put them in a large barrel in the basement. After several months, it was hard cider. If you took the stopper out of the bung hole, you would make vinegar to use with cucumbers to make pickles. We also had cherry trees and grape vines, and Elizabeth would make sure that the children always had apples or grapes in their dinner pails when they went to school. As they came home from school, they might have had an apple that they hadn't eaten for lunch and would throw away the core. Today there are apple trees along the school path where those cores had landed. They are good eating apples, and it just goes to show you that even good apples can come from bad.

Elizabeth and I knew our land and what we had. We understood what was good for farming and what was fallow. It was this knowledge that allowed us to succeed where other miners often failed. On the southwest corner, we had a glen of ancient oak trees in which we saw a mother skunk with her babies. We called it Skunk Hollow.

We had been there many times before, but this journey was different. We were alone but together, bonded as one. I watched as Elizabeth walked on, stopping here and there to look at what God had brought forth. The oak trees had to be two hundred years old ... from a time before even Black Hawk's family had nurtured what God had given them. From the old wood came an ancient melancholy that was somehow soothing to us and much more agreeable than the harsh insentience of the outer world that now permeated our lives.

There was no noise except the rustling of the leaves as the gentle breeze brushed against my mind and filled my heart. Even today, so many years later, I have a fondness for that day, that moment, that memory. Even with the changes that we have endured, I have always loved the inwardness of that remnant of the forest and the reticence of those old trees. It has always been a place where I could go and think ... a powerfully silent but vital presence.

As the land around these ancient trees turned from forest to grassy plain and then to field after field after field, we preserved Skunk Hollow as it was. The trees there would not be cut down and cleared away. This was our parish. This was our enclave of tranquility.

As years passed, I have often wondered why this spot has meant so much to me. Perhaps it was the solitude. Perhaps it was the strength and dignity of the trees. Perhaps it was because this was where we saved the Indian girl. Most of all, it reminded me of my Elizabeth and the beauty, tranquility, dignity, and balance she had given me. The silence of those strong trees, have always meant something else. It meant my love for my wife.

Life is not just about the here and now; it's also about tomorrow. What the eye does not see and the mind does not know simply does not exist, and yet with each day, there was so much more to see and know, and this meant opening ourselves up to the world around us. We found that world in Mineral Point.

Every visit to Mineral Point was different from the last . The town was growing, and with it came so many strangers. Each Sunday, we would head for town and go to church. We hadn't been church-going people in Cornwall, but I liked going to church in Mineral Point. It gave me the chance to talk to God, thanking him for all our blessings, and to get to know our neighbors. We became members of the Bethel Methodist church. I can't tell you why we chose the Methodist religion, other than all of our friends went there. Going to church was an all-day affair ... first for services and then for socializing. The ladies would do their best to create some special meals, with the highlight always being Cornish pasty and saffron bread at Christmas.

We also went to Mineral Point once a month on Saturday. For these outings, we would load up the wagon and take all five children. (I guess I forgot to mention that we added three more to our family; there was

Sarah, of course, then Dora, and finally Mathew, the little one.) They would be all excited about going into town and seeing other children, going into the stores with their mother, and, if times were good, getting a small treat at Tom Tradinick's sweet shop. I really can't tell you if it was the candy that got them excited or simply getting out of chores and not having to wear their Sunday best.

As for me, I would leave them be and go to the blacksmith's or the feed store or, every now and then, when things were good, down to the saloon for a pint. I'm not that much of a drinking man, but a cold pint on a hot summer's day ... nothing better!

I loved to listen to all the men talking and complaining, laughing and joking, bragging and, yes, even arguing every now and then. Most of all, I loved the arm wrestling. Two men, face to face, with no other goal than to see who was the strongest, if only for an instant. It's will versus might. Who is stronger and more determined? When I was younger, I could hold my own, but the years made me smarter than to think that I could keep up with the young ones. You can learn a lot about a man as you sit across the table from him where it's your will against his.

Skunk Hollow

As our children grew, and with them their yearning for knowledge, we knew they needed formal education. It was too far for them to traverse daily to Mineral Point, and so, we met with our three neighbors and agreed to hold our own school where our children could meet and learn. What better place than Skunk Hollow?

There was a small clearing in the dell within the sacred trees which was about the same distance from all four farmhouses. I proposed, and it was agreed, that we would build the school there. I offered the land with the understanding that, as long as it remained a school, the land was for all to use. I also had another rule. The land had to remain pristine, without the changes we put upon the rest of our farms. After some discussion about its design, a school was built with no roads leading to it and nothing more than the schoolhouse set within the glen. With no roads, all of our children would be required to traverse the land upon which they lived, which would give them the opportunity to experience the beauty and joy of the land we loved and to share with others the majesty that can only come from knowledge.

We all got together and built that little country school about 1½ miles from our house. It was only one room, and there was a steeple like you would find on a church with a bell that was large enough that we all could hear it ring when school began and when it ended and in times of emergency. There wasn't much wood, and yet we completed the structure. It was small and poorly lit. The seats were rough benches. We couldn't afford blackboards, and so we put in troughs filled with sand in which our children learned to write, using their fingers as pencils and the edge of their hands as erasers.

It was agreed that we would share the costs and that the school would not be for just our children, but for all children who wished to attend. Be they the children of farmers or workers and even the Indians, all were to be welcomed with open arms to share in the joy of learning and the majesty and integrity of the trees. At our house, the older children were responsible for the younger in terms of getting them to school. None of them seemed to like that much. The little ones had to persevere, and the older ones understood that they couldn't leave the little ones in the middle of a field, pasture, or grove as they traveled to the school. It was called dedication and commitment to education and to each other, and that was what going to school was meant to be.

Education is a privilege. It allows you to look beyond here and now and to learn about the world in which we live. Every family needed to teach their children that learning was important and that knowledge meant sacrifice regardless of the time, inclination, or the Wisconsin weather. There was to be no shirking. In the winter, the children faced the west wind across a high field, and sometimes when they reached school, they would have rosy cheeks or a red nose. From this, they learned about nature and about safety and what to look out for. While it was a challenge that took dedication, we never let it get too dangerous. From walking the land, the children learned about living and also about survival in a Wisconsin winter, where they knew that a frozen cheek or nose turns white instead of red. They understood that to help thaw out, the teacher would need to put snow on them, not as punishment, but as a method of care.

Over the years, each child learned that snow was not an intrusion but an inclusion ... something Mother Earth used to muffle the sounds of summer and keep us aware of her power and might. Each flake meant one more time that she would open her arms and tell us that is was we who were visiting and not her. The Indians were right, as always, in their philosophy: Respect and fear Mother Nature. She has the ability to wreak wrath upon one's soul. Honor her with the beauty and grace of perfect harmony.

Not everything in life is easy, nor is it pleasant. Some winters, when the snow was too deep, I would hitch up a team of horses and drag a log behind the sleigh and make a path for the children to walk in ... but walk they did. The only time we would take them to school or bring them home was when the snow was melting and the floodwater was high in the creek they had to cross. There was to be dedication, but there was not to be danger.

When we built the school, there was no well for water. To get water, the pupils had to take a pail to a spring that was perhaps a mile away. The teacher always sent two to get water. They were allowed to take school time, so it was considered a privilege. I am told that on the return trip some of the water would slop out of the pail. Nevertheless, it was all the water the school had for that day.

The school was heated with a wood-burning stove, and the teacher had to light the fire and remove the ashes. All four families brought chopped wood and stacked it next to the schoolhouse and equally shared in the teacher's wages regardless of how many children they had in attendance. Around the school, there was the beautiful valley where the children could play. In the winter, they took their sleds, as there were hills to slide down. When it was warm, they would play tag, Ante Over, and many other games. We tied a rope to an overhanging branch and made a swing. In the end, I feel that, while the education was basic, these were good times in their lives, and they were happy. That's what our goal in life must be ... simply to be happy ... to feel wanted, needed, and loved ... important within our realm ... accepted for who we are ... children of God.

Education was their requirement ... to learn, to grow, to understand. Our role as parents was, at first, to teach and then to be their counselor. We would share with them the beauty of life and also its dangers. We would express our thoughts and yet compel them to take a stand for what they believed in. We did not prescribe total obedience, as that would narrow their thoughts and stunt their growth like a small tree in the shadow of a mighty oak. Yet we did have our rules, which included honesty, integrity, virtue, appreciation for what God had given us, and respect for mankind and for nature ... never taking more than what was needed, yet never allowing anyone to take what was ours.

The town of Mineral Point continued to grow, and by 1834, it had recovered from the malaise that it had endured. There were a few characters, as I liked to call them ... good for a laugh, good-hearted, people who would give you the shirt off their back if they thought you needed it. None other than Uncle Ab Nichols comes to mind. In 1832, Ab built his Mansion House, which with his magic became the most popular tavern in all of Wisconsin. Ab would say the most popular in all the world, but then he always made grand claims that no one could ever challenge. The town consisted of buildings down in the ravine, across from where the diggings were. At noon, the wives and cooks would fasten rags to poles to summon the miners home for lunch. One day, according to Ab, as he was watching one of the clog "flags" billow in the wind, he thought "shake rag" would be a good name for the village. Now Mineral Point certainly sounded a lot fancier than Shake Rag, and yet the name caught on, and over hill and dale, our village became known as Shake Rag or Shake Rag Under-The-Hill. Elizabeth thought it queer that such a name as Mineral Point could be replaced by Shake Rag, and she never once referred to our town by that name.

Life at Waldwick

I have spoken of Old Ed. This horse had been a member of our family. He had carried us to our freedom. He had stood beside me and hauled the lead that gave us the money we needed to begin our life here at Waldwick. He had been our friend and our supporter. He had been there with us in Kentucky and had pulled the very first plow through the very first foot of ground we ever tilled. As the years came and went, so did Old Ed's strength. We didn't know how old he was, but we knew that age was upon him. While others worked, we let Old Ed retire. His job became one of keeping us in touch with our past. His job became one where we could look back and be thankful for his loyalty to us.

Each day, I would expect that he wouldn't be there and yet there he was, asking for nothing more than a few oats, some fresh grass and, whenever possible, an apple or two. We would let him out of the barn, and he would slowly walk to the crest of the hill where the field grass was the greenest and the breeze the coolest. When it was time to come home, he would turn and walk back to the gate and simply wait for us to let him in so that he could go to bed.

In the fall, after we had picked the apples we needed, we would lead Old Ed into our little orchard and let him feast on all those too small or too damaged for us to worry about. He would eat until his belly was full and then, with that look of contentment, slowly walk back to the barn as if he had gone to heaven.

It was the fall of 1834, and the apples were picked, and we let Old Ed saunter up to the orchard for his annual feast. He was grazing and nibbling and truly enjoying himself. I stood and watched him eat and thought of all that he had meant to us ... his loyalty and compassion, his tolerance and obedience, his trust and gentleness. As I turned, his eye caught mine, and for just a moment, we stood as one, as he nodded his head as if to say "thanks." I smiled and remember looking back thinking what a great friend he had been and thanking him for all that he had meant to us.

That evening, Old Ed didn't come back to the gate, and I knew that he was gone. I walked that long, lonely walk down to the orchard and saw him lying there. His time had come. I knew that my friend had departed in peace, doing what he loved best, eating his apples.

I knelt down beside him and slowly stroked the soft gray hair on his neck. My sadness was as great as if he had been my brother. Even today, as I think of that night, tears come to my eyes. We buried Old Ed in the orchard beneath his apple trees. We read the 23rd Psalm knowing that God had a plan for our friend that only He would know. Life is for living. Death comes to us all.

A lot happened to Mineral Point and to the Terrill family in 1834. First, the Methodist church burned down. It seems that someone forgot to snuff out a candle. All of us got together and decided to build a new one. We took the point where High Street and what was to become Doty Street came together, and this is where we built it. It was fun building the church because it didn't have anything to do with farming. Also, it gave us a chance to meet more of the new people who were settling in. The church was made of limestone and had enough room to seat sixty people. It was a serious place and yet a place filled with happiness and joy. People were married and buried and baptized there, and in between, they came to thank God for what they had and even for what they didn't.

The parson was a very serious soul. I guess that's part of being a minister. I didn't take much to him but listened to what he had to say about God and Jesus and tried to put those ideas in my own life. Honesty, humility, and generosity were the things I got from it. I don't know if it is right or not, but that's what I've been trying to do ever since I started going to church. Also, that year the U.S. government established a federal land office in Mineral Point. The next closest was up in Green Bay. The land rush was on when the miners began to realize that the lead in the ground was not as golden as the crops that could be grown on top. The opening of the federal land office meant the first sale of public lands took place with all of us going into the office on succeeding days to enter our land in the official register.

Now some of the land was still precious, but the land around Mineral Point had become a disaster. While in the distance the land held beauty, around town, it had been stripped of all trees, and the mineral holes had resulted in piles of dirt and rocks strewn everywhere. My God, what pain mankind had wrought upon Mother Earth!

When Wisconsin became a territory that year, we heard there was a lot of bickering between the folks up in Green Bay, a trading post called Milwaukee, and the politicians down here in Mineral Point about where the capital should be. I guess we won, because we had more people than the other two combined. They agreed on the town of Belmont, about fifteen miles from Waldwick.

You know how politicians are. Something is only permanent until they think they can get it changed. In 1836, representatives from all over the territory came to Belmont to draw up the first territorial laws. Knowing how long-winded politicians always can be, I think we were all surprised that they not only wrote forty-two laws but decided where to put roads and railroads and a system of judges in a short period of time. Mineral Point was chosen to be on the rail line, something that would forever change our town.

I wasn't at these meetings, but I can just imagine all that took place with everyone wanting their own little piece of the Wisconsin pie, especially where to finally build the State Capitol building. On a hot July 4th day, virtually every farmer from miles around came into Mineral Point, not only for church, mind you, but that was the day that Henry Dodge was inaugurated as the first governor of the newly formed Wisconsin Territory. During his oratory, now-Governor Dodge explained that the name Wisconsin came from the Menomonee Indian word for "river that runs through a red place." We were finally, officially part of the United States of America.

At the ceremony, some gentleman by the name of Mr. Horner unveiled a seal that he designed to represent the new Wisconsin territory. His flag displayed a pick axe over a pile of lead ore. We learned that his design became the Great Seal of Wisconsin that's still in place. A formal census was taken a few months later, and there were 5,234 settlers living in Iowa County, making it by far the largest county in the Wisconsin Territory.

In the end, it was Judge Doty who must have had the most power. Some say he was from up by Green Bay, but I knew better. He lived near Mineral Point and was a damn good speaker. He got them to agree to not have the capital in any of the three competing areas, but instead to build it on marshland in the area called "Tychobera" by my Indian friends.

Now I have seen many a good salesman in my life, but to get a bunch of lawyers, let alone politicians, to agree on anything is a miracle, and then to have them agree to build a whole new city on swampland ... well, that really takes the cake. Word was that Doty was the shrewdest, most subtle, and suave of all speculators ... a master of the chicane, able to talk a skunk out of its smell. While the name Tychobera might have been OK for the Indians, it wasn't good enough for the legislators, and so they named the new city "Madison" after our fourth president, James Madison. Madison, Wisconsin, was to become the territory and someday the state capital. I guess Tychobera, Wisconsin, didn't quite sound as good, now did it?

One doesn't have to look very hard to figure out why Judge Doty wanted the capital in Madison. I heard he owned most of the land on the isthmus where the new city would be built. It was told that he carried a hastily platted map in his coat pocket of what was to be his good fortune. It was mainly swampland, but that didn't matter. Ah, yes. Lawyers and politicians!

With the change came our first real territory laws. I know they were meant to protect people, but for those of us who had already been here, those of us who had cleared our land, and those of us who had purchased our land from the original legal owners, it also meant trouble. We were all told that we had first right to purchase our land from the government as long as we purchased one quarter section, which was forty acres. The government sent in surveyors, and they plotted all the land around Mineral Point and all the big cities first.

We were lucky ones. Waldwick fit within the same quarter section. If we had tilled a little to the east instead or to the west, we would have either had to give up that land to someone else or purchase two quarter sections, which we just couldn't afford.

While the price of $120 for forty acres seemed reasonable to most, it was still a great deal of money for a single farm family ... especially when you had already been working the farm for nearly ten years. For the only time in our lives, we had to borrow money to buy the land that we already had purchased and cleared and planted so that someone else couldn't buy it out from under us.

I remember the fear we had the day we went into Mineral Point to borrow seventy dollars because all we had was fifty. I remember signing papers at the bank that I didn't understand, promising the entire farm if I didn't pay the seventy dollars. Ten years of work for seventy dollars! It didn't seem fair. I remember wondering where I would get the money when it came due. I remember the long ride home asking myself if we had done the right thing, reminding myself of all that we had gone through to even begin Waldwick ... the losses, the journey, the fears and then remembering my father's dying words: "A man is only a total man when it is his land and all the sweat and tears are simply for himself."

We saved every nickel we could. There was no beer or candy for an entire year. No new clothes either, and when they passed the hat at church, we put what little we could. Unlike others around us, we made our payment, and the land was ours free and clear for a second time.

Some of my neighbors were miners like me, and they didn't know diddlysquat about farming. These folks lost everything and simply moved on. Welcome to the world of farming.

When the land next to ours became available, we bought it from the bank. When the land next to that was foreclosed, we bought that too. Soon, our "little" farm reached 240 acres and then 320, and we began raising dairy cattle and selling milk. Now raising crops is one thing. Milking cows twice a day and taking care of the animals was a totally different way to make a living. It wasn't too long until we had four barns and hired hands to help with the milking. I was the foreman, and Elizabeth the accountant, keeping track of our costs and our revenue, making sure that everyone was paid on time, every time. It wasn't long before visits to the bank meant that I met with the president and not the teller. I had become an important customer, and they made certain that I knew it.

By 1835, even more of our fellow Cornish were following our path to Mineral Point. Working with those who had come before, they added a bit of "home" to our environment, and it made Mineral Point all that much more a welcome spot for us to come to. Nary a week would go by when we would go into town and meet with someone from the "old country." Whether it was a Vivian, Prisk, Edwards, Nichols, Prideaux, or Thomas, it mattered not. Just the tie to what had been home made it all seem worthwhile. We would meet and greet, and life would go on. As the years progressed, they became more like us. We had a history, but we also had a love of our new home that came from pride and above all else ... freedom.

Word spread about the lead, not only throughout America but back home. Folks were told it was easy pickings ... that all you needed was a shovel and you could get rich. As more folks heard the tale in Cornwall and followed our trail, our favorite Cornish food also became common fare. The best is Cornish pasty, which is nothing more than a pie crust filled with meat and potatoes or rutabagas cooked until brown. When I was mining, Elizabeth would make the pasty one day, and I would have it as my lunch the next. To keep our pasties warm, we would start a fire and heat a rock and let the heat of the rock keep the pasty warm without making it too dry. If ever Elizabeth wanted to spoil me, she made pasties.

Now folks from Cornwall had always been used to tough times, and so when they decided to settle down in Mineral Point, they tended to build homes they thought would last. With few trees and plenty of limestone, the homes of this new generation of Cornish immigrants took on a solid feeling of permanence, a deep sense of pride, and a complete commitment to the community in which we lived. While quite religious folks, we all enjoyed a pint, and never, ever, was there one who would not reach out a helping hand to someone in need. It would take them a few years to learn "English" and give up on some of our Cornish words. It was always fun when they got to speaking freely and rattled on about fairies, pixies, and giants from stories they carried with them to the grave. These were the workers who replaced the original settlers and made Mineral Point a town to be proud of, without all the boisterous clamor of those who came only to get rich and squander the wealth of the land.

While the Cornish brought a sense of decorum, there was still the riffraff of those miners who had come for life, liberty, and libation. They would come in from the mines on Saturday afternoon and consume as much raw whiskey as possible until either they were penniless or passed out. Stories were told of gambling and fights and disagreements that would lead to more fights and disagreements, but none, and I mean none, ever tickled my innards more than the duel between a Mister Joseph McMurtry and Colonel TB Shaunce of Dodgeville. Now this argument commenced in a heated rage as both had become intoxicated to the point where neither could hardly stand and concluded in a challenge to a duel by McMurtry to Shaunce ... not with knives or pistols but with rocks at forty paces. At the appointed time, both men appeared, and Shaunce stood at the mouth of his mine and informed McMurtry that he was to take forty paces into the mine, which happened to be forty feet deep, to which the crowd roared. All headed back to the inn, and McMurtry set up a round of drinks for all those witnesses to the duel.

One day, I realized that selling milk to the processor was a rough way to make a living. If I could turn that milk into butter or cheese, I could earn more and not have to worry so much about it going sour. With that, I began to observe the cheese business and realized that with a small investment, we could begin selling our milk to ourselves and making butter and cheese. I also knew that time was such that there was no way I could operate four farms and also a cheese business alone. I looked for someone I could trust. I was always in tune with Tom Wolfe and went to Tom with a proposition. I told him that I would build the factory and purchase the vats needed for the cheese. On the first day, he would own 9 percent of what became Cross Roads Cheese Factory. Each year, he would own 5 percent more until after eight years he would own 49 percent of the factory and would receive 49 percent of all the profits.

Tom thought I was crazy, and yet our partnership began. I only had one other requirement: Our children would pay for the cheese curds just like everyone else. I also had the agreement drawn up that should Tom want out of the business, I would own it in its entirety, and should there be any malfeasance, I would own the factory. I trusted Tom, but money can do funny things to people, and all I needed to do to remind myself of that was to think of my brother. Soon, the milk we were producing wasn't enough to meet the demand for the butter and cheese we could sell, and I turned to other farmers and started buying their milk as well. Business was good ... very, very good.

With the farms going well and then the cheese factory, my thoughts went to starting a brewery. John Phillips had started one in 1835, and I thought we could do better. Boy, was I wrong! We had a large population and a spring that had the purest of water. I thought we could grow hops and brew beer. I invested $4,000 and built a limestone brewery at the head of Shake Rag Street and looked for a partner to operate what I called Mineral Springs Brewery. It was a big mistake. I was terrible at it, and in 1851, sold the business to Jacob Roggy for $3,000. Needless to say, the loss of a thousand dollars left a bad taste in my mouth and it wasn't the taste of bad beer. Jacob didn't seem to have any more luck than I did. In 1854, the brewery was sold again to Charles and Frederick Gillmann, who first named it Gillmann Brothers & Company but later changed it to Wisconsin Brewery under which it stands today.

The Farmhouse

The log cabin was no longer big enough. It was time for a real house ... one made of limestone ... thick enough to withstand the cold of winter and strong enough to fight the howl of a summer's wind. As we began our search, every quarry we went to had stone that was either too soft or too convoluted to satisfy my eye. When you spent as much time under the ground as I had, one learns what is right and what simply will not hold up. This was to be a two-story house. This was to be strong and powerful. This was a house that was to be filled with family and most of all love. There were to be four bedrooms on the top floor, and the main floor was to have a parlor, a dining room, a kitchen and, as Elizabeth asked, or so decreed, a place for muddy boots and overalls.

After nearly a year, we came upon a quarry that we felt would provide the limestone that we desired ... soft yellow in color, yet hard and permanent. The challenge was that it came from Mount Horeb, thirty-five miles away, and this meant each and every stone would need to be cut and hauled a great distance. We did the evaluations and what the quarry master wanted for delivering the stone and came to the conclusion that it would be beneficial for us to hire our own team and have them take a wagon from Waldwick and retrieve the stone and bring it back to our new house. While the milk men were not trained masons, the idea of having them do work between the morning and afternoon milking meant more income for them in what was otherwise wasted time and less cost for us.

And so the process began. The basement was dug, and rocks collected to be used to create the foundation. A root cellar was put in place that would remain cool in the summer's heat to allow us to store what harvest we brought in the year before. The basement walls were to be at least one foot thick, and there would be beams cut from the mighty oaks upon our land but not from Skunk Hollow. That land was sacred! It took nearly one year for six milkers to hand-dig the foundation and to set the floor beams. When it was done, we had our foundation.

Because the task of bringing the stone from Mount Horeb was nothing more than driving four horses from here to there and back again, I looked for two men who were strong enough to control the team but not strong enough to find work in the fields or mining in Mineral Point. I offered them a fair wage with the agreement that each morning they would start off very early from the farm and each night they would return with the stones necessary for yet another piece of the house to be built. The mason and milkers would then add the stone to what was already built between the morning and evening milking, and the house would commence.

When it rained or the ground was too soft for the heavy wagon, I would have the two drivers do tasks around the farm ... things that needed to be done such as mending fences, picking apples, or other tasks that could use their skills. For two years, everyone worked as a team as the house slowly took shape. At the end of the first year, the quarry master thought he had us and wanted double the price for the limestone. I drove to Mount Horeb and looked up this fine, upstanding gentleman, reminding him of our agreement. He must have hit his head, because he remembered none of our agreement and told me the new price. I told him to put the stone where the sun don't shine, if you get my gist.

We ended up in Lyndon Station with a softer stone, but the price was fair. As the stones were laid, we had a two-tone house to remind us always that, in business, a handshake is never good enough. As the walls came to be, the drivers would travel all the way to Madison and retrieve the windows. Fifty-two miles each way meant two full days of travel. I can only imagine what the scallywags did on those nights in the city. But then it was their money and their conscience they had to worry about.

Finally, the house was completed. We had Elizabeth's dream. After three years, we had a real house with wood floors and fireplaces in each room. The first night was a time for celebration, and everyone who had helped create our home was invited. We had lanterns in the trees and music for everyone to dance to. There was food and wine, and even, I might add, a little hard cider and whiskey. We had a house with lace curtains and rooms for the children and a room for ourselves and even some more for guests. We had a home, and we let out the cabin to some of the workers.

During the summertime, the limestone house was cool in the day and somewhat warm at night. Each night we would carry a lamp to our bedroom. It was not a good light and was inconvenient. To keep the lamps working, it was necessary every few days to fill the lamps with kerosene and trim the wicks and clean the chimneys. Often the wicks would be turned too high, and the chimneys would be covered with soot. If Elizabeth or the girls wanted to curl their hair, they would put the curling iron in the lamp chimney to heat.

The family laundry was done by scrubbing it on a washboard. "Rub-a-dub-dub," little Sarah would say. After using the home-made lye soap that Elizabeth would make, the white clothing was boiled, then rinsed through clear water, then again in bluing water, and finally wrung by hand. Drying clothing in winter is difficult in Wisconsin.

There is no place to dry except on the clothesline outside. In the winter, Elizabeth's fingers would almost freeze. Sometimes our clothing would actually freeze hanging there. Sometimes the clothes would still be frozen when Elizabeth brought them into the house and she would put them on a clothing rack near the stove. Washing clothes was hard work, but the fresh scent of clothes washed and dried outside is one of the sweetest smells one can ever imagine.

The first floor of the farmhouse was heated by a woodburning cook stove. If the stove went out at night, Henry or I would get up early and light the fire. The house had an open stairway, and some heat wafted upstairs. Even with the thick walls and down comforters, on January nights, it was still very cold. I guess that's why so many of Elizabeth's and my children were born in October.

While farm life is tough, it isn't without its pleasures. To celebrate Christmas, there were dances held in various farm homes, including ours. Maggie and Bert Stevens furnished the music. Maggie played the violin, and Bert, the piano, if there was one. It meant a great deal of work for the family having the dance as people came and brought their children who would later fall asleep on the beds. There were waltzes, two-steps, and square dances. My cousin came from Cornwall, and he would call the square dances. He so enjoyed calling square dances that made us think, and when we became confused, he would have a large laugh and demonstrate the correct move. He loved the activity.

At midnight, sandwiches and cake would be served. The hostess made home-made buns and ham sandwiches and always saffron bread. The neighbor ladies all brought cakes. When it was our turn, we all danced in the parlor. All furniture had to be cleared out and put down in the cellar. With Elizabeth's hardwood floor in there, she did not like to see it scratched, but it was. It was fun and we all had a good time.

Chores: Every member of the family had a few chores. The little ones had to fill the wood box in the kitchen and also fill the reservoir on the kitchen range with water from the cistern. We used the cistern to catch rainwater from the roof of the house, but sometimes in the winter, the cistern would go dry, and then our drinking water came from the well, which didn't taste very good. To get water from the well, we had to pump it by hand and then carry the water to the house. The little ones would try to carry the pail, but they spilled quite a bit of it carrying it to the house. The goal was to make sure everyone knew that they had a job to do with the understanding that everyone else relied on them to do it.

Another one of children's tasks was to get the cows from the pasture for evening milking. Often the cows were at the end of the back pasture, which was at least a mile away. For some reason, we never have had a good cow dog, so the children always had problems in finding and bringing the cows back to the barnyard. I have to admit, it is quite a job to get the cows in the back pasture. Often the children would have to go back to get a cow or cows they had missed.

As we prospered, Elizabeth had her own horse and buggy. She would drive to Mineral Point taking cases of eggs to trade for groceries. Her horse was named "Charlie." He would often be out in the pasture and not want to come in. Finally we would get him in and hitched to the buggy. Charlie was balky. He would start going up a hill and stop. He refused to go further until someone got out and took hold of his bridle and pulled him the rest of the way. He wasn't mean-spirited; he just had a mind of his own. There were days when Lizzie would come home so exasperated that I thought we would have Charlie for dinner because he was too stubborn for much else. Behind her back, the children and I would laugh at Lizzie and Charlie and the thought of that darn horse being as stubborn as an old mule—just like Lizzie's husband, I might add.

As more people moved to Mineral Point, even more came to visit. Lizzie and I decided that we could take some of the fallow land near the road and build an inn. Nothing fancy, mind you, just a place to supply journeyers with food and drink. At first, we thought it would only be a place to sleep, and then we added food and then a grocery store, and then a pub and a resting area for horses. We did quite well and hired folks to run it, giving them room and food and a small stipend for their efforts. Once again, I developed a partnership where I invested the money and then allowed someone else to run the business. Once again, we were successful. I was two-out-of-three besides the farm.

Every now and then, we would go to town and eat dinner at the City Hotel. The hotel had two long tables in the dining room and served excellent food. The owner of the hotel had a parrot in his office. As I came into the hotel, the owner would call to the parrot and say, "Hello, George." Then the parrot would say, "Hello, George." As I was leaving, the parrot would say, "Goodbye, George." All the children really thought it was great. This same parrot would sit in the window at the hotel and say to passers-by, "Come in and have a glass of beer." If the passer-by did not come into the hotel, the parrot would say, "Go to hell." Needless to say, that would make everyone laugh.

In the winter, if we went to town, it was with a team of horses and the cutter. There was straw and blankets in the bottom and a hot soapstone to keep our feet warm. If the roads were drifted, the fences would be cut, and we traveled through the fields. When we arrived in Mineral Point, the horses had to be tied and blankets placed on their backs to keep them warm. Winter can be very cold in Wisconsin.

Other than my wife and children, I loved my farm the most. One can only imagine what it is like if a person has never roamed the hills, cleaned out the springs, and did work on the land. When you work the land, you never forget the lay as every inch is something that you have turned and cared for. It is a place where you can dig your hands into the rich Wisconsin soil and feel the life that springs forth. Lizzie, the children, and I roamed the hills and gathered wildflowers from the bluff. In spring, the flowers would bloom, and the children would pick them on their way home from school and give them to Lizzie. She would always make a big to-do and put them in the prettiest of vases until they would wilt and be sent away. We worked and laughed and loved the land and each other. We created what our dreams always wanted ... a family who had the bounty of love and respect for each other and for what God had given us.

Even on a land I love, I could never forget that farming is a business. You invest your money and hope and pray to make a profit. It's also a form of gambling based on what Mother Nature throws at you. Other times, it's not Mother Nature who throws you a right cross, but your fellow man. "Trust me." is not a statement I really appreciate. When I hear it, I normally know that whoever said it is a liar.

The Bank of Mineral Point was created in 1836, and its primary owner was none other than James Duane Doty. The bank was established mainly to deal with the smelters who took the lead ore and refined it into lead bars. When the smelters purchased the lead from the miners, the smelters drew orders on the bank to be paid with drafts on eastern banks when the lead was sold. So much for "In God We Trust." Instead of honoring immediate payment, the bank issued "post bills," which were endorsed across the face with red ink. Everyone called them "red dogs," and they were to be paid in two or three months after the date of issue. None of us liked this at all, but we felt our money was safe. We all had just become accustomed to this when the bank changed the rules and said we needed to wait six months to get paid. They began issuing post bills they marked with blue ink that everyone called "blue bellies."

When you're in business for yourself, whether farming or mining or any form of commerce, having to wait six months to collect your money is just too long. As a farmer, you plant crops in the spring and then wait four months for them to mature. If you have to wait another six months until you can collect your own money, you can readily see how that would cause a pinch on many farmers, including us.

Mr. Knapp was the president of the bank, and he and a man named Brace caught wind of a pending audit and high-tailed it out of town. A deputy sheriff and eight men took after them and caught up to them in Galena. Mr. Knapp told the deputy that he had nothing from the bank, just two volumes of Charles Dickens' novels. Now a man quickly leaving town normally doesn't take two books with him and leave everything else behind. The deputy took the books and realized that pasted in the fly-leaves were all the notes and bills of exchange from the bank that represented all the assets.

The red dogs and blue bellies were somewhat worthless, and it really hurt the town of Mineral Point and the Terrill family. This was as close as I think anyone ever got to being hanged in our quiet town. Business and farms recovered, but it was never the same.

Recompense

It was 1841, and we had been in Wisconsin for 20 years when my thoughts of Cornwall and Virginia quietly crept back into my soul. I wondered about the destiny of those with whom our paths had crossed. As the days of summer passed and fall set in, my thoughts of my brother crept into my mind on an almost daily basis. More important to me were thoughts of Clara and Big John and their family and whether, as slaves, they were still together. Twenty years ... time had flown by!

We had survived and then thrived because of the goodness and generosity of those folks, and I began to see that my mission was not to just farm, but to help those who helped me. In church one Sunday, the minister talked of Acts 20:35 and Mathew 6:14-15 about compassion, generosity, and forgiveness, and all I could think about was Old Ed, that rusty musket, and the two five-dollar gold pieces given to us by William's slaves that probably gave Elizabeth and me this life. As we were departing for home, I stopped the wagon in a queer place, and the children looked at me with cocked heads.

"Did you hear what the preacher said?" I asked.

There was murmuring in the back of the wagon, but I knew that they didn't understand.

I spoke of the message in the Bible. I shared with them the responsibilities we had for mankind and for each other. We had never spoken of my brother or of Virginia. We had never told them about Cornwall and Sarah and baby Henry. We had never shared with them how it was that we came to be, and so I asked them all to get out of the wagon and allow me to share with them our story. I had reason for what I was about to say and think Elizabeth knew what was coming.

I was really expounding to our children when I noted that nothing that we experience ever ceases to exist. Some of the experiences are relegated to the unconscious simply because we think they are irrelevant or unimportant to our lives. At the same time, other experiences burrow into our soul, leaving an indelible mark that transcends who we are and what we truly want to be. What we know becomes part of the experience of our conscious being. Once having seen, we cannot unsee. Once we have known, we cannot unknow. Once having done, we cannot undo. Once we have been oppressed, the joy and value of freedom becomes a profound sensation that can permeate our soul and give us happiness.

I looked each of them in the eyes and summarized that what we are conscious of becomes an integrated part of our own personal reality. I explained that the fear and the trembling we may experience when we leave behind the safety of consistency cannot be overemphasized. Change is, for most of us, a terrifying experience. Each person is always profoundly desperate to know that things will work out even when reality says they won't.

In spite of potential rewards, we all fear letting go of safety and the world we know. I attempted to justify my brother's existence. It was profoundly difficult. How could I explain this to my children when we had elicited so much from the compassion of others? From where we were, there was no reference, there was no reality. There was certainly no point by which to judge our own sense of right and wrong. Instead, within my brain lie a jumble of memories of domination, loneliness, and regret that needed one form of affirmation of freedom, liberty, and accomplishment had made anything right as long as I felt there was justice.

In such a state, when someone who is liberated, who has unshackled the bonds that held them appears on the horizon, those unfettered do not know how to act. Should we affirm or deny the freedom? Should we accept or acquiesce the liberty? How can one know what to expect when they have never peered through the darkness of constraint to examine what lies on the other side, especially when the other side contains the ravages of a demon called oppression?

This was the case so long ago when, by chance, my mind crossed with my soul allowing me to share with souls who were held against their will, simply by tyranny, the profound experiences that touched my life to the point that I sincerely felt I could touch their lives as well and feel their oppression, if only it had been cordoned off in a segment of their memories and defeated.

Like them, I was a recipient, and yet, unlike them, I was a participant. I shared with our children, as we stood in a field so far from reality that we could have been in heaven, all of my thoughts, dreams, and prayers! I shared with them my belief that any person could re-experience their existence. Any life could be like a reflection on a quiet pond, where one's consciousness emerges at one, single, precise intersection ... a point in time and space that permits human beings to allow themselves, as individuals, to look beyond their limits of sequestered perceptions and liberate those who were shackled physically, emotionally, or socially ... to seek out the oppressed and simply give them an opportunity, allowing them to bathe in the invigorating waters of freedom.

I expressed that, once you have seen a hidden image, it is easy to see it again. "Once you have felt a cloistered feeling, it is easy to feel it again and again and again. Once you have tasted the sweet, sweet nectar of alternatives that you and only you have the liberty to create, you can always taste it, you can always feel it, and you can always sense it again. Such is the luxury of freedom. It is the profound consequence of liberty that allows those who are free the right to choose, as long as that choice does not impinge upon the freedom of others. Freedom is an opportunity to select a path unbridled by the constraints of others as long as it does not impede the path of others. Freedom is not free. It has its costs that lie deep within our bodies and our souls, impeding, impinging, and controlling any of our urges so that we, who have conscience, accept that there is no such thing as absolute freedom regardless of what our mind and body crave."

As a family, we had done well for ourselves. We were neither rich nor poor, but we were much better off than most. We had worked hard to achieve our place, and, above all else, we had done so honestly. To our children, I expressed that there was nothing wrong with wealth as long as it was good wealth that expanded horizons and allowed you to provide others with the opportunity to achieve their dreams. I explained that a new horizon of achievement takes what we perceive to be here-and-now and moves it closer to a point of acceptance ... of ourselves, of our existence and of our ultimate goal, which should be nothing more than the profound sense called happiness, based simply on the feelings of being wanted, needed, and loved.

"When you have everything, you can have nothing. When you are rich, you can be poor. When you feel the incredible warmth of profound security, it can have no meaning whatsoever if you do not have the confidence that only comes from understanding that you have met one ultimate goal, and that's happiness. How could I possibly be satisfied until I met with those who had restricted our freedom? How could I ever forgive those who had made our journey so perilous ...

from Old Fitzie to my brother? I could not and would not judge until I understood their rhyme and reason and the factors that changed their lives."

I stood beside the empty road and pontificated to a group of children, whose mouths were agape, about all that I knew ... all that I felt ... all that motivated me. I did so with one point in mind ... to express to them that my actions were predicated on the consequence of their actions ... the respondents of my life. My hope that sunny Sunday afternoon was that my children realized that my goal was equity ... to ensure that those who had been subservient became equals, that those who had been victims became survivors, that those who were sequestered by tyranny had the bounds loosened until they too were free. Only when I had given back could there be peace within me. Only when my freedom equated the freedom of others would I find respite from my wandering. We had so much, and yet, even with wealth, I had so little.

The children sat awestruck. Here, their father, a simple farmer, was preaching to them about life, liberty, and the pursuit of happiness as he stood at the edge of a field. I, a common man, had erupted in a passionate discourse that had been building in me since that very first day in Baltimore. I, the husband and the father who wanted nothing more than to build a better life for himself and his family, had evoked a sense of longing, a sense of propriety, and a sense of remorse that I had not done enough, been enough, or sacrificed enough to resolve the pain within my own heart that could only be achieved through freedom for those who had given so much so that we could be free.

We had no idea what it was like at my brother's house in Virginia, nor any thought of what had happened. However, by the time I was done sharing the kindness, the goodness, and the generosity that we had been recipients of, I knew what the answer to my question would be even before I asked it.

And so, it was. The decision was made on a normal Sunday, simply on our way home to Waldwick from a church in Mineral Point, Wisconsin, that Henry and I would travel to Virginia and attempt to convince my brother to free his slaves. And so it was that every member of the family agreed that we would take our life savings of over $5,000 and use it to buy their freedom if need be. And so it was that if my brother did not agree to free the slaves or would not accept payment, then Henry and I would do our best to help those who helped us escape his tyranny by making their way to Canada.

We made our plans. We would go by wagon with two horses instead of one. We would have a special wagon built that was strong enough to hold a family, sturdy enough to traverse all but the most difficult extremes and yet plain enough not to bring suspicion upon Henry and me. We would create a wagon that would allow a family to ride in, hide in, and be free in. It would take time, but I knew that it must be done.

I began quietly reaching out within the folks I thought I could trust in Mineral Point to learn about the Underground Railroad. Quite quickly, people came to my aid with whispers and glances as I learned that the Underground Railroad was neither underground nor a railroad at all. Conversations became whispers as everything needed to be in secret, even in Mineral Point.

To make sure that no one knew what was planned, as there would be a reward on Henry and my heads as well as those of William's slaves, we began talking about the railway even though none of us had ever been on a train. Escape routes were called lines, and safe stopping places were called stations. Those who were willing to help along the way were called conductors. Our friends, those who were attempting to free others, were called liberators. Fugitive slaves, who were known as packages or freight, were transferred from station to station on their way to the Promised Land, where individuals were not judged by the color of their skin but by what they as human beings afforded the society in which they lived.

Every piece of the puzzle needed to fit together as if all of them were cut from the same piece of wood, finely sanded until they would interlock with all the adjacent pieces. One piece out of place, and the puzzle would not fit. One piece askew, and our dreams, our plans, and insurrection would completely fail.

We needed to examine our alternatives and create contingency plans. We needed to memorize the route and plan our method of escape. How could we convince William to sell us what he had become so accustomed to? Virginia seemed so far away, and yet the distance from slavery to the first step to freedom was only a few hundred miles. We learned that there were many routes to freedom from Virginia, which included going back through Maryland, Pennsylvania, and Ohio, the state that had outlawed escaped slaves in 1804, but seemed to look the other way when they passed through. Each route had its benefits, and each route had its obstacles.

The more enticing route was to travel through the Appalachians to Pennsylvania, and from there to upstate New York and then to Canada and the Promised Land. Even with this route, there were obviously some major challenges. First were the Appalachians. These were mountains, and wagons full of slaves meant more people trying to find freedom. Second, there were bounty hunters, called slave catchers, who made a living capturing and returning runaway slaves and who had no idea of justice, no concept of decency, and certainly no belief at all in the words "we hold these truths to be self-evident, that all men are created equal." Finally, there was finding folks willing to help, who understood and accepted the concept that no man should be a slave to another.

In speaking with those to whom we even dared mention our plans, we learned many things. While there were many folks in our area who were against slavery, we learned to look for free blacks or escaped slaves to help us. We knew that in Virginia, there would be no help. No one risked being hanged or their houses burned simply for helping others achieve freedom.

We were in somewhat of a quandary, as we really didn't know if Clara and Big John and their family were even still with my brother or even alive. Big John had the gun and money he gave Elizabeth and me and was ready to escape at one time. Perhaps he was gone. Perhaps our trip would be for naught.

These were the huge challenges, especially when we had no idea what the situation was at William's plantation. We didn't even know if he was still alive, let alone which, if any of the slaves, were still there. The aspiration was there, and so we began.

Designing the wagon and then finding someone who would take that idea and make it reality was not something to take lightly. One false step, one slip of the tongue, and our strategy would be demolished. We were afraid to rely on someone from Mineral Point. We knew everyone, and everyone knew us. We needed a wagoneer. We needed someone who could build what we wanted and do so without the trepidation or the convenient memory that could recall our instruction. The challenge was finding someone who could align us with the task at hand. How does one go about something clandestine? How does someone create an alliance that will manifest itself in a bond, in a level of inscrutable trust that is so deep and so profound that one is willing to stake one's life on the circumstance? It needed someone who understood and venerated our goal and who also had the skills we needed to provide the method of accomplishment. How does one go about such a task when sharing the thought with one wrong person could mean your demise?

We discussed the project at length and began our search. While many folks knew of a good wagoneer, the challenge was one who could not only create what we wanted but do so without the least bit of apprehension. Our search expanded until we heard of a man in Blanchardville who was touted to be a craftsman.

I elected to visit this man personally. Both fortunately and unfortunately, my name was such that people had heard of me. It was my hope they spoke of me as a person who had built his own world, who was fair and honest and forthright, someone that they could trust.

I remember that I approached the wagoneer and politely inquired about his skills. He indicated that he had made many wagons for many different needs and that his skills were such that he could make any type of wagon we needed. I spoke in generalities. He spoke in specifics. I spoke of heading west, yet he knew we were heading east. I spoke of cargo, and he knew that my cargo was not grain nor supplies but freedom. We spoke, and I outlined our needs—something big enough, strong enough, and durable enough to allow for a long ride with the potential for high speed and even great protection.

He smiled.

In his eyes, I glimpsed a flicker of understanding.

He smiled again and noted that God had sent me to him and that what was written in the Good Book was such that he was ordained to help me help those who could not help themselves.

I offered a premium.

He requested nothing.

I offered equity.

He accepted equality.

I asked for a price.

He said that God would pay him in heaven.

I gave him a fifty-dollar down payment and told him that God had told me that his efforts, his tasks, and his blessings were such that he deserved the recompense to allow for another good deed ... if and only if what transpired was between him and me and no one else.

We shook hands and made a pact. We looked in each other's eyes, and I knew that his word was his bond. His handshake, his commitment, his devotion were insurance that he would provide the very best that he could create.

How incredibly strange to rearrange your life in an opposite direction from which you had vowed you would never travel again. Yet, Henry and I began the long, slow journey from Mineral Point to Amity, Virginia. We passed through Chicago and found it still dirty and repulsive, as it had been before. The flat lands of Indiana were filled with farms and farmers, and the routes rutted with those who had gone west as we headed east. Kentucky meant the hills and their majesty. I couldn't find the cave in which we lived, but then didn't looked too hard.

Soon the Appalachians were upon us, and I knew that we were close to where it had all had begun. Along the way, in the many days, I shared with Henry all I could about Cornwall and the ship and baby Henry, Sarah, and William. I wanted him to know and understand all that had happened. I wanted him to realize the journey we had taken and, more importantly, the reasons why we were making the journey that we were on. I wanted him to appreciate the beauty and majesty of freedom and dignity and what it meant when it was taken away. This was our journey. This was our epiphany. This was the time when father and son melded into men, bound together by all that mattered.

Virginia: After five days' travel, I recognized the juncture and realized it was time to turn the wagon towards its destiny. Time does not heal all wounds; it only covers them in scars that shine brightly in the sunlight of memory to remind us of what was and what should have been. Instead, we proceeded on, passing the small intersection until we arrived in Farmville. We had departed in abject poverty and returned with $5,000 in gold coins sequestered within a strong box built within the bowels of the wagon we drove. We had been nervous about the funds and yet confident of our abilities. We watched carefully at every tree and intersection to ensure that no interloper suspected the bounty within. As we met with the city, we entered a large bank, and I inquired about two important parts of my plan ... the processes needed for deposit and the services of the finest lawyer in the city.

I was informed that the bank could handle any level of deposit, and I asked for an armed guard to accompany me to my wagon. Henry and I peeled back the seat upon which we had been riding and assisted the guard in carrying the cache into the vault.

The ordeal was such that the head teller became aware of our activities and inquired as to the source of our funds and our intent.

I responded that I was a successful farmer and was in Virginia for business purposes with the goal of acquiring property.

This seemed to suffice, and I was given a bank note for the sum of the $5,000 deposited.

My inquiry and the amount of money was such that the president of the bank accompanied me to meet with whom he felt was the best business lawyer in Farmville. I was not impressed. As Henry and I were walking to the hotel in which we were to stay, I observed a gentleman, about my age, locking the door on his establishment ... one Martin J. Ward, Attorney at Law. As Henry and I approached, Mr. Ward tipped his hat, something that was rarely done in Mineral Point.

"Gentlemen," he greeted us.

I looked him in the eye and determined his integrity as he returned my gaze.

"Might we have a word with you?" I inquired.

"Most certainly," he responded.

"Not here," I replied.

"My office is now open," was his response.

"Have you ever ridden on a train?" I asked.

A wry smile came across his face. He knew what I meant, and he was a proponent of freedom for all.

With that, Henry and I proceeded to his domain, which was filled with all types of fancy books and oil lamps unlike any we had ever seen. For two hours, I shared our entire story from Waldwick in Cornwall to Waldwick, Wisconsin; from oppression to depression to resurrection to retribution; and told him that our goal was freedom and equity.

He asked about resources, and I shared with him our venture into the bank and our deposit.

He noted that it was a tidy sum and wondered what his role would be.

I indicated that I felt I needed to purchase my brother's slaves and have the legal documents created that would show proof of ownership and the right to transfer my property out of Virginia and away from slavery.

He indicated that there was a huge difference between legal rights and freedom and that, even though their freedom was purchased, we could be killed and those we freed returned to the life from which they came and done so with even a greater risk to their wellbeing.

I asked about hired assistance. He noted that those who purchased hired guns oft-times ended up on the wrong end of the barrel themselves, as the defenders took the slaves and sold them back to the slave catchers.

I asked about routes that we could take that would allow for the greatest security. He noted that individual young slaves had the greatest chance and older families held out the greatest risk of capture. The Underground Railroad was for the young and not for the old. The Underground Railroad was for individuals and not families. The Underground Railroad was something people thought was the way out, and yet in reality, it represented a slim chance of success.

I inquired about options, and he noted that, while not recognized in the North, slavery was truly not something everyone in the South supported. Sadly, even when people were against it, they did nothing, simply hoping that the government would do something about it.

We talked of the reasons why so many people who were against slavery allowed it to exist. His response reverberates within my mind even today. He noted: "History lessons are often incredibly simple and blunt, yet for all our powers of reason, we often miss the most basic and uncomplicated of points: Peace-loving people are made irrelevant by their silence. Peace-loving people will become our enemy if they don't speak up, because the peace-loving people will awaken one day and find that the fanatics own them, and the end of their world will have begun. So it is with those who are against slavery. They let the fanatics own them, dominate them, and control them in the name of commerce."

I had sensed his passion, and it was as strong as mine. At that point in time, we became brothers within one cause ... the elimination of oppression and the resurrection of dignity within mankind. I finally asked what his fee would be to represent Henry and me in case we were charged with violating the law. His response was that it would be his honor and there would be no fee. To which, I reached into my pocket and slid a five-dollar gold piece across his desk.

"Consider yourself my lawyer on retainer. We will authorize remittance from the bank of five dollars per month until further notice."

He understood that we were serious in our intent, and at that point, we had an ally and a confidant, someone within the society who would work for us and against those who harbored ill feelings towards our mission.

After so many months of planning, so many weeks of dreaming, and so many days of traveling, the plans we had made were not something that would happen, unless there was a way that we could create freedom from within.

As we sat and looked at our options, the thought crossed my mind: "What would happen if we purchased William's plantation and its assets? Couldn't I then do what I wanted with my 'property'? If we made the purchase, couldn't we run the operation and allow the slaves to have the dignity of freedom in a cloistered world? If we managed our assets, couldn't we create a world in which all could live in dignity?"

My new friend leaned back in his high leather chair and smiled. He knew that, within reason, we could accomplish our goal and legally achieve our objective. As long as there was structure, nothing could be done to impede our objective of dignity. The challenge became: How could we get my brother to sell the plantation?

As the minutes stretched into hours, it became clear that we had bonded not as client and counselor but as friends. That night, as Henry and I ate dinner at the hotel, I asked what he thought of Mr. Ward. I was asking a critical question, and Henry knew that his answer would determine a course of action.

He nodded and asked, "Do you trust him? He is a lawyer."

I replied, "I looked in his eyes and saw integrity."

Henry smiled. "What are your plans?"

"What if we do like the inn or the cheese factory?" I responded.

"As long as it's not like the brewery," Henry laughed.

Oh, how the children liked to tease me about that brewery. I thought everyone would drink my beer.

The next morning, I went to Mr. Ward's office and asked his secretary if it would be possible for Mr. Ward, Henry, and me to have lunch. She said that it was amenable.

I asked where the worst restaurant in Farmville might be.

She balked. "Fine people like you and Mr. Ward don't frequent such places, sir."

I responded, "Today we do," and said that Henry and I would meet Mr. Ward there promptly at noon.

We arrived on time, and Mr. Ward was seated at a table in the corner with a broad smile upon his face.

"Normally I don't dine with clients in a place like this," Mr. Ward expressed.

"That's exactly why we're here, Mr. Ward," I replied. "I don't want to be your client, I want to be your partner."

"But you have no background in law," he answered.

"Not your law partner, sir. Your business partner."

There was a wry smile upon his face. "In what endeavor?"

"Real estate," I responded.

I laid out my plans and the equity program. Similar to the inn and the Crossroads Cheese Factory, he would start with 5 percent ownership and would earn 5 percent increased equity for every year until he owned 25 percent of each farm that would be established as separate entities. Mr. Ward would provide the local contacts and legal expertise, and I would provide the money needed to do what I wanted to do.

"Interesting," he said while carefully sipping his tea.

"We will be partners, and you will control our mutual Virginia interests in my or Henry's absence."

Henry looked at me in surprise.

"What do you have in mind?" Mr. Ward inquired.

"I want to own some farms or plantations or whatever it is you call them."

"Any in mind?"

"I have two or three that I feel would provide the return on investment that I desire. I would like to invest in the area around Amity, if possible. I will leave it up to you to determine the property and the fair market value. I will not be here for a long period of time, but my son Henry will remain behind to assist you with the finances and the operation."

Henry looked at me at first with disdain until he began to realize my ploy.

"It is my conclusion that we should begin by looking at properties that are either suffering or where the owners are old. I am willing to pay a fair price."

Mr. Ward agreed, and we set a timetable of one week for him to do his research. It was set for one week hence that we would meet again and that he would have the proper partnership papers drawn up and provide a summary of farms that were or could be for sale.

While Mr. Ward did his due diligence, Henry had his first assignment: to determine the plantation's condition and establish some reasons why my brother would be motivated to sell. I was certain that if he knew that I was involved, he would balk. If he knew my objectives, there would be no success. If he had any idea that I wanted to change the course of his life, then nothing could or would ever happen. I accepted that I could not set foot on William's property, but also knew that Henry would be someone who could learn the fate of Big John, Clara, Daniel, and Anna.

The next morning, as we sat in the hotel restaurant, I reiterated the plan to Henry. We would attempt to purchase William's farm, and if it failed, we would purchase the one next door to the north. At the same time, we would attempt to purchase the farm to the south so that William's land would be surrounded by our property. The goal was to squeeze William until he was forced to sell. By using Mr. Ward as the legal owner, William and his neighbors would never know our intent … freedom and liberty for all.

Henry posed the question, "What if the neighbors don't want to sell?"

I responded that this was why Mr. Ward came into the picture. With his stability, time was on our side. We could return to Wisconsin and continue with our lives and still have the insurance that when change happened, we would be there.

I directed Henry to the Tyrill farm and sent him on his way. It was a long day waiting for his return.

Late that evening, there came a knock upon my door. It was Henry.

"Let's get some air," I suggested.

As we walked, Henry told me about his visit. "I went to the farm, and it was just as you had described it. There was an old slave there, and I asked him if he was Big John, and he got a perplexed look upon his face."

"Do I know you?" Big John inquired.

"No, sir, you do not."

"Sir? No one called me sir in my entire life. Who are you?"

"Then the large lady came forth. 'You must be Clara,' I said. She had a frown upon her face."

"Do I know you?"

"No, ma'am, you do not." Again, there was a frown as she shook her head in a questioning way.

"About twenty years ago, you loaned someone two five-dollar gold pieces, an old musket, and a horse named Ed."

Big John's grin began to spread from ear to ear.

"I am here to repay that debt with interest." At that, Henry pulled four five-dollar gold pieces from his pocket and handed them to Big John.

"Lord have mercy," Clara said.

"Who are you?" Big John inquired.

"I am George and Elizabeth's son Henry."

"Oh, my God," Big John whispered. "Let me see your hands."

"Big John looked at my fingers," Henry said.

"Sure enough, and you came all the way from Kentucky to pay us what we gave your father?"

"No, sir. I came all the way from Wisconsin," Henry noted.

"Wisconsin? Where's that?"

"Beyond Kentucky and Indiana and Illinois."

My Lord, to pay back what we gived?"

"No, sir. To seek your freedom."

"Freedom? Freedom from what?" Big John inquired.

"From slavery?"

"Slavery? Why, we too old to be considered slaves. We just livin' here doin' a little work for which we gots a place to stay. We got nowhere to go and don' know how to do nothin' else. When we were young and foolish, we dreamed of freedom, but now that we is old, that freedom idea has no meaning. Where would we go? What would we do? How could we live? This is where our family is."

"What about Joshua?"

"He died," Clara sadly said. "He got real sick, and there was no doctor nor nothing, and he just died."

"What about Daniel?"

"Oh, he's here. He's out workin' in the field," Big John said with a proud smile.

"What about Anna?"

"Miss Priscilla, she didn't like Anna, and she sold her about ten years ago. They wanted her to have babies, and she had none so she had no value to the Tyrills."

Henry noted that he could sense the anger and frustration in Clara's voice. I remembered, "Breeding stock. Return on investment. Two horses." My God.

Henry continued on that Clara noted, "She a housemaid in Richmond. She got it good. She work for a rich man name Bates. She don't have to do no pickin', and she gets to wear them fancy dresses and she gets to take care of her massah, when he in the mood."

Henry asked to see Daniel.

Big John indicated that he wasn't allowed out of the yard for fear that if he and Daniel were both gone, they would try and escape.

"Mr. William, he tells Daniel that iffin' he try to leave, both Clara and I would get a whippin' until we die. Daniel, he believe Mr. William, and so he never try to escape along the railroad to the North."

Big John pointed the way to the field to the south, and Henry said he went to meet his cousin.

"Daniel was a very large man," Henry told me. Much larger than he had ever seen with broad shoulders and muscles in his back and legs that made my Henry, who was not small, feel quite petite.

Henry said that as he got off his horse, Daniel stopped swinging the scythe and looked at him. Henry noted that Daniel had dark curly hair, but his skin was light brown, and his nose was thin and straight as were his lips. Henry said that he went up to Daniel and stopped and looked at him and stuck out his hand. Daniel didn't know what to do. No white man had ever shaken his hand before.

"Hello, my name is Henry Terrill. I think you knew my mother and father once, a long time ago."

Henry reported that a perplexed look came across Daniel's face as if he were rolling back the years to his childhood. "Mr. George and Miss Elizabeth?"

"Yes."

A broad smile beamed from beneath his nose. "My Lord!"

"Your mother and father loaned my parents money when they wanted to leave here, and I came to pay it back."

"My Lord!"

Daniel put his hand to his chin and shook his head. "Your mama was expecting when they left here. We thought they had died and gone to heaven."

"No, Daniel. Wisconsin."

"My Lord. You came all the way from Wisconsin to pay my parents what they gave as a gift?"

"Not just for that. My father has done quite well for the family and has decided that he wants to own farm property here in Virginia."

"What?"

"Yes. He has plans on raising tobacco in Wisconsin and also in Virginia or perhaps create a dairy farm here and a cheese factory."

"My Lord!"

"Daniel."

"Yes, sir?"

"No 'sirs' to me please."

"Yes?"

"I know who your father is, and I know that you are my first cousin. I stand before you ashamed and appalled that my ancestors have kept you in chains while we have been free. Let me see your hands."

With that Daniel stuck out his huge hands, and Henry turned them over.

"Look at your index fingernails. They are fan-shaped, just as Uncle William's, my father's, and mine," Henry noted. "You see, we are relatives, and I give you my word that I will do whatever I can to make it right ... to give you the honor and the dignity that only comes when you can taste the sweetness of freedom to come and go as you please, to be what you want to be, to accomplish all that you can. My father and mother left here with nothing, and today they own four farms, a cheese factory, and an inn. They are not rich, but they are certainly a long way from being poor, and it is because of your parents and their generosity."

"It ain't so bad," Daniel replied.

"It's not bad because it's all you know."

"Why did you come here? Did you come to make me feel frustrated? To make me angry?" Daniel said as indignation rose in his voice.

"I came to pay a debt, and a debt I will pay."

"You gave the money."

"Money is not enough. I want to give you dignity ... to choose what you feel is best for you and your real parents."

Daniel shook his head in disgust.

"You don't know anything about the South. You come in here and think that you can make it all right. Look at my skin compared to yours. I am brown, and you are white. I am in chains, and you can come and go as you please. It has been this way for over two hundred years. If you stir up a hornets' nest, they will come."

"Who will come?"

"Those who don't want change will come at night and kill my parents and burn everything to the ground. Don't you see? None of us is free. Not you. Not me. Not anyone. We are all prisoners. We are all slaves. We are all victims of oppression."

Oppression. Henry's eyes grew wide. The word I had said to him so many times before.

"How do you know so many fancy words?" Henry asked.

"You think that because my skin is brown that I am stupid?"

"No, of course not."

"You think that because my parents don't have proper diction, I cannot?" Daniel's head was held high as he looked down his nose at Henry. The man was incensed, and there was fire in his eyes.

Henry was surprised by the abrupt change in vocabulary and how in an instant Daniel had gone from slave talk to high articulation.

"You think that as a slave I couldn't learn to read and write and do my numbers?"

Henry stood with mouth agape. With each sentence, Daniel's vocabulary and pronunciation became more defined.

"Sir, I am self-taught. I have studied English, history, philosophy, mathematics, astronomy, physics, biology, economics, and religion. If I could, I would go to the University of Virginia. Instead, because my skin is brown, I cannot even use the language I know. 'Yes, massah. No, massah.' Instead I wear a leash around my neck that curtails my thoughts, impedes my emotions, and limits my expression. One false step, and my parents die. One wrong word, and they will be whipped. One nuance of reservation, and they will feel the wrath that we all fear ... the total obliteration of any dreams we might have for a better tomorrow."

Daniel slipped back into slave talk. "I dooz what's you wants me to, massah. I clean your chamber pot an' wash your clothes. I do what's you tell me to. Yes, massah. No, massah. Go to hell, massah."

Henry now stood in awe. Before him stood a powerful, intelligent, articulate man, but a man filled with hate and distrust and, above all else, profound frustration.

"Bear with me please. That's all I ask. Please give us the patience to try and do what's best."

"Do I have a choice, Cousin Henry?" Daniel said with a degree of sarcasm in his voice.

Henry looked him straight in the eyes. "No, you do not, Cousin Daniel. No, you do not."

Henry was moved by the dialogue, and it showed in his expressions. It was so much more than he thought it would be ... the realization of permanence that only comes in defeat, the anger, the frustration, and, above all else, the keen sense of futility. While Henry and I walked, he reported that he and Daniel talked about my brother and his wife. Daniel said that Priscilla had consumption and was too weak and frail to leave the house. He noted that William was also beginning to cough and had night sweats, the first sign that he too was infected. Daniel noted that Clara continued to clean the house and reported that Priscilla was nothing more than skin and bones, rasping and wheezing, coughing up blood, her skin fallow and her eyes sunken. At dinner, Clara only made broth for Priscilla and assisted my brother in feeding and taking care of her. Clara noted that death was at the doorstep and would soon be knocking. She reported that William had turned into a very old man, feeble in many ways, and that his energy had eroded and he stood sapped of any strength.

Henry asked about the farm, and Daniel noted that all the livestock had been sold and most of the fields rented to the neighbors. The North was becoming industrialized while the South continued to farm and use slave labor. By 1841, factory workers in the North had greater income than most farm owners in the South.

While there were canals and roads being built in the East that traversed the Appalachians to the West, the South was in an economic quandary, relying on manual slave labor to do the tasks machines were already beginning to do in the North. With little income and no ability to change, William was living on the rent for his land, which was based on the value of the crops sold and what money he had remaining in the bank, hoping that what little money remaining would last until his days on this earth were done. Gone was the high society that he coveted so much. William and Priscilla rarely left the farm. When William did leave, he always went alone. There were no parties, and no one came to visit.

Henry asked Daniel why Big John and Clara didn't just leave. Daniel indicated they had nowhere to go. The farm was home, and runaway slaves risked a much worse fate than they had to endure. It was then that Henry realized that, even in oppression, there can be degrees, just as there can be levels of happiness and sadness. They were not free, but they were also together, and because of their goodness, they were doing everything they could to care for those in need.

The next day, Henry, Mr. Ward, and I had what would become one of our weekly meetings. I asked Mr. Ward to determine ownership of the land adjacent to my brother's. I still had not let on what my plans were nor what my association was with William. Seven days hence, we met again, and Mr. Ward noted that the land was owned by the Smithsons, who had emigrated from Scotland and were elderly. He noted that the farm was well kept and viable, and included in the property were twelve slaves, eight horses, two barns, four outbuildings, and a house. He added that there was a spring-fed stream that ran through the property and into that of my brother's, from which all water was gathered for both farms.

I asked if the Smithsons had children, and he said he did not know. I asked him to determine if there were any children, where they were residing, and what was their means of employment. Mr. Ward smiled, as he knew my intent. Subsequent to the second meeting, Henry and I elected to visit Richmond and told Mr. Ward that our next meeting should commence in seven days, at which time, I hoped that he would be able to provide the information that we needed.

Richmond

The next day, Henry and I departed for Richmond. It was only sixty miles or so, and that meant nothing more than a day's ride on horses. Richmond was a beautiful city located at the fall line of the James River running through it. I remembered how Elizabeth and I had to pay to cross it by boat twenty years before, and it took almost every penny we had to our names. With the current so strong and large boulders everywhere, crossing by horse was simply too dangerous, and so Henry and I waited for a large bateau to cross into the main area of the city. I marveled once again, as I had done so many years before, at the flat-bottomed boats that were pointed at both ends. While they varied in both length and girth, they were incredibly agile in the water. I could never have controlled one, but the bateaumen who pushed us across the river used long sturdy poles, and we crossed what would have been an otherwise dangerous escapade without incident.

Once in the main city of Richmond, Henry and I took it upon ourselves to attempt to find the Bates residence. We had learned that Anna's owner was part of the upper class … wealthy, to say the least, and not afraid to show it. His home was stately, with flowers and well-tended gardens, and we elected to return after finding a hotel and having a hot bath. We inquired and learned that Mr. Bates was the owner of a trading company that bought and sold tobacco and exported it to New York City and Europe.

The next morning, clean-shaven and in new clothes, we returned to the Bates estate and walked up to the front door. As I rapped, an elderly slave dressed in formal attire opened the door.

"May I help you, sir?" the elderly gentleman inquired.

"Is it possible to see Mr. Bates?" I asked.

"Mr. Bates isn't here today. May I be of service?"

"When will Mr. Bates return?"

"Mr. Bates is a very busy man, sir."

My demeanor was changing, and the smile upon my face had been washed away. "My name is George Terrill, and this is my son Henry. We have arrived from Wisconsin, where I own four farms, a cheese factory, a brewery, and an inn. I am currently in the process of purchasing several farms in Virginia. I am attempting to establish a method by which to sell my tobacco and import goods from Europe. I was informed that Mr. Bates uses his residence as his primary office. I was instructed to come to his home and seek the gentleman out. I appreciate your role, but I ask again, may I speak with Mr. Bates?"

With that, an anteroom door opened, and a man in his fifties walked into the room. "I am Thaddeus Bates."

"Good morning, sir. My name is George Terrill, and this is my son Henry. We have traveled a long way to meet with you."

Bates shook my hand. "Please excuse the efforts of my head butler. He is only doing what he is instructed to do. I have many friends and several enemies, and it is his job to ensure that only my friends are welcomed into my home. Please follow me. And Virgil, please have Anna bring us some tea."

"Thank you, Mr. Bates. As I was explaining to your butler, I am seeking an outlet for what I will be producing here in Virginia and hope to also extend my ability to market my products if it is possible in this area."

We were sitting in the anteroom when the door opened, and Anna's eyes met mine. Even after twenty years, she immediately knew who I was and had a shy smile on her face, but also a look of fear. Why were we here? Who was with me? Would I make trouble for her? I wondered if beneath the shroud of oppression, she too had the profound intellect that Henry had witnessed in Daniel.

She had gone from the little girl my brother had raped to a beautiful woman who stood proud and erect. It is difficult to explain Anna's beauty other than to say that she was spellbinding. Her high cheek bones and soft light brown skin highlighted beautiful white teeth. Her shape and form were such that she looked lithe and limber, and yet she carried herself like a proper lady with her head held high, shoulders square, and long arms delicately balanced on each side. Her huge brown eyes accentuated her face while her thin lips pierced her cheeks and made her look evocative. Her hair was pulled back with pins, and she wore a tiny pink ribbon above her left ear. It was no wonder why so many men coveted her company and why Mr. Bates held onto his prize possession ... not for the comforts she could provide but as a statement of wealth and power, showing the world that he had what many men wanted but could not touch.

Not a hint was given that we knew each other. Not a glance. Not a smile. Not a nod or even a frown. Anna placed the pitcher before Mr. Bates and left the room.

"We heard that you might be of service to our family, but can you please explain your business to me and what services you provide?" I inquired.

Mr. Bates took it upon himself to outline his function and that of his trading partners. He noted that his company had the ability, when so needed, to purchase crops on speculation and that, in doing so, he also had interests in numerous properties throughout the region. I already knew that Mr. Bates was initially overpromising for the crops so that when the land did not produce the return expected, he could acquire a share of the land for pennies on the dollar. He would then sell the land, making a huge profit. It destroyed farms and families. The net result was that not only families but slaves, who had been together for years, were disbursed and ruined along the way.

I described what we wanted to accomplish in terms of farming in the area and noted that our hope was, with the right partnership, we could expand our business and increase our worth.

Mr. Bates' interest seemed piqued. I later found out that he thought I was a rube.

"And how do I fit in?" he asked.

"I want to establish all aspects of my business structure before I make the investment in the property. I want to have my financial, legal, and operational organization in place, along with the method by which I can sell my goods. As you probably are aware, costs in the North are rising rapidly. Labor costs, land costs, transportation costs are all increasing, and it is my belief that production here in the South and then shipping either to New England or Europe will allow me to generate greater profits than keeping all of my investments in one area."

Bates rubbed his chin in consideration. "And so, what you are seeking is a business associate to take your crops or your cheese or butter or whatever and sell it in Europe, the North, or even here in Virginia?

"Yes."

He smiled. "Do you really consider your volume to be such that it would be worthwhile?"

"Eventually, yes. We currently have four dairy farms in Wisconsin. I have ten milkers, and we are buying all the milk we can from all the farms in the area for the cheese factory. We produce over a ton of cheese per week and have the capacity to increase that to one ton per day." Bates' eyes lit up. "By taking our knowledge and exporting it to Virginia, I have concluded that we can open up a new market and expand our business while also protecting ourselves from any form of regional malady."

"Why not closer to home?" Bates inquired, looking at all possible angles.

"We can't go west because of the Indian situation, and we need a major market for our product. The challenge is that as you travel into New York, costs are even higher, and I cannot operate my business on that small of margin. By coming to Virginia and then shipping the products north, I will have better weather and much lower labor costs."

He nodded and rubbed his nose. "In other words, slaves?"

I deceitfully nodded my head in the affirmative.

"Mr. Terrill, I am interested enough to invite you and your son to meet with my partners."

"That would be wonderful. Please tell me when and where."

He called the butler into the room and asked him to send the boys to contact the partners, telling them that there would be an important dinner the following evening.

"Where shall we meet?" I asked.

"Why, here, of course."

"Perfect," I thought. "Perfect."

Henry and I departed, and the first question Henry asked was about the use of slaves to which I responded that all I was doing was making Mr. Thaddeus Bates believe we approved so that I could learn more about his way of doing business. This would be the tactic used to acquire my brother's farm.

The following evening, Mr. Bates' carriage retrieved us from our hotel and drove us to his residence. Gentlemen did not ride horses to fancy houses in the evening. I had warned Henry that we were not among friends and that anything said would be repeated. As we climbed the stairs, the butler opened the door and greeted us with a warm smile. "Gentlemen," he said as he ushered us into the living room.

When you are accustomed to farmhouses, the thoughts of Southern mansions really never crosses your mind. We entered through the same front door as before but were led into a single room larger than our entire house. The chandeliers glistened while in the corner, a small ensemble played violin and harp music. Waiters dressed in fancy clothes brought us drinks as I searched the crowd for Anna. As guests arrived, we were introduced by the butler and began small talk about farming and Wisconsin and cheese. When there were three other gentlemen and their wives present, Mr. Bates made his appearance, and at his side was Anna, resplendent in a formal gown.

We stood there dumbfounded. Was she a slave? Was she his wife? Where did Anna fit in?

Wherever Bates went within the room, Anna was at his side. As he approached us, he bowed gently and introduced Anna.

"Gentlemen, this is my main housekeeper, Anna."

We both bowed and delicately shook her hand. Not once did her eyes depart from ours. Not once was there a point where there was anything but solidarity with Mr. Bates. What Big John had told Henry seemed true ... Anna was well treated.

Dinner was served in the formal dining room with each person seated having their own server. Never had I ever eaten such a fine meal in my life. While Bates sat at the head of the table, Anna sat to his right. All of his partners and their wives seemed comfortable with the arrangement, as if it had been in place for a very long period of time.

As the night wore on, the ladies were excused and sent to the parlor. Bates, his partners, Henry, and I adjourned to the veranda where the warm summer air was refreshed by a soft Virginia breeze.

"I have shared your plans with my partners, and there is interest on our part, Mr. Terrill. Would you mind sharing more details with us?"

Bates announced.

I knew that this was a trap. If they knew my plan, they wouldn't need me. If they felt it was a ruse, they would block my objectives.

"Gentlemen, it has been a wonderful evening of which Henry and I are most grateful. Your Southern hospitality is even more profound than the stories I have been told. However, to share with you everything on our first night would be like a man courting a woman and having her make love to him that very first night. Where would the suspense be? Where would the courtship be? If we are to become business partners, then we will need to learn more about each other over time and not over drinks."

They knew then that I was no rube. As we were speaking, Anna was making her way onto the veranda.

Discretely, I asked Bates, "Is it possible, Mr. Bates, to use the facilities? I have eaten a great deal and had several glasses of your fine wine and I do need to relieve myself."

Bates had no clue.

"Anna, please escort Mr. Terrill to the guest privy."

With that, Anna and I walked around back of the mansion. When we were in out of sight and sound, I stopped.

"Anna, oh, Anna. It is so good to see you. I have come back to Virginia to repay the debts I have to my brother and your real parents. Henry met with your brother, and we learned that you were here. Your true father and mother send their love."

There were tears in her eyes.

"Are you OK?" I whispered.

She nodded in the affirmation and then said, "I knew it was you. I knew you would come back. I knew that you wouldn't leave us forever."

"Your parents said that you were fine."

"Big John and Clara don't know anything. I am like a rag doll. I am Mr. Bates' toy to do with as he pleases. His wife is long gone, and he needed someone to show off—and that's me."

"Is he taking his liberties with you?" I asked.

Anna had a forlorn look on her face. "Everyone thinks I am his mistress, but I am not. I am like a pretty China doll that just sits on a shelf for everyone to look at, but no one can touch. Mr. Bates uses me to make all the others jealous. I am his trophy. I am like his fancy watch. All he wants from me is for the other men to think he is better than they are."

"You mean you and Mr. Bates aren't intimate?" I asked.

"He doesn't like being with women."

"You mean men?" I squirmed to inquire.

"No, not men."

I must have had a perplexed look on my face as Anna continued, "Mr. Bates likes little boys."

"What? You mean ..."

"Yes, that's what I mean. He has them over, and they go to his bedroom. I hear them crying and screaming, and then everything gets quiet. I hear them begging, 'No, no, no.' But he never stops."

"Are these slave boys?"

"Slaves ... white ... it doesn't matter. He prefers the white ones because they are harder for him to get, and when he is done, he knows that he has humiliated them. Then he is ashamed of what he has done, but he doesn't stop. The little black boys, they don't know any difference. They have been humiliated their entire lives, and what he does to them, they think all white men will do. That Mr. Bates, he's one sick man.

My stomach turned at the thought.

Anna explained, "I don't think Bates means to be a bad person. He just has strong feelings towards little boys. He seeks out their company and really thinks that they want to be with him. When he takes a little boy upstairs, it's because he is in love with them just like men and women fall in love. These boys aren't strangers. Mr. Bates selects his little boys carefully, and 'grooms' them over a period of months with gifts just like he did me. Most of the time, the parents are poor, and they need what Bates has to offer. They see Bates as a way for their son to get a better life for themselves.

"It's sad, Mr. George. Many times, I've seen those little boys come down the stairs all ashamed and embarrassed, shaking in fear. He has had his way with them, and it is awful. They wonder what they did wrong to deserve his treatment. They wonder if this is what life will always be like. The man is a thief, Mr. George. He steals land from folks and steals innocence from little boys.

"Oh, God, how I wish I could make him pay," Anna continued. "He knows that I know, and he reminds me that, at any time, he can sell me to someone who will make me a prostitute or worse. He tells me how lucky I am that he takes care of me and puts me in pretty dresses and lets me eat with the white folks. I hate that man. I hate him."

With that, Anna crumpled into my chest and began crying. "I'm here all alone. I'm not white, so I am a slave, and yet because of my 'stature,' the other slaves hate me. I wear pretty dresses and smile and do what I am told and make it all look good and proper like I am his whore, yet he has no interest in me, and so I am wasted. Mr. Bates' friends all want their way with me, but he always makes certain that they understand the answer is 'no.' He likes to watch me put on pretty clothes, and he makes me try to entice all the men just so that he feels the power of knowing that I belong only to him. Oh, Mr. George, please get me out of here. Please."

I held her for just a moment and then knew we needed to return to the party or there would be suspicion ... suspicion that I had my way with Anna, suspicion that something was not right, and that was the very last thing I needed.

I looked at Anna and held her chin in my hand. "Look at me. I came back to Virginia to free you and Big John, Clara, and Daniel, and I give you my word that it will happen. Be brave. Be strong. Whatever you do, do not let on that you know anything at all about me, or it will become that much more difficult. This will take some time, Anna, but I promise you, it will happen."

She nodded, wiped the tears from her eyes, and smiled. We looked around to make certain that no one had seen us and made our way back into the party. My opinion of Mr. Bates had totally changed, and it was time for some play acting so that he wouldn't think anything had transpired.

Bates made his way over to me with an inquisitive look on his face. "Everything all right?" he asked.

"Just a little indigestion is all. I'll be all right."

Bates had no idea that I knew his dirty secret. I vowed I would play his game and someday use it against him to gain Anna's freedom. With that, Anna excused herself and left the room.

One of Bates' partners said, "That's some fine brown sugar you got there, Thaddeus. Fine brown sugar. If you ever want to sell her, you let me know."

Bates replied, "She's also one very bright woman, not your typical woman or slave. I sent her to school, and within a few months, she wasn't challenged. I wanted to send her up to Farmville to attend the University of Virginia, but even Thomas Jefferson himself couldn't get his slaves educated there, including Ms. Sally Hemings, if you know what I mean. Why, just a few years ago the University itself purchased a slave named Lewis Commodore for the incredible sum of $580. Can you imagine $580 for one slave to do nothing but ring a bell. What is this land coming to? I know for a fact that there is about one slave for every twenty students. Can you imagine that? One slave for every twenty students. They should be out working in the fields and not wasting time doing nothing at the high-and-mighty university."

"Does she still keep you satisfied?" another partner inquired.

"In many ways, my friend, in many ways," Bates chuckled.

"If only they knew," I thought.

Mr. Bates was beginning to feel his spirits, and I knew that it was time for Henry and me to depart. As the evening ended, all parties agreed that further business discussions should take place. I indicated that we would be heading back to Wisconsin and that, if possible, they should send a proposal for my consideration. They seemed surprised that we even got mail in Wisconsin. They thought that the Indians were still at war and there was no civilization. Little did they know!

When one twists their ankle, the initial pain is not nearly as great as that felt the very next day. So, it was with our evening with Mr. Bates and the information that Anna had shared. I thought of my own boys and their innocence. I thought of their joy and laughter, and then I thought of this monster taking away the honor, virtue, and dignity of so many others. My intent quickly changed. No longer was beating Mr. Bates at his own game my mission, nor just acquiring Anna's freedom. It was determining a way for Mr. Bates to suffer the consequence of his indiscretions.

The Smithsons

Henry was not aware of the situation, and I felt that it wasn't necessary to share my knowledge with him. He had enough going through his mind without muddling it with more. The ride back to Farmville seemed shorter than the ride to Richmond as my mind traversed all that had transpired.

Upon arrival, we returned to our hotel to find a message from Mr. Ward indicating that we should contact him as he had results from his investigation. I asked that a messenger be sent to contact Mr. Ward and tell him that we had returned and were available for either dinner or breakfast the next day. Within a short period of time, the messenger returned indicating that Mr. Ward would meet us for dinner at the hotel at 7:00 p.m.

As Mr. Ward arrived, he was carrying his leather satchel, and so I knew he had something to tell us. As we sat at dinner, Mr. Ward outlined that the Smithsons had a son who had not been seen nor heard from for a long period of time and that, like many farmers in the area, there was financial trouble, as they owed quite a sum of money based on failed crops, upon which they had borrowed.

I looked at Mr. Ward and said, "And I'll bet dinner that the company they owe money to is Virginia Equity, correct?"

Mr. Ward seemed quite surprised that I knew the name of the company. "You are quite right," he responded.

"Virginia Equity, owned by one Thaddeus Bates."

"Again, quite correct."

"What is the debt?" I inquired.

"It currently stands at $2,000."

I pondered the amount.

"How old are the Smithsons?" I asked

"Late sixties, is my guess."

"How much property?

"244 acres."

"$12.25 per acre?" I asked.

"Yes."

"Real value?" I inquired.

"Twenty dollars per acre," Mr. Ward responded.

Henry was seeing a side of me he did not know existed. Not as a father, but as a businessman whose goal was to achieve the best possible price I could. When someone wants something, you have the advantage. When someone needs something, you have a greater advantage. When someone must have something or they will suffer outrageous consequences, all you need do is determine what it is they are trying to achieve and make certain that it is included. It can be safety. It can be security. It can be freedom or happiness. People are all the same. All you need do is figure out what it is they must have and offer it to them, and then you will succeed.

"What about this? We offer the Smithsons fourteen dollars per acre for the farmland and pay off the debt. They are allowed to maintain residence in the house for as long as they both shall live. We pay off the debt to Bates and take deed to the house and all property, including the slaves. However, we agree to maintain the home in its current condition and provide twenty dollars per month living expenses for the Smithsons?" I asked.

There was a smile upon Mr. Ward's face.

"The Smithsons give up ownership but maintain residence? They have no debt and a place to live and earn twenty dollars per month for as long as they both want to live in the house?"

"Correct," I responded.

"Their note will probably be coming due shortly, and Virginia Equity can be paid in full. We can set up the farm in a trust managed by you, Henry, and me," Mr. Ward reiterated.

"Can this be a blind trust so that no one knows who your partners are?" I asked.

"Most certainly," Mr. Ward responded.

"Go draw up the papers and make the offer, Mr. Ward. I would like to have this completed in the next few days, if possible."

Mr. Ward and Henry visited the farm and met with the Smithsons. Henry said they were at first taken aback and looked somewhat offended until they realized that they could retain their residence and their local status and no one need know that they no longer owned the farm. Mr. Ward turned out to be a good salesman, pointing out that they had no more risk of bad crops or owing anyone any money.

Two days later, Mr. Ward returned with the counter-offer from the Smithsons. They wanted twenty dollars per acre. I responded that we would pay the sum but they would need to leave the residence as we would be forced to rent the house. Mr. Ward returned the next day with a counteroffer of sixteen dollars per acre and they maintained possession of the slaves. Horse trading is what it is called in Wisconsin.

We responded at sixteen dollars per acre and the slaves were our property. We agreed to place $976 in an account in the bank. We agreed that each year, $240 would replace what they had withdrawn as long as they both were living on the farm, ensuring them that the difference between what they were paid and the twenty dollars per acre they asked for would always be there. Mr. Ward also pointed out that without the deal, they could pay Virginia Equity the money owed and probably lose everything when the property went up for auction.

Mr. Ward returned with a smile on his face. I needed no reply. "Welcome to the world of farming, Mr. Ward," I told him.

The closing was set, and all the necessary papers were signed. Henry and Mr. Ward visited the property and inspected the land, the buildings, and the slaves again. Henry held a meeting and informed the slaves that immediately they would begin receiving living expenses of three dollars per adult per month and one dollar per child over the age of five until age fourteen, when it would increase to two dollars per month. Henry notified the slaves that all would be taught to read and write and that all quarters would be repaired, painted, and made habitable to the best of his ability. He also informed them that they did not need to fear sales or separation for the goal was to build the farm based on the community that was there. Henry said he could see the surprise, the relief, and the joy in their eyes, all accentuated by the smiles on their faces as someone stood before them and did one little thing ... showed them some respect.

That night, there was a party, and all but me joined in, including even the Smithsons. There was peace, there was joy, and there was true happiness as everyone felt secure and respected. When asked where he would reside, Henry indicated that he would stay at the hotel and then take one of the quarters as his residence. Mr. Ward reported that Henry told the staff there was a great deal of work to be done and he would be working side by side with them to reach their goal of safety, security, and prosperity for all. That night when he returned to Farmville, Henry had a smile on his face. There was goodness in his heart, and he was filled with the joy that only comes when someone truly knows that he has done something decent and good.

Virginia Equity was paid by the blind trust, and I thought Mr. Bates did not learn what had transpired. My next goal was the property of one William Tyrill. It wouldn't be as easy, as ego has a way of making even the best of business deals fail to happen.

Henry was soon hard at work, and my initial foray into Virginia was complete. I felt uncomfortable traveling alone, and so I asked Mr. Ward to find a guide to take me home ... someone with whom I could ride for reasons of convenience and safety. Before I left, Henry and I developed a set of objectives. The first goal was to determine what we needed to do to make the Smithson farm profitable. The second was to determine what methods we could use to motivate my brother to sell his farm. Nothing bad, mind you, but something that would do to him what had happened to the Smithsons. The third goal was to keep an eye on Mr. Ward and the bank to make sure our interests were protected.

The Visitors

The journey home was uneventful, and yet I enjoyed the company and security of having someone ride with me. Andrew Kincaid was about the same age as Henry and yet quite seasoned and very good with a gun. He was a quiet man and yet also very careful. His pay was for the trip was twenty dollars, and I felt it was worth it.

As we neared Mineral Point, I noticed that Andrew had begun to relax and actually heard him whistle a tune every now and then. After a week of riding together, you get to know a man, and I felt that Andrew might fit right in Mineral Point. I asked about his education, and he said that he could read and write and do his numbers. I asked about his family, and he said they were all in the Deep South. I asked what he thought of slaves, and he said that was why he had left his family because he could not tolerate the handling of people the way his family did with slave masters and whippings and beatings and such.

When your business is growing, you are always in need of good help, and I asked him where he would go next, and he said he really didn't have any plans. I asked him if he would like to work for me in Mineral Point. I told him I needed someone to oversee the milkers and take care of things on a daily basis at the cheese factory. He thought he might like that.

Elizabeth and the children were glad to see me. I had been gone for three months. Everything had continued, and within two hours, I learned all there was to know about changes in Mineral Point while I was gone. I asked about our businesses and was shown the books.

The farms were doing well. The cheese factory was doing well. The inn was doing well. The only failing business was the brewery. It took me several years before I abandoned my hope of turning it around and sold it for a loss. In the process, I learned a valuable lesson. ... a man should always acknowledge his limitations.

That fall, we received a letter from Henry that was quite disturbing. There had been strangers at the Virginia farm, and when they were discovered, they quickly rode away. I wrote to Henry and told him to purchase some rifles and teach everyone how to shoot.

About two months later, another letter arrived explaining that my advice had been followed, and one night, two men came into the farm. Henry noted that they were scared away by gunshots. He would make certain that every night someone would be on watch. He noted it could be Bates trying to get even or other farmers upset with the pay we were providing for what they considered free labor. He noted that the workers were getting quite good with the rifles and were being trained each day.

It wasn't but two weeks later that another letter arrived. Henry wrote that the two men had come back with the intent of burning the barn. This time, Henry and the workers were ready, and as the interlopers were about to light the hay on fire, found themselves surrounded by barrels of rifles all pointing at them. By their common appearance, Henry noted he could tell it was father and son. He wrote that the men were given their choice ... tell them who put them up to the deed or Henry was getting the constable and having them arrested. He wrote that the men laughed and spat and said that they would be free before the sun came up. With that, Henry decided that he had enough and told the slaves to get a rope as it was time for a good old-fashioned hanging.

Henry noted that the men didn't think he would do such a deed until they saw the rope. With barrels pointed at their heads, Henry tied their ankles together and had the rope slung over the board hanging out from the barn. The men were pulled up until they were hanging upside down. Henry told them that with the blood rushing to their brains it wouldn't be long until they would remember who sent them. He let them hang quite a long time before he cut them down. Still they would not speak.

Henry said he was at wit's end when someone suggested that they be dunked in the horse trough. With hands tied behind their backs, they were led to the water and their feet kicked out from beneath them. As they were on their knees, the workers took them and grabbed the youngest and held his head beneath the water as Henry slowly counted to five. Each time they let the young man up, gasping for air, and Henry would ask again and there would be no response. Again, the son was submerged in the slime-filled trough. This time, Henry slowly counted to six with the son again gasping for air. The next time the count was seven … and then eight … and then nine. Each time, the son came up coughing and gasping and wheezing for air.

Henry looked at the old man and slowly counted, "One … two … three … four … five … six … seven … eight." Henry wrote that he looked at the workers and said, "Get a shovel. I think the old man is going to have to dig a grave." One of the workers ran and got the shovel. Henry wrote that he had intimidated the two men, and now they were totally afraid. No father wants to watch his son die.

With that, the young one's head was pushed once again under the water, and Henry started slowly counting, "One … two … three … four … five … six … seven … eight … nine." This time, the son's arms and legs began to quiver as Henry neared the count of ten.

"Stop! Stop!" the older one yelled out. "It was Bates. It was Bates." The workers pulled the young one out of the water, coughing, gasping, and shaking. The son had seen death and was pulled back from its darkest edge.

"Bates. What do you know about Bates? Why should I trust you? Tell me about Mr. Bates and what he was paying you, and I will let your son go. Hold back anything, and I'll let the boys here have their way with the two of you, and no one will ever know what happened. If you think Bates cares, think again. You're nothing to him. Nothing."

With the secret out, the father confessed that Bates paid them ten dollars to come and burn the barn and that if it was confirmed to be destroyed, there would be ten dollars more for them. They said that Bates knew that we had hoodwinked him, and it was his way of getting even. He wanted nothing but trouble and turmoil for us, and it would not stop until we sold the farm to him.

"What should I do with the two of you? Should I let you go free when you wanted to burn our barn? Should I still kill you?"

Henry wrote that he had a plan. He turned to the old man and said, "I'll give you the ten dollars Bates was going to pay and offer you twenty more if you do an errand for me." He wrote that the men were surprised. He outlined that he went to his quarters and wrote a letter to Anna. In it, he told her that the next time Bates had one of his little boys at the house and they were in his bedroom, she was to put a candle in the upstairs left window, and that would be a sign that the sheriff should come. He sealed the envelope and asked if they would deliver it. He knew better than to trust these two scallywags, so he gave them another note that asked the question, "What was Daniel's father's name?" He then instructed the men to deliver both letters to Anna and return with her response. As I read Henry's note, I realized how intelligent he was. He noted that both men got a wry smile on their faces, thinking that they would be leaving and would either tell Mr. Bates or simply throw the letters away.

"Which of you two men rides the fastest?" Henry reported.

The younger one said he did.

He noted that he handed the letter to the older man. "Take these two letters to the slave named Anna and to no one else, and no one is to see you. Your son is staying here. If you're not back in three days, he can start digging his own grave. If you return with the signed note, then, not only are both of you free, but the twenty dollars will also be paid. I will warn you of this. There have been far too many 'accidental' barns burned and dead animals found around here the past few years, and you are now the main suspects. I am certain that the sheriff and many of the farmers would love to get their hands on you."

With that, Henry let the old man go. As for the son, Henry said they put him in the smokehouse with a chamber pot and told him that in two days, he would begin digging his own grave. If on the third day, the father one hadn't returned, he would be dead.

The next day, Henry went into Farmville and called upon Mr. Ward and explained what had happened. Mr. Ward indicated that the sheriff was a friend and that they all should speak. Henry wrote that he explained what had happened and where the barn burner was. He also outlined the activities of Mr. Bates with the little boys and what the plan was. Henry indicated that he was willing to pay for someone to sit across from the Bates house until there was a candle in the window, at which time he would expect the Richmond sheriff to apprehend Mr. Bates for what he was doing.

The sheriff noted that if it was with a slave boy, little would be done except perhaps ruin the reputation of Mr. Bates, if even that happened. Henry said it would be good enough if that was all that could be done.

On the third day, the father returned with the letter signed by Anna, which read, "William."

Henry knew that she had received the letter and that it was time to put the plan in place.

Henry kept his word and released the son and gave them the twenty dollars as promised. He kept their guns and told them that if he ever saw them around the farm again he would let the other farmers know what had happened. They must have understood, as they rode west instead of east upon leaving the farm, and he never saw them again.

Henry met with Mr. Ward, and they hired a private detective in Richmond. For the first few days, there was nothing, and then one night there was a single candle in the window. The sheriff was summoned, and they broke into Mr. Bates' home and rushed up the stairs. As they entered his bedroom, Bates was caught naked and in bed with a twelve-year-old white boy whose parents were sharecroppers on some of the land that he had stolen from them. Bates' secret was up, and no decent lawyer in Richmond would represent him. His partners fled the firm, and Bates was sentenced to prison.

In Bates' belongings was a ledger that contained all the properties the firm had stolen and how much had been paid. As a form of recompense, Bates' house and all the possessions were put up for auction. Standing at the auction stood my son Henry. When it came time to bid on the slaves, he was instructed to be the highest bidder for Anna regardless of the cost. For $900, Miss Anna was free. For $900, all the tyranny that she had been subjected to was over. For $900, the little girl who had been abused for so many years by so many people would be allowed to finally be happy.

Henry wrote that they gathered her few personal belongings, leaving behind all the fancy dresses that had made her more than she ever wanted to be. They rode back to the farm in the carriage and hardly said a word. That night, Anna seemed out of place and without a smile on her face. It would be some time until she felt like she belonged. Henry told her that her job was not to work the fields or clean house. She was to develop a school and teach all the children, and for the first time in a long, long time, she smiled.

Back to Virginia

After spring planting, it was decided that I should revisit Virginia and give Henry a respite from being alone. I asked Andrew to ride along as both company and security. I think he was glad to go home. The ride took five days, and once again we had no problems. Having now done it four times, things were beginning to look quite familiar.

Even with the familiarity, the Appalachians left me in awe as they reminded me of life where there are peaks and valleys, and it is only because of the valleys that the peaks have any meaning. I thought of the valley in which Elizabeth and I had traversed from Cornwall to America and to my brother's farm. I thought of the peaks of the births of our children. I thought of the valleys of the deaths of Sarah and Henry. I thought of the pinnacle upon which I stood, hand in hand with Elizabeth. We had dreamed, and yes, some of it was nightmares. Yet our dreams had come true, and with it came a debt I owed to someone ... everyone. We had gone from being the oppressed to witnessing oppression at its very worst. From slavery to Black Hawk's nation, from drunken miners to Mr. Bates, we had stood and seen what greed and insolence can do to man and how it could take even the best of people and make them bad.

Our Wisconsin business was good ... very good. Mineral Point continued to boom with new people, and that meant the inn was always busy as was the cheese factory. The farm in Virginia had shown a profit in its first year, and there was tranquility. Henry noted that everyone actually had a smile on their face and the days of someone looking down at the ground when spoken to were gone. There was dignity, and there was grace enhanced by humility and passion ... passion for life and passion for each other, not the physical kind, but the passion that comes from simply caring for another being. Above it all, there was pride ... pride in oneself and pride in achieving the goals that were agreed upon for the good of all, enhanced by the sound of laughter.

What had been fallow fields became ripe with bounty. What had been under-performing land became productive. What had taken weeks in the past was accomplished in days simply because everyone cared. Please don't get me wrong. There were good days, and there were bad. There were happy days, and there were sad. There were days when tempers would flair and disagreements occurred, but they were simply differences based on perspective and not personality, differences that only focused on the subject at hand and not on the person.

Monday through Friday, Henry took it upon himself to teach the children and then, late in the afternoon as the chores were done, repeat the process for the adults. Before long, everyone was learning to read and write. Books were purchased along with slates and chalk and even paper and quills. Within three months, everyone could not only print their name but had a signature. There were to be no more "X's" at the Smithson house.

Every month, Henry would meet with each person and ask them what their goals were for the next month and what they had achieved in the past one. In this way, all of our farm family had a method of measuring where they were and where they wanted to go. At first, many had few ideas about what they wanted or were afraid to speak out. After a few sessions, all were inspired about what it was they wanted to accomplish and what they thought we needed to do to improve the farm. Ideas are contagious, and with them, so too can spirits be.

For nearly a year, Henry had stayed away from Daniel and my brother. In addition, we kept it a secret that Anna was living at the farm. We needed to settle in and let nature take its course. Upon my arrival, the Smithsons offered to allow me to stay in their home. I declined and said that I would stay in Farmville. Andrew and Henry shared a cottage, and they began to learn about each other ... Andrew, the quiet one, and Henry, who loved to laugh and sing.

I made an appointment to meet with Mr. Gillingsworth, our banker in Farmville, and also with Mr. Ward. I needed to check the books and also lay out my next step, which was to duplicate the Smithson offer to one William Tyrill. Andrew would serve as the liaison and work with Mr. Ward on the transaction. I was informed that our funds were secure and our investment had reaped enough reward that our account had reached its initial level. In two years, we had made two major purchases ... the farm and Anna ... and the bounty from both was more than I had anticipated. The bank offered to extend credit, but I said "no." We paid cash for everything we purchased. When we were just starting out, the one time we borrowed almost made me sick.

With Priscilla dead and William alone, I thought the offer would be readily accepted. Instead, both Andrew and Mr. Ward were escorted off the land and told not to come back. The challenge became how to change the balance of power so that my brother had no choice but sell without hurting Daniel, Big John, and Clara and even risking William trying to sell them as well.

As I noted earlier, the Smithsons were renting land from my brother, and our spring-fed stream ran through the land. With the times being what they were, many farmers were expanding their fields so that they could try and break even simply by working their slaves harder as they tended to more land. If we didn't continue to rent the land, the fear was that another farmer would take our place. That left only the spring-fed stream as a bargaining chip.

Henry, Andrew, and I rode along the stream and talked about its value to both farms. Without the stream, there would be no water for cattle, and in times without rain, no way to irrigate the fields. The question became, how or where could we divert the water so that it didn't reach the Tyrill land, at least temporarily.

Henry had a smile cross his face. "Why don't we create a lake?" Andrew and I looked at him with deep furrows in our brows. "There is a narrow that the stream goes through," Henry explained. "If we could block the stream in the narrow by building a dam, we could block the water until the lake was filled. This would not only provide us with necessary water whenever we needed it but allow us to control the stream's flow."

We asked how big the lake would be and how long would it take to fill. Andrew couldn't answer. Instead he noted that he knew where we could find out ... the University of Virginia. I remember that all of us had wry smiles upon our faces.

I sent one of the men into Farmville and asked him to look up Mr. Ward and give him a message that we needed the services of an engineer. He returned and noted that the message had been provided.

About a week later, a very rotund man showed up in a wagon. He was simply too heavy to ride a horse. He was sweating profusely and introduced himself as Doctor McLeod Thrumbolt, Professor of Engineering. We joined with him and took him to where we thought the dam could go. He looked it over, indicating that the location was correct, but there were spots that would not be a lake but marsh, and he was concerned that the height of the dam might be such that flooding would occur each spring with the run-off.

I asked if he could determine where the shores of the lake would be, and he indicated that a topographical map could be drawn and that it would cost a great deal of money. When I asked how much, he wrinkled his nose and curled his lips and said a hundred dollars.

I asked when he could commence. He noted that he would need the assistance of three men. I agreed. I asked how long it would take, and he noted about a week. I asked when he could begin. He said, "How about tomorrow?"

The map was created, and we learned that approximately fifteen acres of land would be underwater. It would take nearly four weeks to fill the lake, and during this time, there would be no run-off. It being summer, all workers were assigned to create the dam. First a slew had to be dug around where the dam was to be built so that the water would have an alternate route. Then the dam itself needed to be built where the stream would flow. In the center, large logs were placed, and then on each side, rocks, and then mud.

The dam stood ten feet high by the time the men were done, and then it was time to fill in the slew. As each shovelful of dirt was placed back in its original position, I felt one step closer to redemption. For each foot the stream was blocked, I sensed one step closer to resolving the anger in my heart. For each drop of water that was stopped in its flow, I sensed that we were that much closer to my ultimate objective.

Slowly, the slew was filled, and the water began backing up behind the dam. A little water trickled through the dam, and then even that stopped. There was a smile upon my face.

For five days, the water level slowly rose. Dr. Thrumbolt had been correct. What had been fields became covered in cool clear water. I could only imagine the concern on Daniel's face. I could only hope that Big John and Clara were still all right. This would be a temporary inconvenience.

On the third day, a carriage was seen coming up the drive. It was my brother. He looked deathly pale and gaunt. Each breath rasped within his chest, and when he coughed, a spatter of blood burst from his lungs. I quickly went into hiding in one of the sheds, and Andrew took my place.

"Can I help you sir?" Andrew inquired.

"You know why I'm here," my brother responded.

"Reckon I don't, sir."

"You stopped the stream, and I have no water for my cattle," my brother replied.

"And who might you be?" Andrew inquired.

"You know damned well that I am William Tyrill. Where are the Smithsons?"

"Sir, this farm is owned by Attorney Ward in Farmville. I am the manager of the property."

"What did you do with my water?"

"Your water, sir?"

"Yes, my water."

"Sir, the water comes from a spring located on Mr. Ward's property. Mr. Ward has elected to create a lake for fishing," Andrew lied.

"Well I need that water. I need to speak to Mr. Ward."

"Sir, you had that opportunity when you told Mr. Ward and me to get off your land. Don't you remember that?"

"So that's what this is all about, is it? I'd rather die in hell than sell the land to Mr. Ward."

"Sir, without water, your property is worthless, and when you die and go to hell, you will have nothing to show for all the years that you have worked to maintain your property."

William was weakening both physically and in his intent.

"If you remember, Mr. Tyrill, Mr. Ward had a proposition for you, but you were too disinterested to listen. If you like, I can summarize it for you."

"I'm not interested," William barked.

"Mr. Ward instructed me to inform you that, without water, there would be no need to rent your acreage anymore, and all payments will stop at the end of the month."

"Bastard!"

"Mr. Ward has a fair and decent proposition. I have a copy of it in my office if you would permit me to get it."

Andrew could see that William was weakening.

Andrew indicated that the offer, even without water, was sixteen dollars per acre for all property, including the slaves. Like the Smithsons, William could retain his residence and what was left of his social status, and no one need know that he no longer owned the farm. We again offered to place funds in an account in the bank and each year, $240 would replace what William had withdrawn as long as William was still living on the farm. Andrew also pointed out that without the deal, he could pay to have a well dug and settle up with the lawyers cleaning up the Virginia Equity mess and that he would probably lose everything when the property went up for auction.

William sat in his carriage. Without Priscilla, he was a sad, old, weak man.

"Will my house still be cleaned and my meals made?"

"Yes."

"Will I get to keep my slaves?"

"No. They are chattel and will be part of the purchase, but they will stay on the farm and continue to work."

"I worked my entire life, and what do I get?"

"Sir, you get to live out your days in freedom and dignity. You get to stay on the land and in the house. You will have a secured income, and you will maintain your social status. What you won't have is the challenge of farming. What you won't have is the risk of losing it all. What you won't have is the pressure you have right now. That's what you won't have if you can see it our way. Our offer is fair, and you know it. If you reach out to your other neighbors, I am certain that the offer won't be as generous, and you will be alone, especially after you pay off Virginia Equity the money owed."

William took a deep breath and coughed. He was in deep thought. He knew that the offer was a fair one, and yet the thought of losing his land was almost too much for him to bear.

"When would this all take place?"

Andrew responded, "I can ride into Farmville today and have Mr. Ward draw up the papers."

William nodded his head in the affirmative.

With that, Andrew reported that the old man who had been my brother turned his carriage around and headed down the lane. Unfortunately, it wouldn't be the last time I would ever see him. The papers were drawn and signed, and three weeks later a fine carriage arrived at the front of the Tyrill farmhouse. It was driven by Henry and Andrew, who held their heads up high as Miss Anna, as she had come to be known, sat in the back.

As she stepped from the carriage, there was a loud scream, and Clara almost fainted. Her adopted daughter had come home. There were tears of joy, and even Big John and Daniel smiled and hugged each other. There is no greater joy than a reunited family. Anna informed them that she was no longer the property of Mr. Bates and that she had been on the Smithsons' farm and had begun teaching school. She shared with them how Henry and I had planned everything and that our goal was to purchase the Tyrill farm. Daniel simply shook his head and smiled.

"What about the water?" Daniel asked Andrew.

"Go check the stream," Andrew replied. "It is running. We will keep it as a reservoir in case of a dry spell and also add fish so that we can have another source of food."

Our plan had worked.

A few minutes later, Mr. Ward and I arrived. William was peeking out of window at the gathering. I think he knew right then and there what had transpired.

As I dismounted, I walked up the stairs that Elizabeth and I had climbed twenty years before.

I quietly knocked on the front door of the house that I now owned. Slowly it opened as a thin, gray man opened it slightly.

"George?"

"I've come to pay for the horse I took. Here is twenty dollars."

"Keep it," he whispered, breathing hard.

"No, I owe it to you."

"Give it to the new owner, Mr. Ward," he said sarcastically.

"William, Henry and I own the farm along with Mr. Ward. I came back to pay my debts to you and to Big John and Clara."

He hadn't changed. "By stopping the flow of water to my land and then stealing it from me?"

"William, the water came from my farm. I wanted to build a lake. You were going to be evicted by Virginia Equity. I paid off the debt. I paid you a fair amount for the land. In the agreement, you can continue to live in the house and have the services of my employees, and I am paying you more than you would have earned had you attempted to farm the land yourself. Tell me, Mr. Tyrill, what have I stolen except your pride? I am a man of MY word. I have not promised a single thing that I won't keep. And now sir, if you will excuse me, I want to inspect MY property."

With that, I turned and walked out of the house. Twenty years had come and gone, and still the anger raged within me. Twenty years, and I had not forgotten that ride back from town. Twenty years, and now it was over. I would never speak to or see my brother again. Six months later, I learned they found him dead in bed. He, too, had died of the consumption ... consumption of his body, consumption of his soul, but most importantly of all, consumption of any sense of decency and dignity that had ever resided within his heart. I did not mourn his loss. I was not sad at his departure. I had lost nothing that hadn't been lost so many years before.

I asked Henry who would live in the big house, and a smile came across my face when I learned that Big John and Clara had taken up residence. They were the ones who had taken care of it. They were the ones who had ensured its dignity when there was nothing left to dignify. They were the ones, honest and dedicated, sweet and sincere, who stood by the couple who had treated them as if they were nothing more than Virginia dirt.

When I returned to Virginia the next summer, I noticed a change in Henry. There was a broader smile on his face and a little bit of a spring in his step. I ventured to guess that he had met some young lady and they were in love. Upon my second day back, my suspicions were justified. It was just that I was shocked to see who he had fallen in love with ... Anna. There was a shy smile upon her face, and I watched as their eyes would meet. I could see the emotions fire between their hearts. I had seen it so many times before and knew what it meant.

I took Henry aside and asked him point blank, "Are you and Anna, 'involved'?" Henry took a deep breath, smiled, and shook his head yes. I myself, took a deep breath and wondered what the consequences would be, he a white man and she a mulatto. I asked him if he was certain, and he shook his head "yes."

"Do you understand the consequences?" I asked. "I am happy for you son, but I also think we need to speak with Mr. Ward about this."

The next morning, I went to Farmville to examine the books and found all in order. The properties were secure, and there was no debt. I looked at my partner and asked for some personal and professional advice. I asked him to research the consequence of Henry and Anna's union if there was to be one and to provide some direction.

I guess I was shocked the next morning when Mr. Ward reported that the Virginia General Assembly passed its first miscegenation law regulating interracial marriages in 1691. Although it did not ban such unions outright, the law required that the white partner leave Virginia within three months. A 1705 revision of slave laws included a miscegenation provision that no longer required the white partner to leave; instead, it levied a fine and six months in prison. Henry could go to prison simply for marrying Anna.

Mr. Ward pointed out that this was not a new law. In fact, Virginia lawmakers had attempted to construct a biracial society that clearly differentiated among people on the basis of their race as well as status for nearly 150 years. In fact, Mr. Ward noted that an Act of Assembly, enforced in 1715, directed that all individuals with any African ancestry at all, be labeled as such.

Mr. Ward added that for Henry and Anna to continue to live in Virginia, they would be exposed to great harm and recommended they either reconsider or relocate. I returned to the farm and reported to Henry what Mr. Ward had said ... to love and marry would result in prison. If his intentions were to marry Anna, they would need to return to Wisconsin or at least leave Virginia. Henry was devastated.

"Six months isn't that long," was the response of a naive young man. He didn't think of the risks of lynching and all else that can happen when someone goes against established society and has the law against them.

I replied, "We can return to Wisconsin, and in the fall, Anna can teach at Skunk Hollow. Andrew can run the farms for two or three years. Then I will bring your brother Thomas here to help out. By then, he'll be old enough to learn the family business."

Anna didn't want to leave Big John and Clara but also realized she had no choice. She and Henry had a baby on the way, and they needed to get out of Virginia. It was 1843, and one would think that the oppression was enough. However, in 1848, the Virginia General Assembly increased that penalty to a maximum of twelve months in prison, again just for the white partner. The following year, the assembly declared that all marriages between whites and African Americans were «absolutely void.» Had Henry and Anna stayed in Virginia, things would have been bad … very, very bad.

Daniel

Before leaving for Wisconsin, I went to Mr. Ward and asked for a personal favor. I asked that he look after Daniel and determine his level of intellect. Daniel had a way about him that led me to believe that he was capable of learning almost anything he set his mind to learn. I asked Mr. Ward if it would be possible for Daniel to come to Farmville under the auspices of being his slave and that Mr. Ward determine whether Daniel had the ability to learn about law. Mr. Ward agreed to my request.

I took Daniel with me to Farmville and bought him some new clothes. I took him to the bank and had him walk in the front door with me. I went to Mr. Wallace, the bank president, and asked that we have a private meeting. Behind closed doors, I indicated to Mr. Wallace that Daniel was my nephew and was the son of the late William Tyrill. I noted that I understood the "one drop" law of Virginia that indicated that even one drop of Negro blood meant that Daniel could not be free. With that, I produced a chattel agreement signed by Mr. Ward and me transferring "ownership" of Daniel to Mr. Ward for the sum of one dollar.

I also noted to Mr. Wallace that my nephew was highly respected by me and that any form of indiscretion towards him would not sit well with me and would jeopardize our business relationship, including not only the substantial sums of money that I held in Mr. Wallace's bank but also the commerce that we were building. I also noted that Daniel was to be provided with a sum of twenty dollars per month as his stipend and that I would appreciate it if Mr. Wallace would find appropriate accommodations for my nephew, commensurate with those to which I had become accustomed. Mr. Wallace said he understood.

As we rose from our meeting, Mr. Wallace extended his hand to me, and I looked down and then towards Daniel. Mr. Wallace understood and extended his hand to Daniel. "And what might your last name be, so that we can properly address you when you visit our facilities?"

Daniel stood for a moment and responded, "Terrill. My name is Daniel George Terrill."

"As it is, Mr. Terrill! As it is!"

Daniel and I made our way back to Mr. Ward's office, and the three of us met. At that time, it was agreed that Mr. Ward was to teach Daniel the law profession and that Daniel was to serve as his assistant. Now Mr. Ward's secretary was not too keen on the idea at first, but money, lots of money, can speak much louder than the complaints of one secretary.

The next day, Henry, Anna, and I made our way back to Wisconsin. Needless to say, there was a big surprise at hand when we arrived. Elizabeth held her composure and welcomed Anna to our family. Privately, she expressed her concern for the challenges the young couple would face, and yet the smile on Henry's face, the warmth in his heart, and the joy in his soul melted any trepidation that Elizabeth had like a warm sun does to new-fallen snow on a late spring day.

Henry and Anna settled in. I'm not going to say it was easy, as anything or anyone that is different will be challenged. Elizabeth and I made certain that they always felt welcome at our home, and for the first several times Anna went into Mineral Point, either Elizabeth or I went with her. It was through tacit association that people began to see Anna for what she was … a kind, compassionate, intelligent individual. Her teaching our children and those of our neighbors was never a question, as the neighbors did not see a former slave ... they saw a woman who could help their children love and learn about all that was good and bad in our world.

I would see the frustration in Anna's eyes as people would look at her a little differently than others. I explained to her that whether a person is alone or finds only a handful of others like themselves or is among the majority of mankind is of no importance or consequence whatsoever. Numbers have nothing to do with acceptance. Whether one is alone or not, mankind is at its best when each person is accepted for "who" they are and not "what" they are. To be brave requires perseverance, as it is only through perseverance that people learn about the "who" a person is and forget about the "what." When this is allowed to happen, it truly marks mankind at its highest potential. I noted to Anna that there will always be those who find detriment in difference. There will always be those who judge others not for who they are but for what they are not. There will always be those who, regardless of the circumstance, will reside in the valley of prejudice simply because they do not have the wisdom to climb to the mountaintop and see the beauty of acceptance.

Anna looked me in the eyes and gave me a hug, for she knew that I understood the road she traveled had not always been smooth and the life she chose would never be perfect, but then, it never is for anyone.

I had been focusing on the farm when I received a letter from Mr. Ward. At first, I was concerned that business might have taken a bad turn, but that was incorrect. The subject of the letter was Daniel. Mr. Ward noted that he had already reached a point with Daniel where he felt he could no longer teach him. At first, I shook my head in disgust until I read further. It seems that in just two years, Daniel had perused all of Mr. Ward's law books and become so educated on Virginia law and court procedure that Mr. Ward indicated that he, not Daniel, had become the student.

Mr. Ward noted, "In all my years, I have never met a man so intelligent and so learned as Daniel. I cannot fathom his abilities as they exceed mine beyond my comprehension. To this end, I sincerely now conclude that I am a detriment to his education and not an asset." Signed "Humbly, J. Martin Ward."

With business going well in Wisconsin and my associations expanding to include numerous members of the legal profession, I began inquiring about where Daniel, still technically a slave, could study if given the talent he appeared to have. Harvard was mentioned, as was Princeton and Yale, but the names that came up most often that would allow Daniel to escape the bondage of his past were Oxford and Cambridge Universities in England. There, Daniel would be able to study with the greatest minds in the world and hopefully meet someone with the level of intellect he appeared to contain.

I had my "friend" Judge Doty determine which course of action was best, and he personally took it upon himself to contact a fellow in Washington, D.C., about what steps were needed for a slave to be allowed safe passage and admission to either Oxford or Cambridge University. Within a few weeks, a Major Holmes representing the U.S. Army came to visit our farm and indicated that he was instructed to assist in any way possible to ensure Daniel's safe passage to a ship in New York City to take him to England.

It was time for Thomas and me to visit Virginia, and with that, I offered to meet with whomever Major Holmes would communicate with in Farmville to accompany Daniel and me to New York. Thomas and I made our way to Virginia. Upon our arrival, a Captain Rodgers arrived at our farm from Washington with a squad of six men. He indicated that he had no idea who I was, but that Mr. James Polk himself, the newly elected president of the United States, had personally signed the orders guaranteeing Daniel's safe passage out of Virginia and out of the United States.

It must have seemed queer to those in Farmville when seven soldiers along with Thomas and I rode into town and went directly to Mr. Ward's offices. Mr. Ward was taken aback by the entourage. Captain Rodgers repeated his assignment and its source to Mr. Ward, and I feel that Mr. Ward could have been tipped over by a feather as a huge smile spread across his face.

"Daniel is in the law library," Mr. Ward directed.

"Library?" I inquired.

"A few years and twenty dollars per month can buy a lot of law books, my friend."

We entered the room and saw Daniel reading. Quickly, his hands traversed each page and flipped to the next. In a matter of seconds, each page was registering within his mind. He looked up, smiled, and stood. As he crossed toward us, he extended his hand. Instead, my arms went around his shoulders as I gave him a hug reminiscent of those given to my own children.

"What a wonderful surprise," Daniel said. "And who might these gentlemen be?" He motioned toward the soldiers.

"I have some great news, Daniel," I replied. "These gentlemen have come at the order of President Polk to escort you to New York City and assure your safe passage to England. You have been accepted at Oxford University."

Daniel was taken aback.

"Oxford? Me?"

There were tears in his eyes, and mine too. I had made good on my promise to Daniel and to myself.

"Oxford!" Daniel shook his head in disbelief and repeated, "Oxford!"

I inquired with the good captain if Daniel could first visit the farm to say goodbye to his parents, and it was agreed. We returned to my brother's former farm, and when we rode up, Big John and Clara were sitting on the front porch. It must have seemed odd to them that their son would be surrounded by soldiers, and the look on Big John's face was one of dread and utmost concern.

We all dismounted, and I introduced Captain Rodgers to Big John and Clara and outlined all that had transpired. Their fear turned to joy, their concern to jubilation. Their son was to be educated and to be free. Their prayers were answered. A gala party was held that night with all from both farms in attendance. Andrew brought his workers. The soldiers, while somewhat in disbelief that planters and slaves could mingle so freely and enjoy each other's company, quickly joined in the fun.

The next morning, Clara made a huge breakfast, and then Daniel, seven soldiers, and I departed for New York City. Along the way, many must have thought that Daniel was some sort of outlaw to be surrounded by so many members of the Calvary. However, more than one time in the past, freed slaves had attempted to leave the South only to be taken deeper into hell and never heard from again. With each mile out of Virginia, the looks became less suspicious. With each mile away from oppression, the soldiers relaxed a little more. With each mile closer to New York City, the sweet smell of freedom filled our nostrils with joy.

We arrived in New York, and accommodations were arranged for the horses, the soldiers, and me. While the government had promised protection to the ship, my concern was the voyage itself. Unscrupulous seamen had more than once taken a freed slave and sold him into oblivion. To prevent this, two elements were implemented. First, it was decided that only a ship of American registry would be used and that prior to departure, the ship would be inspected along with Daniel's quarters and that the ship's owners and then its captain made aware that Daniel was traveling under the auspices of the president of the United States and that any act against Daniel would be considered an act of treason punishable by death. The ship's owners and captain quickly understood that the cargo they were transporting was no common person but one of great value and that any event that led to any form of harm or risk to Daniel would result in dire consequences.

My second act was to contract a Mr. Allan Pinkerton for his services as bodyguard, whose only task was to accompany Daniel safely to Oxford. Fifty percent payment was made at the time of departure, and upon arrival, the second half of the service fee would be released from a bank in New York. I was required to pay for the round-trip crossing fee for the detective, but felt the investment was worth the cost, as I wanted the assurance that Daniel would not meet with any harm.

Daniel departed and eight days later arrived in England. There were no problems. Daniel George Terrill enrolled in the University of Oxford, England ... a freed slave who was about to teach the world that intelligence was not a white man's domain.

The Crash

The years were rolling by faster now. I guess that's part of life. Both sets of farms were prospering, as was the cheese factory and our inn. Lead production reached over 43,000 pounds per day in Mineral Point and was used for paint all over America and for ammunition for those who traveled west. Each day would see coaches and prairie schooners filled with settlers and tourists, capitalists and miners, all arriving in Mineral Point and all seeking the same thing ... their own fortune.

You simply could not imagine the amount of land speculation that fueled the area. People were getting rich by doing nothing more than trading paper. The Supreme Court of the United States itself had to rule on ownership of the land that many miners had been working for up to twenty years. To this end, Congress passed a law stating that, once again, we needed to pay for the land we farmed at the rate of $2.50 per acre, which we abided, as did many others.

With land prices this low and growth so fast, there were many speculators and scallywags who would buy a property one day and a few weeks later sell it for double, triple, or sometimes even four times what they paid for it. The city of Mineral Point continued to grow and prosper, with its population exceeding 2,400 individuals.

In just twelve years, from 1836 to 1848, the Territory of Wisconsin progressed toward becoming the State of Wisconsin, and most of its development was centered around our city. Mineral Point was the political center of the territory to the point that all three territorial governors—Dodge, Doty, and Tallmadge—came from our town. The future State Capitol was surveyed and platted by Frank Hudson and his men from Mineral Point. The nickname "Badgers" was conceived in Mineral Point to reflect how those of us first lived in hollowed-out caves in the river's side, and the first banking establishments in the territory and the state were located here as well.

In 1848, we reached the required 65,000 residents, and our territory became the State of Wisconsin. Madison became the state capital, and they set out building a fine palace for all those politicians to commence their arguing. I think my good friend Judge Doty got rich selling some of that swampland between the lakes. Madison's a real pretty place, and they picked a spot high on a hill between two of the four lakes to build the capitol building. Lake Wonk-sheek-ho-mik-la became Lake Mendota, which, I learned, meant "mouth or junction of one river" in Dakota, "the great lake" in Ojibwe, and "the Indian's bed or where the man lies" in the Hocak language. Whatever the Indians called it, the name became Mendota to all.

On the other side of the isthmus and less than a mile away stands a smaller lake. In Winnebago and also named by Black Hawk's Sauk nation, it was called Lake Monona, which meant "fairy water," and also called Či-hipokixake Xetera, or "Great Teepee Lake" by the Hocak nation. But a mile apart, the two lakes are as different as night and day, with Mendota being rough and powerful while Monona is a smaller and more peaceful place to be. I guess that represents government … rough and powerful in the name of peace.

I learned from friends that, for many centuries, Lake Mendota had been much smaller and contained a great deal of marshland around its edges. A gentleman named Simeon Mills, who had been postmaster and a friend of Judge Doty's, determined that by damming the Yahara River that drained much of the area, you could raise Mendota's lake level by about four feet and eliminate much of the marshland. Why would someone go to such trouble? To increase the amount of shoreline Lake Mendota offered, thereby allowing for the sale of more land along its edge. Needless to say, with the government on his side, Mr. Mills achieved his goal, and Lake Mendota became much larger while the marshland simply disappeared ... drowned in man's own definition of progress.

Elizabeth and I visited Madison many times. It stands just fifty-two miles from our home, and we always stood in awe of its natural beauty. Connecting the two lakes of Mendota and Monona, the dammed Yahara River continues to meander south through what were originally called the first and second lakes by the original surveyors. A few years ago, a developer by the name of Leonard Farwell didn't think that people wanted to live on lakes that had numbers for names and had the two lakes renamed ... Kegonsa, which means "Fish Lake," and Waubesa, which means "Swan Lake" in the Sauk native tongue.

As is the case with all politics, what was real does not always reflect reality. Madison became the "four lakes city," even though only two of the four are within its bounds and a fifth, named Wingra, which takes its name from the word for "duck" in the language of the Winnebago nation, is fed by springs which deposits its water into Lake Monona, and isn't mentioned at all.

Several of us were invited to attend the state ceremony by our neighbor, Governor Dodge, and Elizabeth and I did go. It seemed as if everything that could possibly go right was doing just that. We had the farms that were now legally ours. We had our family. We had the cheese factory and the inn, and Thomas had met and was marrying a young girl from Virginia. Add to this the fact that Henry and Anna had given us two beautiful grandchildren to carry on the Terrill name. Life was good!

As I noted, everything that could possibly go right was. However, just like farming, just when you think that all is good, something comes along and kicks you right in the teeth as if it were an irate donkey reminding you that life is a long way from perfect. In January 1848, gold was found by James W. Marshall at Sutter's Mill in Coloma, California. Word quickly spread, and it wasn't long until that little bit of gold became one great big mountain as story after story after story was told, retold, and embellished until incredible wealth was there for all the taking.

The emigration was on. Folks were leaving Wisconsin and Mineral Point by the dozens each day. On one particular day in 1850, sixty—that's right sixty—wagon teams left for California. A total of 260 people who had lived in Mineral Point were gone. With them went their money, and with that went the value of the land that had been bought on speculation. Before it was over, 700 people had departed by land or water, never to return. In a period of less than one year, Mineral Point went from 2,400 active, positive residents to under 1,700, who stood in disbelief and fear that all that they had hoped for, all that they had dreamed about, and all that they had worked so hard to build was collapsing under them like sandstone at river's edge.

Just when it looked as if our community had hit our darkest hour, the town of Mineral Point suffered its first cases of what was called malaria, with symptoms of severe chills and high fever being most prevalent. As soon as the malaria plague was over and things seemed to be settling down, Mineral Point suffered from a cholera epidemic that saw many old and weak meet their demise. With so much sickness, the Terrill family did not venture into Mineral Point for nearly six months, and when we did, we were shocked by the number of empty buildings, empty stores, and empty homes that echoed the long-lost dreams of so many who were now gone.

With the tremendous exodus, business was paralyzed, stores closed, property values fell, and promissory notes went into default. Saddest of all was the gloom on everyone's faces and the reality that the busiest place in Mineral Point was the Old City Cemetery, where so many folks came to rest. Built around the largest tree in Mineral Point, so many graves were dug around its base that the tree died, much like the community.

We thanked our lucky stars that we owned our land free and clear. People always needed to eat. Unfortunately, losing so many people so quickly severely hurt our cheese factory and disabled the inn. Worst of all was our bank, where we lost our savings again, when it collapsed.

I cannot share with you the anger and frustration one feels when a person has done what he agreed to do and others have left him short. I cannot express the frustration towards the high and mighty that had spoken of this and that and then had, for all intents and purposes, stolen our money, for which there was little or no recourse. I cannot define the despicable nature of one's own feelings when you confront one in whom you had trusted and feel as if you had been swindled. What raised my ire was their nonchalance. They had no forlorn look, they had no remorse, and above all else, they had no sense of embarrassment for what they had done.

To go to a bank that has your money and find no one there! To go to a bank that you had trusted and see it deserted! To go to a bank and begin to realize that your money and your trust had been cancelled as if nothing had ever existed ... it made me close my eyes and ask God for the strength to not lash out at the insolence. I attempted in total frustration to barter what was owed for foreclosed land only to be told that it could not happen.

The bank president sat in his fancy home and lost nothing. It was the rest of us who lost something or everything. Fortunately, we had paid for everything. We had what we had and began again at zero. With our bank savings lost, so went our social status, and those high and mighty "friends" of ours who had at one time invited us to dine with them and to be their friends suddenly forgot who we were. What was became what was not. There were no more connections to powerful people in high places. We were back where we began and, quite honestly, that was quite all right with me. Virginia was still doing quite well, and it allowed us to have the security that we needed.

We looked at the cheese factory and determined that we needed to expand our customers to include more than Mineral Point. To this end, we began hauling our cheese to Dodgeville, Mount Horeb, Darlington, Monroe, and even all the way to Madison. The profits were slimmer, but the market more stable. Now instead of selling the cheese to the person who was going to eat it, we began selling it to other stores so that our trips would be shorter and our shipments larger.

Our only business goal was to keep our family together and keep on farming. Foreclosed farms were so attractive, like a young maiden swimming in a lake so innocent, and yet their virtue was purloined … poisoned by the deeds of others, making fertile land fallow with sadness.

Several times we were provided the opportunity to expand and do so at a very reasonable price. Land that had reached twenty dollars per acre in 1848 could be purchased, if you could find the rightful owner, for as little as sixty-five cents. As opportunity after opportunity arose, the urge was there, but the loss of our savings would have meant debt, and we were in no mood for that kind of pressure. We held firm with what we had, taking each day as it came and thanking God for the bounty that we received.

Elizabeth and I stood side by side, shoulder to shoulder bearing the burdens of life. She was my partner and my bastion of strength and reason. She was the glue that held everything together. When I traveled to Virginia, the thing I always missed most was her. When the days were long, my reward was to sit with her in our spot and look out at the valley below, to watch the breeze gently blow her hair and see the glisten of the setting sun explode within her eyes. My love for her exceeded all that ever filled my body and soul. As the years progressed, that love never diminished. As our hair turned grey and our hands gnarled from work, we were still in love, madly in love with each other ... and would be forever.

Elizabeth and I had a business meeting, and it was concluded that the inn would need to close. The value was so little that it made no sense for us to attempt to sell it. Instead, we told Henry and Anna that they could live in the inn and use it as a home if they so desired. They took us up on it and filled all five of the bedrooms with their own offspring. The inn became filled with the love and laughter, happiness and joy that only come when a family is a family. What a wonderful payment.

Elizabeth had not returned to Virginia since our departure nearly thirty years before. I asked her to go with me to see the farms and visit with Thomas and his new bride. At first, she was resistant, and then I mentioned that she could also personally thank Big John and Clara for all they had done for us and see what we had done for them. That seemed to be the log that tipped the scale, and it was agreed. Henry would assume total responsibility for the farms and cheese factory, Anna would tend to the school and keep an eye on Sarah, Dora, and Mathew, who were old enough to be somewhat on their own, yet too young to know any better.

It was June 1852 when we set off for Virginia. Instead of by horse, it was by carriage. Instead of with a guide, it was with my wife. Those five days alone with her were filled with the joy of each other's company as we laughed about silly things, lamented about the mistakes we made, and chuckled at our good fortune.

Upon our arrival at the Smithson farm, we were greeted by the workers and made to feel welcome. From the main house, a young woman appeared. Quite tall and lean with light brown hair. I could see right away why Thomas had been attracted to her. She had a shy smile about her and yet an air of confidence. Her name was Annabelle Lee, but she went by the name of Abby.

As Abby strode across the lawn, there was a bounce in her step, a gleam in her eye, and both Lizzie and I knew right away that we were going to approve. She had that Southern twang to her voice that softens all words and makes them melt like butter on a warm stack of flapjacks. She had manners, too. Everything was "yes, sir ... no, sir!" and "yes, ma'am ... no, ma'am!" She also was educated, knew her numbers, and could read quite well. I also saw a strong spirit in her that said she would take no guff, and that too made me happy that Thomas had found someone to share his life with.

Dinners were spent reflecting on all that had happened ... both good and bad, serious and funny regarding Thomas growing up. I think Abby enjoyed learning about her husband and his tomfoolery.

As our time extended, it was agreed that we would meet Abby's parents, and a grand picnic was planned at the farm. It was to be a family get-together and what many would probably consider a wedding reception. Andrew made all the plans and introduced us to his lady friend from Farmville. I knew that he wouldn't be returning to Wisconsin with us. You could see that in his eyes and feel it in his heart.

As the big day arrived, my Lizzie was quite nervous. With Henry, there had been no ceremony, and what family Anna had was long lost in the world of chattel and subservience. We loved her as if she was our own daughter, and it made no difference. We sat in the shade and awaited the arrival of Abby's parents, not really knowing what to expect. As we peered out into the valley, we saw the approach of a carriage being pulled by two white horses. Seated in front was a black man dressed to the nines. Behind him sat a tall man with snow white hair and a lady dressed as if going to a ball. My God, did we feel out of place.

The carriage arrived, and Abby came out of the house and went to greet her parents. It all seemed so formal and so much more than we were accustomed to. I remember her introducing me to Colonel Borgard Lee and his wife, Isabelle. I shook hands with Mr. Lee and felt his firm grip, something I always appreciated in a man. Small talk was had, and the ladies excused themselves and went into the house. Thomas, the Colonel, and I retired to the chairs beneath the old oak tree.

It is always interesting when you meet someone who is accustomed to authority. There is an air about them. The way they look at you. The way they walk. Even the way they talk. It is so much different than regular folks. The first topics were about our travels ... he from Richmond and us from Wisconsin. He said he couldn't imagine living where it was so cold. I told him that, like everything else in life, you get used to it and that winter was like sleep and always reminded me of peace and tranquility. As the conversation moved on, we spoke of Thomas and Abby, and we both agreed about their happiness and how it was shared by all.

I learned a long time before this conversation that there were two things you never talked about ... politics and religion. Mr. Lee must not have heard that rule, and it wasn't long before the discussion of religion began. He asked my faith, and I said Methodist. He said he was Baptist and assumed that the children would be raised as such. Not wanting to get into any form of extended discussion, I said that it would be up to Thomas and Abby and was certainly not my say. He seemed to catch my drift and let the topic die.

Next came politics. He heard we were paying the slaves and thought that it was ridiculous and set a poor example for other planters in the area. I told him of how Elizabeth and I had come to visit my brother and how, without the generosity of Big John and Clara, we would never have been allowed to leave and move to Wisconsin. He wondered out loud where two slaves came up with ten dollars and made an off-the-cuff remark that it was probably stolen.

He asked what farming was like in Wisconsin, and I outlined the seasons and the milking and the cheese factory. He noted that the money crop in the South was cotton. In fact, nearly one million tons of cotton were grown each year in the South. It took more labor, but the rewards far outweighed the investment. He was incredulous to think that we actually had to pay for help and wondered how we could possibly make money milking cows. I noted that it was hard work, but we had done well and that the only losses we had taken were my ill-fated brewery and when the bank had failed. He noted that the South was all plantations, and without the labor of the slaves, they could not exist.

As the conversation moved on, I could see where he was going. He was pro-slavery and expected Thomas and Abby to rescind the wages and keep the status quo. Now my mind was not to argue with Thomas's in-laws, but it was also my mind to let the Colonel know that our farms were working farms based on mutual trust, mutual respect, and mutual reward and that, in implementing our payment plan to reflect those values, our bottom line had dramatically increased. There was no need for a slave master. There was no need for whips and chains. What there was, was need for more land and more opportunity, and my goal was to continue to expand our Virginia holdings and continue to reap the bounty of our investment.

The Colonel was not a stupid man, and yet he wanted the last word, to which he inferred that, for the good of our neighbors and the good of the South, it was best to return to the way it had been for two hundred years and not try to put false hopes in the minds of others. He noted that slaves were not naturally intelligent enough to be educated and thought our school was for naught. I pointed out that Daniel, who had been a slave, was studying law at Oxford.

I inquired, "if Daniel was too stupid to learn, why was it that in a period of less than oner year he went from student to teacher for Attorney Ward." The Colonel said that he thought Mr. Ward must have been a fool to let a slave teach him law. I noted that it was not by education, but by example. Daniel had absorbed so much that questions asked by Mr. Ward were answered by Daniel before researching the law books, where Daniel quoted laws and decisions that helped Mr. Ward prepare for trial.

The Colonel just shook his head. "A slave at Oxford ... in England," he repeated. "What will happen next?"

I was waiting for the last volley, and it was my time.

"What is coming next is that Daniel has his choice between Harvard and Yale. He is graduating first in his class and is a Rhodes Scholar. He has been offered fellowships to earn his PhD and perhaps either become a judge or teach jurisprudence at either school."

The Colonel sat dumbfounded. "A slave at Harvard or Yale? Well that certainly wouldn't happen at the University of Virginia."

"No, sir, it would not ... not right now anyway," I said with a slight smile on my face.

The conversation was going nowhere, and the goal of the evening was to enjoy each family's company. The ladies were getting along splendidly, but the Colonel and I were far apart on many things, neither of us willing to budge an inch. He coveted keeping all things as they were. I aspired to change so that the words Elizabeth and I had read so long ago on that building in the Baltimore Harbor really had meaning ... "and liberty and justice for all." I know the Colonel and I did not become friends that night, but then I have always picked and chosen my friends wisely.

We were in Virginia but one month, and it was time to return to Wisconsin and home. Virginia was on its own. Once again, I saw that Mr. Ward and Thomas were working well together, and the structure they built in terms of the "slaves" was such that there was honor, dignity, and respect on all sides. The long ride home commenced, and as Elizabeth sidled up next to me, I knew that she approved of all that had transpired and that my decisions had met with her satisfaction.

Our journey home was without incident, and, as always, it was wonderful to sleep in our own bed, in our own house, on our own farm. By now, the young ones had reached an age where Skunk Hollow school was beyond their realm. They coveted more, and so daily excursions into Mineral Point became the norm. On most days, there was just the same routine, every now and then punctuated by this event or that, intended to mark the standard and eclipse normalcy. As summers came, the daily excursions to Mineral Point would wither as the children would assist in helping on the farm.

The Peddler

Being a farmer and the child of a farmer is such that you are more isolated and innocent than those who are raised within the social environs of a town. You become naïve, more willing, more adventurous, more susceptible, and, sadly, more open and prone to the consequences of the actions of others.

Peddlers would periodically come to our farm. It was common that these men would load up their wares and then travel from farm to farm as they headed west. In their wagon, they would have a plethora of bric-a-brac that included everything from pots and pans to the newest of liniments. We were always polite, and Elizabeth would take time from her chores to listen to their claims about this or that and how it would make her life better than it had ever been before.

One quiet summer's day, a man appeared with a wagon filled with his nonsense. He was one of those fast-talkers, and before long, both Elizabeth and our daughter Dora were enamored by his spiel. Elizabeth eventually had her fill and decided against any purchase. But Dora was spellbound by this barker and his talk of far-away places and exotic life. At the age of just fourteen, little did she know of this kind of man.

As he packed his wagon, he asked if she could show him the farm. Being naïve and innocent, little did she realize his intent. As they walked the land, he took advantage of her in a very bad way, taking away her innocence and scarring her for life. He warned her that one word would mean her demise. She buckled under his threats, consumed by tears and remorse. As he walked back to his wagon, he had a smug smile upon his face, for he thought that he had taken advantage of my little Dora and that she would never say a word.

A man's eyes can tell you an awful lot about what is in his heart. When eyes glisten, it is usually with joy or fear! When they are dull, people are nearly dead or ambivalent to all that is good in life, in love, and in other people.

As he was about to reach his wagon, our son Mathew saw Dora and knew in an instant what had happened. Instead of the barker stepping up on his wagon, Mathew drove him to the ground.

I happened out of the barn and commenced to intercede when I saw Dora and immediately realized what had taken place. While Mathew was younger and already stronger than me, he did not have the wrath of a father provoked. I took it upon myself to begin to pummel this man with all my might. The ferocity of my advances were such that within a few moments this monster lie on the ground quivering in fear.

"Get a rope," I directed Mathew. With that, he was off to the barn.

The interloper attempted to get up, but one swift, very powerful kick to his privates sent him into folded pain so great that I thought he would relieve himself right there.

"What are you doing?" he pleaded.

"You know goddamn well what I'm doing," I responded. "You son of a bitch! You took advantage of my daughter."

"I did not," he lied.

With that, I kicked him again, this time in the face. Blood spurted from his broken nose as Mathew came back with the rope. "I should hang you right here. Right now!"

Elizabeth came out of the house and saw the altercation. She glanced at me and then at Dora and knew that my anger was justified. She took Dora in her arms and felt her quiver as her raw emotions poured forth. For the only time in her life, I heard my Lizzie swear. "Kill the bastard," she roared. "Kill him, or I will."

The peddler saw the wrath of a mother whose child had been violated. He felt the heat of her hatred. He knew that what he had done meant grave consequences for him, and yet through it all came a wicked smile.

He tried to respond. "She ... I ... we." But I kicked him again, and down he fell.

My choice was now what to do with this rapist. Did I take him to town and let the sheriff put him in jail? For what, I pondered? So that he could get out and do it again? Did I hang him and toss his body in his wagon and send it on its way? My anger was so intense, my sadness so profound that I did not think that a quick death was good enough for this coward.

Once again, I kicked him. This time in the stomach. He curled in pain, unable to move.

"Tie him up," I directed Mathew. With that, my son tied his hands behind his back and put the rope around his neck and sat the peddler up. He was in pain. His nose spewed forth dark red plumes of blood while he quivered in fear. Even with his demise, he had a look of contempt in his eyes and retained that wicked smile. My heart knew that he had no remorse. My soul knew that the good Lord would not mind if I took the Fifth Commandment and made it mine as I was now certain that this bastard had had his way with many before my Dora.

"A quick death for you is not to be. You need to visit your own purgatory and let God decide where you shall go for eternity."

The peddler had no idea what I was referring to, nor did my family. I instructed Elizabeth to take Dora into the house. I instructed Mathew to get me a hammer. I am certain he thought that I was going to beat the peddler to death. Once again, Mathew ran to the barn.

"For you, there is no punishment great enough, and ye, I have a way that will allow you to wallow in the face of death until that time when you beg to die."

Mathew returned with the hammer as I wrapped the rope tighter around the peddler's neck and tied him to the wagon wheel. I picked up the pitchfork that I had been using and handed it to Mathew. "If he moves, run him through and don't let him out of your sight."

Mathew nodded in total acceptance as he placed the tines of the fork against the interloper's neck.

I was furious. My anger was growing by the moment. My daughter! My lovely daughter! Slowly I walked behind the house and into the privy. I took the hammer and removed the seat. The smell was almost more than I could bear, and yet the sweet smell of revenge filled my nostrils. I walked back and found Mathew and the peddler as I had left them. "Get up," I commanded.

The peddler remained on the ground. With that, I took the pitchfork and stuck it deeper under his throat. "Either get up now or die right here."

He could tell by my earnestness that he had but one option and began slowly to rise. "I need to get the sheriff and let him decide what to do with you. Until then, I need to keep you in a place worthy of your deed."

I grabbed the rope and pulled him to his feet with my son watching my every move. I tightened the rope around his neck so that any move could be his last and threw him over my shoulders as he gasped for air. Leading him behind the house, I spun him around and the peddler's eyes widened with profound apprehension. I sensed that he felt I would lock him in the privy and go get the sheriff. I pulled him into the privy, and his knees buckled when he saw that the seat had been removed and there stood an open cauldron full of human waste. He attempted to block my efforts to force him into the cubicle, but my anger and my strength and the rope around his neck were too much for him.

"No, no, no," he begged, but I was of no mind to change my course of action.

I beckoned Mathew to come and assist me as I took the son of a bitch and leaned him over the open hole. "This is your punishment. This is what you deserve." With that, Mathew and I removed the ropes and dumped him into the hole filled with human waste and watched as he began to sink until he was up to his neck.

He attempted to jump up and grab the opening, and when he had a grip, I took the hammer in my hands and pounded on his fingers until they were smashed, watching him fall again into the muck where he belonged. With that, I pounded the seat back in place. The interloper fell back down into the abyss, and the darkness of his confinement was only overwhelmed by the stench of his existence.

Mathew exited, and I opened my trousers and urinated on him. This wretched man would stand in shit until either he died or the sheriff got him out. As we walked from the privy, I installed one last form of insurance. I nailed a board across the door such that there would be no way for him to escape and no one could get in. I looked at Mathew and he at me, and my son realized that justice was about to be served. "I'll wait until tomorrow and go get the sheriff," I reported.

Mathew looked me in the eye with a sense of wonder, and a degree of admiration fell upon his face. He had not seen this side of his father. For the first time, he saw a man full of anger, full of spite, and full of revenge ... a man who had taught him honor, justice, and dignity ... who now showed him the consequence of wrath so great when someone, anyone, took it upon themselves to harm one of his children.

That afternoon and evening, the shouts from the privy were almost non-stop, their intensity so great that I knew that the peddler's escape would be my demise. I did not waver. I listened for the silence that only comes from surrender, when even the dastardly realize that they have no choice but to abide.

That night, Elizabeth tended to Dora and did all that a mother could to help her wounded child. There were tears and affirmations— "That's all right. That's all right. That's all right"—as Elizabeth comforted my little girl. I knew that she would never be the same. I knew that she walked on broken glass. I prayed that she would recover her joy and innocence. I swore that the man who had been so cruel would never walk the face of the earth again.

Elizabeth asked what had transpired. I quietly told her that the peddler was spending the night in the privy. I did not go into details about where the man was placed—only that he was inside.

We all used the chamber pots, and then in the morning, I went out and poured it down upon the peddler's head. He was still alive, but his anger had turned to remorse. "I'm sorry" was his whisper as I ignored his pleas and opened my pants and relieved myself on him once again.

Mathew and I drove the wagon into town and to the sheriff's office. I explained what had happened and where the man was, and a wry smile came upon the sheriff's normally serious face. "Well, I'm awfully busy right now, George. How about if I stop by in a day or two?

With that, Mathew and I rode our horses home. Nary a word was said as I got the milkers and began digging a new privy about twenty feet from where the current one stood. Two days later, the sheriff arrived, and I took him to see the peddler. The man was slumped and supported by all that was within. We got a pail of water and poured in on the peddler's head, to which he looked up at us with a hollow stare as his head tilted back one last time.

"How's little Dora?" the sheriff asked.

"Not so good," I replied.

"My prayers are with you," the sheriff responded. "I think you need to fill in the privy and move on with life, George. Next time don't make the hole so big that a man could accidentally fall in."

I knew not the man's name, nor whence he came. I knew not if he would be missed or if there was anyone anywhere who would care that he had left this earth ... not as a man, but as a thief ... not as one who stole goods, but one who stole purity and innocence. Had he taken goods or money, I would have asked why. Had he needed it, I would have willingly shared, but to steal what he stole, to do what he did, left me no recourse than to make sure that it never, ever happened again.

With that, the sheriff rode off. Never a word was ever said about what happened to the peddler or why we dug a new privy. None of the milkers were aware of the changes as Mathew and I poured the dirt from the new hole into the old until all that was left were horrible memories. There was no grave, and certainly no headstone. In a matter of weeks, weeds had grown where the hole had been and life went on.

My little Dora was scared and scarred. Her innocence was gone. All she knew was that the man was gone forever. She had no idea that he lay where he did. All that she knew was that the days of silly dreams were washed away like tiny footprints on a dusty road after a heavy rainstorm. With each day, she returned a little bit more, but she never returned to her ways and never did she marry. Instead, she has lived with me and continues to do so even today ... alone, but not lonely, sad but not forlorn, tormented yet appeased to know that her daddy had taken the demon away. How sad it is when a few moments can change the life of another forever. How can a land be so beautiful yet so ugly? How can a land be so free and yet filled with oppression? How can humans be so inhuman as to violate another?

Three times in my life, I had seen it. Three times in my life, I felt it. Three times in my life, I shared the horror and the shame that took innocence and shattered it upon the ground in a million pieces. While there should have been regret for what I had done, there was none. While there should have been remorse for what I did, there was none. While there should have been pain for the dead man buried in my privy, there was none. Instead there was only relief. There was relief that a monster had been destroyed, and with him, the chance that some other innocent young girl would be destroyed. We went to church, and I got down on my knees and prayed to God for forgiveness. As I knelt there, I felt His hand upon my shoulder and sensed that it was all right ... an eye for an eye ... justice had been done.

Mineral Point and the World

From my perspective, the 1840s represented the greatest period of growth for our area. In 1847 alone, fifty new buildings were built in Mineral Point only to double in 1848. Tons of copper—yes, copper—were being smelted each year, and although mining was still king, stores were selling more plows and farm implements to people like me as our fields came closer and closer and closer to the mine shafts that existed.

I have spoken of the challenge of getting lead and crops to market, and even though the roads to Galena and Madison and even Platteville and Belmont had been improved, they were not set for heavy commerce. While changes had been made so that the lead was hauled by oxen to Milwaukee and put on ships in the Great Lakes, we all knew that the answer to getting all of our products to market centered around the railroad.

To this end, the Mineral Point Railroad was finally formed in 1851 with the goal of connecting Mineral Point to the Illinois Central Railroad at Warren, Illinois, thirty-two miles away so that it would connect with the new Illinois Central planned to traverse from Chicago to Galena. Work was begun with stops in Calamine, Darlington, and Gratiot before crossing the state line and reaching Warren. Thus, a connection with the Illinois Central would allow Mineral Point lead and produce to reach the east and allow modern goods to come into Mineral Point.

In 1853, groundwork had been completed and bids let for construction with the winning bid of around $700,000. While dreams existed, reality was such that there wasn't enough money to build the railroad spur, and without the railroad spur, many thought our community would see the return of the social devastation experienced during the Gold Rush of 1849, and no one wanted that. When funds weren't there, the State of Wisconsin authorized all communities that were to benefit from the line to participate in its cost. When that was not enough, the county issued 150 bonds at $1,000 each, but the original company had had enough and pulled out of the entire project.

The second company agreed to complete the project for one million dollars. The work commenced until the second company went bankrupt. Now it was up to the communities to commit to our future. I spoke with our neighbors, and it was agreed that we would become a township. The name Waldwick was selected, and we, the members of the community of Waldwick, committed $10,000 towards the completion of the railroad with Mineral Point, with the town of Mineral Point adding $150,000 more.

Construction of the rail line began in 1856, and the station house was built and the line commenced operation between Mineral Point and Warren in 1857. The single train left Warren each day at 9:30 in the forenoon and arrived in Mineral Point at noon. It left Mineral Point at 2:00 in the afternoon and arrived in Warren at 5:00 p.m. What had taken a day to travel in the past could now be done in two and a half hours. The line carried 9,100 persons that very first year, while also hauling 4.5 million pounds of wheat, 3.4 million pounds of lead, 1.8 million pounds of oats, 190,000 pounds of pork, 78,000 pounds of hides, and 65,000 pounds of corn.

Mineral Point was becoming a commercial center, and those in the community who cared quickly learned that our sequestered life was changing rapidly as we were woven into the tapestry of our country socially, politically, and economically. Gone were the days of isolation and total independence. We were integrated in and not only reaped the bounty of those who had prospered elsewhere but assumed the responsibilities of being American citizens. By 1859, Mineral Point had become a commercial hub. The city covered two square miles and included 637 buildings, of which more than half were brick or stone. There were eight hotels, five churches, two schools, two newspapers, and one bank, along with dozens of retail stores and shops that provided dry goods and food to the residents.

Milwaukee

When one peers into a looking glass and sees an old man looking back, it can come as a shock. The year was 1859. I was already sixty-one years old. I had five grandchildren by Henry and Anna, and Thomas and Abby had given us two more. Henry's boys were reaching the point of being adults when it seemed like just yesterday they sat on my lap and I sang old Cornish lullabies to them. Mathew was married to Mabel Farrell and lived on one of the farms down in Jonesdale. Sarah had met a young man, and her eyes were full of stars, and there was always a smile upon her face.

Elizabeth's and my walk to "our" spot upon the hill each night seemed to take a little longer than before, but that didn't matter as we were together and yet alone, enveloped in each other's lives as man and wife, loving and sharing the bounty we had both worked so hard to acquire. Dora was alone, but at peace in her world of daisies and daffodils that grew in the fields. Skunk Hollow continued to produce young children with open minds and hearts who were never taught why the color of one's skin made one person any better than the next. Thank you, Anna!

The Wisconsin farms held their own, and each day Mathew grew into the man that I knew he would become. Henry had taken his mother's sense and had gone into the world of banking. When the Mineral Point bank failed, Henry sensed an opportunity and was quick to act and became president and part-owner. Thomas and Mr. Ward retained the Virginia partnership and purchased yet another farm adjacent to the two we already owned. They did not switch to cotton like every-one else and continued to grow tobacco, corn, and hay to feed the live-stock. Daniel was at Harvard and was involved in post-doctorate law. Dr. Daniel Terrill ... what a wonderful sound! Later it would become Judge Daniel Terrill. Our hope was for the Supreme Court, but that would not happen.

Henry came to me and asked if I would like to accompany him to Milwaukee. The city was growing rapidly, and he had business there. It was September 1859, the farm was running smoothly, and there was to be the Wisconsin Agricultural Society meeting and agricultural fair. I thought, "Why not?" We traversed the terrain, stopping in Madison and then Jefferson and then Waukesha before reaching Milwaukee. While Henry tended to his banking business, I walked about and saw a city in bloom. The shoreline of Lake Michigan was resplendent with sailing boats, and the water as deep and as blue as I could imagine.

By early Saturday afternoon, Henry's work was complete, and we made our way to the Cold Spring race course. We meandered through the livestock and listened to this and that and were about to leave when we saw a small crowd gathering. I asked a gentleman standing at the edge what was about to transpire, and he said some Illinois Con-gressman named Abraham Lincoln was going to speak on economics.

Henry and I took our place amongst the 200 to 300 fellow farmers in attendance as Mr. Lincoln took his place. He was a tall lanky man with long, bony fingers that he used to make a point as he raised them into the sky.

Mr. Lincoln stood on an empty dry goods box with his tall gaunt body trembling with emotion as he expressed the travails of our land of the free, which he felt to be in imminent danger. I watched as the lines of sadness etched their way deeper across his face and into his heart and soul. Mr. Lincoln was not a very good speaker that day. He spoke in a dry, nonpolitical tone, but his speech did reflect his attention to detail and orientation on economic issues, which I felt our family understood better than most owning land on both sides of the mindset.

As I stood with Henry, my mind wandered. Who was this man? He did not speak eloquently, and yet there was a decency and passion that he evoked. People came and went, and no one thought anything of it. He did not captivate many in the audience besides me. The address itself was such that Mr. Lincoln quietly outlined the ingredients that made our Wisconsin society free as he contrasted two competing economic systems in America ... one in which laborers were hired to work for others and one in which laborers were compelled to work, oppressed, simply because of the color of their skin.

As Mr. Lincoln concluded, applause was polite and yet short, and for many, the attractions of the day were much more than some lanky congressman from Illinois. But Henry and I felt we had seen a messiah ... someone who understood what we felt, someone who could comprehend all our emotions and equivocate them into words.

As the meeting was disbanding, we learned that the next day, Mr. Lincoln would speak again in Beloit, and I urged Henry that we should attend. It was a little out of our way, and yet I felt compelled to listen to the man once again. We traveled the sixty-five miles to hear him again and were even more inspired. We learned that Mr. Lincoln was traveling to Janesville, only fifteen miles away, and would speak again that evening.

Once again, I urged Henry that we should attend. While my words are humble, I leave it to those who were there with us to share what they heard as was reported in the Janesville Morning Gazette.

Mr. Lincoln "enquired why slavery existed on one side of the Ohio River and not on the other? Why did we find that institution in Kentucky, and not in Ohio? There was very little difference in the soil or the climate, and the people on one side of the line loved liberty as well as on the other. The northern portion of Kentucky was opposite free territory, while the southern portions of Ohio, Indiana, and Illinois, had neighbor states in which slavery existed. Indiana while a territory had petitioned Congress three times to allow them to introduce slavery. Mr. Lincoln said there could be no other reason than that it was prohibited by congress. If it had been left to the people, as proposed by Mr. Douglas, a few slaves would have found a place there—if ten thousand had been admitted into Ohio while she was a territory, many questions would have been presented that would have been embarrassing, which would not have perplexed the people if slavery had been prohibited by congress—the question would have come up, what shall we do with these ten thousand slaves? Shall we make them free and destroy property which people supposed they possess? If they abolished slavery what would they do with the negroes?

"These questions would be troublesome and difficult to decide. The power of this amount of property in the hands of wealthy and educated men, who would most likely own the slaves, would in the end prevail and slavery would be established; whereas if congress had prohibited it until the state constitution was about to be formed, slavery and freedom would start upon an equal platform, and without the embarrassing questions named—freedom in this case would prevail and slavery would be prohibited. Slavery comes gradually into territory where it is not prohibited without notice, and without alarming the people, until having obtained a foothold, it cannot be driven out.

"Thus, we see that in all the new states where slavery was not prohibited, it was established. In Kentucky, Tennessee, Mississippi, Alabama, Louisiana, Arkansas, and Missouri, the principle of popular sovereignty prevailed—congress permitted the people to establish the institution of slavery if they pleased. In all these instances, where they had their choice, slavery had been introduced; but, on the contrary, in all the new states, where slavery had been prohibited, and where popular sovereignty had no choice until state constitutions were formed, the states have prohibited slavery in their constitutions; such was the case in Ohio, Indiana, Illinois, Michigan, Wisconsin, Iowa, California, and Minnesota. In California it had been prohibited by the old Mexican law, which was not abrogated before California became a state. Minnesota was a territory five years after the Missouri Compromise was repealed but commenced its settlement with a congressional restriction against slavery.

"It is therefore evident if the principle of popular sovereignty becomes the settled policy of the country, that slavery will have a great advantage over freedom, and the history of the country proves this to be true.

"Mr. Lincoln said that he had failed to find a man who five years ago had expressed his belief that the Declaration of Independence did not embrace the colored man. But the public mind had become debauched by the popular sovereignty dogma of Judge Douglas. The first step down the hill is the denial of the Negro's rights as a human being. The rest comes easy. Classing the colored race with brutes frees from all embarrassment the idea that slavery is right if it only has the endorsement of the popular will."

"Douglas has said that in a conflict between the white man and the Negro, he is for the white man, but in a conflict between the Negro and the crocodile, he is for the Negro. Or the matter might be put in this shape. As the white man is to the Negro, so is the Negro to the crocodile. But the idea that there was a conflict between the two races, or that the freedom of the white man was insecure unless the Negro was reduced to a state of abject slavery, was false and that as long as his tongue could utter a word he would combat that infamous idea. There was room for all races and as there was no conflict so there was any necessity of getting up an excitement in relation to it."

All that I felt for so many years had been expressed so eloquently. Oppression. Repression. Dominance. Subservience. All in the name of commerce and protected and sanctified by a government that promised, in its very foundation, to be the land of the free. I had seen it. I had felt it. I had endured it. For the first time, my thoughts were personified.

I stood and listened, and tears filled my eyes. A man had been sent to open my heart and let it see that my thoughts were not alone ... that other people ... important people ... shared my conclusions. We stayed in Janesville that night, but I could not sleep. The words of a plain, nervous, lanky man from Illinois had awakened my heart and aroused my spirits.

The ride home from Janesville was quiet with both Henry and I deep in our thoughts. When we reached the juncture to continue to Mineral Point or home to Waldwick, Henry and I stopped and dismounted. I looked my son in the eye and he in mine, and we embraced ... a father-son embrace ... that held for an instant too long as we garnered each other's might, knowing that what we had seen was truly right.

I breathed deeply the sweet country air and thanked Henry. Had he not asked, I would have never gone. Had we not gone, I would have never seen. Had I not seen, I would never have learned the beauty and majesty that only comes from dignity. Dignity to stand up in front of others and share your beliefs, your values, and your inspirations. I looked Henry in the eyes and smiled. I needn't say another word.

We got on our horses and headed home. He to Mineral Point and me to Waldwick ... both of us filled with the tension of excitement knowing that we had seen the beginnings of greatness and basked in the glow of a man so humble, yet so spectacular, as to take every ounce of energy in our body and align it with his, in the direction of tomorrow.

What can a man say about war when he has never been? How can a man feel the terror that must reside within the minds of those whose only job is to take the life of another for a cause they may or may not believe in? How can a man fight for something he knows so little about ... especially when it could be brother against brother? How sad the fate of war whose only goal is to destroy ... property, family, and lives.

The storm clouds began to appear on the horizon as the difference in agriculture between what became the North and South became more diverse. The North had cities and industry, and our farming was becoming mechanized with such things as the McCormick reaper that took the work of ten men and made it one. The South had turned to cotton as the Colonel said it would. The problem was that cotton need-ed to be hand-picked, and that meant even more workers were needed to get the job done.

As territories became states, each passed their own constitution that set down the rules upon which each state within the United States was to be governed, including the rights of the residents who lived there. For some states in the North, there were clear rules regarding freedom. For some states in the South, there were mentions of who was and who was not a free man. The challenge came in those states that traversed the Northern and Southern mentalities. Were they to be free states or slave states?

In order for me to write what I am about to share, I had to confer with my nephew Daniel, for he had become an expert on the subject. In his correspondence, Daniel referred to a case that went all the way to the United States Supreme Court about a man named Dred Scott who was a slave. Once again, I turn to the words of another, not out of avarice, but simply to make sure I share the story correctly.

It seems that Mr. Scott was born in Virginia around 1800, about the time I was born, and was the property of a Mr. Peter Blow, who took Mr. Scott with him to Alabama and then, in 1830, to St. Louis, Missouri.

Mr. Blow died in 1832, and Mr. Scott was sold to a Dr. John Emerson, who took Mr. Scott with him in 1833 to Illinois. When Illinois entered the Union in 1818, its constitution included the words, "Neither slavery nor involuntary servitude shall herein be introduced into this state otherwise than for the punishment of crimes." This fancy wording allowed residents who already owned slaves to retain them as property. As Daniel pointed out, this went right in the face of what the federal government had set as law with the United States Ordinance of 1787, which prohibited slavery in the Northwest Territory that included Illinois and Wisconsin.

In 1836, Dr. Emerson was reassigned to Fort Snelling, which at that time was in the Wisconsin Territory, and took Mr. Scott with him. While at Fort Snelling, Mr. Scott met and married a slave named Harriet Robinson, and her ownership was transferred to Dr. Emerson. The doctor left the Scotts behind when the Army transferred him back to St. Louis and then to Louisiana. In Louisiana, Dr. Emerson married a Miss Sanford and requested the Scotts join him there.

The couple willingly moved back to St. Louis, where the doctor died in 1843. Mr. Scott offered Mrs. Emerson $300 for their manumission, which Daniel told me meant their freedom. Mrs. Emerson refused. Both Mr. and Mrs. Scott took the matter to court, filing separately, based on the facts that they had lived for extended periods in the free Northwest Territory and Mr. Scott had lived in a free state. Daniel said that their claim to freedom was based on the 1824 Missouri Supreme Court decision in Winny v. Whitesides, which established the standard, "once free, always free" in cases of this matter.

In June 1847, Mr. Scott's case was tossed out of court on what Daniel called a technicality. The reason given was that Mr. Scott could not prove that he and Harriet were owned by Mrs. Emerson. In 1850, the couple was granted their freedom. However, Mrs. Emerson appealed. In 1852, the Missouri Supreme Court overturned twenty-eight years of Missouri law and took both Mr. and Mrs. Scott's freedom away. It was during this hearing that Mrs. Emerson's lawyer introduced the argument questioning the authority of the U.S. Congress to prohibit slavery in the territories. In other words … states' rights upon which a godawful war was fought.

In 1853, Mr. Scott sued his current owner, who was Mr. John Sanford, Mrs. Emerson's brother. This time, Mr. Scott went to federal court because Mr. Sanford had moved to New York. The trial took place in 1854, where a Judge Wells directed the jury to rely on Missouri law to settle the question of Scott's freedom. Since the Missouri Supreme Court had held that Mr. Scott remained a slave, the jury found in favor of Mr. Sanford.

Mr. Scott then appealed to the U.S. Supreme Court, where Mr. Scott was represented by a Mr. Blair and Mr. Curtis, who had counsel from none other than one Dr. Daniel Terrill, noted law authority at Harvard University. The case was heard by the seven justices, and their ruling was handed down on March 6, 1857, just two days after President-elect James Buchanan's inauguration that was timed to curtail some of the anger brewing on both sides.

Chief Justice Taney delivered the opinion of the Court, with each of the concurring and dissenting justices filing their own opinions. Daniel wrote that six justices agreed with the ruling and two dissented. While this will probably seem long and drawn out, it was so important that I asked Daniel to share it with me, and then I with you.

Daniel wrote that there were three questions before the Supreme Court:

The first question was whether the Supreme Court had jurisdiction to hear Mr. Scott's case. To this Daniel wrote: "It was his belief and what was argued was that the relevant basis for jurisdiction in this case is known as 'diversity jurisdiction,' which is found in Article III, Section 2, Clause 1 of the U.S. Constitution, and provided that 'the judicial Power shall extend to controversies between citizens of different States. ...' Mr. Scott declared he was a 'citizen' of the State of Missouri and that the defendant was a citizen of the State of New York and therefore Mr. Scott was eligible for a trial in a federal court and not that of Missouri.

"However, Mr. Sanford's lawyer argued that Mr. Scott was a descendant of an imported African slave and was therefore not a 'citizen' of any State. Mr. Scott's lawyers did not dispute his ancestry, but said that due to all that had happened and where he had lived, he had been emancipated and therefore could have the status of 'citizen.'"

Daniel continued that the Supreme Court ruled that neither Mr. Scott nor any person of African descent who had been emancipated from slavery could be a "citizen of a state" and therefore Mr. Scott could not bring suit in federal court on the grounds of the diversity jurisdiction.

According to Chief Justice Taney, the authors of the Constitution had viewed all people of color as "beings of an inferior order, and altogether unfit to associate with the white race, either in social or political relations, and so far inferior that they had no rights which the white man was bound to respect." Justice Taney also noted that "the diversity jurisdiction would give to persons of the Negro race ... the right to enter every other State whenever they pleased, ... to sojourn there as long as they pleased, to go where they pleased ... the full liberty of speech in public and in private upon all subjects upon which its own citizens might speak; to hold public meetings upon political affairs, and to keep and carry arms wherever they went."

In Daniel's note, he indicated that this meant that even though he personally was a legal expert and was repeatedly sought as counsel for many of the greatest lawyers in New York City and Washington, D.C., he himself had no rights and was not a citizen.

The second question dealt with the Missouri Compromise of 1820 and whether Congress compliant with the Constitution. Daniel wrote that "despite the first decision that the Supreme Court lacked jurisdiction, it went on to decide the second question regarding the provisions of the Missouri Compromise and declaring Missouri to be a 'free territory.' Here the Court ruled that Congress's power to acquire territories and create governments within those territories was limited solely to the Northwest Territories acquired before the writing of the Constitution and did not include the Louisiana territory, which was acquired well after its signing." I am certain that had Black Hawk still been alive, he would have challenged this decision himself as his entire nation had been eliminated based on laws established by the federal government regarding the territories that the Supreme Court was now saying it had no right to do.

While not there, I could only imagine the seething in Daniel's mind as he witnessed the destruction of something he held dear to his heart … the Constitution of the United States of America.

The third question was whether Mr. Scott or any slave, living in the Wisconsin territory or any free state was entitled to freedom. Daniel responded, "The ruling was once again, against liberty and justice for all, when the Supreme Court had no opinion other than to abide by the laws of the State of Missouri. This meant that Mr. Scott and his family, upon their return to Missouri, were not free, but were the property of Mr. Sanford. If this wasn't demeaning enough, they once again noted that the Circuit Court of the United States had no authority to intercede because Mr. Scott was a slave, and not a citizen."

As I read Daniel's letter, I could feel his disappointment. He had such high hopes. He had such profound intellect and integrity. To be told by what he cherished most that he had no rights must have been especially heartbreaking. Particularly, when it was he who, had he been white, would have been arguing the case before the United States Supreme Court for "liberty and justice for all" and had lost.

I sat with Daniel's letter in my hand and felt I had to reply. For the longest time, I did not know what to say or how to express my frustration or my sadness. I was confounded on how to share my feelings of support for a man so noble as Daniel until at once, it came to me ... one word ... that I scribbled on a sheet of paper and mailed to him ... "Lincoln."

The whole issue of slave states versus free states kept brewing, and the Dred Scott case became a flashpoint. During the Scott trials, Congress had passed the Kansas–Nebraska Act in 1854. This act permitted each newly admitted state south of the 40th parallel to decide whether to be a slave state or free state. Because the 40th parallel was the border between the Kansas and Nebraska territories, one can quickly see how things could get out of hand. With the Dred Scott decision, the Supreme Court appeared to permit the expansion of slavery into the Kansas territory.

Being a Wisconsin farmer, I didn't think much of the law until it was explained to me that adding slave states would mean a loss of political power for the North, as the new slave states would mean additional power in Congress. Why, I asked? Because each slave was counted as three-fifths of a person and would add to the political representation in Congress. All you needed to do to add political power in the South was have more slaves.

I shook my head many times and wondered. If a slave was not considered a citizen, why would he count towards citizenship that determined the representation of our country? Even those of us in Mineral Point, Wisconsin, quickly realized that the decision would only be resolved on the battlefield. The question was not why, but when?

Horace Greeley of the New York Tribune coined the terms Bleeding Kansas, Bloody Kansas or the Border War, which commenced with the signing of the Kansas-Nebraska Act that we read about in the *Mineral Point Democrat*. These skirmishes mainly dealt with folks from both sides trying to pressure the balance of power involving anti-slavery and slavery positions for the State of Kansas.

After the Dred Scott case and all the fighting in Kansas, the country was a mess. The North hated the South, and the South hated the North. The Republicans and Abraham Lincoln supported banning slavery in all the U.S. territories, and they won the presidential election. The man Henry and I listened to thrice became President of the United States. Now, the Southern states felt that banning slavery would be a violation of their constitutional rights. Mr. Lincoln was elected as the first Republican president. However, even before his inauguration, seven slave states, which all grew cotton, formed what they called the Confederate States of America and wanted out of the United States of America. By the time it was over, there were eleven states involved in the Confederacy: South Carolina, North Carolina, Virginia, Tennessee, Alabama, Mississippi, Georgia, Louisiana, Florida, Arkansas, and Texas.

President Buchanan was still in office at the time, and he rejected the secession as illegal. I read in the *Mineral Point Home Intelligencer* that in Mr. Lincoln's inauguration speech he promised he would not initiate civil war. It didn't matter that much as Confederate forces seized several federal forts within the Confederacy. With its larger population and industrial might, many thought the war would last but a few months and consist of nothing more than a few skirmishes. They were wrong. Profoundly wrong.

The war began on April 12, 1861, when the Confederate Army fired upon Fort Sumter. President Lincoln called for 75,000 volunteers. With Lincoln's call, Wisconsin Governor Randall immediately cast his support for the president and directed Major Horace A Tenney to put the Wisconsin State Fairgrounds in Madison near the University into condition for reception of Wisconsin troops, making Wisconsin the first state to pledge allegiance to the cause. This was quickly done, and in honor of the governor, the training grounds were named Camp Randall. The leaders of Mineral Point passed a resolution offering to pay six dollars per month to the families of the first twelve married men who would enlist.

Wisconsin backed unification, and the first national draft was held in 1862 that called for 638 men from Iowa County and thirty-four from Mineral Point. All in all, the state of Wisconsin raised over 90,000 soldiers for the Union Army. Ninety thousand Wisconsin men who marched into war! Ninety thousand Wisconsin men who said goodbye to their loved ones. Ninety thousand Wisconsin men who hid their tears and their fears and walked away from everything that meant anything to them in the name of the United States of America. Ninety thousand Wisconsin men who fought for life, liberty, and the pursuit of happiness for the good of all men regardless of race, origin, or creed!

The Miner's Guard at Mineral Point had been merely a state militia protecting against any Indian "uprisings" and was but sixty members strong. After the call, 130 men joined and volunteered for the front. Although state militia laws limited the strength of a single company to seventy-eight men, no man would surrender his place. Three officials had to deputize fifty-two unwilling men for home duty who were ready to go to war. The Miner's Guard was the first to leave Mineral Point for war and the first to return. In May 1861, they left to the cheers and music of the citizens who supported them. In July 1864, when they returned, the battle-scarred survivors came marching quietly home where they were welcomed with an ovation that was more sincere and stirring than when they had departed. The citizens of Mineral Point honored their men, the country, and our freedom. Farmers were not to be left out, and the Farming Guard was formed, including two Terrills who went off to war. Iowa County and Mineral Point were well served by the men in blue.

The Terrills were Anna and Henry's boys and, I am proud to say, my grandsons. Sarah's boys were too young to go to war, and I thanked God for that. Our family wasn't alone. I heard tell that nearly one in nine Wisconsin men served their country, and that included about half of all men over the age of twenty-one. If they would have taken me, I think I would have gone. There is dignity in standing up for what you believe in, even if it means laying down your life for the good of others. As the war rolled on, Wisconsin was the only state in the Union to send replacements for troops that had already been fielded. Union generals understood and preferred having some Wisconsin regiments under their command.

Camp Randall was supposed to be all about preparation, and about 70,000 Wisconsin men were trained there during the war. However, in early April 1862, about a thousand Confederate prisoners arrived. They had come from the 1st Alabama Infantry. When the first train pulled into Madison, men of the 19th Wisconsin Infantry escorted them to Camp Randall while crowds of civilians stood by trying to get a look at the new arrivals described as being dressed in the dirty, ragged remnants of their gray and butternut uniforms. I always wondered what the reason was for people to stand and wait to see other people. They were described in the newspaper as being in generally good spirits as they marched to the camp. The band of the 19th played "Dixie," at which the step and military bearing of the men improved considerably. Many good-natured remarks passed between the prisoners and the Madison natives. These were young men and boys, away from home, afraid and homesick, just as our boys were. They were treated well, and I think everyone understood there was a common bond ... we were all still Americans.

A few days later, another train arrived bearing some 275 sick men who had not fared as well. Fully one in three who died in war did not die from a saber or bullet, but from disease and infection. Madison's residents were very generous in bringing food, medicine, and clothing for the ill men. A Union surgeon was joined by a Confederate surgeon who had accompanied the men, and also by a civilian doctor as well. I am told that these three men worked tirelessly, but many of the men were too far gone. For the next four weeks, several died each day until 145 had gone to their rest. One hundred forty graves were marked by name and regiment in the Confederate Rest Cemetery plot in Madison, which is a long way from Alabama and the folks they left behind. I wonder if their families ever came to Madison to pay their respects?

Most of our Mineral Point boys fought in Kansas and along the Mississippi, although several regiments I hear also served in Eastern armies, going into Virginia and the Carolinas where Henry and I had been, riding through the countryside where Thomas and Abby lived, past the farms we owned. Those who went away as boys came home as men.

The Civil War brought prosperity back to Mineral Point. It was the regional shipping point for wheat, livestock, and lead as we had the railroad. Mines that had been abandoned were reworked, and new ones opened all intending to make bullets for the soldiers. For the first time in twenty years, a mining boom hit the community as the price of lead doubled and tripled and then hit four times what it had sold for before the war.

Over 12,000 of our troops, including one of my grandsons, did not make it home to Wisconsin. Stephen was lost on August 28, 1862, in the Battle of Gainesville. I would write more, but even after all these years, my heart yearns for that boy. We were not alone. Over 12,000 letters of condolence were written and read, followed by heartache and tears. Over 12,000 times sadness covered our earth as if it were a dense fog, shrouding the sunshine of life and making all seem so stark and so, so desolate.

Death is so permanent. No more goodbyes. No more I love you's ... only memories and regrets of what could have been. When the letter arrived, Henry already knew and was home with Anna and comforted her. There was a silence broken by the muffled sounds of sadness. Stephen Terrill had died in valor, protecting his country, protecting his way of life, and protecting the dignity of his mother so that no other mother would have to be violated in the name of commerce. He was the son of a slave and died trying to stop the tyranny.

As I had learned so early on, death is a strange bedfellow. It seeks out who it wants and when it wants to and leaves those of us behind wondering when it will come again. We had a memorial service, but his body was buried in Missouri. Anna and Henry want to visit it someday. I don't know when. Perhaps when the pain is gone! There is no greater sadness than a child dying before their parent. Every time I've seen it, I always thanked God I was not in their shoes. Losing a babe at birth was enough for me.

The Letter

We all take so much for granted. We all assume the best. We all never really comprehend consequences. Each week, we would go to Mineral Point and to the post office. Before the war, each week there would be a letter from Thomas or Abby detailing all that was happening in Virginia. Elizabeth and I would read their thoughts and smile at their accomplishments and send a note back so that each week, when they went to the post office, there would be a letter from home ... something that would keep us connected, even when we were not.

When the war clouds began to form, the letters began to arrive in bunches delayed by the challenges of decency. I begged Thomas to come home, but he said that Virginia was his home. I said he could go back when the war was over, and he said "no." As the war began, the letters stopped. There was nothing. How deafening the silence of abstinence. For four years ... total silence. We had no idea what was happening. Each week, Elizabeth would go to the post office and look in the empty box and shake her head. The torture of not knowing was worse than all the pain one could possibly bear. I watched as each journey took its toll upon her soul as she aged before me. Her vibrancy was withering, and her steps slowing. A mother just needed to know. I offered to travel to Virginia but was told I could be shot by either side. God, how I missed those letters.

In September 1862, President Lincoln issued a warning to the Confederacy that he would order the emancipation of all slaves in any state that did not end its rebellion against the Union by January 1, 1863. None of the Confederate states restored themselves to the Union. On January 1, 1863, President Lincoln followed through with his promise and signed the Emancipation Proclamation. In a single stroke, Mr. Lincoln took three million slaves and, in the eyes of the federal government and the world, moved them from "slave" to "free." Until his signing of this document, the war was only about keeping the United States united. The Emancipation Proclamation made the Civil War about freeing the slaves.

While this might have sounded like nothing more than more political gibberish in a time of war, it meant that as soon as a slave escaped the control of the Confederate government, by running away or through advances of our federal troops, they became legally free. For every inch that the Union army took, for every slave that it encountered, the result was the same ... freedom! Freedom! As the old Negro spiritual sang, "Free at last. Free at last. Thank God almighty I'm free at last!" That year, the Union's siege of Vicksburg split the Confederacy in two at the Mississippi River. The tide was turning.

Robert E. Lee fought back, moving his army north out of Virginia, to Gettysburg, Pennsylvania. On July 1, 1863, a total of 150,000 soldiers commenced and fought to the death in one field outside Philadelphia. One can only imagine the terror as 23,000 Union and 28,000 Confederate soldiers fell as casualties in ten days of battle. More than 50,000 men piled like logs, frozen in time with grimaces of pain and disbelief upon their faces ... dreams vanished and hearts broken. These were men and boys who wanted nothing more than to go home and live their lives in peace. My God, how sad!

As the stories of the battle reached Mineral Point we stood in silence and shook our heads. At that time, I thought of those boys and could do nothing more than share what I felt it must have been like by penning a short poem that was published in the *Mineral Point Home Intelligencer:*

Look In a soldier's eyes and what do you see?

Blood and hate and battle and needless misery.

Breathe through a soldier's nose and what do you smell?

The pungent odor of death, the rancid fumes of hell.

Eat with a soldier's mouth and what do you taste?

The tartness of desolation. The bitterness of waste.

Listen through a soldier's ears and what do you hear?

The moans of a wounded comrade. The screams of a child's fear.

Grasp with a soldier's hands and what do you touch?

The shattered lives of people and the pieces that they clutch?

Walk with a soldier's feet and where do you tread?

Across the shallow graves of children, so innocent, yet so dead.

And live with a soldier's heart and what do you feel?

The awesome disbelief that anything so horrible could actually be real.

Some folks didn't like what I wrote, but I didn't care. They didn't bury a grandson or understand the peril of not knowing where your loved ones were.

No man had ever seen a war like this, and we can only hope that no man ever sees another with battles so fierce, hate so deep, sadness so profound that even the word forlorn cannot do it justice. Our interest remained keen on the actions taking place in Virginia because the battles reported were near our land and where our son was living. As the stories were reported, we knew of the places and the people and wondered what the consequences were to our family, to our land, and to the United States of America.

The war was turning, but not fast enough for those who continued to lose their lives. The Southerners suffered mightily with food rations key to military desertions and constant changes in authority within the Confederacy. General Ulysses S. Grant was on the attack and General Robert E. Lee on the defensive as Grant pushed Lee's men back through Wilderness, Spotsylvania, and Cold Harbor to the city of Petersburg, Virginia. In June 1864, General Lee entrenched his troops in this city south of Richmond only to be matched by those of General Grant from the North. This was to be General Lee's point of operations from which food and logistics could be controlled. The Confederate Army was starving, living on nothing but cornmeal and beef and a periodic rat or two.

To protect Petersburg, trenches were dug and reinforced and men stationed against any form of attack. To counter, General Grant literally built a new city called City Point at the junction of the James and Appomattox Rivers. There was a stalemate with periodic but disastrous overtures between the two generals, none of which was worse than an ill-advised attack by the Union soldiers on July 30 when they rushed headlong into a bomb crater in which nearly 4,000 Union soldiers lost their lives.

In November 1864, President Lincoln was re-elected, and the war continued on through the deep, dark, dreary winter that saw General Lee's men ill-equipped in summer clothing and ill-prepared in terms of rations, while to the south, the North's General Sherman marched across the land and to the sea.

Each morning, Lizzie and I would take the buggy into Mineral Point at the break of dawn to acquire a fresh copy of the latest news from the *Home Intelligencer* with hope that our family, our farms, and our workers were spared. News was reported from the front to New York City and then telegraphed via the Associated Press to all the big city newspapers. From there, it was transcribed and distributed to newspapers such as *Mineral Point's Home Intelligencer,* where the editors would print the previous day's war information.

While news had previously only come via letter or courier and newspapers reported on events in the past, the invention of the telegraph allowed even those living in Mineral Point, Wisconsin, to know, for a penny, what was happening in Virginia. Unfortunately, the news we received for our penny was not what we had hoped for, and the look upon Lizzie's disappointed face expressed her melancholy as we made the sad, quiet trip home to Waldwick to wait another day.

Although outmanned and outgunned, General Lee's men held off General Grant for months. Beginning on April 1, 1865, it took but nine days to finally bring a ceasefire to the area where Thomas and Abby lived on our land. Let me share with you all that transpired, as it will all make sense a little later on. As the Army of Northern Virginia retreated, the Union Army advanced. With each step back, there was one step forward. With each regression, there was an answered progression that resulted in the demise of all that had been whether by those departing or those arriving. War is hell on earth, and its ravages consume all that is good and use it as fuel to keep the fires of misery burning long after the cries of battle go silent.

On Saturday, April 1, 1865, General Grant's troops cut the railroad between Petersburg and Richmond, and its fall was eminent. At dawn on Sunday, April 2, 1865, General Grant's army attacked Petersburg in full force. General Lee's men put up a good fight that lasted long enough for General Lee to keep General Grant's troops occupied to save what was left of the Confederate treasury, along with government papers, all loaded into railroad cars and moved on the only open railroad toward Danville, Virginia. With this, the city was burned as the Confederate soldiers were in retreat. As the fires were contained, looters took to the streets, and mayhem broke out. Thank God they took those papers or so many lost men would have never been found; so many lost souls would have simply vanished, and their legacy would have evaporated as smoke in the wind.

On Monday, April 3, 1865, Union troops entered what was left of Richmond. On Tuesday, April 4, General Lee and his men reached Amelia Court House expecting food and supplies from Richmond via the railroad. None arrived! On this day, President Lincoln arrived from City Point to see the Stars and Stripes fly once again above the city of Richmond. News spread quickly of his presence, and throngs of now-free slaves came to pay homage and simply see the man who had given them their freedom.

President Lincoln walked into the Confederate White House and sat behind the desk that only forty-eight hours prior had been that of Jefferson Davis. Later, Mr. Lincoln visited the hospital where boys of both sides were being treated. It was reported that there was no joy, no celebration—only relief that what had been was no more, at least not in the city of Richmond, Virginia.

Meanwhile, the battle raged within Amelia Court House and along the road to Amelia Springs, which traversed Amity and our farms. The Union soldiers repeatedly attacked the area around Amity, seeking to end the war with a show of force so great that no man could misunderstand might for valor. Battles were hand-to-hand, man-to-man, with soldiers fighting, dying, and wishing only that all would end. While less than 300 men died in battle, these were still 300 men who never went home and the devastation to all living creatures within the area was enormous.

On Wednesday, April 5, 1865, Union General Sheridan captured the railhead at Jetersville, Virginia, and blocked General Lee's exit by rail to the south. Without food for four days, no ammunition, and few with dry boots, General Lee's troops moved on. On April 6, the same General Sheridan cut off the rear-guard forces of General Lee, and 8,000 Confederate troops surrendered. Given nothing more than Union rations, the boys thought they had been invited to a feast.

Friday, April 7, 1865: General Lee was down to his last tactical maneuver. It was his intent to have General Longstreet burn the bridges across the Appomattox River, but Longstreet was beaten at High Bridge, and this meant there was no way to stop the onslaught of General's Grant's army.

Saturday, April 8, 1865: General Sheridan's cavalry beat what was left of General Lee's supplies at Appomattox and Lee's last line of retreat. The newspaper reported that General Lee announced to his men, "There is nothing left me to do but to go and see General Grant, and I would rather die a thousand deaths."

Sunday, April 9, 1865: General Lee and General Grant met and came to terms of surrender. Acting without authority, General Grant promised that the 28,000 soldiers of the South would be paroled and "not disturbed by United States Authority" and certainly not imprisoned or prosecuted as long as they obeyed the laws and did not take up arms again. General Lee spoke to his men and thanked them, telling them to go back to their families and be peaceful citizens.

The following are General Lee's words and not mine. However, they reflect the emotions so much better than I could ever do ...

"After four years of arduous service, marked by unsurpassed courage and fortitude, the Army of Northern Virginia has been compelled to yield to overwhelming numbers and resources. I need not tell the brave survivors of so many hard-fought battles, who have remained steadfast to the last, that I have consented to this result from no distrust of them; but, feeling that valor and devotion could accomplish nothing that could compensate for the loss that would have attended the continuation of the contest, I determined to avoid the useless sacrifice of those whose past services have endeared them to their countrymen. By the terms of the agreement, officers and men can return to their homes and remain until exchanged. You will take with you the satisfaction that proceeds from the consciousness of duty faithfully performed and I earnestly pray that a merciful God will extend to you his blessing and protection. I bid you an affectionate farewell."

There were no winners in this war ... only those whose lives were lost to sanctify the beauty of the passage, "life, liberty, and the pursuit of happiness."

General Grant also wrote so much more eloquently than I. "When I went into the house I found General Lee. We greeted each other, and after shaking hands took our seats. What General Lee's feelings were I do not know. As he was a man of much dignity; with an impassible face, it was impossible to say whether he felt inwardly glad that the end had finally come, or felt sad over the result, and was too manly to show it. Whatever his feelings, they were entirely concealed from my observation; but my own feelings, which had been quite jubilant on the receipt of his letter were sad and depressed. I felt like anything rather than rejoicing at the downfall of a foe who had fought so long and valiantly, and had suffered so much for a cause, though that cause was, I believe, one of the worst for which a people ever fought, and one for which there was the least excuse. I do not question, however, the sincerity of the great mass of those who were opposed to us."

Peace was at hand, but not quite in place. I can only imagine the queer feeling of those who were in battle to, at least sleep a night without fearing attack on either side. I heard tell that the captured Confederate soldiers were a ragtag lot who hadn't eaten in a long time and that those of the Union Army shared their rations so that all could enjoy the beginnings of the healing that we so desperately needed.

Tragically, war's casualties did not all end on that last day of battle. There was still more death and destruction in the name of freedom. On Saturday, April 15th, 1865, word spread that President Lincoln had been assassinated. The man whose decency and compassion had saved a country from itself was gone. I heard that there were many who celebrated. We were not amongst them. This man made the ultimate sacrifice for our country as did so many more, all casualties of commerce and a perception of right and wrong and a way of life. How incredibly sad! Black bunting hung from the windows of every building and every home in Mineral Point. Church bells tolled, and there wasn't a smile on a single face. The toils of war meant no spoils of war other than sadness and the loss of our great leader, which gave heavy hearts to those that prevailed.

On Wednesday, April 26, 1865, General Joseph E. Johnston surrendered his troops to General William T. Sherman at Bennett Place, North Carolina. Six weeks later, on Friday, June 2, 1865, the war ended. The South surrendered. While it should have been a time of celebration, it was a time of relief. The pressure was gone, and with it the fear. The North had mobilized over two million men, and the South, a million themselves.

After four years of Americans fighting Americans, over 700,000 citizens were dead, and much of the South lay in ruin. The Confederacy collapsed, and once again, we were the United States of America. I still shake my head ... 700,000 people ... 700,000 souls lost their lives ... 700,000 people simply gone. One in ten of all men in the North and nearly one in three in the South. I wonder how and why man can be so inhuman.

In December, the 13th Amendment was put in place. Over 20,000 men gave their lives for each of the following 33 words: "Neither slavery nor involuntary servitude, except as a punishment for crime whereof the party shall have been duly convicted, shall exist within the United States, or any place subject to their jurisdiction."

We fight for peace, that's what they said, so many boys who all are dead. What a tragedy. The only reward was that, at last, there might be peace. At last our country might have the slightest beginnings of that preamble Elizabeth and I had read so long, long ago: "life, liberty and the pursuit of happiness." My nephew Daniel must have cried in joy. For the first time in his life, he was recognized for what he was ... a man. Not a Negro man. Not a former slave. A citizen. A proud, honest, and honorable man capable of walking the streets with head held high in Boston, New York, and even in Amity, Virginia, if he so desired.

Peace did not mean immediate safety or the ability to travel, and so we waited several months to see if the letters would start again. When they did not, it was decided that Mathew and I would make the trip to Virginia and determine the fate of Thomas, Abby, and the farms. Little did I expect to see what we saw. Little could I comprehend the magnitude of destruction I found. Never would I ever forget that war truly is hell.

Mathew and I departed for Virginia but did so by train. We rode first to Warren, then to Chicago, and then made the long trek to Philadelphia and from there Virginia. Elizabeth was forlorn. It had been so long, and while she needed to know, she was afraid of what she would learn. The travel through Illinois and Indiana saw little change from when I had passed so many times before. As we traversed Pennsylvania, all seemed well.

We spent a day in Philadelphia, and Mathew and I visited Independence Hall. This was a wonderful respite that we needed as what we were about to encounter was far beyond anything we could have imagined. Our travel south saw subtle changes begin to show. Farms weren't as well kept, buildings not as neat and clean as they had been before, and there was no livestock anywhere. Damage here! Death there! With each mile, the frequency increased.

The further we traveled into Virginia, the more devastation we saw. Wherever we looked, there was carnage ... burned buildings, broken fences, scars upon the land. My heart was sinking, and with it, my hopes that things were all right. Our train ride stopped in City Point, which had been the center of the Union effort in terms of the railroad. When the war was nearing its end, General Grant began the siege of Richmond and Petersburg from City Point, setting up the rail depot from which he provisioned his army. At least 100,000 Union troops and 65,000 animals were supplied out of the town that was also the site of the Depot Field Hospital, which served 29,000 soldiers as well as the final resting place for those who never made it home.

How stark to look out upon a cemetery filled with hundreds, if not thousands, of the same markers. The sadness inspired me to write the following in my journal.

Little white crosses side-by-side, for each of them one soldier died.

Little white crosses row-by-row, for each of them a life we show.

Little white crosses in a field, for each of them a life did yield.

In '76 and 1812, from '62 to '64, we fight for peace, that's what they said, a million men who all are dead.

With little white crosses on a hill and one more grave that we must fill.

Upon arriving at City Point, we purchased two horses and their tack and began our journey towards Amity. With each turn in the road, with each hill whose peak we crossed, with each town we came to, we were reminded of the devastation of war. Regardless of where we looked, we could not escape its wrath. As we entered Farmville, we saw burned-out buildings. The bank, where our money had been, was only a hulking shell ... a blackened skeleton of a time gone by. With its demise went the demise of dreams created in small layers as deposits were made that would never be honored and lives changed, if there was still life to be had. Hope had transformed itself into reality and then to depression. How sad. How profoundly sad.

Mathew and I went to where Mr. Ward's office had been and where Daniel studied law, and there was simply nothing there. No building. No people. No commerce. I had no idea how to seek out Mr. Ward, and inquiries at what was left of the town hall were fruitless. My heart was sinking deeper into my chest. I think I already knew what I would find, and yet there was still a slight glimmer of hope.

We traveled to the intersection where we were to turn to Amity, but there was no sign ... no sign of the town, no sign of the land and, worst of all, no sign of life at all. I stopped to get my bearings, and Mathew asked if I was all was right. I told him yes, but it all seemed so different and so incredibly sad. We progressed to the turn to go to the Smithson farm where Thomas and Abby were living and came over the hill. I gasped. There was nothing there. All that showed were tall weeds. The barn was gone. The house was gone. The stables were gone. The quarters, where the workers had lived, were gone. Life was gone. Mother Nature had taken back all that had been. We stopped where the house once stood, and there were burned pieces of the front stairs woven into the weeds, as if begging to let them rest in peace.

I searched for any clue and could find none. It was as if the farm had never existed. But what about all the people? Where had they gone? Where were Thomas and Abby? I was getting more despondent by the minute. Mathew and I continued in the direction of my brother's farm. Where the lake we had created had been, there were only weeds and tall grass. We rode between the hills and saw the remnants of the dam. It had been exploded, with broken timbers lying like bodies upon the hills, bleached in the sun ... skeletons of what had once been.

As we crossed the next hill, I saw smoke coming from what had been my brother's house where Big John and Clara lived. That gave us a glimmer of hope. As we proceeded, a man, about the age of forty-five, appeared on the porch with a shotgun. We sidled up and dismounted. One needs to be polite when one has a gun pointed at them.

I looked at the man and could tell he wasn't of any level of education. He was wearing dirty underwear beneath his overalls, and stains of sweat made rings beneath his arms. He had not shaved, nor had a beard, just scruffy, unkempt, and filthy. As he smiled, his yellow-brown teeth showed the consequence of chewing tobacco, verified as he spit its juice upon the ground.

"What can I do fer ya?" he asked.

I was careful with my words, as Mathew slowly loosened the pistol in his holster. I knew that if shots were fired, someone would be dead, and there had already been enough of that to last more than one lifetime.

"My name is George Terrill, and this is my son Mathew," I said.

"What you want on my land?" the interloper questioned.

"Before the war, this was my property, along with the Smithson farm and the Gilbertson farm next to that."

"Ain't no more" was the curt reply. "You on my land now, and this is my house, and you are tresspassin'."

I weighed the consequence of the shotgun and surmised that any argument would be lost. This would be up to the constable and a court of law to decide.

"Can you tell me what happened to the young couple who resided on the Smithson farm?" I inquired.

"Been no one there for years. The Confederate Militia burned it to the ground in the name of the cause. Seems them folks didn't like the way things were around here, and let's just say, they didn't quite fit in."

"But do you know what happened to them?"

"Nope."

"What about the folks who lived in this house?"

"You mean them two old nigras? Slaves livin' in a fancy house like this? They didn't belong here. They were just slaves. All uppity and such, livin' here all high and mighty."

"Sir, do you know what happened to them?"

"Sure do. Both dead! Buried them myself up on the hill. Uppity nigras! Should've left 'em and let the vermin eat 'em!"

I wanted to pull my gun and return the deed, but the interloper had his finger on his trigger, and I knew better.

"You best be goin' now, you hear, and if you ever come back, I'll use this gun on you just like I did to them."

There was no cause for altercation, but there was cause for retaliation, and I vowed right then and there that the plight Big John and Clara suffered would be compensated.

Mathew and I carefully backed away. This man thought he had won, and yet his war had just begun.

When we were out of sight, Mathew inquired about my intent, and I indicated that we needed to first find out the fate of Thomas and Abby, then the fate of Mr. Ward, and then reclaim our land. With such a disheveled mess in Farmville, my thought was to go directly to Richmond and investigate all three tasks at the same time. Mathew thought it would be best to return to Farmville and determine any knowledge from there. After considering the matter, I concurred.

In Farmville, the pace was that of a lame man trying to walk as fast as he can. Progress was slow, but at least there were people. We went to where the town hall had been and found that it was intact. The Union soldiers had used it as a command post and had honored the records kept within. We visited with a Mrs. Gorgen and explained our situation. She indicated that she knew of Mr. Ward and that he and a group of slaves had headed north into Ohio when the war began. She could not say where they went or what their consequence had been, only that Mr. Ward and about ten slaves had left one night right after the Emancipation Proclamation had been signed.

I asked about Andrew, Thomas, and Abby and whether they had accompanied Mr. Ward and she responded that she did not know. I asked Mrs. Gorgen about property deeds and if they were still in place and she said "yes." I informed her of our "visit" to my brother's farm, and she responded that there were squatters living in many homes and that it would take the sheriff to remove them.

I asked if I could meet with the sheriff and if eviction notices could be drawn up and a formal complaint filed regarding the deaths of Big John and Clara. She said eviction notices could legally be created but it would require a lawyer. She also noted that, in time of war, there was no actual proof that the squatter did actually kill Big John and Clara. For all anyone knew, he could be just saying that to make us afraid so that we would go away. I told her I understood.

I inquired about my son and daughter-in-law, and she indicated that there was a great deal of conscription and that we probably needed to go to Richmond as it was the capital of the Confederacy and all records would be there. With Abby's last name being Lee and her father a colonel, all we had to go on was the fact that the general of the Confederate army was Robert E. Lee. I had no way of knowing whether he was related to Abby or not. All I knew was that I needed to find out.

I felt we learned all we could from Mrs. Gorgen and that it was time to head for Richmond. The squatter could wait, and with him, the secrets he held within. I sensed that he knew more than he was sharing, and my goal was to get it from him just as Henry had done so long ago with those who had come to burn the Smithson barn.

Mathew and I began the trek to Richmond, and with each mile, the devastation grew worse. Gone were most buildings. Gone were most trees. Gone was any form of life ... all replaced by a sense of desolation that one cannot comprehend.

As we reached the St. James River, I stood in total shock. While the journey had made me somewhat immune to the carnage, nothing could prepare me for the sight before my eyes. Across the river, this beautiful city was asunder, blackened by the ravages of bombardment and the attempts of its own citizens to leave nothing of value behind as they burned buildings and attempted to escape the onslaught of the Union Army.

We crossed the river and entered the city. Everywhere, Union troops were still on watch, and this was over a year after the end of the war. Richmond had been the symbol of the South, and the victors wanted to make certain that anyone, everyone, realized that the war was over and peace was at hand.

Mathew and I made our way to where the Bates house stood and saw a shambles before us ... a burned-out frame, pockmarked with bullet holes and black soot coming from each broken window. We learned that the Bates house had been one of the Confederate headquarters and had been attacked as the last few of the Confederacy, who could not escape, fought on to the very end.

We were incredulous at the damage we saw in Richmond. Nothing could have prepared me for how my senses were assaulted. Never do I hope to see such carnage again. I inquired and learned that a Confederate general named Ewell had directed all the tobacco warehouses, then full of tobacco, be burned and that the burning was to commence when he provided a certain signal. The plan was to start the buildings on fire and, in the ruckus, have his troops pass over the St. James River on Mayo's bridge and retreat south towards Appomattox. From the level of destruction, General Ewell's plan had worked, and the beautiful city was decimated as flames leapt from building to building.

I read an article in a newspaper written by a woman named Eliza Frances Andrews. This lady said it so much better than I ever could, and I hope that I do her justice: "We made a brave fight but the odds against us were too great. The spell of invincibility has left us and gone over to the heavy battalions of the enemy . . . As I drove along from the station to the hotel, l could see that preparations were being made to evacuate the city. Government stores were piled up in the streets and all the horses and wagons that could be pressed into service were being hastily loaded in the effort to remove them. The rush of men had disappeared from Mulberry St. No more gay uniforms, no more prancing horses, but only a few ragged foot soldiers with wallets and knapsacks on, ready to march Heaven-knows-where ... I heard fresh rumors of Lee's surrender. No one seems to doubt it, and everybody feels ready to give up hope. 'It is useless to struggle longer,' seems to be the common cry, and the poor wounded men go hobbling about the streets with despair on their faces. There is a new pathos in a crutch or an empty sleeve, now that we know it was all for nothing."

Shortly after the war, President Grant and Congress realized that rebuilding Richmond was a noble task and set about in earnest, restoring this great and beautiful city. Everywhere that Mathew and I went, we saw reconstruction and the rebirth as it was taking place. While there were five military districts of the U.S. Army following the war, Virginia was the smallest in terms of size and was successively commanded by Brigadier General John Schofield when we visited.

With such hubbub, it was difficult to get answers, and yet we persisted. Our only lead was that of Colonel Lee and whether he was in fact the brother of the famous general. We attempted to seek records, but all leads led to dead ends. I determined that the only way to find a solution was to seek out General Lee himself.

After numerous inquiries and many false leads, Mathew and I learned that General Lee was not in prison as so many Union soldiers had told us. In fact, after the surrender, he simply went home. He had spent a few months with his family in Richmond, but the pace was such and the pain so deep that he wanted to retire from public life. General Lee had been the superintendent of West Point, and this caught the eye of the leaders of Washington College in Lexington, Virginia, and they made him their president.

It was but a two-day ride of 138 miles from Richmond to Lexington, and it was our last hope. We made the journey and set out to find the famous general. We met up with him as he sat working at his lap desk at the college. I was surprised first by his stature, being much smaller than I had expected, and then by his nature, which appeared one of a calm and gentle spirit. This famous general put down his spectacles and listened to our story and how many dead ends we had met in simply trying to find out the circumstance of my son. He was soft-spoken, and yet there was an aurora of authority about him.

I asked if Colonel Lee was his brother, and he said "no." He knew of Colonel Lee and his family, as they had met several times. He recalled Abby and reflected that she was a beautiful young girl. I asked if he knew the whereabouts of Colonel Lee, and he indicated that he thought Colonel Lee had died in battle. My heart sank. He asked if I knew that all military records for the Confederacy were intact in Washington, D.C. I told him I did not.

As he leaned back in his chair, his eyes and mine met, and we spoke man to man, father to father. "I am sorry for your troubles," he said.

With that, Mathew and I stood and were about to leave.

"One moment please," the general said. "With that, he took a pen and scribbled a note upon which he wrote instructions and signed it "Robert E. Lee." "Take this to Washington. It will help."

I folded the paper and put it in my coat pocket. All three of us shook hands, and we retreated for the door.

"I truly am sorry—truly," he whispered as we closed the door.

Washington

It was a three-day ride to Washington, and Mathew and I made it the best we could. Upon arriving at the Bureau of Records, we were informed that only government employees were allowed access to Confederate files. I removed the folded letter from my pocket and placed it in front of the clerk. His expression changed immediately.

"One moment please," he said as he exited the room.

Within a matter of a few minutes, a gentleman appeared. "My name is Oswald Hornsby. May I be of assistance? I hear that you have been sent by General Lee."

"Yes, sir, that's correct. Here are the directions he provided."

"General Lee has been a help to many who have lost a son, and we all respect the dignity of the gentleman in assisting those in search of others. Come with me please."

We entered a very large room that was stacked with files. Each box was numbered, and within each were countless sets of records. Mr. Hornsby pondered for a moment and thought out loud.

"Let's see. Amity, outside of Farmville, let's start there."

We walked to a long row, and Mr. Hornsby found a stack of boxes containing the records of all those who served in the Confederate Army and were conscripted or volunteered in Farmville. All names were alphabetical, and the files were neat.

"Terrill, Terrill, Terrill," Mr. Hornsby said to himself, shaking his head as his search came up blank.

Mathew interjected, "What about Andrew Kincaid? He worked the farm with my brother and his wife, Abby."

Mr. Hornsby walked to the box marked J-K-L and opened the file. Beneath so many others, were the records of Andrew. Date of birth, date of conscription, and date, cause, and location of death. Andrew had been drafted into the Confederacy Army in 1861 and was a corporal who died in battle and was buried at Gettysburg. I guess the eventuality of what we had assumed insulated us from some of the sadness. Yet, to see the life and death of someone we knew written before us still resonated in my heart.

"Do you think your son could have been drafted at the same time?" Mr. Hornsby asked.

"I have no idea," I responded.

"Let's check the Richmond files and see if there is anything there," Hornsby replied.

Again we walked the long rows of lives lost within the Virginia enclave until we came to those that represented Richmond. It was a long shot, but it was our last shot. Mr. Hornsby went to the box with the letter Te-To on it as many more had come from Richmond than Farmville. Quietly he opened the box and sorted through the files. His eyes looked down and then up and then at us. He had found Thomas's folder. I took a deep breath and said a prayer as Mr. Hornsby opened the file. "Should I read it to you?"

"Yes please," I replied.

"Thomas Michael Terrill, born October 11, 1829, in Waldwick, Wisconsin. Farmer of approximately 200 acres owned in partnership with Martin E. Ward, conscripted in Richmond, Virginia, on October the 23rd of 1861. Was trained and used for troop support and logistics for Colonel Borgard Lee in the battle of Gettysburg."

My heart was filled with sadness as I thought my own son had fought with the rebels.

"It was determined that Sergeant Terrill was a spy for the North when he was seen communicating confidential messages with them. He was charged with treason and was shot by a firing squad before the battle commenced. It was determined that the messages he shared with the enemy were such that it had saved hundreds of Union lives. He too is buried at Gettysburg, but it was done so on the Union side."

I took another deep breath and put my hand on Mathew's shoulder for support. Tears welled within my eyes. I was sad, yet I was proud. My son had served his country and helped end a wretched war. He had lived two lives. His years of living in the South hadn't changed him. His body may have been in Virginia, but his heart was in Wisconsin. I thanked Mr. Hornsby for his generosity of time and reflected that my only regret was not knowing what happened to Abby.

With that, Mr. Hornsby smiled. "You said that Colonel Lee was her father?"

"Yes"

"Let's check and see."

With that, we went to the "L" boxes and learned that Colonel Lee had taken leave to South Carolina in 1862. Mr. Hornsby surmised that Abby and the rest of the family thought they would be safer there than in Virginia. Mathew and I walked out of the building with heavy hearts, and yet we knew that Thomas had died a hero. We never learned the fate of Abby. We just considered her "gone." I likewise never learned the fate of the children. War plays a funny game with this thing called life. The only thread that had bound Abby to us was Thomas, and that thread was broken at Gettysburg.

I thought our journey had ended and we should head for Philadelphia and the train home. On our way, we visited Baltimore, and I showed Mathew the building where we saw the slave auction and where Sarah was buried. We put flowers on the spot where we thought her grave would be and said the Lord's Prayer. Finally, I took Mathew to where his mother and I first set foot in America. I pointed to the sign above the door. "We hold these truths to be self-evident that all men are created equal." Little did Elizabeth and I know when we arrived the terrible cost of equality. We painfully learned that being free does not come without cost. It is a precious commodity to be honored and dignified by one's treatment of their fellow man.

When we arrived in Philadelphia, Mathew asked if I wanted to visit Gettysburg, and I said "no." My heart was already too heavy. We caught the train to Chicago and then another to Warren and finally home. Elizabeth knew before we got there of Thomas's demise. She had the sense, and all she needed was closure.

Home at Last

As I saw her sitting alone in the garden, I walked slowly up to her, and we embraced ... a long, careful, embrace of two people who had loved so much, shared so much, and done so much together. I filled her in on all the details as we sat in our spot upon the hill. She didn't cry for she already knew. I made the only promise to her that I never kept ... I promised to take her to Gettysburg to see Thomas's grave. She died before we could make it.

Sunday, May 9, 1869, was one of those glorious spring days in Wisconsin. The sun was warm, and the flowers had begun to bloom. Elizabeth hadn't been out of the house for several weeks. I asked if she would like to go to our spot upon the hill, and she smiled. She was but a wisp of herself, and I could easily have carried her. Instead, we took her wheeled chair and slowly made way to our vantage point. The birds were chirping, and the first signs of the summer's insects were abuzz.

I looked at my wife, and a faint smile crossed her face. I told her I loved her, and she nodded. I looked out over the valley and reflected back on Cornwall and Old Fitzie. I talked about the trek across Ireland and then upon the sea and of Henry and Sarah and the baby. I reflected on the auction house in Baltimore and William and Old Ed. I laughed about the bear and Black Hawk at our cabin and then about our children. I smiled as I talked about our trips to Mineral Point and even Skunk Hollow. I told her again how much she meant to me and how my life could not have been better. When I was done reflecting,

I looked down, and she was gone. Somewhere in my reflections, her soul had departed. I had lost my Lizzie, the love of my life.

We buried her that Thursday where she last sat upon the hill. It is her final resting place. It was a sad day, and many friends came to pay their respects. I wrote the following poem that Henry read ...

Today will be yesterday, tomorrow.
And with it,
Will go another bit of our future,
Slowly slipping into the past.
I cannot remember each today,
And some I wish I could forget.
I only know that all todays must turn to yesterdays,
And slip slowly into the past.
Yesterdays ... once so near, slowly slip beneath our todays
That were once tomorrows,
Before they too
Slip slowly into the past.
Soon, all of our tomorrows become yesterdays.
Making today's today and tomorrow's todays,
Only nothing more than yesterday.

When all were gone that warm May day, I sat alone upon the fallen log that had been our chair and told her simply, "I love you."

My Last Words

I contacted Daniel by telegraph and noted Elizabeth's passing. I explained the situation with the farms in Virginia and asked his advice. He offered assistance and the land was cleared of the vermin who had overrun it. A man from Pinkerton was hired and went with a deputy sheriff that the squatter did not know. A conversation took place about the land and about Big John and Clara. Once again, this ill-kempt man bragged about their deaths. This time, it was to the wrong people, as he was arrested and eventually hanged for murder, just as it should have been.

I offered the land to Daniel, but he said "no." I suggested we donate the farms to the State of Virginia with only one requirement ... that the land be used as a park in perpetuity so that all folks ... colored or white ... could be welcomed to come and enjoy the peace and tranquility that the land offered. Daniel responded that the partnership with Mr. Ward would impede the gift and that the State of Virginia had so many other pressing issues that creating a memorial park was not on their list of priorities. We agreed to rent the land to adjacent planters and that the revenue should be used to establish scholarships for area children to attend school with Daniel acting as the trustee.

I asked that a memorial be placed where Big John and Clara were laid to rest. Daniel agreed to implement the activity and took it upon himself to have the project completed. We had headstones carved and put in place upon which we put their names, both ending in Terrill, with the words, "free at last" inscribed below. I am told the masons kept their word as I have never returned.

Daniel elected to leave Harvard and was appointed as one of the first Negro judges in America and continues today to serve. He looks only in a man's eyes and never at a man's skin when making decisions, and he is known for his honesty, integrity, and brilliance.

Henry and Anna continue to live in Mineral Point where no one thinks less of her simply because of the shade of her skin. Their children all moved to Madison. I guess the wanderlust of a bigger city made them feel that there would be a better life there. Anna has been involved in all good causes in the name of the children throughout Iowa County, Wisconsin, and America and is a member of the Eastern Star of the Masonic Temple while Henry is a 32nd degree Mason.

Sarah is married to a young man named Wright, who is also a farmer, and they have nine children. She lives in Richland Center, and I see them often. She comes to visit, and we share memories. Dora lives with me. Alone and quiet, and yet she visits Sarah and Anna regularly, and they do lady things. She has taken over teaching in Skunk Hollow and lives vicariously through the lives of her students and those of her nieces and nephews. Mathew is my partner, and he and his wife, Fanny, live in the inn where Henry used to reside. It won't be long until he will live in this house as I plan on joining Elizabeth quite soon.

Each afternoon, near sundown, I go and visit my Elizabeth and, when they are in bloom, I bring fresh flowers. I sit upon the log where we always sat and reflect upon the day and all that transpired. Each night before I leave her, I say a little "thank you" to the good Lord for bringing her into my life. She was my wife. She was my partner. She was my best friend. I cannot think of a better life or a better wife and thank God for all that's been. We were a family ... husband, wife, sons and daughters, brothers and sisters, joined by a common bond called love ... love of life, love of family, and love for each other and the land which we call home.

On the day I join my Elizabeth, I hope to see my friend Henry, my son Thomas, and my Sarah. My thoughts are done. I pray that I have done justice to those I have written about. I cannot write another word for my well is dry. I only ask that, after I am gone, what I have written is read and that a child of the next generation continues the tradition I have begun. If we do not tell from whence we came, how will one ever know in what direction they should travel?

As I lay awake so many years ago in a land so far away and dreamed of a better tomorrow, I could not have had a better dream, for I have found the happiness, contentment, and joy that I thought would never be mine. I listened to my father and followed my heart, and it led me to Waldwick where I became a man.

I have seen so much, felt so much, and done so much. I have laughed a lot, lived a lot, and tried to be a good father, husband, and citizen. I have experienced oppression from both sides and seen its ugly head. In the end, I can only hope and pray that each man, every man, will be given the opportunity to reach for their own greatness as I have. That is what life should be all about ... attaining those magic words ... life, liberty, and the pursuit of happiness.

George Terrill ... August 2, 1871

Disclaimer

This book is a work of fiction. Some of the events and experiences detailed herein are true and have been faithfully rendered as researched by the author to the best of his abilities. The information contained in this book is intended to provide helpful and informative material on the subjects and events addressed and written as an interpretation of his learning. No part of this text may be reproduced, transmitted, downloaded, decompiled, reverse-engineered, or stored in or introduced into any information storage and retrieval system, in any form or by any means, whether electronic or mechanical, now known or hereafter invented, without the express written permission of the author.

I am a descendant of miners from Cornwall. There is a town called Mineral Point, Wisconsin, where my childhood was filled with magical moments and marvelous memories. There is a village called Waldwick that remains nearby and is the birthplace of my grandmother and mother. There are many Terrills living in the area who are my relatives, and I hope and pray that I have done the family name justice by what I have written, for they are the kindred spirit upon which our country was created. There is no reality to the names used as they are all of consequence.

If the tale I weave meets your fancy and your interest is piqued, I highly recommend visiting the wonderful area just southwest of Madison, Wisconsin. The scenery is spectacular and is only exceeded by the honor, dignity, and warmth of the people who reside there.

I have written this book as a tribute to my grandmother who was a Terrill and from whom, I learned the value of integrity and honesty and the joy of acceptance that only comes from an open heart and a profound sense of decency that she emanated with each breath.

The End

About the Author

Kenneth Linde was born and raised in Madison, Wisconsin. Each summer, he would visit Mineral Point and his widowed grandmother who shared stories of her growing up and living on the family farm in Waldwick. During his visits, Ken would meet his grandmother's siblings, who would share more stories and provide the joy and laughter and profound sense of decency that he has hopefully expressed throughout this book.

Like his mother, Ken loved to write and, after attending the University of Wisconsin, where he majored in communications, Ken entered the world of broadcasting as a writer. After marrying and moving outside Milwaukee, Ken's career evolved into executive sales and marketing where he matriculated to a senior executive level at several national and international companies.

In 2010, Ken was afflicted with 70 blood clots from too much travel and too little exercise and was given less than a 5% chance of surviving three hours. While hospitalized in intensive care, Ken came up with the idea of revisiting his first passion, writing and upon recovery, wrote "Survivor...Death and How It Saved My Life" that addresses social dynamics which became the foundation for "Waldwick".

Ken and his wife Denise have been married 43 years, have two daughters and sons-in-law and five grandchildren and Ken continues his lost-love of writing where "Waldwick" represents just the beginning followed by "Little Spirit", "Driftless" and "the Hayflick Limit" that continue the story and address social issues of the past, present and future. The author hopes that he has done justice to the people and the area that has always filled his life with great stories and fond memories.

Next: *Waldwick* continues with *Little Spirit!* It's 2016 and descendent, George Terrill the Fourth shares his love, life and belief in the magical place called Waldwick. Read along as "Q", as his friends and family call him, stands up for what is right and defends the land he loves. Share in his passion for dignity, honor and equality and meet the woman who simply changes everything. Available soon from Little Creek Press.